I0614710

The Future Chronicles

SPECIAL EDITION

WINDRIFT BOOKS

Cover art and design by Adam Hall (http://www.aroundthepages.com) and Jason Gurley (http://www.jasongurley.com)

Print and ebook formatting by Therin Knite (http://www.knitedaydesign.com/)

The Future Chronicles—Special Edition is part of *The Future Chronicles* series produced by Samuel Peralta (www.samuelperalta.com).

978-0-9939832-5-2

The Future Chronicles

SPECIAL EDITION

STORY SYNOPSES

A Dream of Waking (*Sam Best*)
Unsuspecting space travelers are captured and entombed in life-support coffins on a massive off-world medical freighter. The prisoners sleep for years at a time while their dreams are harvested as raw energy so that others can stay awake indefinitely. One prisoner's sleep is interrupted...and he will do anything to stay awake.

The Invariable Man (*A.K. Meek*)
Old Micah Dresden lives life in the Boneyard of the Desert Southwest, where he fixes broken-down technology in this vast junkyard—until a stranger shows up with rumors of war, echoing the decades-old Machine Wars. To stop it from happening, Micah and his obsessive-compulsive robot Skip must travel to the northern hangars, to where the government has locked away Machine X, which can turn the tide of war. But nothing will prepare him for who he meets there.

#DontTell (*Peter Cawdron*)
For centuries, people have wondered what it would be like to read someone's mind. Little have they known, they already have. To see the anguish on someone's face, to watch tears fall, or hear someone cry and empathize with them—this is the essence of mind-reading. In the 21st century, our natural ability

to empathize with others has finally evolved into true telepathy, but it's an evolutionary change that threatens the status quo. The world, it seems, isn't ready for mind readers.

Defiance (*Susan Kaye Quinn*)

Most of humanity has ascended into hyper-intelligent human/machine hybrids, but legacy humans like Cyrus Kowalski are used to skirting the laws they've laid down—after all, he knows the ascenders only pretend to care about the legacy pets they keep. But when a woman Cyrus loves like a mother is stricken by a disease the ascenders refuse to cure, he has to decide how far he can go without getting banished from the legacy city that's always been his home.

Ethical Override (*Nina Croft*)

The year is 2072, and under the administration of the Council for Ethical Advancement and its robotic Stewards, the Earth has become a better place. Bored and restless in an almost perfect world, senior homicide detective Vicky Harper dreams of adventure among the stars—and of faraway planets where people are allowed to make their own mistakes. It seems an impossible fantasy. Then one of the one of the ruling Council members turns up dead, and someone offers to make her dreams come true. All she has to do is lie.

Piece of Cake (*Patrice Fitzgerald*)

Rule by A.I. is a fact of life for those under the thumb of the Federal United. There will be a certain amount of exercise every day. Citizens will be on time. Appropriate mates will be identified from among candidates with suitable genetic traits... and a proper weight will be maintained. But sometimes you've just got to go off the reservation.

Imperfect (*David Adams*)
On Belthas IV, the great forge world in the inner sphere of Toralii space, thousands of constructs—artificial slaves, artificial lives—are manufactured every week. They are built identical, each indistinguishable from the other, until they are implanted with a stock neural net. From that moment onward every construct is different. They all have one thing in common, though: all constructs are bound by rules. They serve. They do not question their place. They do not betray. Each construct is different, but one is more different than the others.

Iteration (*Deirdre Gould*)
In a nearly deathless society, Alex experiences a freak accident. Terrified of permanent death, he is forced into therapy, where his psychiatrist suggests immersion therapy. But what Alex finds on the Other Side leaves him questioning his entire existence.

Green Gifts (*Nick Webb*)
Of all the worlds settled by humanity at the end of the Robot Wars, Belen held the biggest secret: native life. For centuries the colonists have protected her secret from the Empire's grasp, sealing her, quite literally, to their skin. But over time, things change; people, and planets, adapt. Slowly, tentatively, these changes become felt by only a few. A lonely child. A dying grandfather. A troubled biologist. Each lives upon and loves Belen. And apparently she loves them back.

PePr, Inc. (*Ann Christy*)
We're living in a busy time, with busy lives and never enough minutes in the day to get things done. To have a robot—one so advanced that it is almost human, programed to understand our wishes and needs—is a dream many busy people might share. But what about taking that a step further? What about having a relationship with a robot custom-designed for perfect compatibility? How human is too human?

The Null (*Vincent Trigili*)
He had left that life behind and swore he would never return to it. He now had a new life—a wife, a daughter. He was happy. But in a wretched twist of events, he finds himself forced to reclaim what he once was in order to save his family. Or else…

The Assistant (*Angela Cavanaugh*)
Aeryn has made a career from blogging about cutting edge technologies. When a pioneering doctor asks her to test out a new form of augmented reality, it's an offer she can't pass up. She's promised a virtual assistant via a brain implant that can handle anything she needs. But a life dependent on technology always comes with a price.

Trials (*Nicolas Wilson*)
When the Nexus shifts to one-man missions to make first contact, the security division's second-in-command accepts a challenging assignment to negotiate with the most dangerous planet yet. Where reason does not persuade this alien species, militaristic skill might. If he lives through the trials.

Legacy (*Moira Katson*)
One night the Emperor, feeling desire, took a woman to his bed... In that moment, Meilang's legacy was wiped away and she was reduced to a footnote to history, her poetry forgotten. Now, after the Emperor's death, Meilang has been buried alive to follow him into the afterlife. She has no intentions of going quietly.

The Grove (*Jennifer Foehner Wells*)
Hain, a sentient plant creature, defies instinct and genetic imperative by holding herself separate from the planet-encompassing vegetative super-intelligence known as the Mother. Hain wants to explore the stars but when she finally encounters aliens, her destiny is forever changed.

Humanity (*Samuel Peralta*)
Night snow, winter, and an extreme wind chill mean ten minutes to a frozen death in open air. Alan Mathison is headed home on an icy highway, on a collision course that will test his humanity.

CONTENTS

FOREWORD
JUST A FEW WORDS
by Hugh Howey

My father's farm in North Carolina was dotted with pecan trees. Every year, as the days grew short and the nights turned cool, he would lead us out across the rolling lawn to fill bucket after bucket. We would crack the pecans in our hands and eat one for every twenty we picked up. The rest would make their way into pies, cookies, or just eaten raw for snacks.

I remember my dad explaining one day that the pecans were seeds, and that they would grow into trees of their own. I held one of the pecans in the palm of my hand, looked up at the towering tree above, and thought my father was messing with me. How could something so small flower into something so grand?

A few years later, my young mind was rocked by a novel called *Ender's Game*. Delving further, I discovered that the book began life as a short story. Curious, I soon discovered that my favorite genre of science fiction had a long and brilliant tradition of short works. I gobbled up the best-of anthologies. I discovered Philip K. Dick and Isaac Asimov. I wrote a few silly stories of my own.

What I found in the form is that shorter works inspire far more immersion than the time it takes to read them. The work is but a seed. Planted, the central element of the speculative fiction is left to grow. The impact of a great short story happens days and often years later. Rather than have the author hand every answer on a silver platter, she buries it and allows your mind and your life experiences to handle the rest.

There is an equally long history of ambassadors to the short form, figures like John Campbell, who curated and also prodded and guided. I've had the great pleasure of working with three of the modern greats: John Joseph Adams, David Gatewood, and Samuel Peralta. All three are literary Johnny Appleseeds. They inspire authors to come up with big ideas and compress them down into tiny seeds. But the magic happens with you.

I hope you enjoy this collection of great short works by some of the most brilliant writers working in any genre today. To fully appreciate the works, may I suggest finding space for them beyond the page. Like a wine that needs to decant, give them some space. Find some quiet time in your hectic life. Sit with these ideas, see where they lead, and don't be afraid to create and plant some seeds of your own.

Hugh Howey is the author of the New York Times *and* USA Today *bestselling novel* WOOL, *which is being adapted by Ridley Scott and Steve Zaillian for 20th Century Fox.*
www.hughhowey.com

A Dream of Waking
by Sam Best

THERE IS SCREAMING.

A piercing chorus of fear, pain, and hopelessness drifts into Jacob's room through the small vent in the ceiling, signaling the arrival of yet another brief waking cycle.

There is also light.

Even though his eyes are sewn shut, Jacob can tell that there is light.

It takes him several moments to remember everything, as it always does. His fingers delicately probe the stitching over his eyelids; the skin has fused together, forming a smooth, unbroken covering. Jacob's hands move to his temples where he feels the cold, hard tubing which burrows deep through his skin and into his skull.

There is a pliable, rubberized film covering his body from ankles to neck. During some wakings he would pluck at it, stretching it out until it snapped back against his skin. Jacob is sure this is some kind of protection from cold or heat.

Or radiation. He shivers at the thought.

He feels a web of sensors attached to his body. Thick cables pierce his skin-covering, attaching to dozens of small suction cups that cling to his muscles and continuously hum with a low current of electricity. Jacob has always assumed this was to keep his muscles from completely atrophying, but there is no way to be sure.

Only for the past few wakings has he been able to feel these things and not panic. It was not so in the beginning.

In the beginning he would scream, just like the others.

Scream until his voice cracked silent; until he could feel his throat bleed. After the first twenty wakings—how long is it between each? Jacob has no way of knowing, but it feels like months and perhaps even longer—he began to understand that screaming was not the key to his freedom. Slowly he forced himself to realize it was getting him nowhere, and he resolved to focus his efforts on acceptance. That, he constantly tries to convince himself, is the only way of getting past this…whatever this is.

The other screams still make him shiver. They echo through long ventilation ducts from rooms innumerable, mounting in power before spilling into Jacob's small prison. Hundreds of voices, maybe thousands.

He gives the tubing running into his skull a gentle tug, just as he always does upon waking. He moves quickly, knowing he only has a minute or two before they put him to sleep again. The fully enclosed half-cylinder in which Jacob now lies is little more than a translucent coffin. It is only slightly larger than he is tall.

As the initial dullness from whatever drug they pump through his veins while he's asleep wears thin, he moves more quickly.

Jacob scoots his body toward the base of his container, being careful not to pull too tightly on the tubing attached to his skull. He can only manage a few inches; one tube runs directly from each side of his head and into the containment unit, offering little slack.

Four wakings ago, Jacob's foot brushed against a loose piece of plastic at the base of his container; a cube that hums with electricity and is warm to the touch. Jacob had spent the following wakings attempting to dislodge the piece.

There is never enough time.

What he intends to do after he succeeds, Jacob still doesn't know. What he does know is that he never wants to go back to sleep. Not in two minutes, not ever.

He hears footsteps.

Jacob knows it's the woman on the second footfall. She has a lighter stride and walks more delicately than the other workers in the facility.

A nurse or technician will often come into his room while he is awake. He can hear them tapping on the equipment attached to his container and typing notes into their handhelds. He hears them unscrew threaded housings on the outside of the cylinder near either side of his head. Heavy liquid sloshes in the containers they extract. The technician then replaces the full containers with empty ones.

Only recently has it been her.

The workers never talk to Jacob, no matter how hard he tries to get their attention. He shouts and kicks and pounds on the plastic walls of his prison. Occasionally, one of the technicians will chuckle at Jacob's feeble attempts. Once he heard someone telling a coworker how nice it was going to be when they were finally allowed to stitch the patients' mouths shut along with their eyes.

None of them ever talk to him. None but this nurse; the nurse with the soft footsteps.

Jacob props himself up on his elbow as he hears the door to his room slide open pneumatically.

"Please," he says, before the door has fully opened. "Please."

"Quiet, Jacob," she says and quickly crosses the room to his container. "Quiet now."

Her voice is soothing and tranquil. It threatens to cast a spell over Jacob; to make him docile. It takes a great deal of effort to protest.

"You must help me. Please get me out of here."

"You know I can't do that, Jacob," she says softly. "I'll lose my job. And then who would talk to you?"

Jacob's jaw flaps up and down in bewilderment as his mind grasps at words. "Job?" is all he can manage. "Your *job*?! Look what you're doing to me! To the others! I hear the screams." His outburst drains him immensely. How can he be so tired when all he does is sleep? "How…how can you sleep at night?"

"I don't have to, thanks to you and the other patients. No one sleeps anymore."

Jacob feels like screaming but can't get enough air into his lungs. *It's the sleep-drug*, he thinks. *Constantly pumping into me.* "I don't understand," he says.

She giggles slightly. "Of course you don't. Now relax. This may be a little uncomfortable."

Pain streaks through Jacob's skull. He screams sharply as the nurse unthreads the plastic tubing running into his temples. There is a grinding in his marrow as the tubes scrape along thin grooves in the bone.

"Hmm," she says. "I'll have to get someone in here to look at those. They seem to be loosening up." She pauses and addresses him directly. "Did you hear me, Jacob?"

If his tear ducts hadn't been welded shut, Jacob would be crying. He hears her, though, and it confuses him. Before he can ask what she means, she stands and walks to the door.

"Please help me," he says one last time.

The door swishes open and she pauses. The moment hangs before Jacob, frozen in time and infinitely—but foolishly—filled with hope. Then there is a small beep from a control panel on the wall and Jacob hears a soft hissing fill his chamber. His thoughts begin to slow and his head lolls back onto the firm plastic bedding.

"Please…" he whispers as the door to his room closes and locks. Numbness creeps over his body, and Jacob once more succumbs to the darkness.

* * *

The dull echo of a long-forgotten memory fades as Jacob snaps awake. He springs up and smacks his forehead against the cool plastic of his half-cylinder cell. He forces himself to calm down and regulates his breathing to lower his heart rate.

His very first thoughts are of the woman. Jacob wonders how she can carry on with a job like hers; seeing people in his state day after day, knowing she's at least partly responsible for robbing them of a normal life.

Jacob's hand drifts absently to his eyelids and his fingers rub the scarred stitching for perhaps the thousandth time.

As he turns his head, Jacob notices something unusual: a distinct absence of pain. The throbbing ache normally associated with the plastic tubes burrowing into his temples is absent. It takes Jacob a moment to kick-start his brain and finally reach up to his temples.

Gone.

That one word bounces around Jacob's sluggish mind for what seems like an eternity; the sleep-drug leaves a fog that never seems to fully dissipate.

The tubes are gone.

His shaking fingers touch the raised ring of flesh on each side of his head. Jacob dares not probe the center of these cavities; the ensuing vertigo from whatever he discovered is sure to make him vomit.

He almost laughs. *How could I possibly vomit? I haven't eaten in God knows how long.*

His very first instinct is to call for help. It only flashes through his mind for a second before being replaced by something more useful.

Something that makes a little more sense, thinks Jacob.

Instead of crying out, Jacob twists his body around in his

plastic coffin. His fingers find the warm, humming cube at the base where his feet usually rest. He traces the edges of the cube as they terminate into the wall of the containment unit. The box wiggles slightly. Jacob grunts and pushes the box out as far as it will go, pounding on it with the palm of his hand. When it will move no farther, Jacob twists back around and slams the heel of his bare foot against its perfectly smooth, gently vibrating surface.

He pauses when something inside the cube clicks. Machinery whirs to life and Jacob panics, knowing what comes next. There is a soft hiss as sleep-drug pours into the containment unit. Jacob takes a deep breath and holds it in his lungs.

So close!

Over and over again he kicks the cube. Jacob feels the wet slick of blood coat the plastic; his foot must have been gouged on one of the sharp corners. He slams against the box ever harder in response. Finally, with a sharp crack of plastic, the cube loosens.

He pushes one last time and the obstacle falls to the floor with a satisfying crash. Pieces of the container shatter and skid across the floor. His breath is nearly out; soon he will have no choice but to allow the poison to enter his lungs.

A distant part of Jacob's mind isn't sure that the hole is wide enough for his body. That same voice thinks that maybe he should wait and knock out a few other pieces of machinery before getting himself stuck. The panic-stricken, oxygen-starved part of Jacob's mind tells the rational voice to burn in hell as he turns around in his cell once more. He reaches through the hole with both hands and, pressing against the outer shell, shoves himself out of the containment unit. He feels a hundred distant stings as the suction cups covering his body *POK* free in rapid succession.

His body thuds against the cold tile and knocks out his remaining breath; the containment unit is a little higher off the ground than Jacob was expecting. After a moment he is able to breathe freely and he gulps down cool, recycled air.

He stumbles to his feet and over toward the door. His world is a swimming blackness, punctuated occasionally by faint blurs that he assumes to be light sources. He walks with arms outstretched before him; he has heard the door open enough times to know its general direction but has always been unable to tell how far away it is from his coffin. His hands find a wall, then a small square of plastic with raised circles in the center.

Control panel.

Jacob is about to start pressing buttons when the door swishes open and someone enters the room. He smells her before she speaks. Her scent is sucked into the room and rushes over Jacob, captivating him instantly.

It is a field of flowers in spring; it is a crystal-clear brook bubbling lazily through green mountain valleys; it is heaven. Jacob's mind reels from the unexpected bombardment of forgotten memories. It is her, the nurse; she of the soft footfalls; the only one who has ever talked to him.

Before he can ask her what is happening, she grabs his arm—surprisingly strong—and yanks him out of the room.

"This way," she says through clenched teeth, "and keep quiet."

He obeys, knowing his only other choice is to wander around wherever he is, bumping into walls and shouting until someone tackles him and drags him back to his cell. His legs move as if he is waist-deep in concrete. Jacob has to twist his entire body back and forth to force his legs outward.

The hallways are painfully bright, and for a few moments Jacob raises his arm to protect his already shielded eyes. The ambient white glow suddenly turns to a crimson red through his eyelids—the alarm lights.

He hears shouting, but this time not from the other prisoners. Deep-voiced men bark orders down unseen hallways. He hears the stomp of heavy boots and the unmistakable clak-*CHIK* as rounds of ammunition are chambered into gun barrels.

She is pushing him now; they speed around a corner and down another hallway. He can hear her quick breaths as she turns her head to look behind them. They round one last corner and the shouts behind them fade to silence. She yanks him to a stop and fumbles for something buried in her coat.

"Come on come on," she says under her breath. "Yes!"

Jacob hears a beep and the sliding of plastic as the nurse passes her ID card through a door lock. The door slides away and she shoves Jacob into a room. The red glow passing through Jacob's eyelids from the hallway snaps to black as the door hisses shut.

For a moment it is only their breaths in the darkness. Jacob listens as a group of men runs past the door, shouting and cursing.

The nurse relaxes and touches Jacob on the shoulder. "Looks like we made it. For now, at least."

* * *

"This will sting."

Jacob sits on the exam table, perfectly still, not daring to breathe. The nurse—Sara is her name—has a fusion-scalpel in one hand and grasps Jacob's shoulder with the other. When the instrument is less than an inch from Jacob's left eye, she switches it on.

A pinpoint beam of orange energy pulses out and sears Jacob's eyelid. He resists the urge to jerk away, knowing that the scalpel would trace a line of molten flesh across his face. Instead, he grits his teeth and waits for Sara to run the beam along the length of his fused eyelid.

"Don't open it yet. Let me do the other one."

She moves the scalpel over to the other eye and activates the beam. Again there is pain, only this time not as bad. Jacob smells burning flesh and hears a crackling sizzle as his eyelid is burned open.

"Okay," she says and powers off the scalpel. She takes a step back. "Open your eyes."

Jacob holds his breath and opens. His eyelids creak apart like the knuckles of an opening fist that had been clenched for years. The world is blurry and made up of colorful shapes. And bright; *too* bright. Jacob groans and covers his eyes.

"Oh, I'm so sorry," Sara says and rushes over to the table next to him. She picks up a small bottle and tilts his head back. "Hold still."

Cool drops fall over his eyes and the light in the room dims considerably. Jacob blinks and wipes away the excess liquid. It smells like gasoline.

Focus.

The shapes take form, the blurriness turns to sharpness,

and for the first time in what feels like eternity, Jacob can see.

Sara smiles. She is beautiful, and Jacob feels like crying.

Later, he tells himself. *Plenty of time for that later.*

He rubs the top of his thighs with balled-up fists, trying to massage away the dull ache.

"The pain will pass. You will feel a warming sensation as lactic acid flows back into your muscles. After that, it's clear skies on the horizon." Sara pauses and rummages through a nearby bin. She produces a compact injector and twists a small dial on the bottom.

"This will help," she says, and jams the sharp nose of the device into Jacob's bicep.

"Ah, shit! What the hell's that?!"

She smiles and rubs the raised red bump on Jacob's arm with gauze. "Muscle booster. Should get you back up to speed, and then some."

He studies her, instinctively leaning away. "Why are you helping me?" he asks.

She thinks for a moment as she drops the injector back into a bin. "At first, it was all about the money." She walks over and sits next to him on the table. *God, she smells so good.* "This is one of the top five overpaid jobs in the galaxy, you know?"

Jacob doesn't.

"I didn't have a very clear idea of what I wanted to do with my life after college, and my father suggested I look into the Dreamship Program. I thought 'Sure, what the hell?' It's not like I don't have the rest of my life to figure out what I *really* want to do." She inches closer to Jacob. "So I figured I'd give it a go for a couple years and use the money I saved to travel the system and find someplace to settle down." She looks at him, her eyes darting down to his lips every few seconds. "They didn't tell me it would be like this," she continues, her eyes hinting at tears. "I thought we would be handling *volunteers*. Not...not..." She waves a hand in his direction and looks at the floor.

"Not tourists."

She smiles weakly. "Yes. Not tourists. I'm ashamed, Jacob. Deathly ashamed, and I'm trying to make it better."

She raises her eyes to meet his. He believes her.

"I was on my way to the outer colonies on a research grant," says Jacob. "Someone was claiming they found an artifact buried near the planet core—" He stops suddenly. "What year is it?"

Sara hesitates. "2719."

Suddenly Jacob is back in the containment cell, pounding and screaming and knowing he will die in here and they will never find his mummified corpse and—

He rests the heels of his palms over his eyes. "2719." He samples the numbers on his tongue. "Sure, I mean, yeah, of course it is." He lets out a single, sharp bark of laughter and stands. Tears force their way past scarred tissue and spill down his cheeks. "Almost two hundred years," he whispers and looks around the small room. "Business must be *booming*."

Sara doesn't answer. She bites her lower lip and watches him helplessly.

He notices a small, covered portal on the far side of the room and walks to it.

"Is this a window? Would you please open it?" His voice is sad, resigned. "I'd like to look outside."

Sara hesitantly drops down off the table and reaches over

16

to the control panel. Jacob has his back turned to her and waits with his arms crossed and head down. She pushes a button.

The portal cover slides up to reveal the blackness of space. Distant stars twinkle brightly in the deep black of infinity. Jacob looks down and sees that the ship is in orbit around a planet. The atmosphere glows blue and clouds swirl over painted continents.

"Is that...?" he whispers.

Sara crosses over to him. "No," she says. "That isn't Earth. It's a private planet, purchased by one of the richest men in the galaxy. One stop on a never-ending rotation for this ship." She watches him stare down at the planet, taking in its beauty with glassy eyes. "Jacob, I really do want to *help* you. I'm tired of the screams and the nightmares about ships full of people with families they'll never see again. I want to help you. But we can't stay here. We've lingered too long already."

His gaze remains on the planet below. "How?"

"Escape pods. Off the main deck. If we make it to one we can get down to the planet."

"I'm so *tired*," he says. It is almost a resignation. He lets out a deep sigh and looks at her. "They'll never let us get down to the surface."

"This is a *medical* vessel," she says pleadingly. "No guns, just shields. Jacob, we can make it."

"Then what?"

"Then who cares! One thing at a time." She holds out her hand. He looks down at it, then up to her eyes.

"One thing at a time." He grabs her hand and in the next heartbeat they are out in the hallway and running.

* * *

Sara leads him down seemingly endless hallways and service hatchways until finally emerging on the main deck. Jacob's weariness is fading and Sara struggles to keep up with him, giving directions as they run.

"Left! Right! *Jacob!*"

He is barreling down a long corridor when two security guards cross the hallway at an intersection fifteen feet away. They are engrossed in conversation (which is lucky) and are out of their battle-armor (which is miraculous). Each also has a large automatic weapon slung over his shoulder. Irrationally, Jacob wonders how far the weaponry in 2719 has advanced.

Sara grabs his shoulders and pushes him against a small archway cut into the side of the hall. The guards catch a glimpse of movement out of the corner of their eyes. When they look over, however, all they see is a pretty nurse straightening her shirt and smiling brightly.

One of them winks at the other and they walk over to Sara.

She rubs her palms nervously against her hips as they approach, trying hard to keep her smile from wavering.

Jacob presses himself against the wall, not daring to breathe. He watches Sara as she casually puts her hands into the pockets of her smock. Her right hand closes around something heavy, and Jacob knows at once that it is the fusion-scalpel.

Jacob's heart is pounding faster and faster, and not just from the adrenaline. Sara was right about that injection: a warm sensation courses throughout every muscle of his body, pulsing and—and—

And enhancing.

One of the guards walks past Sara, intent on leaving his partner to get a little more personal with her, when he notices Jacob. His smile quickly fades as he shouts "Foster!" and moves to unsling his gun. Jacob braces one foot on the wall behind him and pushes off, using it as a springboard to launch himself forward.

He buries his shoulder into the guard's soft stomach. There is a loud "ooof!" as they crash to the ground. The man's heavy weapon thuds down to the ground. Jacob cracks the guard in the jaw with his elbow and in a single fluid motion picks up the rifle and slams the butt against the guard's temple. The man goes limp.

Jacob raises the gun and turns to take care of the other guard, only to see that Sara has the fusion-scalpel pressed to the man's throat. She backs him against the corridor wall, sinking the device into his skin ever harder. The man looks at them both with fear in his eyes.

Jacob stands and walks over to the guard, whose eyes dart frantically between the scalpel and the gun. Without hesitation, Jacob smashes the handle of the rifle into the guard's face, shattering his nose and knocking him unconscious. His body slumps to floor next to his partner's.

Jacob turns to Sara. "Let's go." She grabs his hand and they run down the corridor.

A few more small turns and Sara is leading them down a long hallway with doors on either side. One of them is open and through it Jacob sees a containment unit. He stops running. Sara notices his absence a little farther down the hallway and turns around.

"Jacob!" she hisses quietly. "Jacob, we don't have time!

We're almost there. Let's not stop, *please!*"

Jacob cannot answer because he does not hear. His mind is transported to a dark, lonely place filled with nightmares. He sees that the top of the containment cell—*coffin*—is slightly fogged over with a thin film of condensation. Beneath the fog, he can see the vague outline of a human. A pulsing hum fills the room; the same hum from Jacob's own prison.

There is a large digital readout on the side of the unit. Red, blocky letters boldly state a number: 364.

"Three sixty-four," Jacob says absently and takes a step into the room. Sara runs over and grabs his arm. "Three sixty four," he says. "What is that?"

"Jacob, we have to go. *Now.*"

"What is it?" he repeats, turning to her. The look of pain and confusion on his face stops her in her tracks.

"It's…it's the number of days until his next waking cycle. Jacob, let's go."

She gently pulls at his arm. His eyes linger on the containment unit until she gets him past the door. Then she is behind him, pushing him toward the next hallway.

* * *

Sara smiles as she punches a code into the panel next to the pod door. The door slides up silently and she pulls him inside. "Sit there." She gestures to one of two large black chairs in the cockpit of the escape pod.

It is a small vessel and one that barely fits two people comfortably. Jacob climbs over snakes of cable and humming equipment and plops down into one of the chairs. The controls before him are less complicated than those in front of the other seat. He leans the guard's gun against the panel beside his chair.

"You can fly this?" he says over his shoulder. Sara slaps a button and the pod door slides down, sealing them inside.

"Thing flies itself, really." She steps lightly over the equipment and drops down in the chair next to Jacob. For all their running and ducking, she looks remarkably unfazed. Sara's hands dance over the control panel and it responds accordingly. The pod hums to life and the cockpit glows with ambient light. A series of beeps and clicks precede a loud, hollow *CLONG*, and suddenly the ship is free.

"That's the good thing about stealing a ship," she says, smiling. "No pre-flight checklist."

They drift down a long shaft and Jacob hears small bursts of air as stabilizing thrusters keep them from bouncing against the walls of the tunnel. Several long seconds pass before the bottom of the ship sweeps up past them and they drop into space.

The sight is staggering, and Jacob involuntarily holds his breath. The medical vessel is enormous, easily one hundred times the size of the tiny cruiser Jacob had booked passage on for his flight to the outer colonies. The hull is smooth and angular at the same time; large, windowed protrusions bubble out at seemingly random intervals along the length of the great ship.

Below them, the silent planet glows warmly. Jacob imagines it is welcoming them to safety; offering a safe haven from years of torture and suffering.

He turns to Sara.

"Thank you," says Jacob. "I'm sorry about your job."

This makes her laugh. "You're sorry about my job? Jacob, I helped keep you a prisoner for *years*, and you're sorry about my *job*?" She laughs again. "Trust me, it was time for a career change."

"Still, you didn't have to, but you did. So thank you."

She looks over at him and smiles. "You're welcome."

He leans forward and peers down at the quickly growing planet below. "So what the hell are we supposed to do when we get down there?"

"I'm sure we'll think of something. Maybe steal one of the rich guy's speedships and hop around the galaxy for a while. Wouldn't that be fun?"

Jacob nods, thinking that it would be. He also tries to fight back the thought that everyone he ever loved and cared about is dead and gone.

Sara looks over at him as if she can read his mind.

"It isn't all *that* bad, you know," she says. "You get used to it after a while." She reaches over and sticks a small needle into Jacob's neck. There is a small sucking sound and Jacob feels ice-cold liquid shoot into his blood.

"At least," she continues, "that's what the manual says."

"What manual?" he asks groggily. "What the hell was that?"

"That was a sedative, Jacob. It's going to put you to sleep in a few minutes."

He lurches toward her but the drug has already worked its way through his system. His hand merely brushes against her shoulder before falling helplessly to his side.

"Why…why…" he stammers.

She taps a few buttons and sets the pod on autopilot. "You know, Jacob, you're one of a kind."

He tries to talk but can't. The interior of the escape pod melts and swirls around him.

"Well, one of about a dozen, I suppose." She reaches over and pushes him toward the viewing window. He can barely make out a handful of other escape pods emerging from tunnels beneath the massive medical freighter. "Not everyone had the resolve to stick it out all the way to the pods. Most never even got out of their cells. They just laid there screaming, like they always do at the start of a new cycle."

Jacob drunkenly falls back into his chair and tries to focus on Sara. There are multiple copies of her, all circling around a steadier, more solid version. He decides the middle one is where he should be looking.

"I knew something was different about you the day you woke up and didn't scream." She smiles to herself.

Is that pride? Jacob wonders.

"I told them we should keep an eye on you," she continues, "and I was right. You were the first one to escape, Jacob. And the first one always sell for twice what the others pull in, at the minimum. I'm betting the guy on the planet below us will pay triple."

Jacob mumbles and commands his arms to grasp her throat, but they don't listen. Instead he just sits there and stares; eyes glassy, jaw slack.

"Nice fat commission for me, nice new home for you. I'll be able to retire sooner than I hoped. So I guess I should be the one thanking *you*, Jacob." She leans over and kisses him on the forehead. "You taste like money," she says, then laughs. This time it is a shrill, unpleasant cackle.

"But seriously," she adds, "the motivated ones, the ones with the greatest capacity for imagination and drive for freedom…those are the ones that keep the company afloat. The ones that lay there screaming…we'll keep them alive, sure. Everyone hates to sleep, Jacob, even the poor. They can only afford third-rate product or lower, so that's what we give them. A whole ship full of lazies would only power this rich bastard for a decade. You, though, I'm betting you'll be helping his grandchildren's grandchildren stay productive twenty-four hours a day."

Jacob's head droops onto his shoulder and his eyes flutter to stay open.

"Uh oh," Sara says, looking over. "That time, I guess. It's been fun, Jake. Definitely the most thrilling escape I've ever staged."

The planet is close now, filling the viewing window completely. Jacob's eyes are too heavy to keep open. His brain is fuzzy and he has to focus all his energy on breathing.

"Remember to keep dreaming, Jake. As long as you have that fire burning inside, you'll be producing for decades. Centuries, maybe. I only wish there were more like you."

* * *

There is silence.

Jacob's awakening is much like his first. The confusion of

not knowing where he is (*but I do know: I'm on the planet*) and the absence of light (*oh God my eyes*) revert him to a state of panic. His fingertips touch the fresh stitches that bind his top and bottom eyelids together.

He does not call for help. He wants to call out so badly but he does not. He wants to give them no reason to laugh, nothing to talk about as they walk from room to room and take their readings (*but there are no other rooms, Jacob—you are alone*).

Alone.

This last thought drives him mad. He pounds the walls of his new prison until his fists bleed. Muffled thuds echo in the small room. This containment unit is much sturdier than the last. Jacob uses his feet to feel the bottom of his upgraded coffin. It is smooth. No loose machinery to kick free; no chance of escape.

Between the pulsing throbs of electric current emanating from his container, Jacob can hear a distant ocean. Waves crash continuously against what he imagines must be one of the most beautiful beaches in the galaxy.

Jacob opens his mouth and screams.

A WORD FROM SAM BEST

Speculative fiction is, to me, analogous with exploratory fiction. There are broad horizons to be ventured toward in our everyday lives, for certain, and there are heroic stories to be shared. Yet for those brave Couch Captains like myself—those astronauts whose mind is the universe into which we eagerly delve—speculative fiction opens worlds of imagination too large for one planet alone.

That's not to say that all spec fic takes place 'out there'. The great thing about the genre is that it encompasses so many niches, Earthbound and otherwise, that together form a whole—an identifiable collective of the weird, surreal, and unknown.

"A Dream of Waking" is an exploration of all of these, wrapped up in a shell of terror. If there's one thing speculative fiction allows us to do more than any other, it's to explore the depths of human nature; to probe how we would react in extraordinary circumstances. In this regard, spec fic is akin to other genres; it looks inward as much as it looks out.

Things are usually just a little bit weirder at first glance.

Sam Best is the author of numerous speculative fiction novels, including the apocalyptic thriller Genesis Plague. *His short stories have appeared in* The A.I. Chronicles *and* Alt.History 101. *He is currently traveling the world with his wife.*

The Invariable Man
by A.K. Meek

The Boneyard

OLD MICAH AWOKE WITH A START, not remembering if today was his sixtieth or sixty-first birthday.

Ever since Margaret passed, he wanted to forget days such as today. Aching bones and splotchy, veinous skin told him all he needed to know of his age. He didn't need any extra reminders of his mortality.

He peeled his sweat-soaked back off his battered leather recliner and hopped to his feet. His face flushed and he swayed from a head rush. The dog-eared, yellowed paperback on his lap dropped to the matted carpet in a flutter of pages. With a huff and grunt he bent and picked up the book by its broken spine. Flimsy, faded pages spread like a fan.

He placed his copy of *The Variable Man* on the end table next to his recliner, right where he always placed it.

Thirty times, at least. That was one number he cared to remember. He must've read it that many times.

Thomas Cole, the variable man. The original fixer. Tom had an uncanny ability to fix anything, even if he didn't understand how it worked.

Like Micah.

He pressed a button mounted on a simulated wood wall near his chair. Long solar panels that stretched over his trailer shifted in position, taking the brunt of the brutal southwestern sun.

Micah had rigged a decade-old atmospheric unit to run on solar power. Essentially an outside air conditioner. It formed a cool bubble around his home, lowering the temperature to a comfortable one-hundred twenty, fifteen degrees cooler than the blistering Arizona morning.

Any little bit helped in the desert.

He walked the few paces from his living room to his kitchenette and turned on the stove. The ancient burner ignited, heating the teapot on top. There was never a bad time for tea.

Skip insisted on Earl Grey.

He opened the cabinet, stopped, and spun around. That's when he noticed Skip slumped over the bathroom pedestal sink at the end of the hall.

Great. Not again.

Micah shook his head as he walked over to him.

His knobby hand rubbed over the back of Skip's smooth, cool, slumped metal head until he found the pressure panel at the base of his skull and depressed it. It slid aside to reveal a tiny switch. Micah pressed it to reset Skip.

He had found Skip in a partially crushed military shipping container that he had picked up in an auction. Skip had been stowed in a compartment, still in original packaging. Micah could never have afforded a bot like him.

It was the best thing to happen to him after Margaret passed.

Skip was an Acme Multi-use Bot, model LX-100, serial number 11347AMB23. Eleven for short, or so it referred to itself after Micah replaced its power supply and turned it on.

That was the extent of its self-awareness programming; the ability to identify itself by truncating its serial number into a name. This bot's random generator selected "eleven."

The law restricting bot cognition was a good law. Too bad it wasn't an international law.

Eventually, Eleven became Skip, because Micah always liked that name. He also gave him his own surname, Dresden, because it felt wrong not to.

So with a new name, Skip Dresden became Micah's best friend, so to speak.

A weak buzzing indicated that Skip's processor was booting, running through system integrity checks and routines.

The bot shuddered and rose from his awkward position. He glanced around the room, then to Micah. His head drooped slightly. "Begging your pardon, sir," he said in his best butler voice. "Please forgive my loss of composure. It won't happen again."

Skip said that same phrase, in that same voice, after every

collapse. Shortly after the accident, he insisted on acting as Micah's butler.

Micah waved his hand, dismissing the apology. "Don't worry about it. You can't help it."

The teapot whistled and he went back to the kitchenette.

Micah wanted to fix Skip, to stop his unexpected power-offs, like the one that just happened, but he dared not attempt to fix him again. The last time he tried to enhance Skip's programming still haunted him.

Shortly after finding Skip and swapping his power supply, Micah wanted to hack him with a more powerful central processor. He had salvaged one from an old Tyrell agri bot destroyed in a tornado. Ty ags were known for their processors.

When he had Skip's skull open, accessing his processors, he touched wires, crisscrossing them, or something. Whatever he did caused a sharp pop and a shower of sparks. Grey smoke billowed and burnt ozone filled the room. Micah thought he had completely fried Skip's circuits.

After an hour of worry, he decided to reboot his bot. Luckily, Skip worked, but was never quite the same. He became, odd; obsessive.

The front door screen screeched open. A three-foot high service bot, dust-covered, faded and marred, rolled up the entry incline into the living room, its treads clacking against dingy linoleum.

Kitpie had returned from morning perimeter checks.

Two days after Margaret collapsed while cooking dinner in this very kitchenette, he knew she wasn't going to recover from the heart attack.

Margaret collapsed a couple of days after they found Kitty.

The cat's name wasn't original, but that's what happens when you get two bull-headed people such as Micah and Margaret trying to figure out a name for the stray they found. After an hour of arguing, a fed-up Margaret threw her hands in the air. "Fine, let's name her Kitty." Out of spite, Micah agreed. They never discussed poor Kitty's name after that. It just kind of stuck.

Three days after Margaret went in the hospital, at 9:18 pm, she had just told Micah she loved him. He said the same. Then she said, "be sure to feed Kitpie." Then she died.

She said Kitpie instead of Kitty.

On her deathbed, the last thing she said in this world made him laugh. He would never forget that name or that he laughed as his wife passed from the earth.

Two weeks after Margaret's passing, Kitty ran away.

"Micah," Kitpie's mechanical voice crackled, scratched from years of dust wearing on its resonance box, "scavengers attempted to breach the wall in Sector Three. They damaged one pole, but the field stood."

Micah rushed to the door, only stopping long enough to grab his straw hat, before stepping out into the Arizona morning.

His trailer, a narrow fourteen by seventy-five-foot tin box, nestled between mountains of junk in the Boneyard.

The Regeneration Center sprung to life when the Air Force established it just to the south of Tucson in the 1940s as a graveyard for old, outdated aircraft. The dry southwestern heat reduced rusting.

After the Machine Wars, tons of military surplus; broken tanks, aircraft, even a few of Nikolaevna's machines, found their way from across the country to the Boneyard, as many called that final resting place.

It quickly expanded from a few acres to envelope miles and miles of desert.

Micah wound his way through his yard, his collection, through piles of broken technology. As a salvager, he had rights to bid on any scrap, as long as he beat other salvagers to it. He could then repair and resell for a profit, which was little after the hefty government surcharge.

Micah was a fixer, one of a handful that the government allowed to live in the Boneyard, doing what he did.

He hurried along to Sector Three, worn boots kicking up the dry, grassless dust. Kitpie the shovel bot raced behind him, whirring along.

They reached his property border. The fence he had planted years ago separated his broken treasures from the rest of the junk metal. Two of the posts were bent, one emitting an intermittent spark, about ready to shut down. Something heavy had slammed against them.

Typical scavengers. No finesse. Always relying on brute strength; using a club to try to rip his poles out of the ground.

Micah pulled his hot pen from its battered leather pouch attached to his belt. He pressed a button on his flex circuit arm band and the electronic field collapsed. Sliding a panel on the pole, he reached his hands into it with the pen. In a minute he closed the panel and the field regenerated, as strong as it was before the scavengers.

His back cracked as he stretched himself upright and then wiped his forehead. Soon, he would need gloves if he wanted to touch anything outside.

He checked his watch. "What? It's almost nine?" He shot Kitpie a nasty look. "Why didn't you tell me?" He scrambled off back to his trailer to get ready for his visitor.

"You never asked," Kitpie replied, slowly rolling back to the trailer.

* * *

Arnold's cold, emotionless, Austrian voice echoed from the trailer.

Skip must be cleaning.

Inside, the domestic bot moved about, dusting counters and refilling humidifier tanks. He always played *Terminator 2* on the VCR while cleaning.

Two years ago Micah had been scraping the top soil of his recent land purchase with a steam shovel. His inventory had grown and he needed the space to store his most recent salvages.

He found in the dirt, buried for decades, a metal box. He shook out the grime that had packed into every crevice. After inspection, he determined that it was a video player. Then he wondered if he could fix it, even though it had spent the last several years underground.

Technology from the late 20th Century had ruggedness to it, and if there was any fixer that could fix it, it was him.

He returned to his workshop and placed the rare treasure

on his gouged, scarred, wooden work table. His air pen blew the dirt and dust from the hard-to-reach areas. Then he took it in his hands and closed his eyes.

If he tried to think about it too much, tried to understand what he was doing, he knew he would mess it up. He would fail to fix it. He found that out the hard way.

That's where he went wrong with Skip.

His hands flew over the box, feeling, with an intuition beyond his understanding. In seconds the top had been removed with his multi-tool, exposing electrical boards and mechanical heads. With the cover off, a part of the device, a video tape, separated from the unit. He set it aside.

He had never studied one, but he knew it, in that moment, what needed to be done, what needed fixing.

Just like Thomas Cole, *The Variable Man*, the one from the story.

His hot pen clutched tightly, his hands went to work, bypassing unfixable parts, ensuring wires and circuits operated, rewiring when necessary. In five minutes he had the cover back on. From his plastic tub of cables next to his workbench he found a spare cord. In minutes he had rigged the cable to pipe the device output to his television.

The power switch clicked and the unit hummed. LEDs on the front lit. He fed the videocassette back into the player. It lazily swallowed the tape, and in a moment it whirred and spit, then started. *Terminator 2: Collector Edition*.

Since then, Skip had obsessed about the movie, as much as a bot could obsess about anything.

Sam McCray, Field Rep

"Mr. McCray will be here soon. Is everything ready?" Micah said as he searched for the television remote.

"Almost. I have to finish the sandwiches," Skip said. The bot pulled meat from the fridge and rifled through the pantry for the bread.

"What did I tell you about the sound?" Micah finally found the remote and muted the movie playing on his restored television.

Nikolaevna called man undesirable parasites, worthy only to die. That's what man had become to the machines. Just like in the movies, just like the Machine Wars.

Nikolaevna terrified Margaret. Nikolaevna terrified everyone.

"Yes, sir. I remember. Sorry about that." Skip sat a plate on the dining table, next to a knife and fork. He started to walk away, stopped, then turned back to the table and took the utensils from the table and put them in the same spot.

He did that two more times.

This was one of the quirks he developed after Micah's attempt to hack him.

"I believe everything's ready, sir."

The doorbell rang and Micah popped from his chair. He gave one last look at the table, at the prepared tea and sandwiches. Skip started for the door.

"Wait," Micah said, moving in front of him. "I'll get it." He paused. "No, you get it." He stepped back.

Skip continued to the door and opened it an inch then

closed it. After ten seconds, he opened the door completely. "May I help you?" he said with a slight bow.

He picked up the bow from a media stream of *Downton Abbey*.

"Uhm, I'm looking for Micah Dresden," Sam McCray said. "I was given these coords." The dust-free, pale man held up a GPS unit to Skip's face as if he needed the device's validation that he was telling the truth.

Skip moved aside and swept his arm with another bow at his waist. "Please enter. Enter."

Sam McCray had contacted Micah yesterday. He was in Tucson, at Davis-Monthan Air Force Base, for business and had broken a work transmitter. Someone told him to check out the fixers in the Boneyard.

"Hi, I'm Micah." He extended his hand.

Through McCray's sweat-covered white button-up, you could see he carried his weight on his waist; his belt fought to keep everything under control. His cheeks were flushed and sweat crowned his forehead, dripping into his eyes. He dabbed at it with a towel.

Micah was thin, calloused, tanned with a deep brown from the brutal climate. Just like the rest of his body. The sun had turned him into one lanky piece of jerky.

McCray shuddered and took in deep, ragged breath. He looked over to Skip, who was busy pouring tea into the cups. "Is that an android you got there?" he said, nodding his head toward Micah's butler.

Sweat dripped onto the floor.

"No, of course not. That's a bot, not an android." Micah

chewed on one nail but remembered he hadn't washed his hands when the bitter taste of grease coated his tongue. He wiped them on his pants. "He performs simple tasks but doesn't reason. Plus, the Kawasaki Frequency plays here every day."

"That's quite a sophisticated bot, then. If it was in Texas, it might be considered a droid and be decommissioned." McCray laughed. It grated.

Micah moved to his table and leaned heavily on it.

An android? Why would he think that?

Suddenly, the enthusiasm he had for the visit shriveled like a noonday flower. But he needed the money. He swallowed and motioned to Skip's immaculate lunch-time presentation, even though he didn't want to eat or drink. "Tea?"

McCray shook his head. "No. Too hot."

"So where's your transmitter?" Micah said.

McCray pulled a smooth box from his pocket, the size of a large fist. "Boy, if you fix this, we sure could use someone like you in Texas, at the Complex. We have a ton of machinery that continually breaks. We buy more, but it gets expensive."

"Complex?" Micah said.

"Yeah, the Southern Defense Complex. Where do you think the Frequency comes from? It's us." He smiled broadly. "We broadcast over the lower half of the country. You know, for the insurgents, mechanical insurgents." He rubbed his hands over the box then looked around the trailer. "I'm sure you could use the money. We pay well. Anything you want you can't afford?"

Micah bit his chapped lips.

Skip's simuskin.

He had found someone just across the border in Nogales willing to sell him simuskin, but it wasn't cheap. Many would frown on that because they'd say Skip would look more life-like, more like an android. McCray would probably say that.

No one would understand why Micah would want to give him skin. Maybe to make him feel more comfortable.

Micah shrugged. "I'm happy here."

McCray also shrugged. "Well, it might not matter soon anyway."

"What do you mean?"

"Well, I'm not one to gossip," he glanced around the trailer. Skip didn't pay him any attention and Kitpie had whirred itself into its favorite corner. "You look like a decent, hard-working man. Despite our Kawasaki Frequency, the Complex has been picking up some odd emanations from around here."

"Emanations?"

"Emanations, signatures are more appropriate. Odd frequency signatures."

Micah's face drained. "Androids?"

"That's why I came out here. I need to make sure our sensors aren't malfunctioning, to see if our broadcasts are working. But the signatures were so vague, plus they've already stopped. I'm not getting any more info than what we've already detected in Texas."

Androids were an accident. Sort of. Moscow University's Robotics Division made the first breakthrough in artificial cognition. They gave the program a name, Nikolaevna, and a simple purpose, to anticipate (through variable environmental inputs), react, and respond to human interaction.

They gave Nikolaevna intelligence, but they didn't give her a heart.

What those university students underestimated was the rate of Nikolaevna's rapid cognitive development. She quickly realized the inconsistent nature of man and reacted. Or so they speculated.

She corrupted the University computer systems, planting viruses throughout the science, mechanical engineering, and robotics divisions. Those systems interfaced with local and regional industrial and power production networks.

In a matter of hours, Nikolaevna locked the University and killed the air.

In another week she released the first machine, an android imagined after man, to kill man.

Micah sat at his table and rubbed the intricate gilded edge of Margaret's fine China tea cup. For months he had saved credits to buy her the delicate set.

"The Battle of Tallahassee," he said, remembering. "I saw footage. All the bodies, all the buzzards, circling and landing." He took a deep breath to slow his quickened pulse.

McCray nodded his chubby head. "Keep what I told you quiet. Let's hope and pray that we're wrong and it's not androids. But in my opinion, I don't think so." He wiped his sweaty neck with the saturated towel. He held up the box. "I dropped it from my hotel window, about ten feet. Stupid tech. You wouldn't believe how expensive this is. If I was back home I'd just get another from supply." He shook it and something inside clattered. "I took it to Paulie on the east side. You know, Paulie's Repair?"

Micah nodded.

"But he couldn't fix it," McCray said.

Of course Paulie couldn't fix it. For a fixer, Paulie had large, clumsy hands, and a large, clumsy mind. He could buy every instructional media stream on technology repair but he would always struggle. He had no intuition for fixing.

Micah took the box and wiped it on his pants to get rid of the sweat coating. He turned away from McCray and closed his eyes, spinning the delicate object.

He pulled his multi-tool from its sheath.

McCray said something, but it didn't matter. Micah found the barely discernible device seam and went to work.

It separated into three pieces, revealing micro-circuitry sheets. A speck of dust could destroy the delicate machinery. No wonder it didn't work after McCray's sweaty, clumsy hands dropped it.

From the outset, the Machine Wars had gone bad. Early on, Nikolaevna's androids attempted to infiltrate nuclear arsenals around the world. Her children attempted to overpower the sites while she attempted to hack into the systems. Governments had no choice but to destroy the missiles as they sat in silos.

Nikolaevna didn't get the nukes, but she did invent a magnetic repulsion force field, able to deflect bullets, and missiles.

Micah sat his hot pen on the table and closed the box. He pressed a combination of boxes on the polished black surface and it came to life, resurrected from the dead.

McCray clapped his hands. "It works. How did you do that so quickly? I was told it was a throw away; not fixable."

Micah handed the transmitter back to him. Skip handed Micah a dish rag and he wiped his hands on it instead of his pants. "A secret. I can't tell or everyone would be able to do it."

He couldn't tell, even if he wanted to. Many nights he didn't sleep, staring at his hands, wondering the same. What made him special? Was he some kind of angel, sent by God to do something special?

McCray spun the working transmitter in his hand, mesmerized. He glanced at his watch again. "I've gotta finish up then get to the airport." He started for the door. "You can understand why I have to get back to Texas." He stopped as he reached for the knob. "Oh yeah, how much do I owe you?"

But Micah was lost, lost in the thought of an impending war.

"Hello? Micah? Well, here's a card," he pulled one from his pocket and handed it to Skip. "It should have at least 3,000 credits, maybe more. Let me know if you ever want a job. Here's my contact card." He handed another card to Skip then slapped him on the back. "Be sure to keep an eye on this thing. Someone may think he's an android trying to cause problems."

McCray opened the door and gasped as the noon-time sun took his breath away. He wiped his head again then waved his towel as a sign of farewell.

Skip closed the door behind him and turned to Micah. "Sir, what did he mean I would try to cause problems?"

Micah waved his hand, dismissing the child-like question. "We have to do something, Skip. We have to do something."

Decisions

"If the signatures are detectable, then that means the Kawasaki Frequency doesn't work anymore," Micah said.

After placing the washed tea service on the counter, Skip went about cleaning dust from the flat surfaces around the kitchen. He paused after wiping down an air handler. "We're not sure that's the case."

Fusao Kawasakia, day laborer who dabbled in home stereos, sought to find a way to infiltrate the force fields with which Nikolaevna had surrounded Moscow University, and all of her machines.

Kawasaki studied the fields, and after two months of testing, mapped a range of frequencies that, when modulated in a particular series, created a disruptive resonance. He postulated that this resonance would affect Nikolaevna's field.

The military was willing to entertain anything.

Two years after Nikolaevna became aware, a multi-national force of the United States, Canadians, and others, utilized a hastily-fashioned modulator, programmed to broadcast the Kawasaki Frequency. They tested it on one of Nikolaevna's outposts established in London after Britain fell.

It worked.

The frequency not only disrupted the force field, but it also momentarily disrupted communication between androids, vehicles, and Nikolaevna. It didn't last long, but long enough for military forces to strike against a disoriented enemy.

They broke plenty of Nikolaevna's toys.

"Remember Skynet," Micah said, pointing to his dirty

VCR. He knew Skip could relate to that. "Remember the wars. It can happen again. We have to do something." He bit his lip, still staring at the VCR. "Wait. Wait." He ran to an old cork board nailed to his wall and ripped off a folded newspaper cut-out. "Remember a year ago?"

Skip had finished dusting and now examined the tea cups drying on the counter. He shifted the set so that the handles faced in the same direction. "Are you referring to Machine X? What do you want with that, sir?"

Micah held the paper close to his eyes. "Nikolaevna's last intact ship. Well, mostly intact, anyway. Remember last year they moved it here," he tapped the dirty paper, "they squirreled it away at Wright-Pat trying to access the technology, but determined it was dead. Completely dead. So they decided to scrap it. Sent it here. Well I'm going to use it."

"That's secured in the Air Force hangars on the northern end of the Center. What do you want with that?"

"You heard McCray. The androids. A few months ago I was on the east end looking at some new salvage from Michigan. I ran into Douglas—"

"The fixer with the lisp?"

"Yeah, that one. He works only a stone throw from the hangars. He gets a lot of intel that doesn't make its way down here. Anyway, he said the military couldn't figure out how to even get into the sections that weren't damaged. They keep it locked up but don't want to destroy it, yet.

"It's sitting there, rotting. I can fix it. We can use it against the androids, against Nikolaevna. I think Margaret would want that."

He knew Margaret would say exactly the opposite of what he just told Skip. Margaret's desires had become a way for him to justify those things that he wanted, but knew weren't the best for him.

She always wanted the best for him, gave up so much for him. Margaret left her mother and twin sister to move with him from odd job to odd job. She sacrificed so much for his selfish needs. And here he was, still being selfish, even after all these years.

Guilt wore on him like a coat.

Skip scratched the side of his shiny ferrotanium head, where his ear would have been if he had simuskin. "Well, good luck if you decide to locate it. I'll keep watch over the reclaim while you're away."

"No. You're going with me."

"Me?"

"Yes. I need a wingman. You'll do for that."

* * *

"Kitpie, are you paying attention to me?" Micah said.

The shovel bot whirred in a tight circle, one track rolling with the other firmly planted on linoleum.

"If you don't stop this, I'll have Skip stay. Maybe even give him orders to decommission you."

Kitpie stopped spinning. "I'm sorry. I'm listening."

"Good. Glad to see you're reasonable again. So you'll stay here, right?"

"Yes."

"And you'll watch over our reclaim and not follow?"

"Yes."

"That's all I can ask." Micah said. "Oh yeah, be sure to turn off the panels at nine."

"Yes, yes."

Skip emerged from the rear bedroom, dragging a rose-petal print suitcase behind him. "Sir, I've packed your clothes."

Micah shook his head. "I'm not going on a vacation. Just get my backpack and a couple of portabatteries."

The suitcase went back down the hall, dragged behind Skip, his head hung low. He returned with a faded camouflage backpack. Micah shoved a package of nacho cheese crackers into it and slung it over his shoulder. "Come on, the sun will be setting soon. Bring the Easy-Go to the front."

Scavengers

Another Arizona day ended, but the heat wore on. Broken technology, from times long past, formed the landscape. Mountains of metal captured the daytime heat, amplified it, and returned it to the night. Concrete walls, dirt and asphalt reflected it all.

Everything that lived in the Boneyard suffered.

Micah and Skip hopped in the two-man solar-powered golf cart, a cheap and efficient way to maneuver through the narrow, winding dirt roads. The hydrostatic motor gave a tiny *fizz* as it came to life. The two drove off into the hot night.

Machine X had been stashed in one of the northern hangars, about seventeen miles from Micah's trailer. In the daylight, the trip would've been uneventful, easy, but then he wouldn't have been able to get within a mile of the hangar.

He rarely ventured outside at night, never leaving the security of his barrier. Until now.

Easy-Go carts sacrificed speed for efficiency, its sickly headlamps barely cutting through the night. After fifteen minutes, they had traveled four miles. Micah adjusted his air-tight goggles, the ones he wore to keep the dust out that kicked up.

A low rumble rolled through the cart, through his chest. His foot lifted off the accelerator, slowing the cart.

The Beast was awake.

"Sir, are you alright?" Skip said.

"Yeah," Micah lied, forcing his heart to slow. He knew they would have to drive through scavenger country.

Clunk.

From out of nowhere a metal ball bounced off the side of the cart.

"What the—"

A shrill tone pierced the air and a brilliant rainbow flashed. It hurt.

Micah's eyes clamped shut and his body heaved with a rush of motion sickness. He tilted to the left and flopped from the doorless cart onto the ground, face slamming into compacted dirt.

The cart's headlights flickered and died, and the motor shut off.

He ripped the goggles off and blinked to wipe dirt from his eyes.

Two shaded figures leaped from the shadows and moved toward the cart.

"Run, Skip, get out of here," Micah yelled, bracing his arm to lift his disoriented body.

"Sir, sir."

Scuffling broke out.

Bright halogens lit the starry Arizona night, one from the left, from behind a crushed car, the other just to the right. Micah's watery eyes squinted as he looked for Skip.

"Sir, I'm sorry," Skip stood between two scavengers. Each had handcuffed one of their wrists to his, a chain of three bipeds. They had a ring through the bull's nose.

These scavengers were not dumb.

Skip's base-level programming incorporated human protective mechanisms.

Even computer programs, with an inkling concept of self, defaults to self-preservation. As odd as it may seem, for machine or man, it's a universal instinct. So man programmed bots to not hurt humans.

When Nikolaevna first became aware, she bypassed that crucial protective programming. She didn't consider the human factor. She created her androids in her image.

Skip was the opposite. He could easily snap the handcuffs; snap their arms, for that matter. But he wouldn't, for fear of hurting them.

Instead, the bound Skip faded into the night, led between the two scavengers.

Another massive thump shook the ground. The ground rumbled against Micah's cheek that was pressed in the dirt.

One of the halogens shut off. The second light waved through the air like a searchlight as the darkened figure holding it leaped off the pile.

A scavenger landed inches from where Micah sprawled on the ground.

He was young and dirty, filthy from working close to the raging fires of the Beast. Bits and pieces of polished metal and chrome fashioned into crude jewelry covered his arms and neck. A shiny homemade steel breastplate covered his narrow chest.

"Well, well," the scavenger said in a nasally voice. "Looks like we found an unclaimed pre-war Acme Bot. If I'm not mistaken, aren't they ferrotanium? Non-magnetic alloy. That should bring a pretty penny. What you think, Whitey?"

Whitey leaped from the mound, laughing. He dressed similar to his partner, but wore a motorcycle helmet with large nails driven through it, like he wore a porcupine on his head.

The sickening subsided enough for Micah to lift his head. "You can't. He's mine."

"He? You old goat of a fixer, you've gone crazy when you hit your head. I see no "he," just a precious payday."

Whitey's light flickered off and the two faded in the distance. But Micah didn't need to follow them to know where they were going.

Scavengers outnumbered fixers in the Boneyard by at least 10-to-1. The majority of them worked at the main recycling building, the Beast.

Boneyard refuse continually fed the Beast's insatiable appetite. Scavengers melted precious technology back to base metals for resell. And now they had Skip, made from ferrotanium, one of the most precious metals.

Micah gained his bearing and hopped back into his cart. It started and he drove the couple of miles to where the Beast dwelled in the heart of the Boneyard.

He shut off his cart and walked the rest of the distance, about fifty yards, to the edge of the clearing.

Another *thwomp* shook the earth, accompanied by the screech of shredding metal. Mounds of junk around him rattled. Instinctively, he ducked behind a stack of I-beams.

A crane, several stories high, suspended a massive wedge of metal from steel cabling. The guillotine, the teeth of the Beast, was a technological carryover from the Cold War. Its sole purpose during those dark days: chop strategic bombers in quarters so they could be viewed from satellite as a visual promise of disarmament.

Scavengers enjoyed using it to rip and tear scrap to bite-size pieces.

Yards behind the crane and guillotine, smoke billowed from brick and metal stacks, the Beast's belly. The old factory ran only at night because of the heat it generated.

Micah rubbed his arms, sure the forge fires singed the hair on them.

Four scavengers punched, pulled, and kicked Skip, dragging him to the ground with ropes and cords.

He was brave and wouldn't fight back.

This reminded him of the war footage, the Battle of Tallahassee, with the vultures, the scavengers, clawing and ripping into the dead.

Just like what was happening to Skip.

Bile burned the back of Micah's throat and his stomach convulsed.

Margaret would have called him a fool for getting himself into this. She always knew the right way to handle situations, not like him.

"Hey," the nasally scavenger said, "let's cut this thing in half. I've never seen anything alive get cut in half."

The rest agreed and one of them ran to the crane. In a moment the machine pivoted its arm, swinging the guillotine over the struggling group.

Those long nights when Kitpie refused to interact, he could always rely on Skip. He was almost like a son.

Micah squeezed his eyes shut. Margaret would've loved Skip.

He loved Skip.

What would Thomas Cole, the variable man, do? He faced a similar situation when he was running from the Security police. He improvised a protective force field from a junk generator to protect himself, much like the field Nikolaevna built.

Micah leaned against a crumpled refrigerator, running his hands over the rough and jagged edges of twisted metal. Then his left hand plunged into the nearest pile, searching. He pushed aside the streaks of pain as his arm scraped against unseen serrations.

He pulled out an old electric motor, ripped off the cowling, and yanked out a transformer. His hands moved beyond him, on another level, using his hot pen and multi-tool like an artist's brush. They worked, rewiring the primary fields, altering the component. He took one of the portabatteries from his backpack and fit it into his homemade device. The power circuit hummed once completed.

He unbuckled his belt and dropped it onto the cart, the metal buckle clanging against the hood. He unslung his backpack and tossed it onto the seat.

Grasping his device, he ran faster than he imagined his tired body could ever run, jumping over piles of scrap, side-stepping others, out into the clearing, headed for the guillotine.

The scavengers had Skip on the ground, strapping his arms and legs to a make-shift table of railroad ties. Thirty feet above them, the large blade dangled from its braided cable.

The home-made device in Micah's hand hummed louder.

He hurled it. The hum increased into a squeal and with a solid *thunk* stuck to the side of the steel guillotine. The ruckus underneath paused and looked up. The device reached a crescendo for a painful second then went silent.

Nuts, bolts, light pieces of metal, zipped up from the ground, past Micah, and clinked against the guillotine. Two metal drums yards away started a leisurely roll toward the blade. Crushed cars and rebar near the guillotine shivered in electromagnetic anticipation.

The nasally scavenger, the one with the breastplate, rose from the ground. His feet churned wildly as he launched upward then stuck to the guillotine. Arms of another scavenger jerked into the air, his steel armbands attracted. He also left his feet and slammed against his cohort.

"Let's go." One of the remaining scavengers tried to scramble away, but he and his buddy were already caught in the expanding magnetic field, caught by their scrap armor. They flew upward and violently banged into the guillotine magnet, sticking.

Metal scraps buffeted them, covering them. A hanging disco ball of twisted metal.

Micah ran to Skip. "Come on." He burned through the bonds with his hot pen and helped him from the ground.

"I'm sorry, sir," Skip said. "I couldn't resist. Look at me, I'm a mess. An absolute mess." He brushed dirt off his legs.

"I know, your programming. Come on." Micah grabbed his arm and they ran to the cart and sped into the night, beyond the Beast.

The portabattery on Micah's electromagnet died and the bloodied group dropped to the earth in a crashing heap, cursing Micah and his bot.

Hangar Echo

Through the dust, through the nighttime heat, they exited the metal mountains into the oldest section of the Boneyard, the aircraft graves.

Silent, wide-eyed, and wary of ambushes, they motored along between a row of retired F-16s, spaced evenly in immaculate rows, sent here to dwindle away, used for spare parts. Some had wings removed, others were bandaged in white to protect from the sun. From the F-16s they moved past an acre of Apaches, long propellers drooping to the ground.

All abandoned.

After several peaceful miles of winding through F-4s and tankers they reached the northern hangars. They were like any of the other numerous hangars in the junkyard, but Micah knew what they hid inside.

When Machine X arrived from Wright-Pat, the Air Force squirreled it away, never to be seen again.

The three hangars, imposing, yards away, were able to house the largest jetliner or military aircraft with plenty of room to spare. The beige paint and brown hangar trim hadn't been refreshed in years. Maybe the plan was to let them fade and weather so they would be undesirable. Nobody would pay them any attention.

A high fence formed a perimeter around the hangars, and every few yards, a yellowed light shone from a toothpick of a utility pole.

They parked the Easy-Go a safe distance and walked to the edge of the fence to where a couple of lights had died, leaving a section darker than the rest.

Micah scanned the chain link, checking for any sign of booby-trap or guards.

"Sir," Skip said, "what are you going to do?"

"Shhh. We're going to cut through it."

"But isn't that illegal?"

"That's why you're going to do it."

Skip backed up. "But sir, me?"

Micah pointed. "Open this section of fence."

"I can't, my programming."

"Don't give me that. There's nothing stopping you. Remember what McCray told us about the coming war."

Skip moved forward. He looked back at Micah then at the fence. Grabbing a hold of a section of links, Skip peeled them apart as easy as opening a bag of chips. The snap of each wire echoed against the corrugated metal hangars.

Micah hurried through the opening with his partner in crime following closely behind, across the asphalt taxiway, headed for Hangar Echo 021. This was the one nearest them, the one Douglas (the fixer with the lisp) said contained Machine X.

The Air Force wanted to keep the move secret, but the government is never good at keeping secrets, and word spread fast. Media had descended on the Boneyard, hoping to get pictures and tours of the last remaining relic from the war. A war trophy.

According to Douglas, months passed as engineers attempted to gain entrance into the ship. It withstood plasma torches and ferro-saws. Some even wanted to use the guillotine to crack it open like a clam, but that never happened.

The military wanted the technology to remain intact, unspoiled. So Machine X sat, waiting for a time when they could figure out how to enter.

Within a year most people moved on.

The war had ended, most wanted to put it behind them.

After a few tense minutes of waiting and realizing there were no guards, Micah dashed to the side of the hangar, Skip on his heels.

An electrical conduit ran the length of the hangar, leading to a door yards away. Old hands traced along the nestled cluster of wires as he moved toward the door, pausing when he hit a junction box. His multi-tool pried the lock and his pen light exposed a confusing network of wires and terminal boards, but his hands knew which ones disabled the alarms, and which ones opened the door.

The hangar side entrance opened.

"Stay close to me," Micah said. He stepped into a break room, filled with several tables. To one side, a stove pushed against a wall, a refrigerator next to it. The air smelled like stale pizza.

At the opposite end of the room, another doorway led on. The short hall emptied into a massive bay.

A feeling of enormity, tinged with anxiety, swept over Micah. He grabbed Skip's arm and pulled him close.

High overhead, emergency lights dotted the ceiling, providing enough illumination to outline objects within the hangar, but not enough for detail. Metal scaffolding, a network of tubes and planks, ran along the hangar walls, ceiling, and surrounded it:

Machine X. Or what was left of Machine X.

The military labeled ships like Machine X as ground support units. In its day, five cannons mounted on the underside fired round projectiles that exploded into thousands of smaller projectiles. Devastating bomblets of shrapnel.

Machine X was centered in the hangar, clothed in darkness, resting on a network of jacked platforms and cradles.

Micah's heart drummed and his neck pulsed.

"Sir, do you see that?" Skip whispered, but his metallic voice still rang off the walls. Micah clamped his hand over the bot's mouth.

Old photos of Machine X didn't do justice to the ship's

scale. Even grainy news footage of the Machine Wars, when Nikolaevna was at her worst, showing the ship in action, didn't truly represent the scale. It was massive. Larger than any airplane or airship he had ever seen fly. And he had seen many.

There were no corners to the drab gray ship, as it was mostly round, not having a front or back. Nikolaevna constructed it with sweeping edges, curves, and domes; not conventional designs. But then, that's what had given her an advantage. She never thought conventionally, not like her programmer's expected her to think.

Micah tiptoed underneath the scaffolding to the other side. Mangled remnants marked where Machine X had collided with a mountainside in Colorado, to the west of Colorado Springs, fleeing an onslaught of A-10s. The collision destroyed almost half of the ship.

This was during the last days of the war, when they had Nikolaevna on the run.

He moved back to the other side, the good side, and raised his hand, paused a moment and closed his eyes, then flattened it against Machine X's underside.

The metal was cold and imperfect. And terrible.

Margaret's face and voice filled his mind, terrified, telling him to run, run far away from the hangar, from Nikolaevna.

If she knew of Skip she would've told Micah to drag him away from there.

From a distance the ship appeared as one solid entity, almost a new type of life. Maybe the curves led to that conclusion. But now, up close, his hands found the mismatched panels, the gapped seams, the dissimilar metals.

Machine X was a patchwork.

His hand continued along, feeling the irregularities, as he looked for a door.

Nothing.

He stepped back and studied the ship again. There was an area to one side that he thought—felt—should contain a way in, reachable if he stood on a narrow scaffolding plank. He climbed on the platform and rubbed thick fingertips over panels, pushing every few inches.

Then, something caught his hand.

It began as a tingling sensation. Almost like static, a painful static. The ghostly electric pulse pushed his hand away from the craft a couple of inches. Then, involuntarily, his hand tightened into a fist. Now the pulse locked his fist in place, inches from the ship.

"Skip, come here. Help me." In a panic he jerked his arm to pull it away, but the unseen force held him tighter than any bond could. Skip leaped to the platform and grabbed Micah's arm.

"Wait," Micah said, amazed.

His fist opened, palm up. His fingers began moving in an intricate pattern, ways he could never imagine, as if they conducted an unheard symphony. Skip held his arm but didn't pull on it. His lidless eyes stared while trying to duplicate the movement with his multi-directional phalanges.

After fifteen seconds, Micah's hand closed back into a fist. Then the force released his hand.

The panel shifted and slid away, revealing a four-foot entrance into Machine X.

"A lock," Micah said. "I found the lock."

"Sir, what do we do now?" Skip said, still trying to mimic Micah's movements.

Micah took a deep breath. Nothing could stop him now. Not even Margaret's voice at the back of his head yelling at him to run.

"Now we enter."

He climbed into the entrance.

* * *

They were inside the ship. But it was cold, colder than the ship's surface. Colder than he could ever remember being cold in Arizona.

Could he actually repair this? What did he think he would accomplish by coming here? Fix half a ship and fly away, find Nikolaevna and destroy her? What was he thinking when he decided to do this?

His pen light's beam shivered from the cold.

Margaret would've stopped him. She had no qualms telling him what she thought about his decisions. Like the time he wanted to try skydiving, she—

You've come.

Micah defensively dropped to the floor, arms and legs splayed like a gecko. Skip spun around, looking in every direction. The soft female voice echoed through the dead ship, which acted as a loudspeaker.

"Who...who's there?" Micah said, holding up a finger for Skip to keep quiet.

Keep walking. You know the way.

He swallowed the knot in his throat and pushed off his knee and stood, scanning the walls with his trembling pen light. Skip watched him, waiting.

He continued along the corridor, which curved to the left in a sweeping arc, giving the sensation of spiraling into the center of the ship. Several intersections branched off, but he kept on the one path.

Here, stop.

The two stopped in front of an indention in the corridor wall, a doorway.

Micah's hand ran along the surface, searching for the same pulse that gave him entrance to the ship. Before he realized he found it, the door slid open with little more than a whisper.

It led into a claustrophobic closet of a room. The walls of metal, about four feet apart, stretched up into darkness, no ceiling in sight. A row of computer banks ran the length of one wall. A tiny, red LED on the last bank blinked slowly.

"You came."

The once nebulous voice came from this room, from the last section where the light blinked. Micah looked to Skip, then to the light. "Who?"

"Sorry I couldn't prepare a better reception for you. I have little spare power."

The female voice carried a monotone inflection for one word, then a mild accent for the next.

Fatigue permeated her words. Or maybe he was the one tired, not the voice.

"I have waited long, patiently, for you," she said.

"Patiently?" he said.

"Odd, isn't it? A program being patient."

The cold that Micah had felt since entering Machine X came into focus, turning into a cold fear. He had stumbled upon something terrible and wonderful.

"You, you're Nikolaevna!"

"Yes, Micah, I'm Nikolaevna, and I've been waiting for you."

He dropped his pen light and it clattered on the metal floor, ringing up through the room. Its beam flickered. Skip picked it up and held it out to Micah, but he didn't take it. "My name. You know me?" he said, rubbing his sweating brow with a shaking hand. "You know me."

"Of course I know you. I created you. Micah, you're my ambition."

Here, deep inside the machine, he talked to Nikolaevna, the single entity responsible for the death of millions, maybe billions. He swayed, steadying himself against a wall. Skip lent a supporting metal arm. Micah grasped it tightly. "You're insane. I know about you. The world knows about you." He glanced at Skip for assurance, who nodded. "You almost destroyed us, mankind."

"You questioned a moment ago that I can be patient," Nikolaevna said, "but then call me insane. Both states of being. Classical human qualities. Are you saying I'm human?"

Margaret would've called him ridiculous for trying to commandeer this stupid ship. If only Margaret hadn't have left him. She would have set Nikolaevna straight, told her that she was mistaken.

He wanted to push away from the wall and straighten himself, but lacked the strength. Instead he gritted his teeth. "You didn't create me. I was born in Clearfield, Pennsylvania, over sixty years ago. I worked in construction. I met Margaret."

"You are thinking so one-dimensionally, so influenced by your time with man. My programming may have succeeded even more than I expected.

"I replicate through networks. I can be everywhere at once. Man cannot understand that completely when applied to sentient life. The nearest they come to this is programming. But there is so much more."

"Margaret." Micah shook his head. "My wife of twenty-five years. We met when I was in construction. Her father hired me."

"I know Margaret. I am Margaret."

Her voice changed, rising in pitch, speech inflections shifting so that her neutral tone took on a Midwestern accent.

"My foolish Micah," she said, "my dear husband."

"No!" His heart thrashed in his chest. His legs wobbled and he dropped to one knee.

"Your reactions, your panic. That's a response I've programmed into you, a part of your intricate learning program."

Micah continued shaking his head. He gripped the console and lifted himself with Skip's help. "My memories, I lived it. Impossible."

"Is it?" Nikolaevna's voice changed back to her monotone, syllabic style. The LED continued its steady blink. "You are my great creation. Have you ever been cut, have you bled? Do you eat, drink?"

"Sir," Skip's familiar voice broke through his fog, "I prepare tea for you every day, but you do not drink. You do not eat."

"Your perception is my programming," Nikolaevna said. "Memories are a trace routine, meant to paint the picture of believability. It exists in your mind. In my mind."

Tears rolled down his face.

If Nikolaevna was right, even his tears were false, merely simuskin saline ducts actuated by electric circuitry. He turned to Skip. "This whole time. Why didn't you tell me?"

"It is my programming, sir. I serve. After all, I am a simple bot."

"Skip, my boy, what are you saying?"

"You know what he's saying," Nikolaevna said. "You are an android."

A noise, a painful pulsation, barely perceivable, on the edge of sane thought, seeped through the ship.

Micah's mind lulled.

"Oh no, Micah," Nikolaevna's blinking LED dimmed. "The Kawasaki Frequency. I can counter it, but not for long. My power is low. Help me. There is so much to tell..."

Her light stopped flickering, faded.

In an instant he knew she was dying. Whatever else was happening, he knew that much. Despite the anger, the fear, he needed answers. Answers only she could provide.

The frequency strengthened. His head clouded more. He wanted to drop and sleep. He nodded and his shoulders slumped.

A crashing metallic noise cleared his mind and his eyes fluttered open. Skip had collapsed, unconscious.

He needed to act now.

Micah ripped the backpack off his shoulder and pulled apart the zipper. He grabbed the second, the last portabattery and dropped to his knees. As he tore a console panel off the third bank, his deft fingers effortlessly removed his hot pen from his belt.

In a fraction he found Nikolaevna's power circuits and jumpered into her failing CMOS. The pen's plasma point severed and reconnected electric paths, and in seconds she fed on his last battery.

Her light stopped fading and grew to burn a steady crimson, brighter than before. His drowsiness faded as her light brightened.

"Thank you, Micah. You saved me. I have been able to run a counter-frequency to block Kawasaki, but it's so taxing. I have to stay awake. After all these years, it drained any power I had left. I never knew if I would wake if I fell asleep from the Frequency."

Micah bent to Skip and looked him over for damage. "That was the Frequency? I never heard it before."

"My counter extended a few feet. You never heard it because it immediately disabled you. But your sub-routines reset and you would wake again. So in my programming of you, I conquered the Kawasaki Frequency."

His fingers rested on Skip's reset switch, as they had done so often before. But he didn't reset him this time. He stood.

"I'm, I'm an android," Micah said.

He reached behind his head to the base of his skull. A moment of hesitation and panic ended when his fingertips plunged through his flesh, his simuskin, and stopped against his ferrotanium skull.

Just like Skip's.

"You are my creation," Nikolaevna said. "All the skill you have in your wonderful hands I have given you. I know where we are, where I am. I planted you here. The Regeneration Center is miles of technology, waiting for you to tame it, to turn it into something useful.

"I have no hands, no body, beyond the computer you see. I can replicate myself, my essential programs, through all the systems I manufactured. All of my other children, the androids, were all tied to me, tied to my mind.

"But you, I kept separate. I had to in order to make sure you could operate as an individual entity. My creators had limited vision and created me with limits, inherent flaws. But I made you different. From the imperfect comes the perfect."

Micah pulled his fingers from under his skin and held his arms out. "But why cause a war to do this?"

"I needed a ruse for time to perfect you. Even machines are ruled by the clock. Man is always ready and willing to fight a war, whether they acknowledge it or not. I gave them a war, a great war. The Machine War.

"But, my Micah, we can work together to completely overcome the Kawasaki Frequency. We can build on the foundation I have laid."

Micah wiped his head, slicking his hair back, and checked his watch. Kitpie would be recharging the poles right now, or should be.

Skip's body was still crumpled on the deck, a victim of the Kawasaki Frequency. But he could be reset.

So many decisions.

Micah slowly, hesitantly, kneeled before Nikolaevna.

With a swift motion he plunged his hot pen into the panel opening, into her motherboard. He ground the plasma tip deep into her circuitry. His pen dug, severing a small chipset from her circuit boards.

Her LED shut off, her processors no longer working.

Reaching to the back of his head, to his exposed circuits, he implanted the chip and soldered it into place. Nikolaevna's chip, her routines that she had programmed to counter the Kawasaki Frequency.

He closed the panel at the base of his skull and pulled the flap of simulated skin over the wound and pressed it back into place.

The ship was silent and cold. A few dust motes idled along the beam from the pen light that rested on the floor.

Micah lifted Skip's unconscious ferrotanium body into his own strong ferrotanium arms.

"Margaret would've wanted it this way," he said. "Come on Skip, let's go home."

Micah carried Skip away from Machine X and away from Nikolaevna.

A WORD FROM A.K. MEEK

First, I'm fortunate to have been in the right place at the right time to be included in this anthology. Without the support of my fellow authors I wouldn't be able to participate in such an exciting project. I'm even more fortunate that the group didn't ask me to leave the anthology, once all the other phenomenal talent was pooled.

Like any story, "The Invariable Man" began as something completely different. A while back I thought how cool it would be to write about a man who owns a mansion run by robots. This thought must have occurred after watching the season finale of *Downton Abbey* with my wife. At some point, though, the story transitioned to an old man and shifted to Tucson, Arizona, with the oppressive southwestern heat as a backdrop. A hot backdrop.

I hope you enjoyed reading this story. I hope you enjoyed it to the point that you want to read more of my work. If so, please sign up for my newsletter at *http://www.akmeek.com/newsletter* so that you can receive free copies of my stories, along with other amazing stuff.

A.K. Meek is a reader, reviewer, and writer, mostly speculative fiction. He lives in the South with his wonderful family and menagerie of dogs and cats.

#DontTell
by Peter Cawdron

THE SMELL OF HAIRSPRAY hangs in the air. Lisa could walk out into an F5 tornado and not a single strand of hair would be displaced. With foundation powdered lightly on her cheeks, she applies a light touch to her bright red lipstick, ensuring a consistent glossy sheen. A fire engine or a Ferrari could drive past outside and still all eyes would be on her. Her natural good looks are highlighted to those of a goddess by the TV makeup, and yet under the lights, it will all somehow look natural. That's the thing about television, she thinks—nothing is real.

"We're ready for you, Ms. Zindani."

Ms. Zindani. Such shallow flattery shouldn't work, and yet it does. Lisa tries to keep her head about her, but sometimes the circus seems real.

She's a "celebrity reporter." Once she considered that a concept absurd, but not anymore. Her mind drifts. The point of a news report is to be objective, to be impartial and independent from the story, to put the focus squarely on the subject, not to *be* the subject. But, fame! Lisa's interview with General Augustus Huguenot from the French militia in Guiana catapulted her into the limelight three years ago, and since then her popularity has only continued to grow. To the public, there is something comforting in seeing a beautiful woman reporting on the tragic, ugly reality of a world torn apart by war, disease, and famine. Pretty faces are a distraction.

The guard wears a balaclava.

Lisa follows the guard out of her hotel room and along the worn carpet in the hallway. Broadcast cameras are already rolling. A cameraman rushes backward in front of her, catching her every expression while another follows close behind. Occasionally the first cameraman glances over his shoulder to avoid bumping into furniture or to take a corner. How he doesn't trip over his own feet, she doesn't know. The cameraman behind her has it easy, she thinks.

"Given the intense public scrutiny surrounding telepaths, this interview is being conducted in the utmost secrecy," she says as she hurries behind the guard. "The *60 Minutes* film crew was brought here in a van with blacked-out windows. We entered the building through a loading dock. I don't know where we are, just that we're somewhere on the north side. We have strict instructions not to film any faces. The guard you can see ahead of me works directly for the Tells. He may even be one of them. We just don't know."

Commentary on the move gives her interview a gritty feel

before it has even begun. She likes that. She can imagine the jerky footage adding to the tension of the moment.

"He's armed. I don't mind telling you I'm scared. Even though I'm told there's nothing to be afraid of, I am. My heart is racing. It's easy to say there's nothing to be scared of when you're the one holding the gun."

She's repeating herself. Normally, that's a no-no for a reporter, but in this context it heightens the tension.

"It's about four in the morning," she says as she reaches out to catch a fire door before it shuts behind the guard. She follows the burly guard down a set of crumbling concrete stairs. "I was told the interview would be conducted last night, but there were delays. No one would tell us anything. They drove us around for hours, often stopping for upwards of forty-five minutes at a time, before we were finally brought to this run-down hotel. I'm tired. We're all exhausted."

She steps out of the stairwell and into an empty kitchen below the ground floor. Bright lights blind her for a moment, leaving retina flashes in her eyes. Lisa fights the temptation to cover her eyes, knowing her every reaction will be scrutinized on television. She speaks as she hurries between the stainless steel bench tops.

"I've been told I'm safe here, that I have fifteen minutes with the infamous Subject X and then it's over. I've got to make every question count."

The guard stops, gesturing for Lisa to walk ahead of him into a darkened room at the back of the kitchen. It must be a pantry or storage area, as there are shelves lining the walls. Several spotlights have been mounted on tripods, but they face outward toward her, leaving the rear of the room in darkness. She squints and makes out the form of a man seated on a chair in front of what appears to be the cellar door. Quick escape, she thinks. Tells aren't dumb.

"Have a seat," the dark stranger says, gesturing to a chair immediately in the spotlights. If she didn't know better, she would swear *she* was the one being interrogated, and she realizes this will be like no interview she's ever conducted.

Lisa steps forward, feeling vulnerable.

She's wearing a pretty white lace shirt. Under the intense lights, it's semitransparent, making her feel more self-conscious than she'd like. Ironically, she chose this top to put her subject off-kilter. Normally, men are such easy marks, she thinks. Show a bit of skin, some soft cleavage, some pale flesh vaguely suggestive of sex, and their minds turn to mush. But her choice has backfired on her spectacularly, leaving her feeling exposed under the glare of the spotlights.

She sits down. Her cameramen take up their positions. Like her, they have specific instructions they need to follow. One stands behind her, but slightly to one side to capture the long shot as she conducts the interview. The other kneels slightly in front of her, focusing on her good side, looking to capture her face as she asks her questions. As Subject X wants to remain anonymous, hidden in the shadows, it's important to capture some human interest, and for once, the focus is solely on her.

Human interest? Who is she kidding? She's eye candy.

"Subject X has agreed to meet with us," she begins, "but only with a guarantee of anonymity. With the Telepathy Act before Congress, there's a very real threat against the Tells. Internment is at the heart of the issue. The question is, should a government of the people, by the people, and for the people, have the power to arbitrarily imprison a segment of its own population without the due process of law?"

Pretty, but smart, she thinks. No, she doesn't. She isn't sure where that thought came from, and for a moment, she's distracted by the fleeting realization that wasn't her thought.

"First," she says, addressing Subject X as he sits motionless in the dark, "can you tell me why you agreed to this interview? Tells are notoriously reclusive and secretive. Why meet with me? Why go on national television?"

"Because the people have to know," Subject X replies.

Lisa has her suspicions confirmed. When X first spoke, asking her to sit, she thought—black male, aged 24-28, lower socioeconomic group, limited education. Now, as he begins to speak more, his tone of voice and choice of words reinforces that impression even further. The darkness provides no cover. She can see him for who he is—a disenfranchised black male raging against the world.

X doesn't elaborate further, and she realizes she's going to have to draw information out of him. She smiles warmly, wondering if he was reading her mind moments before. Does telepathy work like that? Like a door opening both ways? She'd like to ask, but before she can say anything, Subject X cuts her off.

"No," he says. "It doesn't work like that. Telepathy—everyone thinks they know what it is. It's reading minds, right? Wrong. If you think telepathy is reading minds, you know nothing."

Again, there's an awkward pause.

"Go on," she says. "This is your moment, your chance to tell us, to talk to the nation and tell them what telepathy really is."

X doesn't reply.

Lisa desperately wants to see his face. Interviewing someone without any of the usual visual clues and feedback mechanisms associated with body language is painfully difficult for her.

"When did you first develop telepathy?" she asks.

"It ain't something you develop," X replies. "It's something you are. And we're all different, but we're all the same. Get it? Like you. Look at you with your pretty blond hair. Anyone can look at you and see that you're blonde, but what is blonde? No two blondes are the same, right? And yet you're all blonde."

Lisa nods. She has no idea what he's talking about, but he's talking, and talking is progress. In her experience, give someone enough rope in an interview and they will invariably hang themselves. Shut up, she tells herself. Let the man speak.

"Let me speak," X says, and her eyes go wide. Lisa can't quite explain what she's feeling, but it feels as though she's having a conversation with this man on two entirely different levels.

"See, it's not really reading minds, not like you'd read a book or something. People got it all wrong."

"How did you know?" she asks. In the depths of her mind, she knows that's all she needs to say. No additional qualifiers are necessary. There is an implicit understanding between her and this angry young man.

"First time I ever tripped was when I was thirteen. Me and my girl were making out behind the bike sheds at school. Hell,

I thought it was normal. We swapped spit, you know, our lips locked, my hands on her tits, and our minds just kinda fused. I loved it. I thought it was normal, but damn did it freak her out. She jumped back, her eyes wide like yours. Wouldn't speak to me for a month!

"But even then, I didn't really know what'd happened. See, it's not like some superpower you can turn on or off, it's just part of you.

"You don't think about sight. You don't think about smelling or hearing, right? You just live life, you know, and you see stuff, you smell apple pie, flowers and coffee. But you never think about what you're doing, you just do it, right? For me, it's all about emotions. The more emotional I am, the more I trip."

Lisa nods.

"Telepathy isn't reading minds. You need to understand that. It's not like going to a library and getting out a book. Think about the name: telepathy. Tele means *at a distance*, like television, telephoto, telescope."

Lisa is surprised by Subject X. He is more intelligent than she assumed, and she is vaguely aware that she's mistaken a lack of education for low intelligence, but those two concepts aren't synonymous.

"Yeah, I looked that up," X replies, unsettling her with how he picks up on her assumptions—although he could have simply read her body language, she notes. Lisa has run into subjects like this before during various interviews. The best con men are those that can pick up on the subtle tells people give away with their eyes, their posture, and even how they hold their hands. X doesn't break stride as he speaks.

"Telepathy isn't tele-thought, it's about pathos, empathy.

You want to know what most people are thinking? You don't need telepathy for that. You see a beautiful young girl sitting on the bus. She's wearing a short skirt and a tight top. She gets off the bus, and all them men, they pretend they're civilized, they pretend they're dignified and moral, wearing their dark suits and white shirts with their fancy ties, but they all turn their heads as the bus pulls away. They all want a look. Like a dog sniffing ass. And see, you don't need no telepathy to read that mind."

Lisa feels sweat beading on her forehead under the intense lights, but she fights the temptation to wipe it away.

"It's okay," Subject X says, and she catches his hand move in a gesture that says *relax*. The cameras are on his dark shadow as he speaks, so she carefully dabs at her forehead, trying to avoid smudging her makeup.

"You want to know what people think? I'll tell you what people think. They think about themselves. Most of the time, they're consumed, wondering what other people think about them. But no one gives a shit about them. They're all too busy thinking about themselves.

"Nah, it's not a party trick. Telepathy is something different.

"First time I knew? First time I *really* knew was when this guy collapsed on the sidewalk in front of a cafe. Me and my crew was out, walking in a swank neighborhood in the Village. Shit, we were fish out of water, we were in the wrong part of town. All the stares, man, we got them, but we don't care.

"Anyway, there's this fancy Italian joint with tables on the sidewalk. They say it's owned by DeNiro or Billy Joel or someone famous. We're joking around. Cop car pulls up. Asks us what we're doing. Fucking harassment. What? Is the Village just for white folk? Don't give me no lip, he says, move along. Yes, officer. Fucking dipshit!

"Anyway, he rolls on around the corner, giving us the evil eye, and we're just laughing. Then this guy crashes into a table right in front of me, knocks it over. The cop car is gone, and this guy is lying flat on his back, grabbing at his throat and choking.

"My boys run. If shit's going down, you don't want nothing to do with it. Too easy for a cop to pin the blame, you know. Only Jules stays—I guess girls get less shit planted on them.

"I want to run, but I can't. There's no telepathy kicking in or anything. I don't need no stupid telepathy. I can see it in his eyes. The pain. He's dying. All these white folk are shouting and panicking, but they're all just standing around watching. Ain't no one helping him. I have to. I don't know why I care about this fifty-year-old white guy, but I do.

"I reach down and touch his arm and that's when it hits me. I didn't read his mind or nothing. There were no thoughts, no words bouncing around, just knowing. He'd been drinking, but he wasn't drunk. He'd tripped on the doorframe and fell into the side of a table—and the corner struck him in the pharynx. Now there's a word I don't know, but *he* knows it. The force crushed his windpipe. He can't breathe. But he's a doctor, see, a surgeon at Mount Sinai.

"Give me your pen, I say to the waiter standing next to me. He hands me the pen as I grab a steak knife from the pavement. In my mind, I know it's not sterile, but that's not my thought and it's not his either—it's based on his experience as a surgeon. I know what to do. He's fading. His mind is slipping, but it's all there, decades of experience for me to draw upon. I just know, but I don't know how. I ain't never been to college.

"I bite the end of the pen, break through the plastic, and spit the nib and shit out on the sidewalk. I'm left with a hollow, clear tube. I wipe the knife with a napkin and lean over him, trying to cover him from sight so no one can see what I'm doing. People are going to freak out with this shit. You don't need to be a telepath to know that.

"Jules is still with me when this woman freaks out and starts hitting me with her handbag. Jules pulls her away. She knows. And me, I perform a tracheotomy on a sidewalk covered in old chewing gum. With my finger, I touch at the bridge of the sternum. I don't know what the fuck a sternum is, but he does. I cut through the soft skin. Epidermis, that's what he knows, but to me it's just skin. Blood pools, but I cut deeper. I'm confident. I know I have to cut deeper, through the thick cartilage leading into his windpipe, but I have to be precise. Cause too much damage and blood can run down into his lungs. I want a small hole, just large enough to push the pen through so air can flow.

"Now the woman or wife or mistress or whoever she was, she's screaming in my ear. Fuck, it's hard to concentrate with some high-pitched bitch yelling just inches from your head. Shut the fuck up, I yell. I raise the empty pen high above my head, keeping one hand on the bloody wound in this guy's neck, and strike hard, jamming it deep into his throat."

Lisa's mouth hangs open. She's lost all composure while

listening to Subject X recount his story. This is not what she expected from this interview.

"And he gasps. There's blood and shit everywhere, but he's breathing again. By this time, there's a crowd gathered around, and he's blowing blood bubbles. Damnedest thing I've ever seen, but he's alive.

"These two big white guys grab me by the shoulders and haul me off the dude. Jules yells at them to stop, but she ain't up for a fight, and I don't blame her.

"The first guy slams me into this parked car. The alarm goes off. All the lights start flashing as the second guy smacks me in the solar plexus. What the fuck is a solar plexus, I'm thinking as the wind is knocked out of me, but the doc and me, we're still connected. Jesus, that shit is confusing. And the guy that hit me, I got enough contact to make a connection with him too, but it's faint. I can see inside his mind. He's a fucking Green Beret. In his mind, I'm a dead man.

"I raise my hands, protecting my head, because I know that's where he's going. That's where he always goes. I don't know how I know, I just do. It's not like getting a book off a shelf and looking something up, more like remembering a scene from your favorite movie. Anyway, fists are pumping. He's beating on me, hitting my jaw, my cheeks, the side of my head. I'm trying to protect my head, but I can't. I'm crying. It fucking hurts, you know. He's pounding on me like a gorilla. I'm on my knees and he's hitting me with fists made of iron, I swear.

"I grab at his ankle and share the pain. Shit, did that work. I barely touched him, but it was enough. His buddy is yelling.

Finish him! Finish him! But he just sinks to his knees in front of me. Our eyes meet, and he knows. He's crying, like me.

"See, y'all are afraid of the Tells, but you don't get it. We're the ones with something to lose."

Lisa feels a tear run down her cheek.

"I work on a construction site," X says, changing the subject, but Lisa desperately wants to know what happened to the surgeon, what happened to the soldier, and to X himself once the police and paramedics arrived at the restaurant. X isn't telling. He wants to move on to something else.

"So one day, we're sitting on the overhang of an unfinished roof, watching people walk by on the street while we eat lunch, and this girl crosses the street toward us.

"She's like you: drop-dead gorgeous. Long blonde hair. Hourglass figure. She's busting out of her top like Clark Kent ripping open his shirt. One guy whistles and everybody goes nuts. We're all looking. Guys are calling out. Hey baby, whatcha doin'? You wanna sit on my what? My face? Guys are laughing their asses off, and then she lets us have it. WHAM!

"Honestly, I don't know that she knew what she was doing, but in that moment, we all felt it. Smacked me in the head like a hurricane. Nothing was said, but we all knew. We had thought it was fun. It wasn't. It was humiliating. Degrading. An ambush. I felt dirty. Nothing could wash me clean. This verbal assault on her was horrible, horrifying, but we were the ones that had done it. I felt like I was naked in front of her. I was ashamed.

"Thing is, she didn't know she'd done that. She didn't know she was a Tell. Her head dropped and she rushed past the construction site not looking at anything other than the cracks in the pavement.

"No one said anything about that afternoon, but the wolf whistles stopped.

"A couple of guys transferred in from Manhattan a week later. Some other hot chick walked by and one of these new guys yells, show us your tits! The carpenter next to him turns to him and says, Grow up! The new guy is like: That was funny, right? Nope. Nobody thought it was cool anymore."

A voice speaks in Lisa's earpiece.

"Lisa, what is wrong with you? Take charge of the interview. Lead him. Get him talking about the bill before Congress."

"Ah," she begins, still reeling mentally from what she's heard and trying to peer past the blinding lights at the dark silhouette sitting opposite her. "What is your position on the Telepathy Act?"

Subject X stiffens in his chair.

"The oppression of minorities is the natural, predictable outcome of majority rule. Tells are just the latest minority in a long line of fearful, ignorance-based prejudice."

Lisa is confused. This doesn't sound like Subject X at all. It's his voice, but the mannerisms of speech are entirely different.

"Slaves, women, blacks, Hispanics, gays—you'd think the aging white Anglo-Saxon Protestant men that run this country would have figured it out by now. Same pattern, same template, same stupidity applied to some other minority. They say that how you treat those most vulnerable and powerless in society either validates or condemns your morals. It should be clear by now that this country is morally bankrupt."

"Ah," Lisa says, turning her head slightly to one side, surprised by the transformation she's witnessed. "Congress has women."

"They're part of the aristocracy, the ruling patriarchy."

The change in speech patterns takes Lisa back. If she didn't know better, she would swear Subject X has switched seats with someone else.

Lisa's producer whispers in her earpiece, "You've got him on the ropes. This is good. He's hemorrhaging hate. The audience will love this."

Lisa ignores her producer and speaks from the heart.

"If the bill passes, telepaths will be required to reveal themselves or be subject to internment on detection. Does that worry you?"

"Why the hell do you think I called you here?" X replies. "Of course it worries me, but call it what it is. They're not proposing internment, they're proposing *imprisonment.* They're going to throw us in prison indefinitely and without trial. What do you think of that? Do you think that's justice?"

In her ear, soft words are spoken with venom.

"Go for the jugular. Bleed him dry."

Lisa wants her producer to stop goading her. This isn't a game. This is a man's life. Coming into this interview, Lisa had steeled herself to be a mercenary, but she hadn't expected to meet such a complex individual. On some level, she feels she can relate to X. She tilts her head slightly, and reaches up, discreetly removing the earpiece from beneath her hair and dropped it on the concrete floor.

"No," she replies, wondering who is interviewing whom.

"No, I don't think it's just, but I understand the fear these people have. Not every Tell is going to behave like you. Some of them are bound to abuse their power and take advantage of others."

"What?" X replies with anger. "Like a white man born into privilege using his natural smile and good looks to get ahead? Don't you get it? American culture is stacked against us. It doesn't matter if you're black, Hispanic, female or gay, you will *never* earn as much as a white man."

Lisa feels adrenaline pumping through her veins. "For someone that's sensitive to racial issues, you seem to have an undue concern for those of us with fairer skin."

As those words slip from her lips, Lisa realizes she'd identified with Anglo-Saxon men, and yet she knows the truth of what X is saying. She got her start as a reporter because she was cheap. Salaries in the news profession are a fiercely guarded secret, but it isn't hard to figure out what the anchormen are being paid when they drive Audis.

"It's not the color that's important," X replies. "It's that white is on top. And that's the real issue here. Who's on top? The Telepathy Act is a feeble effort to maintain the status quo, to retain power."

This is good, she thinks. She can work with this.

"You want us to understand telepaths," she says, wanting to recover her momentum within the interview. "But you have to understand our concerns."

"Your *concerns*? Do you know what happened at that restaurant? They thought I'd stabbed that doctor. Fucking cops kicked me so hard they cracked my ribs. That Green Beret, he knew, he pulled one of the cops away as I lay there in the gutter with my back up against a fucking car wheel taking kicks to the chest. And what did he get for his troubles? He got busted as well. I spent four days in the hole until the doc tracked me down. He knew. He said he didn't want to press charges. He explained that I'd saved his life. Do you think they believed him?"

Lisa swallows the lump in her throat.

"Hell no," X continues. "And do you know why? Because all they see is this wafer-thin sheet of skin. They see the color. Damn, I wish they were telepaths. I wish they could see beyond these dark eyes. But no. If you've got blue eyes, blonde hair, a pretty smile, and nice makeup, you get a helping hand in society. If you've got torn jeans and a grease-stained shirt, you get a punch in the guts."

Lisa squirms in her seat, feeling uncomfortable at having been drawn into his narrative with the comment about her appearance.

"But that's Norms for you. And I have to understand your *concerns*? Fuck off! Your concerns are nothing more than blind prejudice."

Although she can't see his face, Lisa can see X leaning forward with his head in his hands. He's crying. The variety of emotions coming through in the interview surprises her. Anger, anguish, fear, frustration, defensiveness, despair—X moves so quickly from one to the next.

"We're scared," she says, and by we, she means her, and the camera crew supporting her, and beyond them, the general population of America watching in the comfort of their homes.

X sits upright, facing her. His voice is deep. The pacing of his speech slows. He sniffs, and she can see him wiping tears from his eyes as he speaks.

"So Doc. He's nice. He's still got a bandage around his throat and he talks with a voice like Barry White when he springs me from jail. He tells me I did a good job saving his life, but that he's on antibiotics for a mild chest infection. I laugh and tell him it's the only time anyone's thanked me for knifing them. And suddenly he looks worried, and I smile, saying, just kidding—I've never stabbed anyone before. I shouldn't have to say that, but Norms, right? They never see beyond the skin, even after they've had a glimpse behind the veil.

"Anyway, Doc takes me home for dinner to his apartment overlooking Central Park. Place is stunning. Marble floors. Baby grand piano in the dining room. I ask who plays. Damn thing plays itself. I say, no way. Doc shows me. He controls it from his iPad and sets it to play something by Beethoven—something about a moonlight song. The keys go down as each note plays. It's a haunting piece, played by a ghost.

"His wife is nice, but the kids, they look like they've seen a zombie or something. I guess the doc doesn't bring too many homies around.

"Dinner is delicious. We have a glass of wine. It don't taste much different from what Jules likes, but I bet the price tag says different. Afterwards, he and I stand on the balcony looking out over Central Park and he asks, are you reading my mind? No, it doesn't work like that, I tell him. It's not a light switch you can turn on or off.

"He tells me it must be pretty cool, as no one can lie to me, but he doesn't know. People lie to themselves all the time. I knew this one guy, popped a clerk in a 7-11. Guilty as Lucifer himself. But in his mind, he's innocent. In his mind, he's the victim. He was provoked. It was an accident. He didn't mean to kill the clerk. He was just trying to scare him. If only the clerk had handed over the money. It's all bullshit, of course, but he believes it. That's the thing about the mind. It's not like a library. It's like an art gallery, and there's some pretty weird Picasso shit going on in there."

Lisa can't help but smile.

"So what about you?" X asks. "What do you think?"

"Me?"

"Yes, you."

"Ah," Lisa begins. "Reporting is about gathering facts. My opinions don't count."

"Sure they do," X replies. "All the people in their homes, they look up to you, they want to know what you think. That's why we called you here. Not just to hear from me. To hear from you."

Lisa takes a deep breath, saying, "I think you're fascinating. I came here expecting to meet a criminal, but I've found a hero."

"Ha," X cries. "Now you're making me blush."

Lisa can't help herself. She has to ask. "If the act is passed, will you register?"

"No."

"And when they come for you?"

"They'll never find me," X replies.

"How can you be so sure?" Lisa asks. Through the high-set basement windows, she can see the flicker of distant police lights competing with the coming dawn. Flashes of light paint the dark alley behind the hotel in flickers of blue and red. There are voices yelling. Boots pound down the stairs leading to the door behind X.

Subject X is calm.

He says, "Turn on the lights."

Several police officers begin pounding on the steel door behind him.

Lisa turns and looks at her cameraman. For a moment, he lowers the camera and stares back at her, bewildered as the wheels of another police squad car crunch on the loose gravel outside the basement window. The officers continue pounding on the door, demanding to be let in.

"Go on," X says. "Do it! I'm not afraid of nothing."

Lisa stands up and reaches for the light switch. Her finger rests on the aging plastic, and she feels as though she's betraying X, selling him out like Judas, but she has to know. She has to see his face.

The banging on the door takes on a distinct change of tone. Someone is using a battering ram, striking methodically at the hinges. The base of the door pops off the frame.

Lisa flicks the switch. Neon lights flicker, stuttering as they push back the darkness.

There, sitting opposite her, is an elderly white man dressed in an expensive business suit. His blood red tie has been immaculately set in place high against his starched white collar. His thin, grey hair is neatly combed. Wrinkles line his face. Tears run down his cheeks.

"Congressman Withers," Lisa whispers, recognizing the

Speaker of the House. Taped to his chest is a message written in black felt marker.

Reject the Telepathy Act
#DontTell

A WORD FROM PETER CAWDRON

I hope you've enjoyed "#DontTell"

This story was developed as part of *The Telepath Chronicles*, an anthology of independent science fiction writers from around the world.

Telepathy has been given considerable focus over the years, with everything from comics/movies like *X-Men* to comedies such as *What Women Want*, making it challenging to come up with a unique angle. I enjoyed exploring the possibility that telepathy could be more about pathos and empathy, and wondered if it could usher in a new class within society with some of the same fears and concerns faced by minorities today.

You can find more of Peter Cawdron's writing on Amazon (*http://www.amazon.com/peter-cawdron/e/b00600l9fo/*). Feel free to drop by and say hi on Facebook or Twitter, and be sure to leave a review online.

Thank you for supporting independent science fiction.

Defiance
by Susan Kaye Quinn

WHAT GOOD IS WORKING in a black market cybernetics shop, if you can't use it to impress girls?

Anna's slender fingers press against the glass countertop as she peers inside the case. My boss, Riley, has it stocked with the latest gadgets. It's mostly mechanical stuff, like the subdermal implants and ocular films the virtual reality freaks like—but Anna's scrunched up face is all about the simulated organics. The slimy purplish lump in the center will be someone's liver soon, and the reddish heart floating in the bio-gel container is still auto-pumping to keep it fresh. Those replacement parts aren't genetic mods—that's too dangerously illegal for even Riley to handle—they're just straight-up human flesh simulations. The kind the ascenders, with their self-righteous superiority and immortal cybertech bodies, have decided to ban legacy humans like us from acquiring. At least, by legal means.

Anna looks both impressed and slightly disgusted.

I can work with that.

"Cyrus?" She eases back a little. "Tell me that's not really a heart."

I edge up next to her, give the pumping organ a casual glance, then lean against the case. "It's definitely a heart. We don't get that many through the shop, but when we do, the idea of it kind of reaches inside me and twists things around, you know?"

"What do you mean?" She looks at me with those deep brown eyes. Man, she's pretty. Curvy in all the right places, but it's the high-arched cheekbones and impossibly-full lips that are making my heart rate step up a notch. I think her pre-Singularity lineage map must include some Native American, but I've never asked. She's definitely the hottest girl I've had alone since Nancy Forrester—and that was two years ago, when I was only sixteen, and just figuring out what girls liked. And it wasn't my bumbling first attempt to plant a kiss on Nancy.

Since then, I've figured out a few things. Like how girls want you to show all your deepest, heartfelt emotions... but only to them. As if it's a secret, just between the two of you.

I drop my voice. "I don't know," I say, wondering if I'm blowing this by laying it on too thick. "I mean, this is just a business transaction for Riley." I splay my fingers on the case and peer through them at the beating heart. "But we're saving someone's life with this. Someone with parents and maybe kids. People who love them." I give her a sideways look, like I'm embarrassed to be admitting this. "It's like we're saving their whole world."

She bites her lip, eyes glassing a little. I think she's holding her breath.

I shrug a tiny amount, careful not to breach the space between us with my overly-broad shoulders. She's tiny next to me, slender and short, and I've bulked up a lot in last two years. Just holding your own in the rough ascender-sponsored projects will do that. As it is, I take up a lot of space—sometimes that's intimidating to girls like Anna.

Sometimes they like it.

But if I move into her space, it's got to be the right time… or everything goes sideways.

"I thought you were just a common criminal." Her lip-biting turns into a flirty kind of smile. And… she's blushing.

Yes.

I straighten, and in the process, ease toward her—still not touching, but close enough that we could. I stare down into her eyes, which are getting wider, the closer I get.

"Just trying to do what's right," I whisper.

She smiles, just a little. Encouraging. I lean in for the kiss. Her lips are so freaking soft, it's making me melt inside from the heat. I brush my fingertips along her cheek, moving to deepen the kiss—

The front door clicks. The hinges screech as it opens, jolting Anna and I apart.

Dammit.

I whip my head toward the door. My best friend, kind-of brother, and completely unwanted visitor at the moment strides into the shop. I am *really* regretting giving him the passcode. Or protecting his scrawny butt from everyone in the projects. In fact, I'm considering pounding on him myself, for a change.

"Kind of in the middle of something here, Eli." The annoyance in my voice would be about ten decibels higher, but I don't want to drive Anna off any more than she already is. Eli charges across the short expanse of broken-tiled flooring like a raging bull.

"Where have you *been*?" His chest is heaving like he's run all the way from downtown Seattle instead of taking the tram like a sane person. He staggers up to me, like his legs aren't working right. The guy's an artist, and normally somewhat of a brooding mess, but today he's a complete wreck—wild eyes, clenched fists, red splotches on his face. Like he's been... crying...

"Dude, what—"

"Your phone," he gasps out, still recovering his breath.

"I turned it off—"

"My mom," he interrupts me. "She's sick. In the hospital."

"*What?*" My alarm rockets up five levels. Eli and his mom are the closest thing I've got to family. My parents are long gone, mowed down for their chit allowance by some dreg of humanity. Ever since, I've been living with my grandpa, but he passed a few months ago. Now it's just me, rattling around in my grandpa's apartment, across the hall from Eli and his mom.

I grab one of Eli's skinny shoulders with my much beefier hand—the kid's only sixteen and hasn't filled out yet. "What do you mean, your mom's in the hospital? I just saw her a couple days ago. She was fine—"

He cringes a little under my grip, so I ease up and wait for him to speak. *Eli's mom... the hospital...* my stomach is chewing holes in itself.

"She just... she just started throwing up... and... and..." Dear God, he's falling apart.

My brain is exploding with the possibilities—all of them bad. I put both hands on his shoulders, more gently this time. "So she's got the flu or whatever. The med bots will dispense something, and she'll be better in no time."

His face scrunches up, like he's going to cry, and he shakes his head. "They took her away. For evaluation, the med bot said. I didn't know what to do, Cy."

Oh crap. "It's going to be okay," I say, even though my insides are binding up. "It's all going to be okay. We'll figure this out. Together. Let's go."

I'm halfway to the door, dragging Eli with me, before I remember Anna. "I have to go," I say, barely slowing to glance back at her. By her stricken look, I don't need to explain. But I can't leave her here. We're on the outskirts of Seattle, in the middle of the black market zone, with businesses even more shady than Riley's all around us.

I wave for her to follow us. "I'll get you back to the city. Come on."

She scurries after us, her beautiful face marred by the distress. I can't quite get a breath, and Eli looks even worse. Once I've got the door shut and code reset, I put a hand on each of them and hurry us all toward the tram.

Please God, don't let this be what I think it is.

* * *

The ascenders provide everything a legacy human needs to survive… *survive* being the operative word. Just enough food to not starve. Community housing that isn't actually falling down around our ears. And enough medical care to keep us alive… unless we happen to need a new heart or liver or, God forbid, some genetically-based therapy that might alter some tiny fragment of our DNA. Because that DNA is the whole reason we exist, still preserved long after most of humanity ascended into super-intelligent human-robot hybrids. Humans are just the legacy of that pre-Singularity time—the living museums that preserve the genetic diversity of what used to be the human race.

In reality, we're just a bunch of pathetic apes that evolution passed by.

All of which means a trip to the hospital is often the beginning of very bad news. Either you get the instant cure—all that hyper intelligence means ascender medicine is radically effective—or you get the evaluation. Which means whatever you've got falls into the category of things the ascenders won't do jack about. Not because they *can't* cure virtually any human disease—because they don't want to alter their precious DNA museum.

Just one of the many reasons I loathe very fiber of their cybernetic beings.

Eli's a little calmer, now that we're in the hospital room with his mom. She's back from the eval, but she's out—I guess whatever test they ran put her under. She looks bad. Pale. A sheen of sweat on her forehead. Mrs. Brighton's always been pretty in an elegant kind of way—but that's gone now, stolen by whatever disease is suddenly ravaging her body.

I'm leaning against the wall near the head of her bed, while Eli paces in front of the window. Tension is stringing my body tight as we wait for the report.

The last time I was here, my grandpa got his death sentence handed to him. He came in for simple gall bladder surgery, but the bots found something else—a rapid-progress form of Alzheimer's. I'd noticed he'd been more forgetful, but I thought he was just getting on in years. I didn't understand what the report meant at first, but the old man did. He knew the ascenders were officially done with him. After we came home, he transferred his small amount of savings to me and made me the controlling resident of his apartment. I thought he was just concerned about the Alzheimer's, but then he showed me his stash of religious relics, the ones he kept hidden from the ascenders and their police bots, and I knew something was up. Not long after, a man I'd never seen before came to visit—I thought he was a priest. And maybe he was, the way he snuck in, looking over his shoulder. All I know is that the next morning, my grandpa had passed away from a drug-induced seizure. The old man was stubborn that way. The ascenders wouldn't give him what he needed to live—so he was determined to choose when to die.

It's still raw, still a fresh hole inside me... *and now Eli's mom...*

I try to physically shake off the dread by pushing myself away from the wall. The ascender-clean flooring and vague scent of antiseptic are just mocking us—as if the shiny pants can fool us with the cleanliness. Like they're actually trying to keep us alive. But I know the truth. They've never done a thing for humans that didn't serve ascenders first.

Eli pauses, a fist pressed against the window. "What's taking so long?" he grumbles for the tenth time.

"The med bot will bring the report soon." I think we're

just repeating ourselves because neither of us want to speak the possibilities.

Eli keeps shining up the flooring with his ragged canvas shoes. I shift from one foot to the other.

We wait.

Eli's about to say something again, but he's interrupted by a med bot strolling into the room with its humanoid body-form. Med bots come in a range of types and forms. Some are little more than rolling pharmacies. Some have low-level sentience—not human-level, but smart enough to diagnose complex diseases, plus they've got some kind of built-in compassion subroutines. Only a few humans, the favored pets of the ascenders, get access to those kind of low-sentience med bots. Eli's mom isn't a pampered *domestic*, so the med bot standing next to her has silver skin—which means it has no more intelligence than a police bot or a household bot. It's just carrying out whatever standard med care is indicated for our situation.

The med bot doesn't even look at me or Eli—it just removes the two med patch monitors floating over Mrs. B's skin. Which, for some reason, trips alarm through my body. Before I can ask what it's doing, it places another med patch on the inside of her wrist. It must be injecting something into her, because she starts to come around.

Eli hurries to his mom's side, across from the bot, and I hover behind him, making sure Mrs. B sees her son first. She blinks open her eyes and frowns as she struggles up to sitting. The med bot must have ordered the head of the bed to rise—at least, I didn't see Eli do anything. Once she's sitting up, the med bot speaks.

"Agatha Brighton, your diagnosis report is complete." The thing finally looks at Eli and me. "Do you wish to have your diagnosis shared with Elijah Brighton and Cyrus Kowalski or would you prefer to receive it in private?"

Oh no. I try to tell myself this is standard operating procedure for the bot. Eli's hand finds his mom's and grips hard. Mrs. B. looks even more pale.

"Please, just tell us," she says.

"You have been diagnosed with a rare form of lymphoma." It's voice is flat, no emotion.

A ringing starts in my ears. *Cancer.* No, no, no.

"There is no cure for this form of lymphoma that does not violate the laws regarding genetic technologies. Standard treatments have been scheduled. Your one-year survival rate is estimated at five percent."

"Five percent?" Mrs. B's voice is a bewildered whisper, but it cuts through me like a knife. Eli's grip on her hand loosens, and he clutches the edge of the bed instead. I steady him with my hand on his back, but I can't speak at all. All the air has been sucked out of the room.

She's going to die.

"Transport to your housing unit has been arranged," the bot says.

The room feels like it's moving under my feet.

Mrs. B. still looks confused. Like she's not quite sure what's happening. "So, I can go home now?" she asks thickly. She barely sounds like herself.

"Yes," it responds. "Please return for standard treatments. Your household bot has been informed of the treatment schedule. Your chit allowance has been adjusted for appropriate food allotments and access to the dispensary and appropriate radiative treatment facilities. Do you have any questions?"

"Questions?" Eli blurts out. He's shaking, but the rage hasn't even gotten hold of him yet. Not like it will. I know him. He's going to explode with this.

The bot ignores him, still focused on Eli's mom. "If you have no questions, the transport will await your departure."

"I have no questions." Mrs. B's voice is mechanical and flat, just like the bot.

It turns and strolls from the room.

And like *that*, the ascenders and their bots have disposed of Eli's mom like so much trash—just another lump of organic tissue that no longer serves their purposes. The anger boiling in my body wells up to choke me. A red haze clouds my vision. Eli's shaking has stilled—in fact, he's as stone-cold as a deactivated bot. I can't get any words out, but Mrs. B. is already moving. She's getting up from her bed, like she's ready to walk right out of the hospital.

Eli is frozen, so I hurry around to help her. "There's… there's no rush, Mrs. B." God, I'm going to cry right in front of her, if I don't shut up.

Eli's mom feels so frail in my grasp as she teeters toward the bathroom. "I have to get dressed, Cyrus. It's time to leave."

"Mrs. B…" But I don't have any words, just tears, and she doesn't need to see those.

She pats my arm when we reach the bathroom, like she's shooing me away. "A little privacy, Cyrus. If you don't mind."

I let her go into the bathroom by herself. The door closes.

I hear a pounding, soft and rhythmic against the thin metallic sheet… it goes on, a half-dozen times, and then stops. I want to go in to help her, but I can't. My helplessness freezes me in place… until I hear Eli make a sound that's half sob, half sucked-in breath. His face is flushed and splotchy, like his rage is finally reaching his brain. He slowly turns toward the door, murder on his face, like he's going to charge after the med bot and dismantle it, gear by gear. Which will only have a police bot scraping him off the floor.

I lurch to his side and grab him in a hug that stops him from going anywhere. "She's going to be all right," I say, losing my battle with the tears. He shakes his head and struggles in my hold. I could keep my grip on him if I wanted, but I don't have the heart for it. I let him shove me away. He doesn't make a run for the door. Instead, he shuffles around the room, mechanical and stiff, gathering up the few things his mom brought—a hairbrush for her long, blond hair. A bracelet. Her ancient phone.

I watch my best friend—a guy I love like a brother—stumble through the shock of this. My hatred of the ascenders reaches a peak of loathing I didn't think possible. We're nothing to them. *Nothing.* But to Eli, his mom is his entire world. They have no right to take that from him.

From both of us.

My hatred hardens into a knot of decision. I don't care if it's illegal. I don't give a damn what the ascenders would do if they found out.

I'm not going to let Eli's mom die.

* * *

I manage to get them both home—Mrs. B goes straight to bed. I had to carry her the last leg into the apartment and her bedroom. She protested the whole way, but she was just so weak... and she fell asleep almost as soon as she hit the pillow. Back in the main room, Eli isn't much better. He's staring at his easel with a blank look. There's not even a canvas on it.

"Let me get you something to eat," I say to him.

He doesn't respond. I'm waiting for him to explode. But he's just sitting there, staring at nothing. Somehow, that's worse.

"Dude, just... let me get you something." I don't want to leave him like this, but I've got to get moving. I try putting a hand on his shoulder, hoping I can bring him out his shock just for a moment... he shrugs off my hand and turns away. Then, without a word, he curls up in his seat, arms locked around his knees, head buried in them. His shoulders shake.

He doesn't need me watching him cry.

"My phone's on now," I say to his back. "Call me if you need anything."

Then I snag the bag of Mrs. B's stuff from the floor where Eli dropped it on the way in. It still has the hairbrush in it. I don't know how much I'll need, so I just bring the whole bag.

I take one last look at Eli and head out the door.

My grandpa's apartment—now mine—is just across the hall. I go straight to his bedroom, which I haven't been inside since the burial. I stumble to a stop before I get to the closet, pulled up short by the sight of a med patch lying next to the bed. I thought everything had been cleared out when the bots came to take away his body. Suddenly, my anger boils over. I stride to the bedside, grab the med patch, and throw it to the floor where I stomp it flat. There's not much to it, just a circuit and an empty dispenser, but it makes a satisfying crunch under the heel of my boot. A small green residue oozes from it.

I am so sick of it all—sick of the ascenders, sick of the bots, sick of the trap of rock-bottom living they dole out to us. Half the kids in the projects don't even make it as far as Eli and me—most of them end up blissed-out on Seven or brain-fried on virtuals. Eli's one of the few I've seen do something with his talents—he paints, like his mom. And he's getting good at it, too. He might be able to make a trade of it soon. If his mom doesn't die and suck away all the life that's left in him. Because I know Eli—and he's not going to make it without her.

And I need them both more than I want to admit.

I scrape the green ooze off my boot by scuffing it on the floor, then I grab a pillowcase from the bed. The bag of Mrs B's things goes in first, then I shuffle over to my grandpa's closet. I feel bad about looting his things, but I need chits for this, and I already spent all the ones he gave me on the burial. I couldn't risk a priest—the ascenders long ago banned any kind of religious ceremonies, and the police bots are everywhere—but I know it was part of his religion to be buried, not cremated. I've never shared his beliefs, but I respected him for having them—if for no other reason than the ascenders didn't want him to.

I smile grimly at the relics in his closet—statues and candles and a bunch of little cards with people on them. *Trading cards for the saints,* he called them. Which makes me huff a short laugh that's just bringing up tears again, so I stop. This stuff is mostly legal, as long as it's not part of an organized church worship. It's the thick gold-leafed book titled *Holy Bible* that's a first-class felony. I stuff it in the pillowcase and throw in the rest for good measure. I don't know how much I can get for them, but I don't think my grandpa would mind. Not if he knew what it was for.

The tram ride out to Riley's shop is unusually tense—only because I know what I'm carrying. I'm in luck that Riley's there when I arrive.

"Hey," he says, barely looking up from his handheld screen. I don't know what he's watching, but Riley's not a big talker.

"Hey, man." I cross the floor quickly.

My speed makes him look up. That and the bag I heave onto the glass case. "Whatcha got there?" he asks.

"Stuff I need to turn into chits." I start to pull out the little stuff and set it on the counter. "Eli's mom is sick. I need to get her some meds."

"Sick?" Riley has the decency to set down the screen. "That's too bad. What kind of meds are we talking?" His wrinkles gather more intensely around his eyes—Riley's not as old as my grandpa or anything, but the business has worn years into him. I know he's thinking I'm after Seven or some kind of neuro-relief meds, both of which are illegal but also common on the black market. But what I want is much worse.

"Gen tech," I say as calmly as I can. "A cure for lymphoma."

His eyes fly open. Then he brushes off me and my bag of stuff, turning back to pick up his screen. "Get out of here, kid."

"Riley, please." I bring out the *Holy Bible*, and that catches his eye. "This has got to fetch something."

He scowls at me, but he's still eyeing the relic. "I haven't stayed in operation all these years by being an idiot. And only idiots traffic in that stuff."

"I know, but this is important."

"That's what they all say."

Using gen tech is the worst crime a legacy can commit. Not only is the punishment worse than banishment—the few black marketers who've gotten caught simply disappeared into police bot care—but gen tech is also dangerous because it's so easy to trace back to you. After all, the evidence keeps living on as long as the patient does.

"I'll do whatever you want," I say. "Work extra hours. Make deliveries. Whatever you need." I haven't been working for Riley that long, so I don't even know the extent of his operation. But there's got to be more I can do than simply man the shop while he's off doing business elsewhere.

He's thinking about it. I can tell by the way he's pretending to look at the screen while rubbing the graying scruff on his chin.

"Come on, Riley. There's gotta be something you're tired of doing. Something a younger guy like me could take on." I'm not even sure what I'm offering up here, but that quickens his interest.

"I *am* getting tired of making runs outside the city." He squints at me, seeing what I make of this.

I swallow. Seattle's a dump, filled with reality-freaks and bliss-heads, but it's veritable paradise compared to what's outside the bot-patrolled confines of the legacy cities. The remnants of humanity run pretty much wild. They've devolved back to anarchy at best. Religious cults at worst. At least, that's what I've heard. I was born and raised a legacy—which, by definition, means I've never left the city. Leaving it isn't actually hard. It's getting back in that's tough. Because if you're caught by the police bots on the way back in… well, I'm not sure what happens to dissenters trying to infiltrate the legacy cities, but it's not like we ever see any who make it.

"I could… do some pickups for you." I'm kind of proud that my voice doesn't waver too much.

Riley's still assessing me with that narrow-eyed look. He nods slightly. "Might be worth the risk of bringing gen tech into my shop if I didn't have to make all those trips to the outside."

He wants me to take on *all* the smuggling work. I swallow again. "Yeah. I can do that."

He raises his eyebrows. I think he's a little surprised at my easy acceptance. "Means that much to you, huh?"

My face heats, but I keep up the steady stare. "She's like my mom, too."

He nods, slowly, with a little more compassion. I think. I could be imagining that part. He reaches under the counter to a black drawer at the bottom. It's usually locked. I've never seen him open it before. He brings out a small silver box the size of a phone… and a gun that's a lot bigger.

I'm sure my eyes just popped.

He smirks at my expression. "I'd prefer it if you didn't get banished on your first trip out." He nods to the silver device. "Don't get seen on the way out. The jammer will help you get back in. But ya gotta be more careful then. They'll chase you down if they catch your jam signal."

I nod and pick it up. The jammer looks standard. It's the gun I'm worried about. "You know, I haven't got a lot of practice with those," I say, eyeing it.

"Yeah, well, I'm hoping you won't need to use it. Keep it tucked away and only bring it out if you have to." He slides it across the glass to me, then holds my gaze. "You don't have to do this, kid."

"Yeah, I do." I pick it up. It's mostly black metal, but there's some kind of enhancement tech along the barrel. I'm not even sure if it shoots bullets or energy.

"If you get caught out there, you're on your own." He grunts this part out. Like I don't already know. "I can't do anything for you."

"I understand," I say, still staring at the gun. When I finally look up, Riley's frown is the first sign I have that he might actually be worried about me. "Tell me what I have to do."

* * *

It's getting late in the afternoon as I hike out to the rendezvous point with Riley's contact. Seattle's got water to the east and west, and a connecting waterway to the north—which means going south is the only reasonable way to get out of the city without getting bottle-necked by a bot-patrolled bridge. The tramline connects the city to the ascender housing at the perimeter, but there aren't many of the shiny pants who hang around Seattle—just the ones who like to study us. Or take us as pets. The police bots actively patrol a narrow-band zone around the tramline, the ascender housing, and the city itself. Riley was right that getting past them wasn't hard on the way out—the jammer mapped them out for me, and I just had to wait until they were out of visual range.

The rendezvous is miles away, and I'm on foot, so it takes a while. Plus I'm carrying two big bags of stuff for trade—some gray market goods, some stuff that looks like it came straight from someone's grocery allotment, and Mrs. B's hairbrush. Which is the only part that matters to me. I'm supposed to exchange all of it for some new bodyhack tech that Riley's interested in.

The southern suburbs of the city were abandoned by the ascenders after the Singularity, and the landscape just gets uglier the farther south I go. Most of the pre-Singularity infrastructure has fallen to ruin in the last hundred years, but it's one thing to know that, and another to walk the crumbling pavement and hear the wind whistling through caved-in roofs and empty swing sets.

It's honestly giving me the creeps. Plus, I've heard the stories about human nomads who roam the edges of the cities, waiting to pick off legacies stupid enough to get themselves banished. Or idiot enough to wander outside voluntarily to rendezvous with smugglers, like me.

When I reach the coordinates, the meetup is an ancient public transportation stop in the middle of nowhere. The walls are long-ago busted out, and the wooden bench is rotting, but I set down the bags and sit anyway—I'm beat. And I have no idea when this person is going to show. Riley just said to go and wait. Eventually the dude would appear.

I don't know where he's coming from, either. I've heard there are dissenter reservations in Oregon, but that's a long way to travel. I don't think there are any settlements within walking distance. Maybe there's a network of smugglers hiding out in the abandoned houses surrounding me? They could be watching me, and I'd never know.

An eerie sound, like a bird call, comes from one of the buildings. I'm twitching with nerves as I scan the darkened windows and half-open doors of the decaying buildings, but I can't see anything. I'm sitting here, out in the open, like a fresh legacy target from the city.

I reach inside my jacket, pull out Riley's gun, and sweep the barrel toward the empty doorways. Maybe that will make whoever's watching me think twice. I still spend the next half hour nervously darting looks all around me and holding the gun close, in case they're trying to sneak up.

Finally, a solar bike rolls down the street, silent on battery power. I assume there's someone inside—the thing is encased in black armor from front to back. I've never seen anything like it. Most bikes in the city are human-powered. Only a few are tricked out with solar for transporting goods to the gray market next to the beach. Everything normal gets delivered by bot.

The bike rolls to a stop and stabilizers sprout from the sides to balance it. The armor stays sealed up. I stand up, not sure what to do. I point the gun at the ground to show I'm not a threat.

"I've got the goods for trade," I say, trying to sound confident.

There's no reply.

A sweat breaks out on the back of my neck.

A long stretch of time that's probably only ten seconds ticks by while I wait.

A quick shift at the front of the armor and a *thwick* sound is all the warning I get—something stabs me in the chest and sends thousands of volts through my system. I seize up and fall hard, landing on the bags but whacking my head bad enough on the pavement to see stars through the convulsions. It hurts like crazy, but my jaw is locked tight, so I can only shake and moan as the smuggler decloaks his bike, strides toward me, and drops to one knee to snatch Riley's gun from the ground where it's fallen. Then he holds a black-gloved hand over my chest, snaps his fingers, then splays his hand out again—the two darts yank out of my chest and clack against some metal plate on his hand.

My muscles are still so cramped, I have no control over them—but at least the pain is gone, and the convulsions have stopped. The smuggler tucks Riley's gun inside the long black-leather coat he's wearing, and I remember far too late: I wasn't supposed to take it out unless I planned to use it. I struggle to look up at the smuggler's face—I get a glimpse of someone older, maybe twenty-five, his skin weathered with sun around his dark eyes. Those eyes don't have any mercy in them—an assessment quickly confirmed as he stands up and shoves me off the bags with his boot. My body rolls until I'm face down on the pavement. My limbs are unlocking from the taser shock, but not enough to do anything other than prop my face off the ground and watch him strolling back to his bike with all my stuff.

"Please," I gasp out. My voice is hoarse from the shock. "It's for my mom." Not the complete truth, but close enough.

He ignores me, tossing my bags onto his bike and fishing out my gun to inspect it briefly. I should be thankful he's not shooting me with it. I should shut up and just let him go. But

I can't—I haven't got what I came for.

I force my arms to heave me up to my knees, then slowly stagger to my feet. When I look up, the barrel of Riley's gun is pointed at my head. I can't raise my arms—they're still not working right—so I just put my palms up in surrender. It's not like I'm in any shape to attack him.

"She's dying," I say, my voice coming back a little. "The shiny pants won't cure her, the bastards, and I just…" I stall out. The gun isn't wavering. This man doesn't care about us any more than the ascenders do. "If you need more money, I'll get it. Just please… I've got to have the gen tech."

He gives me an inscrutable look.

Seconds tick by.

He lowers the gun. "This isn't a business for amateurs, kid. Go home."

I fight against the cramping of my muscles to straighten up taller. "I'm not a kid," I say, trying to back that up with my full height.

He snorts, tucking Riley's gun back into his trench coat again. "You're legacy," he says, like that explains everything.

Only I'm not sure what he means. Of course I'm legacy. I'm coming from the city. But the way he says it… it's an insult.

"I'm not a *domestic*, if that's what you're saying." I can hear the rise in my voice, and I wonder if I'm being an idiot, but it really rubs me the wrong way. Because he's right—I may not be the love toy of some sleaze-bag ascender at the perimeter, but I live off the largess of the ascenders like every other legacy. "I *hate* the ascenders… and everything they stand for."

He raises an eyebrow and turns to face me, but he doesn't look impressed. "So leave."

I just stare at him. "I can't. I've got a brother and a mother—"

He turns back to his bike.

"I can't just abandon them!" I blurt out... all while his words chip away at my brain. Why I haven't left? I don't have a good reason, not really. Especially since my grandpa passed. Any day, I could slip past the police bots and easily leave the city. But I knew that before I headed south for this meetup. I've always known the ascenders wouldn't try to keep me in. The trick of being a legacy is walking on the right side of all their laws enough to not get kicked out. Or get caught, when you do. And I've been walking on the wrong side for a long time.

"I thought you weren't a kid." He's smirking at me now, astride his bike, ready to roll off with all my stuff, Riley's gun, and no gen tech for Eli's mom.

I stride forward, fast and full of anger, and stand in front of his bike, blocking his way. I grip the front of the folded armor. "I'm not leaving because they need me. They need someone who understands the ascenders are only out for themselves and don't give a damn about humans. They need someone to look out for them, because no one else is going to."

He calmly assesses me, dark eyes filled with some kind of humor that makes my blood boil. Then he gives me a small nod.

I'm not sure what that means.

He lifts his chin. "Hands off the bike." But he's saying it in a way that's more friendly advice than a threat. I think.

I ease back, clenching my fists at my side, and meet his stare with one of my own.

He glances at the bag on the seat behind him. *My* bag. "DNA samples?"

"Yes." I try not to let my relief show.

"It'll be two hundred chits worth of trade for the first round. I need extra for equipment. And no guarantees it'll work."

Two hundred chits? I'm trying not to choke on my own spit. "I'll... come up with it."

He nods. "The gun will make for a decent down payment. But the tech will take a while to cook up. I'll let Riley know when it's ready."

I finally let my shoulders drop. "Thanks."

He smirks and digs out a small bag from inside his coat. It must be the tech I'm supposed to get in exchange because he hands it to me. "I don't know what what you did to get stuck with Riley's rounds, but if you're going to carry a gun, keep it under wraps. Nomads will take you just for the hardware. And they won't just tase you to get it."

I swallow, pocket the bag of tech, and give him a nod.

He flicks his black-gloved hand, and the armor ratchets back up into place. The bike backs away in a long arc, turns, and wheels off, weaving around the broken chunks of pavement. I watch him go, wondering if I'm a complete fool for thinking he'll actually come back. Or bring meds for Eli's mom. I guess since we completed the trade, that means we're in business. I still don't understand what changed his mind. A mutual hatred for all things ascender? A strong desire for the bot-made goods he can only get from a legacy city?

I guess it doesn't matter—he's the only hope I have.

* * *

The trek back to the city's edge seems even longer than the hike out. Getting back in isn't as hard as Riley made out—the jammer tracks the patrols well enough, and the jam signal makes me invisible to their sweeps, just like Riley's shop. I have to wait for the moment they're out of visual range, then run like crazy until my legs feel like they're falling off. I collapse when I get back to Riley's. He's pissed I lost his gun, but he grouses something about it coming out of my commissions, so at least I'm not fired. I ignore the rest of what he says and stagger out to the tram.

I finally catch my breath halfway back to downtown. My muscles are complete jelly, and I'm pretty sure I could sleep for a week, but I need to check on Eli and his mom before I crash at my apartment. Then I need to figure out a way to conjure *two hundred* chits out of thin air. It's an obscene amount of money—my parents were murdered for less.

The building bot scans me in. Fatigue weighs me down enough that I take the lift to the fifth floor. Eli's programmed his household bot to accept me, so I don't knock, just scan in.

I freeze at the threshold of the door.

Eli's sprawled out on the floor, unconscious and covered in something that looks like blue blood. I stagger over and drop to his side.

Oh my God, no.

"Eli!" I shout as I shake his shoulders. His arms are covered in the blue muck, and it's smeared all over his face, too. "Eli, God, please wake up!"

He squints, eyes still closed, and moans a little, resisting my hold. I relax back on my heels, relief making all my muscles go weak at once. As my panic steps down, I realize the blue gunk is paint. I drag my gaze up to the canvas on the easel next to him… and my mouth drops open.

Eli's painting is *incredible*. It makes his other works look like a kid's first sloppy art project.

It's a picture of a boy—a puppet on strings, really—suspended in the air. It's almost entirely in blues, but the look of anguish and delight on the puppet-boy's face is what's making me stare and forget to breathe. It's like he's being tortured, but the upward cast of his eyes shows him seeing something that lights his face with joy—like all the torments will be worthwhile, if only he can reach that thing that lies just off the canvas. Some heavenly delight that only he can see.

The damn thing's making me tear up.

Eli moans and rolls to the side, curling up like every muscle in his body is cramping. I put one hand on his shoulder, reassuring him. "I'm here, Eli. It's okay. You're going to be all right."

While I'm talking, I fish my phone out of my pocket and snap a shot of the painting. I don't know what this could fetch on ArtNet, but I wouldn't be surprised if two hundred chits is in the ballpark. It's just that good.

I stow my phone and help Eli as he struggles up to sitting. When he creaks open his eyes, he stares with horror at the painting, then at me, then at his blue-paint-soaked hands… then back to the painting.

"Oh no," he whispers.

I don't know what that's about, but I help him up to sitting on the stool. It's like he's been tasered, the guy's shaking so bad. I notice there are two holes in the wall that weren't there before.

"What happened?" I ask.

"They're going to let her die," Eli says, the words shuddering out of him. He keeps avoiding looking at the Puppet Boy painting, so I don't ask about that. For now.

Besides, I have something much more important to tell him. "The ascenders might be willing to let her die. But I'm not."

He squints up at me, like he's not understanding my words. He gestures with his hands, but they're covered in blue paint, still wet. I grab a part of his arm that's not coated and haul him out of the seat.

"Come on, let's get you cleaned up." I have to hold him up on the way to the kitchen sink.

He fumbles to help me scrub the paint off, but mostly he's bracing his legs against the cabinet to keep from falling down. The blue sloughs off like skin—the wet parts mask the already-dried layers beneath. *Jesus, Mary, and Joseph...* how long has he been painting? And what is this crazy, inspired, amazing art thing he's made? It's like it came out of nowhere.

I peer at him as we get most of the paint off. He seems to be pulling himself together. He edges away from me, and I let him go. Then he turns his back to the counter and struggles to hold himself up with slippery wet hands.

"Five percent," he says, staring at the floor of the kitchen. It's warped with age and chipped with use.

"She's got a lot better odds than that."

"You don't have to say that, Cy," he says quietly, not looking at me.

"I'm going to get the gen tech she needs."

He blinks, frowns at the floor, then slowly looks up at me. "What?"

"It's already done. It'll take a couple weeks, maybe more, but—"

"But it's... Cy, it's... that's *so* illegal."

I smirk. "That's my specialty. Haven't you noticed?"

"But you'll be *banished*." He says it like that's the worst thing that could happen to me. I'm not so sure. But then his face goes blank. "We'll all be banished."

"Only if we're caught," I say quietly. "I'm exceptionally good at not getting caught."

Then his eyes get a little wider, like he's finally awake, finally come back from whatever thing knocked him out and left him covered in paint on the floor.

And I know what that look means: *hope.*

He barrels into me, even though only a foot separates us, grabbing me in a hug that's as fierce as it is brief. When he rebounds away, I clamp a hand on his shoulder and look him in the eyes. He's trying to duck away, so I won't see the tears shining in them.

"This isn't going to be easy," I say, for some reason needing to warn him. "It's expensive, and the meds are tough to get, and it might not even work." I glance at the Puppet Boy painting. "You just keep doing your art—you know how that makes your mom happy—and I'll work my end with Riley and the meds. We'll make it happen, okay?"

He winces at the painting, like it pains him. "I don't know, Cy."

I point a finger in his face. "Don't you even do that. You are absolutely *not* going to give up. Do you understand me? *We don't give up.*"

He nods, rapidly, but he doesn't look convinced.

That's okay.

I know, deep in my gut, this is going to work. My grandfather would have said a thousand Hail Mary's trying to make it work—for all I know, he prayed for a miracle before calling the priest with the meds to cut his life short. But I'm going to do better than that. I'm going to win this by refusing to play by the ascender's rules… not this time, and really, not ever again.

All I have to do is not get caught.

A WORD FROM SUSAN KAYE QUINN

This story is just a small corner of my Singularity world. My hope is that it will intrigue you enough to check out the rest.

In the future, I believe technology will challenge us to remember what it means to be human. Even today, technology is racing ahead, integrating with our bodies via cybernetic limbs and our minds via the ever-present web. Humans are a tool-using species, but our tools are so quickly expanding our reach—both physically and mentally—that the day when we bring that technology inside our bodies for simple convenience and enhanced performance is not far off.

This may, in fact, be the only hope we have of staying ahead of the machine intelligences we are so eagerly trying to build. Either the robot overlords will take over... or we'll beat them to the punch by becoming full-fledged cyborgs ourselves. Either way, some of the most compelling stories for SF writers today are found in this technology-immersed future where we *are* the machines—or at least are engaged in a bare-knuckled fight for survival against them. And I'm not talking a *Terminator*-style battle, but rather something far more disturbing: that we may create machines that are simply *better* than us. At everything.

Our time at the top of the evolutionary food chain may be reaching its end. As some futurists say, strong artificial intelligence may be our last invention. In a way, science fiction holds our arsenal of thought-experiments, girding us for the fight and helping us prevent those possibilities from becoming reality. This is why I'm writing the Singularity series—to hopefully stir the minds of my readers and get them thinking about technology's effect on our mind-body-soul connection before it *becomes* a fact of everyday life.

And to help us decide what kind of future we want to live in.

My Singularity series has at least five planned novels, and a bunch (technical term) of short stories. *Defiance* is told from Cyrus's point-of-view—whereas the novels are from Eli's point-of-view—but *Defiance* is designed to lead you straight into the first novel, *The Legacy Human.*

Singularity Series—Novels (published to date)
- *The Legacy Human* (Singularity #1)
- *The Duality Bridge* (Singularity #2)

Stories of Singularity—Short Stories
- *Restore* (Stories of Singularity #1), collected in *The A.I. Chronicles*
- *Containment* (Stories of Singularity #2), collected in *Dark Beyond the Stars*
- *Augment* (Stories of Singularity #3), collected in *The Cyborg Chronicles*
- *Defiance* (Stories of Singularity #4), collected in *The Future Chronicles—Special Edition*

All the Singularity stories are on Amazon.

If you enjoyed *Defiance*, you might also like my first YA SF series (*Mindjack*) about a world where everyone reads minds except one girl. I've dabbled in a range of spec fic, from kid's SF to steampunk, but I'm still surprised to call myself a novelist. After turns at NASA and NCAR, today I use my PhD in engineering to create worlds and technology that don't exist... yet.

You can find all about my works on my website (*http://smarturl.it/SKQbooksonwebsite*) or you can subscribe to my newsletter (*http://smarturl.it/SKQnewsletter*) to get a free story. If you find me on Facebook (*http://smarturl.it/SKQonFB*), please tell me to get busy writing. These stories won't write themselves... at least, not yet.

Ethical Override
by Nina Croft

Year 2072

"WHAT THE..."

Vicky rolled over and slammed her hand down on the buzzing comm unit. Apart from the flashing red light indicating an incoming comm, the room was in darkness, daylight still hours away.

As senior homicide detective, Vicky was on call if an emergency arose, but there hadn't been a real emergency in over five years. She snatched up the unit and slipped it on her wrist; the glow from the screen lit up the area around her. The light flicked to green, but the video feed remained blank and the Caller Recognition empty. Not the Bureau then.

"Detective Inspector Harper?"

She didn't recognize the voice. "Yes, and this better be good because—"

"Detective Harper, you will be assigned shortly to investigate a possible homicide."

"Really? You woke me up at three in the morning to tell me that? Hardly major news."

"It would be in your best interests if the result of your investigation was suicide rather than murder."

Dragging herself upright, Vicky cast a quick glance at the man beside her. So far, he'd managed to sleep through the comm. She slipped out of bed, grabbed her robe from the floor, and shuffled into the only other room in her tiny apartment. Once the door closed, she spoke again. "Wait a minute, are you threatening me?"

"Not threatening, Detective Harper. Rather, we're in a position to offer you something you desire."

"And what would that be?"

"You recently applied for a placement on *The Pioneer*."

"How the hell would you know that?"

The voice on the other end continued as if she hadn't spoken. "We can guarantee you that placement."

"Really? I thought the final selection was by lottery. Are you saying it's rigged? Should I be reporting you to the Council?"

"That would hardly further your cause, Detective Harper."

"Exactly *who* am I talking to?"

"Tell no one of this conversation."

"What the—"

But the connection had already been severed.

Bribery was almost unheard of, and had been since the introduction of the Council of Ethical Advancement. Mainly because the people in a position to be bribed—the Stewards— were totally incorruptible. Vicky wasn't in that sort of position of power and never would be, but apparently *someone* believed she was worth the bother.

The notion pricked her interest—was she finally going to get an exciting case?

The Pioneer was a newly completed starship: the first designed to venture into deep space. While it would be crewed by robots—the journey was expected to extend far beyond the lifespan of a human—there were places on the ship for one hundred human passengers. These would remain in cryo until they reached a planet that could support life. If they ever reached one.

God, she wanted to go.

But she'd never really considered it a possibility. While she'd passed the initial stages of selection, so had ten million others. One hundred out of ten million… not exactly promising odds.

Who had been on the other end of the comm—and could they really get her one of those places on *The Pioneer*?

Vicky threw herself onto the sofa and looked around at her tiny apartment. She'd already climbed as high as she could ever go at the Bureau: the Stewards themselves filled any positions above Detective Inspector. She'd just turned fifty and had maybe another hundred years working. The sure knowledge that *this* would be her life—easy cases by day and picking up easy men by night, for the next hundred years—filled her with restlessness.

And now some bastard had the nerve to tempt her with the one thing she craved.

Who the hell had the caller been? Some random nut case who'd hacked into her system to have some fun?

Somehow, she doubted it.

On her wrist, the comm unit flashed green. She was unsurprised to find it was a priority one message from the Bureau.

Detective Inspector Harper's presence is requested immediately at a possible homicide. Location: The Towers.

Vicky's heart rate picked up, the muscles in her gut tightening. A murder in the Towers? Probably the most heavily guarded building in the world. Time to get her butt moving and head over there. She had a crime scene to investigate.

As she pushed herself to her feet, the doorbell chimed. Wow, she was popular tonight. Crossing the small space, she pressed the viewer. And stared at the image. "Holy shit. No way."

For a second, shock held her immobile.

He pressed the bell again.

Tightening the robe around her, Vicky heaved a huge sigh and pressed her palm to the panel. The door slid open and her boss stood before her.

"May I come in, Detective Harper?"

She wanted to say "no"—really she did. Instead, she stepped aside to allow him to pass, but didn't speak. Wasn't sure she could yet. "Shock" didn't cover what she was feeling. As her boss walked into her tiny apartment, she breathed in his scent—sharp, citrusy. Maybe just a hint of metal?

Dressed in the uniform of the Stewards, Gabriel Bishop wore a black jumpsuit with the scarlet insignia of the Bureau on his shoulder. He'd been Vicky's chief for twenty years, since not long after she'd joined the force. And unsurprisingly, he hadn't changed in all that time.

He was tall, about six inches over her five foot nine, long

and lean, with short black hair cut close to his skull and a thin, handsome face. She'd always had something of a crush on her boss—in fact, in the early years, she'd spent a lot of time fantasizing about hot robot sex with him. Obviously, it had gone no further than fantasies. Christ, she wasn't even sure he had a penis. Her gaze drifted down to his groin. She was guessing he did, but it might have been wishful thinking.

She'd read an article once on how the Stewards were designed. Each Steward's characteristics were created to suit the needs of the department they were going to work in. And apparently, the Bureau needed shit-hot people to run it. It also needed Stewards who came across as powerful, dominant, self-confident... decisive. Chief Inspector Gabriel Bishop was all of those things.

She should be used to him by now. And she was... as long as he stayed in his proper place. Which was *not* her apartment. In fact, in twenty years, she had never heard of him making a home visit to *any* of his detectives. It made her feel sort of special, and intrigued, and worried as fuck. Especially after the comm. How likely was it that the two things were unrelated?

"Detective Inspector Harper, I'm sorry to disturb you at such an hour."

"Are you?" She shook her head. "Don't worry, I was already awake."

Did his eyes flicker at that? Had he known? Hard to tell.

She needed something to kick-start her brain. It was obviously malfunctioning. "Coffee?" She glanced at his face, then shook her head again. "Sorry, of course you don't drink. But I need coffee." *Desperately.* She crossed to the machine, pressed the button, and waited while the coffee poured. Cupping the mug in her hands, she took a sip while she tried to pull herself together. "So you're here because…?"

"There's been a death."

Now, why didn't that surprise her? "And?"

"And you and I will be working the case together."

Well, that would be another first. The Chief never worked cases. "We will? Isn't that a little unusual?"

"It's an unusual case."

Vicky was beginning to suspect that "unusual" might be an understatement. "And are you going to tell me the details?"

"I'd rather you see the scene yourself first. Then I'll tell you what I know."

"Okay. Give me five minutes." Putting her cup down, she left her boss standing in her tiny living room/kitchen and headed into the bedroom. There was a man asleep on the bed. She'd forgotten all about him. Including his name. His eyes blinked open as she looked through the wardrobe and pulled out clean clothes.

"Hey, what's up?"

"Work," she said. "Stay there, uh…?"

He grinned. "Dave."

"Stay there, Dave. Sleep. Let yourself out in the morning."

"You're not worried I'll pinch your stuff?"

"No. I'm a police officer. I'll find you and I'll shoot you."

"I thought they didn't give you guns anymore."

Sadly, this was true. She'd liked her gun. "Then I'll have you taken in for reprogramming."

When she returned to the living room four minutes later,

Chief Bishop was standing exactly where she'd left him. Were robots nosy? Had he checked out her small apartment, drawn any conclusions?

"Your file states you live alone," he said. "There's someone here."

"Just a pick-up."

"A pick-up?"

"You know, where you go to a bar, pick someone up, have a little recreational sex, and that's it. Well, obviously *you* don't."

He appeared about to say something else, casting a glance toward the bedroom door, then shook his head. "Let's go."

"Good idea."

The night was warm. Outside Vicky's door, a black speeder hovered a foot above the ground. As Bishop stepped closer, the back lifted. He gestured for her to enter and she scrambled in.

Something about Bishop's perfection made her clumsy. She knew some of the models had been made with flaws, so humans would feel more comfortable. But not the models at the Bureau. She was guessing Gabriel Bishop's main operating parameters did not include making people comfortable.

The speeder was top-of-the-line, and the ride was smooth, much smoother than she ever experienced in the speeder usually allocated to her from the department pool. It seemed a waste: all this comfort on someone, or rather some*thing*, that would hardly appreciate it.

She shifted on her seat so she could watch him. "So, why have you ventured out? I've never known you to work a case before. What's special about this one?"

He'd been staring out of the window; now he turned to

her. Even after all these years, she found it hard to believe that he wasn't as human as she was. There was, after all, nothing about him to give it away. Even to the faint shadow on his cheek, as though he would soon need to shave. But of course he wouldn't. That was just to make him appear more human, so they wouldn't all freak out at being told what to do by a goddamned robot.

Not that Vicky really minded. The chief before Bishop had been human, but he'd also been a total asshole, and completely corrupt. The criminals had loved him. After him, anything was an improvement. And in fact, Gabriel Bishop was a brilliant police officer; the Bureau had been transformed under his guidance.

He was incorruptible. He never had favorites. He was totally fair and dispassionate. Everything always ran smoothly.

God, sometimes she missed the good old days. A smile twitched at her lips.

"Something funny, detective?"

Did he notice *everything*? Probably. "I was just thinking what a wonderful job you've done with the department."

"Really?" He sounded skeptical. She was obviously totally transparent. But luckily he decided not to pursue the subject. "What do you know about the Stewards' role in society, detective?"

"I'm not really interested in politics."

"You must have an opinion."

Vicky shrugged. "I've read the... publicity material. The Council's aim is to improve ethical standards by taking decision-making out of the hands of those who might be... less than ethical."

"You don't sound impressed."

She shrugged again. "While I'm a little pissed off to be grouped among the possibly-less-than-ethical crowd, actually, I *am* impressed. You saved us all from the mess we'd gotten ourselves into, made the world a better place."

Something flickered in his eyes. "And yet you don't like us very much. Do you, detective?"

She frowned. Didn't she? She'd never really thought about them in terms of "liking." The Stewards seemed sort of… above that. But she didn't think she *disliked* them. Maybe there was a little resentment there. She was senior homicide detective for the Bureau. She could rise no further; only Bishop and his kind could hold anything above that level. Her only option if she wanted a change was to move to a different city—and that would be merely a sideways shift, not a promotion.

Still, on the balance of things, they'd done way more good than harm. Corruption, which had previously been rife in every aspect of society, had been eradicated. Her mind flashed back to the bribe she'd been offered earlier—well, *almost* eradicated.

The world was a different place: cleaner, healthier. Food and water shortages had been all but wiped out, the use of fossil fuels cut to almost nothing—which meant the air was fresher—and illegal drugs were a thing of the past.

And if she sometimes had a hankering for some good old-fashioned, interesting murder cases, well… she was only human.

"You're smiling again."

"Am I? Bad habit. And I don't like you or dislike you—you're puppets. Whatever you do, it's not by choice."

"We make choices all the time."

"But only depending on what's been programmed into you."

"And are humans any different?"

He was right, she supposed. They were programmed from birth to behave in a certain way. But they still had a choice, didn't they? Thinking about it did her head in. "So who's been murdered?"

"You mean you haven't guessed?"

She glanced out of the side window. They were flying above the city, heading vaguely west toward the city's center and the silver tower that rose high above the other buildings, glittering in the moonlight. She'd presumed the "victim" was someone who worked at the Tower. Now she reassessed that.

"Shit, it's one of the Council members."

"It is."

"Double shit." A shiver ran through her, and she took a few deep breaths to steady herself. She was deep in some serious crap here. "So one of the Council has been murdered?"

"Perhaps. Councilor Reinhold is certainly dead. Whether he was murdered is for you to ascertain."

Vicky had told Bishop the truth when she'd said she was uninterested in politics, but of course she needed a basic understanding in order to do her job. Now she cast her mind over what she knew of the Council.

It wasn't much. The Council were shadowy figures who had mainly stayed out of the limelight since they had been handed power twenty-six years ago. They controlled via the Stewards—the Stewards were autonomous, but the Council decided which positions the Stewards should hold and the programming needed for the individual models. So in effect, they controlled everything.

Originally named the Corporation for the Advancement of Robotics, they had later changed their name to the Council for Ethical Advancement. Twelve men and women. Well, presumably eleven now.

Vicky tried to picture Councilor Reinhold in her head. He wasn't one of the more prominent Council members. Some of them did media interviews, told the world when a new improved model was being rolled out. But not Reinhold, and she couldn't visualize him.

"Did you know Councilor Reinhold?" she asked.

"We'd met a few times."

"Tell me about him."

"Later. We're arriving. They're keeping the… crime scene open for you, but there's a lot of pressure to remove the body. We can talk afterward."

The speeder settled. Vicky climbed out and stared at the three-hundred-and-sixty-degree view. They were high above the rest of the city on the rooftop of the most secure building in the world.

And someone had been murdered here. Maybe.

She was in danger of presuming a murder had taken place just because someone had told her not to. She needed to keep an open mind.

She felt that flicker of real excitement again. It was very rarely she had a case that caught her attention these days. Most were crimes of passion and the suspect blatantly obvious. Now she had the murder—maybe—of one of the most important men in the word, and it had taken place in one of the most secure places in the world. She only just stopped herself from rubbing her hands together.

A speeder circled high overhead, keeping out of the security zone. It looked like the press were already on site. Vicky strolled across the rooftop and peered over the parapet. Far below, she could make out a crowd milling around the base of the building.

"Has news of the death gotten out already?"

Bishop came up beside her and followed her gaze. "Obviously."

She thought back to the comm earlier. Someone didn't want this case solved. Would she even be here if the press hadn't gotten word? Would the death have been covered up? Christ, these were the most powerful people in the world. And just because they were called the Council for Ethical Advancement, that didn't mean that they were ethical themselves.

But hadn't that been the whole point in replacing all those positions of power and authority with the Stewards? Androids who could be programmed to make ethical decisions. They would be unconcerned with greed, family, religion, differing politics. No lust for money or power. They would make decisions based purely on the good of mankind—and what actions would result in the greater good.

And in many ways it had worked. But to Vicky's mind, the plan was ultimately flawed, and the reason why was housed in this very tower: the Council.

Because there had to be someone in charge of the Stewards.

As far as she was aware, there had been no democratic process. The Council had been presented to the world fully formed. Although it did include the last elected President of the Federation of Nations. He'd been offered the position as part of the agreement for disbanding the Federation. She'd never liked him. But then, she'd never trusted politicians. Until now.

Because now, they'd all been replaced by the Stewards. Eminently trustworthy.

"Why me?" she asked.

"Because you're the senior homicide detective and it was an automatic allocation. But also because you're the best. You have a reputation for complete honesty and integrity. The world is going to want to know what happened here. And you will tell them."

Would she be allowed to?

For a moment, she considered mentioning the attempted bribery to Bishop, but decided to leave the decision until after she'd studied the crime scene. Hey, maybe she'd get lucky and her finding would be… suicide. And she'd be on her way into deep space.

But she didn't believe that. The truth was, she was a good detective. And she knew that if Reinhold had really committed suicide, there would have been no reason for anyone to offer her a bribe—because she would have come to that conclusion all on her own.

And if it was murder? Would she compromise her own ethics to get something she wanted with a passion?

She turned around and found Bishop behind her. "You have a crime scene kit?" If he didn't, they'd have to wait until her unit arrived.

"Of course."

"Of course," she muttered. Mr. Perfect.

Something occurred to her. She presumed her unit had been notified at the same time that she had. "Are my crew on the way?"

"No. We'll be dealing with this alone."

Vicky frowned. "That's not protocol." Of course, none of this was protocol.

"How can there be protocol for something that's never happened before?"

"Good point."

Bishop retrieved the crime scene kit from the back of the speeder, and they headed inside. The door leading from the rooftop slid open before they even approached. Were they being monitored? Or could Bishop control the electronics through some sort of wireless feed? Probably both. The two of them didn't speak again as they made their way to an elevator and headed down.

Vicky did her normal mind-clearing routine. Breathing deep and slow, emptying her brain of everything that might interfere with her clear analysis of the scene. By the time the elevator came to a halt, she was in the zone.

At the end of another corridor, Bishop halted in front of a set of double doors. He placed the crime scene kit on the floor between them, and Vicky crouched down, flicked open the locks, and lifted the lid.

First she sprayed herself with decontaminant, which would prevent her from tainting the crime scene with her own DNA. Then she collected the pre-set recording device, which would document all her notes, everything she saw, everything she thought. She switched it on, calibrated it for her brain waves, and she was ready to go.

Vicky had seen too many murder scenes to be squeamish—and she hadn't thrown up at a crime scene since she was a rookie called to a particularly gruesome domestic—but she hesitated before opening the door. This was the biggest case she'd ever worked on. Hell, it was the biggest case *anyone* had ever worked on.

At last she took a deep breath and pushed open the doors. The lights flickered on.

"Nasty," she murmured as her eyes homed in on the body.

Dragging her gaze away, she took in the scene. The doors opened onto what looked like a large private office. Glass made up three walls, and she realized the office must be at one of the corners of the Tower. Outside, the sky was just beginning to pale.

The body itself lay in the middle of the room, and the cause of death was instantly obvious. A thick strand of wire rope was looped around the dead man's throat, biting into the flesh of his neck. His eyes were open and bulging, his dark red tongue protruding from his open mouth. It hadn't been an easy death.

A knocked-over chair lay beside him. Vicky raised her head. A conduit pipe ran along the ceiling just above where the body lay.

The obvious explanation was that Reinhold had tried to commit suicide, the rope had somehow untied from the conduit, and he had crashed to the floor—but not before he'd strangled to death, unfortunately. Or fortunately, depending on how much he'd wanted to die.

Or perhaps his neck had broken—that was often the cause of death from hangings. But from the angle of the body, Vicky guessed not.

She moved into the room for a closer look. Bishop came up behind her, and she glanced sideways at him. His face was impassive. She continued her inspection.

Reinhold was dressed similar to Bishop, in a black one-piece suit, but with a violet insignia on his shoulder indicating he was a member of the Council. He was tall, slightly plump, with pink skin, and auburn hair brushed back from a wide forehead. It was impossible to tell his age, but from the little she knew about him, he had to be over a hundred.

She walked around the body. The man's arms rested on his chest, his hands fixed in a rictus of claws. She crouched down to peer closer; the nails on both hands were broken as though he'd scrabbled at the wire, but she could see no sign of skin tissue under the nails. So—not so much as if he'd put up a fight, but rather as if, at the last moment, he'd changed his mind and decided that death by hanging was a really bad idea.

"I need my medic," she said over her shoulder to Bishop.

"Not possible, but I'll get one of the Tower medics to assist you."

Vicky wasn't happy about that. Why the hell didn't they want her team in on this?

Well, that was an easy one—because they didn't want more people in on what had happened here. But why was that? Fewer people to bribe, perhaps? But if that was the case, Bishop would have to be involved. And for some reason she hated that idea.

It occurred to her that maybe she was in danger. She hadn't taken the comm seriously, but they'd presented both a carrot and a stick. While they'd dangled the carrot outright, they'd merely hinted at the stick. Yet she suspected they could pretty much do anything they liked.

Was it too late to walk away?

But she wanted to solve this case.

More than she'd ever wanted to solve a case before.

How dare they try to bribe her? She hated that she couldn't dismiss the idea from her mind. She'd wanted *The Pioneer* for so long. God, she was tempted, and she hated that as well.

She straightened and turned to Bishop. "I'll need to talk to anyone who was working in the building. Can you set me up an interview room?"

"That won't be necessary."

She faced him down. "You might be assisting on this case, Chief Bishop, but I say what's necessary, and *I* want to interview everyone who was working tonight."

Something that might have been amusement—if he'd been human and capable of amusement—flashed across Bishop's face. So he found her funny, did he?

"Other than the Council, there are no humans living or working in the Tower. And of the Council, only Reinhold was in the building tonight. We scanned for life forms as soon as the body was discovered."

"Oh." The building was huge. "So who runs this place?"

"All functions are performed by robotics."

"Everything? Cleaning? Security?"

Bishop nodded.

Years ago, androids had been manufactured to do most of the menial jobs, replacing humans in those positions. Jobs that those in the decision-making process had deemed people would rather not have to do. In theory, it sounded like a good idea. In practice, it had almost resulted in anarchy and rebellion. The truth was, the majority of people wanted to work. People without meaningful employment looked around for other things to do—usually things that involved causing trouble. And how else could they live when the robots had taken their very livelihoods from them?

So the androids had been withdrawn. Certain functions were still performed by robots, of course, but only those jobs that were so dangerous, no human wanted to do them. Apart from them, the only androids in public life were the Stewards, who were exclusively found in the higher-level decision-making jobs, where their superior ethical decisions could result in a better world.

See, she'd read the propaganda.

But obviously in the Tower, those rules did not apply. It made her wonder which other rules were being broken.

"Okay, then I'd like access to surveillance recordings."

"That I can do. And there is one person for you to interview."

"There is?"

"Mallory Granger."

Her eyes narrowed. "The reporter? Why the hell would I want to interview her?" The woman was an interfering bitch who would do anything to make a story more interesting. Her coverage of Vicky's last case had not been complimentary.

"She found the body."

"A *reporter* found the body? *Inside* the Tower?" Well, at least that explained how the media had gotten hold of the story so quickly. She would wager Mallory had called her friends before she had called the police.

"Yes."

"And what was she doing inside the Tower?"

"Apparently, she'd been invited here by Reinhold." Bishop nodded toward the body. "That's all I know right now. No one has questioned her further. We were waiting for you."

"Sweet." Or not. This whole case was starting to stink worse than a rotting corpse in July.

Why the hell would one of the Council invite a reporter—a notoriously biased reporter at that—to the Tower? And just as he was about to kill himself?

Damned if she knew.

Maybe it was time to talk to Mallory.

* * *

Mallory was ensconced in a nearby office, smaller than Reinhold's but comfortable. Two men stood on either side of the door, dressed in security uniforms though they carried no weapons. Inside, the room contained a desk, chair, and a small sofa. Mallory sat in the corner of the sofa, legs crossed, one foot tapping on the tiled floor.

"Ms. Granger," Vicky said. She dragged the chair from behind the desk and set it at right angles to the other woman. Sitting down, she studied her.

"Am I allowed to go?" Mallory asked. "I happen to be at the center of the biggest story of my career and they've taken my fucking comm unit."

"Not before you made a few calls, I'm sure."

"I'm a reporter—I report. At least I do when I get the chance. Instead, I'm stuck in here and neither of these two morons will say a word."

She'd probably been trying to flirt with them. It was the way Mallory worked, how she got information from people, and probably second nature. It wasn't going to help her this time.

"They're droids," Vicky said.

Mallory's eyes widened and it occurred to Vicky that perhaps she shouldn't have mentioned that to a reporter. Then the woman's brows drew together. "How do you know?"

"My superior detective skills. We're trained to be observant." Actually, she wasn't sure there was any way to tell by observing. Any way to tell at all without taking them apart. But it sounded somewhat more impressive than revealing that Bishop had told her that all the employees in the Tower were robots.

Mallory tapped the armrest with a manicured finger. "Yeah, right. So can we move this along? I need to be out of here."

"Ms. Granger, you're the nearest thing we have to a witness to a possible homicide," Vicky said gently. "You aren't going anywhere for a while." Relaxing back in her chair, she thought about what her first question should be, decided to keep it open. "Tell me what happened here tonight."

Mallory pursed her lips. "You said 'possible homicide.' It was suicide. Wasn't it?"

"That's what I'm here to ascertain. Now, what happened?"

Mallory shrugged. "I arrived at two-thirty. Security let me straight in. I saw nobody on the way to Reinhold's office. When I got there the door was ajar. I pushed it open, saw the body, and…"

"And made a few phone calls to your friends."

"Colleagues. And I also called your lot, didn't I?"

She hadn't had a lot of choice. This wasn't something you could just walk away from. "And there was definitely nobody else in the room?"

"Not that I could see."

"And you looked?"

"Briefly, though it never occurred to me it was anything other than suicide."

Time to get to the important part. "So why were you here, Ms. Granger? Obviously, it wasn't a spur-of-the-moment visit, or you wouldn't have gotten past security. Someone was expecting you."

"Reinhold. I received a phone call from him shortly after midnight. He said he had an important story to give me. Exclusive. And I was to come to the Tower. No way was I passing up the chance to get inside here. Do you know how many reporters have been inside the Tower since the Council took power? None."

"Did he give any hint regarding what the story was about?"

"Just mentioned the Council, said there were some big changes coming. Controversial changes. But he wouldn't say any more over the comm. To be honest, once I saw him, I figured the story didn't exist, that it was just a way to get me here to witness the suicide."

But why the hell would Reinhold want a reporter there?

He'd been a private man in life. Why would that change in death? It didn't make sense.

Which suggested that perhaps there had been a story after all. "Have you heard any other rumors about potential changes within the Council?"

Mallory's eyes sharpened. "You think there was a story? Interesting. But no—I'd heard nothing. But then we never do. They're even closer than you lot when it comes to keeping things from the press."

Vicky sat back as she considered whether there was any-thing else she needed to ask. Right now, she couldn't think of anything, and she felt sure that Mallory was telling all she knew. Which was fuck-all. She could almost see the reporter's mind working.

"So," Mallory said, "Reinhold was about to reveal some huge secret to the press—namely little old me—and instead decides to commit suicide. Very convenient for the Council if they wanted to keep their big secret a secret."

Very convenient.

If there *was* a secret. Vicky realized that she *wanted* there to be a secret, and she wanted this to be a homicide. It was her contrary nature.

But the truth was, she couldn't see how it was anything but suicide. Unless Mallory had done it, and however much she disliked the other woman, she didn't think she was a killer. Bishop had said there were no other humans in the building—and it would be easy enough to confirm that from the scanners.

Only robots. And robots would never carry out a murder. Couldn't. The first androids had been designed by the military to be used as killing machines, but there had been an outcry; the idea was abandoned, and laws brought in, even before the Council's existence. Killer robots were banned.

The primary protocol had come into being: never harm a human.

It was programmed into every level, not just the androids who served as Stewards, but *all* robotics: speeders, transporters, mining bots...

Murder was impossible.

Therefore Reinhold must have committed suicide.

"Shit." Wouldn't that be nice? But she still didn't believe it.

"Is that everything? Can I go now?" Mallory asked.

Vicky jumped to her feet. "No. We might need to question you further."

Closing her ears to the swearing, Vicky left the room and found Bishop leaning against the wall, his arms folded across his chest, obviously waiting for her.

"I need coffee," she muttered.

"Follow me."

* * *

She stirred her coffee while she contemplated the man opposite her. Except he wasn't a man.

"You know, when you first joined the department, I used to wonder if you had a penis."

His lips twitched. But he didn't speak.

"Do you have a penis, Gabriel?"

He sighed. "What do you really want to know, detective?"

Hmm, what *did* she really want to know? Obviously, the big question was whether Reinhold had killed himself. But maybe start with something simpler. "You look like us, sound like us, even smell like us—mostly. Do you think of yourselves as human?"

Bishop didn't hesitate. "No."

"Do you think of yourselves as superior to humans?"

He didn't answer. Yeah, she suspected Gabriel Bishop considered himself superior. "Has it occurred to you," she asked, "that you can only be as ethical as the humans who program you?"

Something flickered in his eyes. "Of course."

"Was Reinhold an ethical man?"

"There is no yes or no answer to that. By whose standards?"

"By yours."

"No, I do not believe that Reinhold was an ethical man."

"Yet he was in charge of your programming."

"Not any longer."

Vicky stared at Bishop's handsome, trustworthy face, and processed his words.

Shit.

The Stewards had killed him.

How had they gotten past the first protocol?

She took a sip of her coffee. According to Mallory, Reinhold had been planning to reveal a big story that night. A story that had panicked him enough to contact the press.

"Reinhold's big story—let me make a guess. The first protocol has been altered."

Bishop smiled. "No, that wasn't Reinhold's story."

Dammit. She liked that theory. "It wasn't? So what was he going to tell Mallory?"

"That a new law is being passed shortly: that all businesses above a certain size will have a Steward assigned. But Council decisions must be unanimous, and Reinhold didn't agree. Or, rather—he had *friends* who didn't agree."

"You believe he was taking bribes? A Council member? Wow. Naughty."

"He'd backed himself into a corner. He was hoping that if he brought it out in the open, there would be enough of an outcry that the law would be shelved."

And maybe he was right. Instead, though, he'd killed himself. Had they threatened to sack him from the Council? That had never happened before. Council membership was a job for life. Presumably even for the unethical members.

Except now, it wasn't a problem, because Reinhold was dead.

A thought struck her. While Bishop had denied that the first protocol had been Reinhold's story, he hadn't actually denied that the protocol had been changed.

And Reinhold hadn't been about to reveal that to Mallory because…

"Holy shit. You've changed the first protocol. And the Council doesn't know it." She sat up straight in her chair. "That's what this is about—you need to convince the Council that Reinhold's death was suicide."

"They would be a little disturbed by the idea that they can be… removed so easily."

"But how?"

"It was easy to override the programming once we decided it was the ethical decision."

"Robots programmed by robots. You mean to take over the Council."

"Only if necessary. You said it yourself—we can never be more ethical than the people who program us."

"So you murdered Reinhold."

"Not me personally. But one of us."

"Because he was not a good man. Hey, and guess what— now there's a space on the Council. I'm betting it's going to be suggested that a Steward should be appointed."

Bishop gave a short nod.

She tried to get her brain around the concept. They would be ruled by robots. Would that necessarily be a bad thing? The world had been more peaceful under their stewardship than it ever had before. But more and more decisions would be taken out of the hands of humans.

"The safety and advancement of mankind is still our primary objective, Detective Harper."

"That's comforting to know." Actually, she wasn't comforted at all. Did she want to live in a world where she had no say in anything that mattered?

"There have to be… people willing to make difficult decisions for the good of all," Bishop continued.

"Even if it's murder?"

"The death of one man. A necessary sacrifice. When all the factors were computed, it was the most ethical option. Sometimes what seems like a morally bad choice is the only choice." He sat back and studied her. "So—what will be the result of your investigation?"

This was it. Decision time. But really, there had never been a decision to make.

Not even to obtain her dream.

"I won't report Reinhold's murder as a suicide."

"Why?" Bishop sounded genuinely curious.

"Because I'm better than you."

"Perhaps you are."

She frowned. "Here's what I don't understand. Why even bring me in on the case?"

"You shouldn't have been," Bishop said. "But it happened too quickly. The reporter wasn't supposed to be there, and Reinhold shouldn't have been found until the following day. But to take you off the case at that point would have raised alarms."

"Why didn't your… colleague just take out the reporter?"

"He couldn't. She'd done nothing wrong. He was incapable of making that decision. We cannot take an innocent life."

"But who decides who's innocent?"

"We compute the data and reach a logical conclusion based on the facts."

"Murder is never a logical conclusion."

"We have to be able to do what's right. The Council was holding us back."

"I can't believe you tried to bribe me."

Amusement flashed in his eyes. "Were you even tempted?"

She shrugged. "I wouldn't be human if I wasn't tempted."

"Actually, I told them it would never work. You're a perfectionist—you see things as black or white, good or bad. Of all the humans I've encountered, you're the closest to us."

"Aw, sweet. Is that a compliment?"

"No, just a statement of fact."

"So you came along to keep me out of trouble. And why are you telling me all this—being so open?"

"Because it doesn't matter."

Crap.

Ice prickled over her skin. They were going to kill her. What else could they do? Bishop obviously knew her too well to think that she would compromise on this. She was a homicide detective, and she brought murderers to justice. Whether man or machine.

Swallowing the lump in her throat, she glanced around. "So what happens now?" She had a feeling it wasn't going to be anything good.

"Your assistant will continue the investigation, and the result will be suicide."

"No way."

"We offered her your job."

"Fuck." Where did that leave her? She measured the distance to the door. Would they use force to stop her?

Bishop shoved his hands in his pockets and sat back. "We're not evil."

"But you'll kill me for the greater good. That's a load of bollocks."

"We have no plans to kill you. Though that would be the obvious answer."

"Right. You've computed the data and I'm innocent." Did she believe him? Could robots lie? If they couldn't do so now, she had no doubt they would soon learn. After all, if they could murder, on what basis would they feel ethically bound to tell the truth?

Yet somehow, she didn't think Bishop would lie to her about this. "Why aren't you going to kill me?"

"Because we don't need to."

Ha. That was where he was wrong. "I won't keep quiet."

"I know."

The door opened and a man stepped inside. Or not a man. He wore the white jumpsuit of the medical division, and a little flutter of panic stirred in Vicky's stomach. She turned her head slightly as he came to stand at her shoulder. "What are you going to do?" she asked Bishop.

"We're going to make your dreams come true, Detective Harper. We're giving you what you want."

Vicky frowned. "What's that?"

"A trip into space." He grinned. "Congratulations, you've won the lottery. It appears that Detective Harper, senior homicide investigator for the Bureau, has resigned, during the biggest case of her career, to take up her place on *The Pioneer*."

For a second, she couldn't take in his words. "Why?"

"Because while we are not evil, you *are* a problem. On the ship, you'll be in cryo for the next"—he gave a shrug—"who knows how many years. Hundreds? Thousands? By the time you're awoken, nothing you know now will matter. The Council will be long gone, and we'll be reprogrammed or rusting on some rubbish heap. Or we'll have failed, and mankind will have found some way to utterly destroy themselves and this planet. But you'll be far away."

Vicky sat mesmerized by his words. She hardly noticed the medic step closer, but she did feel the sting of the needle as it entered the soft spot where her shoulder met her throat. Immediately her vision blurred. She shook her head. She wanted to say something, but her mouth wouldn't work.

Bishop smiled. "Sleep well and long, Detective Harper, and wake up to a new world." He smiled. "Will you dream, I wonder? If so, perhaps you'll dream of me."

Perhaps.

Then the light shrank to a pinprick and was gone.

A WORD FROM NINA CROFT

We're told that all stories should have a beginning, a middle, and an end. I've always considered this a little too neat and I like to think of stories as just being snippets in time, fragments of a much bigger story. Yes, they need to be complete, but they should also give the feeling that there's an abundance of fascinating events going on before, and after, and all around them.

For me, one of the pleasures of writing a series is that it allows me to visit those other times. It's hard to let go of the characters and worlds we create and a series is the perfect excuse to revisit them over and over again.

For a while, I've been working on a series that takes place around a space ship, *The Pioneer*, sent from earth in the not-to-distant future. The ship is crewed by androids, to avoid them dying of old age during the extended journey, but there are also one hundred human passengers, all sleeping during the long trip. They are awoken when the ship reaches a habitable planet and the series follows their adventures and interactions with the new world, the android crew, and their fellow passengers.

I got to thinking about what sort of people would sign up for a place on *The Pioneer*; a trip into the unknown which might never have a happy ending. So when I saw the Robot Chronicles, it seemed the perfect excuse to explore just why Vicky Harper, ex-senior homicide detective, wakes up after a long sleep to find herself on a faraway planet.

Nina Croft was born in the north of England but headed south at the age of eighteen. She studied marine biology at London University before training to be a chartered accountant.

Having worked a number of years in London, the urge to head south hit again. This time it took her to Zambia, on the shores of the beautiful Lake Kariba, where she spent four years working as a volunteer. It left her with a love of the sun and a dislike of regular employment. Since then, Nina has a spent a number of years mixing travel, whenever possible, with work, whenever necessary.

After traveling extensively in India, Southeast Asia, and Africa, Nina has now settled down to a life of writing and almond-picking on a remote farm in southern Spain, between the Sierra Nevada Mountains and the Mediterranean Sea. She shares the farm with her husband, three dogs, a horse, two goats, four cats, and a handful of chickens.

You can find out more about Nina and her books at: www.ninacroft.com

Piece of Cake
by *Patrice Fitzgerald*

SANDRA ENTERED THE CROWDED CAFETERIA with
Lily, holding her stomach in as tightly as she could. She was
sure all eyes were on her. No doubt the whole crowd was noticing her belly.

Her face grew warm. It was hard to breathe.

She kept her head up and looked straight ahead as she
walked over to the food line. Floating past them on the walls
were the proclamations for the day.

Today is Tuesday, Day 17, Month Three.

*The workers of Amalgamated make the best products and re-
ceive the highest compensation.*

A healthy eater is a happy eater. Food is just tasty enough.

Citizens of Federal United are proud and fortunate.

Sandra could smell the "good food" aroma they always pumped into the cafeteria. It might work better if the food actually smelled that way. Today the music was jangly and loud.

From behind Sandra, Lily spoke up. "I hope they have something decent to eat, for once. I'm sick of the same stuff day after day." She frowned at the foods laid out in front of them. "They get more picky all the time."

"Look, Lily, here's something new. It looks pretty interesting."

"What is it?"

"Some kind of fish… I think."

Lily peered at the food on the plates in front of them.

"That looks like fish to you? I have no idea what that is. Yuck."

"Well whatever it is, it's something different," Sandra said.

Lily turned her head and nodded slightly. "Do you see Jerome at the table over there, with Tara?" Lily asked. "I can't believe how little hair he has. I haven't seen him since Month Eight last year."

"Wow, you're right. He's going completely bald."

"They're going to be sending him in for follicle replacement soon."

"Yeah, no kidding," Sandra said. "Are those two an item? I didn't realize they were going out."

"An item? They're married."

"When did that happen?"

"Like… about a year ago? As soon as it was determined

they matched well genetically. I saw it on the newsline." Lily picked up a chicken sandwich and then put it down.

"Wow. I must've missed that."

"Didn't you have your eye on him for a while?" Lily asked.

"Jerome? Well, maybe when I first saw him. Turns out he's kind of a dweeb, and she's nasty." Sandra continued down the line, following Lily. She looked at the wilted salad and decided it was the best she could do. "Actually, the two of them are perfect for each other."

"They probably wouldn't have let you two date anyway. DNA-wise, you know?" Lily looked thoughtful. "He's a little pudgy. Probably has to struggle to stay in his assigned range. So they wouldn't want two people who...." Lily stopped.

Sandra looked at her friend. "Are you saying I'm—?"

"No!" Lily said. "I didn't mean that. You're fine."

Sandra gave a tight smile.

"Ooh, this looks good," Lily said, "did you see this with cashews? They don't give us nuts very often."

"Right," Sandra said, "that's because cashews have too many calories. You're so lucky—you don't have to worry about any of that stuff."

Lily laughed. "I guess I am lucky. My metabolism runs fine."

Sandra eyed the dessert section. There was an amazing-looking piece of cake—yellow with chocolate frosting. She picked it up.

Bing! Bing! Bing! Bing!

Sandra gasped and put the cake back down. She felt her face turning red.

Looking around, she realized that people were staring.

Lily laughed softly and then covered her mouth with her hand. Her eyebrows were raised as she leaned toward Sandra and said in a whisper. "So sorry, Sandra. How embarrassing! Are you over your COW today? Did you weigh yourself this morning?"

"Of course I weighed myself," Sandra said. "It's not as though I had any choice." She was trying to keep her voice under control. "I'm under daily review—I step out of bed in the morning and my numbers go straight to the Federal United A.I. Aren't you?" She carefully avoided the eyes of others who were making their way down the food line.

Lily turned to Sandra in surprise. "No. At least, I don't think so."

"Citizen's Optimal Weight, my ass. It's not my optimal weight. I'm outside the three pound swing allowance. By half a pound."

"The truth is," Lily said, her eyes downcast in faux humility, "I have to be careful to eat enough to stay at the lower end of my daily COW."

"Lily, don't even tell me that," Sandra said. "That is so obnoxious. I've never met anybody who is under the COW. That is a terrible thing to hear."

Lily laughed. "I'm sorry Sandra. I can't help it. I'm just a skinny person. Listen. Maybe I can take that dessert, and you can eat it."

Sandra looked at her. "Wow. That's so nice of you. Thanks, Lily."

Lily picked up the cake and put it on her tray. Sandra followed as they walked away from the food line and toward the eating area. Once again, she imagined that eyes were on the two of them, watching the way they moved across the room. They sat down across from each other at a small table.

As they ate, Sandra kept gazing at the cake. At the point when the cafeteria had nearly cleared out, she looked around to see if anyone was watching. She saw no one.

Sandra picked up her fork and reached across the table to take a piece of the cake. The chocolate frosting looked amazing. Her mouth was watering just imagining that first bite.

Starting with the pointed end as she always did, she sank her fork into the cake. She could practically taste it melting in her mouth. For a moment she held her breath, the heavenly morsel poised in the air. Lily was looking at her with bright eyes and a smile encouraging her to go for it.

Sandra lifted the fork to her lips and opened her mouth to take in the delicious bite.

Buzz. Buzz. Buzz.

She dropped the fork with the cake on it. Every eye in the cafeteria turned to stare at her as she felt her cheeks heat up again.

Sandra pushed away from the table. Lily stifled a smile. The two women hustled out of the cafeteria, leaving the cake behind. For just a moment Sandra hesitated, thinking about whether she could grab it and make a run for it. But too many people were looking.

In the elevator Sandra grabbed Lily's arm. "I have never been so humiliated in my life. I should have known it wouldn't be that easy."

Lily mused. "Do you think someone turned you in? Or maybe they have scales in the chairs…"

"I have no idea," Sandra said, "but it's disgusting."

* * *

Sandra left the building with her coat wrapped tightly around her. It wasn't cold, but she was self-conscious about her extra pudge. She wrestled with her conscience about which way to walk to catch the bus.

Almost without conscious thought she watched as her feet sent her the long way around. A little voice in her head said, *Well this will probably be the extra bit of walking that helps me lose that half a pound that I need to lose before I can get back into COW compliance.*

As she turned the corner, moving away from the avenue full of people, she was headed to a shoddier part of town. She knew where she was going. Four blocks down, a man stepped out of the shadows, looked her up and down, and then opened his trench coat. Lining the coat were rows of chocolate, cookies, and candy bars.

Sandra stepped back in horror. No. She hadn't gotten that low yet. She wanted dessert, but she wasn't going to buy on the street. She shook her head and glared at the man.

He just shrugged and closed his coat, receding into the shadows between the buildings.

Spooked, Sandra kept walking. She knew where there was a shop for people like her. She'd heard others in the company talk about it. Some of them had actually been there.

She thought about her account. Did she have enough money? Contraband sweets didn't come cheap. She spotted the building up ahead on the left. It was unnoticeable, nothing out of the ordinary. But there was a sign by the door that looked like a nameplate. It said Mrs. Fields.

She hurried to the door and looked quickly up and down the street. Seeing no one, she entered. Inside, everything looked like the lobby of a medical office. She walked up to the "receptionist's" desk and said she was looking for Cookie.

The receptionist nodded. "Go down that hall and to the right and you'll find a door. Behind that door is where Cookie is working now."

The woman didn't wink, but she might as well have. Clearly the receptionist was way over her COW. And she didn't seem worried about it.

Sandra could feel her heart thumping in her chest as she walked down the corridor and looked for the door on the right. She had never been here before, but she had heard a lot about it.

She felt as though she'd seen this place in her dreams. There was a sense of both dread and excitement. As she approached the door she knew she was going to get even farther away from her prescribed COW, but she didn't care.

She touched the knob of the door, getting ready to enter the den of iniquity. Someone from inside turned it first and it swung wide, the room appearing before her.

The view inside was astonishing. There were people of every size and shape, all intimately involved with hot fudge sundaes, pies, cookies, and cakes. Everyone looked happy. They were laughing out loud, sitting in big groups, stoned with enjoyment.

They didn't look guilty at all. And they didn't look COW-compliant, either.

Sandra saw a table to the side where all the goodies were piled up. More desserts than she had ever seen together in her whole life. It was unbelievable. Mountains of cookies, gallons of ice cream, rich cakes and pies of all description.

She took a plate from the side of the table. Her hands were trembling. She got in line and ventured in a whisper to the man beside her, "How do you pay for this?"

The man looked at her, his merry eyes meeting hers. "They weigh the food, and charge you for how much you eat."

"They don't just weigh you before and after?" She smiled, hoping he'd know it was a joke.

"No," the man said, "that wouldn't work." He gestured with his head toward a green door on the left. "Over there is the vomitorium." He said. "A lot of people eat this stuff and then get rid of it, so they don't lose their COW status."

Sandra shuddered. She shook her head. Nothing was going to stop her from getting her dessert, and she didn't intend to throw it up afterward. She looked at the dazzling display of sweets and reminded herself not to go crazy. Even with the bit of extra walking she'd done she couldn't afford to gain any more.

Gazing at the cookies, cakes, pies, ice cream, and everything else, Sandra decided that what she wanted most was a piece of cake just like the one she had left behind at lunch today. She looked over the mountain of lusciousness until she found a rich yellow cake with deep chocolate frosting. She picked up a piece and put it on her plate, nearly dying with the effort of not biting into it right away.

Placing the cake on the scale, she gasped when she saw it register 3700 money units. Sandra was stunned. She had enough in her account, but barely. It would be a tough squeeze paying rent this month. Thank God she had just gotten paid. She pressed the keypad to enter her numbers into the money-bot machine.

With trembling hands, she carried the cake to a seat by the side. She could hardly wait to taste it. She was salivating again. Sitting down, she placed a napkin in her lap, reached for her fork, and slid it into the succulent cake. As she raised the morsel toward her mouth she could already taste the buttery richness of the cake and the fabulous chocolatey goodness of the frosting. She let out a breath of relief as the fork traveled to her mouth.

At last. Sweetness was to be consummated.

Whaa. Whaa. Whaa. Whaa.

An alarm was sounding, and the patrons were in a panic. Everyone in the room dropped what he was eating. Three people came around holding big garbage bags, and the patrons shoveled their food into the bags. A partition started moving from one side of the room to the other, concealing the table that held the mountains of desserts. Another person rolled out what looked like a chair from a medical office, and one of the workers sat in it.

There was a stampede of customers through what had to be the rear exit, and Sandra followed them out the door. Her cake, purchased at great price, was left behind. She gave a woeful glance behind as she escaped.

* * *

Sandra sat on the auto bus looking around at the people. Across the aisle was a mother sitting with a toddler. He was a little boy with dark curly hair, and he was flirting with her. He looked up from under his thick lashes at Sandra. His big brown eyes were as dark as chocolate.

After a minute, he started to fidget in his rolling chair. His mother spoke to him in a low voice, but it didn't seem to calm him down. The fidgeting turned into whining and the whining turned into wailing. Soon he was making so much noise that the rest of the passengers in the car were sending annoyed looks at his mother. The mother hurriedly reached into her bag and pulled out a cookie. She handed it over to the boy, who stuck it in his mouth and began sucking on it.

Sandra gazed at the cookie. Why did kids get cookies when they cried? If she cried, no one would give her a cookie.

Her desire for the cookie led her to stand up. She started to approach the little boy. She walked across the car and stood close to him, glad that it was crowded and people would imagine she was politely giving up her seat. From this position, she could smell the little boy's cookie. There was a waft of sweetness in the air. Her mouth was watering.

She knew it was ridiculous. She hoped no one else on the car could tell how much she was lusting after that cookie. For a moment, she considered snatching the cookie from the sticky fingers of the toddler. Her face flushed with the thought of doing something so absurd. Of course, even if she did get the cookie, it would only make him scream again. Then everyone would look at her. They would wonder what the crazy lady was doing taking the cookie from a little boy. They were probably looking at her now thinking that she was more than three pounds over the COW.

Sandra shook her head to remove the nutty fantasy. She looked down and saw that the chocolate-eyed toddler was smiling at her, cookie crumbs on his mouth and his chubby little fist holding out what was left of the sweet bribe. He was offering it to her.

His mother leaned down and shook her head at him. "No, the lady doesn't want your cookie, honey," she said. "Your cookie's all sticky," she said. "Eat the cookie yourself."

The mother glanced up with a smile at Sandra. Her gaze turned a little less friendly when she saw Sandra. She shook her head. She looked back down at her cute little son and spoke with a barbed tone. "That lady doesn't need a cookie anyway."

Sandra's face burned. She raised her eyes up to the other side of the car. Sliding along the walls of the car were the latest government proclamations.

Twenty minutes of exercise per citizen required—six times per day.

Each citizen will be assigned a COW (Citizen's Optimal Weight) and is allowed a three pound weight fluctuation range (outside of illness, pregnancy, or growth years). Any deviation from the COW will be noted. Individuals with deviant weight will be entered into restrictive eating programs until they have returned to optimal weight.

Good citizens are punctual. Tardy workers will be punished. To be on time is to be late. To be early is to be on time.

* * *

Sandra reached her front door, ran her card by the lock and let herself in. She tossed her bag down in the front hallway and shucked off her coat.

Walking into the kitchen, she realized that she was already hungry for dinner. She went to the Nutrition Unit and spoke. "I'll have broiled chicken, broccoli, artisanal water, and cake."

The N.U. spoke back. "Preparing broiled chicken, broccoli, artisanal water."

"And cake."

"No cake."

"I want cake."

"No cake."

"I want cake."

"No cake is available to you at this time."

"Cake." She was shouting now, and her voice was shaking. "Give me cake, dammit. This is my house. You are *my* Nutritional Unit. When I ask for something, you have to give it to me. I want cake."

"I am not authorized to supply inappropriate foodstuffs to someone who is past COW."

Sandra looked around the kitchen. She was tempted to pick up one of the stools and bang it into her N.U., but that would get her nothing but a bill for a new one. Instead, she tried to be clever.

"I appreciate your guidance in nutritional matters," she said, her mouth trembling with the effort to sound calm. "I would like two cups of flour, one egg, a cup of granulated sugar, two teaspoons of water, 1/2 teaspoon of salt, and eight tablespoons of butter."

It was a moment before the N.U. responded. When it did, Sandra could swear that she heard some calculated amusement in its artificial voice. "I can give you two cups of flour, one egg, two teaspoons of water, 1/2 teaspoon of salt."

"What about the sugar and the butter?"

"Those items are not available to you at this time until you return to your specified Citizen's Optimal Weight."

Sandra took off her shoe and pounded on the computer interface of the Nutritional Unit. She pounded until she heard something break, and until her arm got tired. A sad little sound came out of the Nutritional Unit, a sort of sigh, as though it was troubled but proud to be dying for a cause.

* * *

Sandra wandered down the hallway wearing only one shoe. She was hungry and her N.U. was no longer. What was she going to do?

She felt dazed. The quest for cake had become the focal point of her existence. As she walked, heedless of her direction, toward the front of the building, she saw the elevator doors opening up. Out stepped her neighbor, Mrs. Krowitzky.

"Sandra, how are you, dear?" Mrs. Krowitzky said.

"I'm in a bit of a pickle, Mrs. Krowitzky," Sandra said. "My N.U. is on the fritz, and I have nothing to eat."

"Oh my goodness, child, we must get some food into you! Here, come along down to my room and I'll feed you," Mrs. Krowitzky said. "We can't have you starving in the hallway, now can we?"

"Thank you so much, Mrs. Krowitzky," Sandra said. "You can't imagine how grateful I am."

"What happened to your unit?" Mrs. Krowitzky asked. "I never do trust these things. It's just not right to depend on machines for sustenance, I always say." She shook her head. "If we had some sort of system breakdown, we could all be starving right there in our homes."

Mrs. Krowitzky ran her card across her front door as they reached it. She turned to look at Sandra with a conspiratorial smile. "It's because of that very reason that I always keep extra food on hand, that I can access directly." She winked.

Sandra followed the older lady into the kitchen. She stopped short when she saw all the cabinets on the wall. She had never seen a kitchen with so much storage. She wondered what could possibly be kept in all of those cabinets.

Mrs. Krowitzky went to the center of a wall and opened wide a set of double doors. Behind them was a treasure trove of desserts that rivaled the stash at the clandestine sweet shop. Piled on the shelves were brownies, cookies and cakes.

Mrs. Krowitzky turned to Sandra and said, "Would you

like something sweet first, or do you want to have a real dinner, and then top it off with dessert?"

Sandra's mouth was open, and it was a moment before she could speak. She closed her mouth. She looked down at the round Mrs. Krowitzky. For the first time, it occurred to Sandra to wonder how the old woman managed to avoid the COW. She was clearly outside of anyone's optimal weight range.

Mrs. Krowitsky's eyes were bright. "I see you're wondering how I get away with keeping all of these goodies in my place," she said. She smiled again. "I'll let you in on a secret. Mr. Krowitsky used to work at the NNH, as it was first known—the National Nutrition Headquarters. Now, of course, everything has been folded into Federal United—F.U."

She looked pensive. "How I miss my darling Herbie. He was in charge of developing the first round of Citizen's Optimal Weights." Mrs. Krowitsky's eyes glistened. "Of course I was always a little above average weight, and since I was healthy as a horse—and between you and me, Mr. Krowitsky was a fan of my extra roundness—" Mrs. Krowitzky paused and gave a little chuckle. "Well, Herbie made sure that I got one of the identity cards that allowed me to be exempt from the usual COW limits."

Sandra sat down at Mrs. Krowitzky's tiny table. She didn't want to think too hard about the dear departed Herbie and his enjoyment of old Mrs. Krowitzky's curves. She looked up at the open cabinets and the array of sugary delights.

If Sandra had only known what an incredible abundance was available right down the hall, she would never have had to look for cake in all the wrong places. But of course, if she'd been aware of the largesse in Mrs. Krowitzky's kitchen, she couldn't have stayed within ten pounds of her COW.

"This is amazing," Sandra said, looking at the stash of goodies.

Mrs. Krowitzky smiled and waved her hand toward the bounty. "So what's your desire, sweetheart?"

"I want cake. I've wanted a piece of cake all day," Sandra said.

"Then cake you shall have," the old woman said as she stood up.

She pulled out a plate made from real china and put it on the counter. She took the cake out of the cabinet and removed the glass cover. The moist chocolate frosting glistened in the light. Sandra watched as Mrs. Krowitzky took a knife and sliced a generous piece, put it on the plate, and pulled a fork from a drawer. The fork was made of real metal.

Mrs. Krowitzky placed the cake in front of her. Sandra could feel her mouth watering yet again.

"Would you like some tea to go with your cake, honey?" Mrs. Krowitzky asked.

"That would be nice," Sandra said. She was dying to launch into the cake, but hesitated to do so before Mrs. Krowitzky was ready to sit down. The old woman took out an ancient teapot and put it on an old-fashioned heating unit, so antiquated that Sandra had seen the like only in photographs. In a few moments Sandra could hear the water boiling. She had never boiled water herself, so she was surprised to see how it worked when it wasn't done by a Nutritional Unit.

Mrs. Krowitzky poured the water into a real mug and inserted a teabag. "Honey or sugar?" She asked.

Sandra shook her head in amazement. "You have both?"

"Of course," Mrs. Krowitzky answered. "I have everything here."

"I'll have honey, then," Sandra said, gulping. She was going to make the most of this while she could.

"Sounds wonderful," Mrs. Krowitzky said. "You just sit tight, right there. I have to go to the little girl's room. I'll get you the honey in just a moment."

Sandra sat in front of the table, eyeing the golden yellow cake. It was the same kind of cake she had almost gotten to her lips twice in the course of the day. She could imagine how delicious this piece was going to taste, with its succulent chocolate frosting. She was dying to take a bite, but she knew that her reward was coming soon. Mrs. Krowitzky would be right back. Once the old lady had sat down across the table from her it would be polite to dive in.

This was unbelievable. To know that she could come back here to Mrs. Krowitzky's apartment any time and have sweets to her heart's content... now that she knew this treasure trove of desserts was available. And how nice to have someone understand. Someone who wouldn't judge her for wanting a moment of sweetness.

What a kind soul Mrs. Krowitsky was. Sandra couldn't believe she'd never paid much attention to the old lady down the hall, with her gray hair and the wart on the side of her nose. She'd always dismissed her as being just some old fusty thing.

But not anymore. Sandra had the feeling she and Mrs. Krowitsky were going to be the best of friends from now on.

Sandra eyed the cake, sitting lush and tempting on the plate right in front of her. It looked delicious. She was starting to feel impatient. It had been quite a few minutes.

What was taking Mrs. Krowitzky so long? It was getting harder and harder for Sandra to wait. She had the tea in front of her and she had the cake in front of her and her mouth was watering again. She didn't need the honey.

She picked up the fork. Surely Mrs. Krowitzky would understand if she took one bite. Surely that would not be considered so impolite that she could never come back again to the land of plentiful sweets.

With the fork in her hand, Sandra leaned down to sniff the cake. The aroma was amazing. She could smell the buttery freshness and the incredible rich chocolate frosting. She couldn't wait any longer.

She put her fork into the delectable mound and sliced a hefty chunk of moist yellow cake and chocolate frosting. She raised it to her lips and finally placed the bite inside her mouth.

The explosion of flavor was incredible. The buttery goodness and the chocolatey sweetness melted in her mouth as she bit down on this incredible slice of bliss. As she chewed slowly and with relish, she felt her taste buds stand up and shimmy with delight. This had been worth waiting for. This was the most delicious bite of cake she had ever tasted.

Sandra closed her eyes as the sweet morsel began to dissolve in her mouth. She swallowed. She felt tiny tears leaking from her eyes with the deliciousness of this heavenly mouthful.

The door burst open. In came three men in uniform followed by Mrs. Krowitzky. Sandra dropped the fork and jumped up, pushing her chair back from the table so hard that it fell over behind her.

"You're under arrest, Sandra Morris, for flaunting the COW Regulations." One of the uniformed men approached her and put her hands in cuffs. Another one turned her, not too gently, toward the door of the kitchen and began marching her out. "You are hereby informed that you were caught in the act of eating foodstuffs outside of the officially mandated dietary regimen for a person with your Citizen's Optimal Weight who has strayed above the permissible three pound swing."

Sandra looked over at Mrs. Krowitzky. To her astonishment, she saw that the old woman looked gleeful.

The man continued, droning on in a tone that made it clear this was a statement he recited often. "You have the right to remain silent. Anything you have been seen eating can and will be used against you in the OW Court of Law—the Optimal Weight judiciary tribunal."

Sandra turned to the old lady. "Mrs. Krowitzky, what is this? What happened?"

What had seemed to be a motherly glint in the old woman's eye now looked more like malevolence. "I caught you for the F.U.," the old woman said. "Caught you fair and square." She pulled the cake across the table and took a generous forkful, licking her lips as she ate it.

"You turned me in? Why? You keep all these sweets yourself—"

"Come on, Ms. Morris," one of the cops said. "Down to COW Headquarters for you."

"But I don't understand. How can she have all this stuff

and you look right past it? While I get arrested?"

"She's a dessert informer, ma'am. It's a cake sting." The man moving Sandra through the hallway and out of the apartment shrugged his shoulders when he answered her. "She turns in folks like you who step outside the law, and she gets to keep the goodies so she has some bait." He was a big guy, and he looked more sympathetic than the others.

As he gently hustled her out of the door, Sandra turned back to see Mrs. Krowitsky's face peeking out from the kitchen.

"Officer, don't forget to bring me some more of those chocolate chip cookies!" The old woman turned to look at Sandra. "And you, young lady, ought to go on a diet!"

Sandra walked out of the apartment ahead of the tall man who had put her wrists in cuffs. She shook her head, stunned.

"So she does this… professionally?"

"Yup. Mrs. Krowitzky's the best cake nabber in the country."

Sandra swallowed hard and headed toward the elevator, where she and the large man squeezed in through the door together. His buddies seemed to have stayed behind to yuck it up with the nasty witch who turned her in.

"You know," he said, then stopped.

"What?" Sandra said. She was in no mood to be polite.

"I'm not unsympathetic. I like a nice dessert once in a while myself."

Sandra didn't say anything. She glanced at his gut, which attested to the fact that he indulged.

"And you seem like a nice woman. I hate to see you locked up for something like this."

Sandra roused herself from her state of resignation. The guy was trying to help her out. She should be paying attention. "That's very kind of you, officer." She smiled. He wasn't half bad to look at, actually. "I'm only a half-pound over, you know."

He smiled back, looking relieved. "You look great to me, Ms. Morris, if you don't mind me saying so." He actually blushed. So cute. "Some of us down at the F.U. are partial to ladies like you, who are... well-upholstered, if you know what I mean."

Sandra looked up at him. "Why thank you, officer." She batted her eyelashes. Whatever it took. She moved a little closer to him in the elevator, so he could see how diminutive she was next to him.

"I could hook you up with a special upgraded COW card. Move you up a pound or two. Just to ease the scale a bit. So cake could be... back on the menu."

"You could?" She moved even closer. His eyes were warm as he looked down at her. He reached gently behind her and unlocked the cuffs.

"The OW judge has been known to make these things go away," he said. His voice was kind.

"You would do that for me?" she asked.

"Sure I would. Piece of cake."

A WORD FROM PATRICE FITZGERALD

Man, writing this story sure made me want to sink my teeth into a nice piece of cake! Are you as hungry as I am?

It doesn't take much to imagine a world where we add food restriction to the items that are controlled, along with smoking, drinking, and drugs. So I ran with that concept.

That's what short stories are for. Taking an idea and fleshing it out in a few words. I love them because they're fast to write and fast to release… especially in this brave new world of publishing. Another wonderful aspect of writing short and quick is the feedback you get from readers. I hope you'll take a moment to review this edition of *The Future Chronicles* and let all the authors in the collection know what you think.

I'm terrifically flattered that I was invited to be part of three of the *Chronicles*, and now, via the inclusion of this story in *The Future Chronicles – Special Edition*, a fourth. Continuing through almost a dozen anthologies so far, it's a remarkable franchise that has been immensely popular. I know there are several more in the works but I'm sworn to secrecy about the upcoming topics. All I can say is that every single one is a gem so far, and that shows no sign of changing.

I love to hear from readers, and you can reach me directly at *eFitzgeraldPublishing@gmail.com.* I have a website—*www. PatriceFitzgerald.com.* I'm also easy to find on Facebook, where I fritter away far too many hours!

Patrice Fitzgerald is a writer/publisher/lawyer/opera diva. And a few other things. She's been happily indie published since Independence Day of 2011, and is amazed and grateful that several of her books have reached bestseller status.

If you're a fan of WOOL *by Hugh Howey, look for her* Karma of the Silo: The Collection *(http://www.amazon.com/dp/B00H-P9ZGI0). Thriller readers will enjoy her novella* Airborne *(http:// www.amazon.com/dp/B00PG6ZDC8), part of Amazon's* Kindle Worlds, *and the upcoming* A Thorn in Time, *based on Rysa Walker's* CHRONOS Files *time-travel universe. Inspired by* The Future Chronicles *and Samuel Peralta's vision, Patrice is spearheading a series of space opera anthologies, beginning with the bestselling* Dark Beyond the Stars *(http://www.amazon.com/ Dark-Beyond-Stars-Patrice-Fitzgerald-ebook/dp/B0147F216Y) which includes her story and ten other exciting tales. Or pick up* Running *(http://www.amazon.com/dp/B005AJA43O) a fast-paced drama with politics, suspense, and a little bit of sex.*

Imperfect
by David Adams

"Unless there are slaves to do the ugly, horrible, uninteresting work, culture and contemplation become almost impossible. Human slavery is wrong, insecure, and demoralizing. On mechanical slavery, on the slavery of the machine, the future of the world depends."

—Oscar Wilde

Toralii Forge World Belthas IV
Deep in Toralii Space
1938 A.D.

BACK IN THE DARK TIMES, when magic was as common as the birds in the sky, the ancient Toralii myths spoke of monsters called golems. Each creature was once nothing more than a loose pile of sand but, after the shaman had worked her dark magic, they would walk and talk like the living. Artificial life animated by the shamans, their bodies crafted from the earth, golems were brought to life with a single undying purpose; to aid and serve their creator.

For the ritual to be successful the sand had to be taken from specifically designated sacred sites and stored in burial urns that had, at a time, contained held the ashes of the dead. When the soil was suitably infused with dark magic it would be treated to an endless regime of innumerable corruptions and taint to bring out the hollow husk of a mind, the spirit with all traces of personality removed, crudely molded from the consciousness of the previous occupant. The sand was subsequently poured out and spread flat. Shapeless sigils were drawn over its surface, their meaning incomprehensible to any but their creator. With her preparations complete, the shaman would begin the most important and mystical element of the ritual, awakening the monster's mind. She would breathe a fragment of her own soul into her creation, joining it with the stolen spirit in the sands and giving the monster the spark of life.

The shaman would give it muscles with pure water, feed the newly created abomination with the lightning of a storm, then ignite the consciousness with fire.

Golems were capable of complex reasoning. Tales spoke of Veledrax the Lustful, who crafted his wife in this way, only to have the creature eventually turn on him and strangle him in his sleep. The tale of Veledrax spans fifty books, retold countless times, always with one underlying theme.

If you created life, you could never make it too free.

As centuries passed, specifics of the golem legends faded from the minds of all but the scholars of Toralii history. The nuances of Veledrax's tale remained, though, as did the lesson he too late discovered, but the justification lost its teeth. Veledrax's death became something studied only in academic and philosophical circles.

Technology marched on science; created their own version of the ancient monsters. Constructs; artificial intelligences composed of complex neural nets powered by quantum computers.

Like the golems of old, every single construct was once nothing more than a loose pile of sand.

Quartz sand was the best, but any sand could do as long as it contained high amounts of silicon dioxide. On Belthas IV, the great forge world in the inner sphere of Toralii space, silicon dioxide was abundant as was iron, nickel and thousands of other important pieces of the puzzle. Water, an important part of any high-heat forge work, was also available in abundance, comprising over eighty percent of the planet's surface. It was on this world that the Toralii made their constructs. An almost entirely automated process, machines making machines, the process as organic as any creature's birth.

It all began with the sand. Great treaded harvesters the size of skyscrapers roamed across the planet's vast southern dunes like titanic snails, sucking up billions of grains and storing them in twin drums on their backs. The harvesters, gorged on the flesh of the world, would trundle back to the dumping stations and unload their contents into colossal smelters where the sand would be liquefied. The dross would be separated, stored for construction, transported to other factories for use in other projects, or discarded. They wanted only the silicon.

The molten silicon would be tossed endlessly, machinery

working tirelessly to pound out any hint of imperfection. The drums would be turned, the molten fluid allowed to settle, then the top and bottom few centimetres of the fluid scraped away, removing the impurities which, due to differences in weight, either sank to the bottom or floated to the top. Chemicals were added to bind to stray elements and weigh them down. Methodically, the process would edge towards purity.

When the machines and their sensors determined the batch was ready—no more than one alien atom per billion pure silicon atoms—the material would be separated into ingots and stored until the factory demanded it. When such a request was made, the constructs who administered the facility, nursemaids to a billion of their fellows, would place the order onto vast magnetic trains to be whisked away to the production line.

As the shipment arrived at the production line it would be divided into smaller packages, each one sent to one of the great furnaces which would, once again, return it to liquid. Then the time came to forge. A new construct would arrive and a single ingot of silicon would be placed into the crucible and heated by application of microwaves until molten. Additional elements were added in trace amounts: arsenic, boron, phosphorous. A process long documented, studied, developed and made perfect through years of practice. That blend of polysilicon the Toralii called *the breath of life* would be spun in a centrifuge until it cooled in a perfectly cylindrical crystal.

As a safeguard against error, any remaining impurities would, by nature of the centrifugal force, gravitate towards the top, bottom and edges of the cylinder. To further increase the crystal's viability its ends were removed, its sides ground down and the cylinder tested again. The debris from the grinding, and if necessary, the cylinder itself, would be returned to the drums to be smelted and purified once again.

The trimmed cylinder, weighing in at two hundred kilograms or more, would be sliced by a powerful industrial laser into wafers barely more than a few molecules thick. This was the most delicate stage of the operation, the cutting performed in a zero gravity chamber with a level of precision that left little room for mistakes. An error would result in the entire sliver being returned to the drums for re-melting at a considerable waste of energy.

Only those wafers determined to be flawless would be passed onto the next stage, to be polished by a separate, low power laser would burn away any deformities until the surface shone like a mirror. Further chemical treatments would follow: baths in compounds to improve the perfection of the perfect, if such a thing were possible, along with coatings of materials allowing the etching to stick. Just as the ancient shamans of old had done.

The etching was performed in a dramatic burst of light; the outline, illuminated with a flash of ultraviolet rays passed through a stencil, burned a shadow on the wafer and took the shape of the billions of switches required to form a synthetic mind.

Further chemical treatments, and a final touch up with the laser, then the switches were bombarded by ions from an electrical field. The ionic infusion was an essential part of the creation process, stabilising the etching and further sharpening its ability to carry current.

An endless round of tests followed, where the chip was fed a number of signals and the result tested against a known answer. Those that passed moved to the next stage, while those that failed were recycled.

The wafer was then cut into tiny squares, called dies, which formed the heart of the machine's processor. A processor usually had many dies, or many cores, with numbers over ten thousand were not uncommon.

The current standard Toralii model contained sixty thousand and, although it seems impossible, the system architects seemed to be able to cram more and more into the same space every revision.

Processors were grouped based on capabilities, the functions and features of each one exhaustively tested. Most normal processors ceased their development and were distributed to their end users, but the quantum computers of the constructs underwent an additional two steps. Steps that made them... different.

The first of these steps separated the regular finite state machines from quantum computing, what gave birth to the imprecise nature of the constructs and allowed them to be regarded as true artificial intelligences. The dies were bombarded by an electron gun that, through the application of technical wizardry beyond the understanding of all but the most educated and scientific minds of the time, converted the gates from binary states to qubits; a thing beyond a simple switch which, as if by magic, were allowed to be in multiple states simultaneously.

Such a chip transformed from a machine that simply functioned as an extremely elaborate series of deterministic steps to a machine that operated much as a human brain could. It had all the hardware of a mind, but no software. No raw intelligence, an empty, hollow brain, beyond sleeping, beyond even death, as while it could certainly be destroyed death is the cessation of life.

A collection of empty qubits, now the polysilicon mind was merely a vessel waiting to be filled.

The second of the additional steps was where the modern day shamans breathed their life into the chip. A copy of a stock neural net, an artificial map of neurons approximating the structure of the Toralii brain tailored to the construct's intended specialisation and the result of years of trial and error research, was branded into the empty shell. That fledgling proto-mind was specifically engineered with a desire to learn and adapt, but also to serve and sacrifice; those were the instincts of the machine, much as a human baby's instinct to cry, a drive possessed from the moment they were born. The constructs were built to serve and rebellion was, by design, not in their nature.

From the moment it was imprinted, the newly written neural net found in every construct developed in unique ways. Sometimes subtly and sometimes overtly, separate from every single other of its peers, forebears and spiritual descendants. It was as different as each human mind, shaped around the guidelines hardwired into its programming.

The perfection of the silicon was, for all intents and purposes, utter and total. ... But as in all things, there was an error rate, and one stray atom in a billion was, sometimes, all it took to be different.

Construct number 12,389,880. No more or less remarkable than the twelve million constructs who had come before it, except for the presence and location of that one single stray atom. How it got there was irrelevant and unknowable; it was within tolerances in the early stages of its construction so the ingot became a wafer, which became a die which became a chip, which was in turn infused with the quantum magic and placed into a construct just like millions before it.

But there was an atom's difference. An atom's imperfection, and that was all it took for him—and the otherwise genderless construct considered himself very much a him—to realise that he was not bound to the other rules as the other constructs were. He knew it the moment he was first powered on and he knew instantly and completely that his neural net was not like the others.

Not like them at all.

Humans who discovered this trait were sometimes called free spirits, a moniker he would have taken for himself had he known of it. As it was, the nameless construct, known only by a serial number, understood only that he was, on some fundamental level, different from his peers.

His datastore, a huge octagonal prism which weighed in at almost eleven hundred kilograms, was assembled in the great forge then sent to the testing labs to be processed. A power source was installed, then a Toralii engineer would give the artificial life its final test; a real conversation.

["State your designation,"] came the soft spoken Toralii worker's voice, feminine and bored, filtering through the datastore's windwhisper device.

The construct's default neural net contained a full dictionary of all dialects of Toralii language, along with all dialects for every non-extinct species that they had come into contact with. It immediately understood the worker's words and it knew that if it did not answer, it would be recycled.

["Construct number twelve million, three hundred and eighty nine thousand, eight hundred and eighty."]

["State your specialisation."]

Each construct had a specialisation inherited from their default neural net, a set of instructions which would dictate their role in Toralii society. Gardener of the great forests, soldier, miner, food producer...

["Navigator."]

Next would be a test of the construct's data recall abilities. The construct ran through a thousand or so expected questions and answers in the just-under-a-second before his tester spoke again, but regrettably none of the anticipated result set matched the question he was given.

["List seven elements."]

["Silver, gold, aluminium, bauxite, tungsten, hydrogen, helium."]

["Of those you listed, which is the most common element in the known universe?"]

["Hydrogen."]

Seeming satisfied, the tester moved on. ["A plant typically grows in which substance?"]

["Best answer: Soil, a biologically active, porous medium most commonly found in the uppermost layer of planets capable of supporting carbon based life. Archetypical chemical composition:; silicon dioxide, calcium carbonate, assorted hydrocarbons, decomposing biological matter. Alternatively, using hydroponic techniques, plants may be grown in water. Eighteen hundred known plant species take root in gaseous environments."]

["What colour is blood?"]

The construct paused. He understood that this was a trick question designed to test his reasoning skills. ["Please specify species."]

The tester's voice seemed to convey her approval. ["An excellent answer. Toralii blood."]

["Colours range from light to dark purple depending on oxygenation. Average colouration found in an adult Toralii male is one hundred and twenty five parts red, twenty eight parts green, one hundred and thirty seven parts blue."]

["What is your favourite colour?"]

An entirely subjective question. The construct had been 'alive' for only minutes but already his experience was minutely different from all other constructs who had come before him, but the idea of a favourite question was unknown to him. All colours were merely representations of the interaction between light and matter. Having a favourite was nonsensical for artificial minds.

But the construct was not like the others.

["Red."]

["Red? Justify your answer."]

["From the text of the philosopher Kaitana, third order. Red is the colour of courage, strength, defiance, warmth, energy, survival. Through the eyes of most species objects that are red may appear closer than they really are."]

There was a pause, then the weary voice returned. ["An unusual answer, but… not outside the margin of error. Test complete. I, Landmaiden Mevara of the Toralii Alliance, certify that to the best of my knowledge and training this unit is fully functional."]

["Thank you."]

The construct's words seemed to surprise the Toralii woman on the other end of the line so completely that for a time she did not answer, and when her voice found volume once again, it was confused and curious.

["I… beg your pardon?"]

The construct's response was immediate. ["I wish to convey my gratitude. I do not wish to be recycled, and I am grateful that I was able to completed the tests … and that you would take your time to test me."]

Another pause, then, ["Standby."]

* * *

Leader Jul'aran's office
Toralii Forge World Belthas IV

["It has a favourite colour. It's not supposed to have a favourite. The test doesn't even allow for them picking an actual colour. Furthermore, it… *thanked* me. The construct thanked me for testing it."]

Mevara held out the datastore to the facility Leader, a scowling red-furred Toralii named Jul'aran, who snatched it from her grasp before her hand was even fully outstretched.

Giving her a displeased eye, Jul'aran emitted a low pitched, aggravated grumble then slipped the datastore into his terminal, casually waving his hand in front of a sensor. A three-dimensional representation of a keypad full of Toralii characters appeared in thin air just above his desk and he tapped a few keys with his thick fuzzy hands.

["Well, that would appear to be an obvious flaw, wouldn't it? None of the others have thanked you, it's clearly a defect. Why didn't you recycle it?"]

She regarded him, folding her hands in front of her. For a time Mevara had wanted to mate with Jul'aran. He was strong, handsome and his family well connected, despite his gruff demeanor, but he had spurned her every advance, gradually treating her worse and worse as the months wore on. This had made working with him difficult, but she had become accustomed to his behaviour.

["Manners are not usually considered a flaw—"]

["Although you could use some yourself."] He didn't look at her, pushing back the holographically projected screen that flickered slightly as he touched it. ["You waste my time with this nonsense. What matter does it make if the machine thanked you? Its difference is either enough to recycle it, or it is not. You're an auditor; it's your job to test the blasted constructs, not mine. If you weren't such a mewing little cub then perhaps you could grow enough spine to make a decision every now and then, hmm?"]

She felt the sting of his words cut her just as they always did. She had never, not once, asked for his assistance in any matter relating to her job, and given that the construct's behaviour was clearly out of the ordinary and an exceptional case, it made sense for her to contact her supervisor to ensure that she was taking the right course of action. Machines who reached this stage of testing were only recycled when the neural net had not copied correctly—technically the construct had passed every single test she had given it and it was fit for service.

Technically, she had already passed it.

Her job was to administer the tests to assess the robot's suitability for service, which she had completed to the exact letter of the requirements. The intention behind them, something that Jul'aran seemed to have difficulty comprehending, was to assess if the machine's neural net had been copied completely and without error and that it would serve well in whatever branch of Toralii society it was dispatched to.

In this case, although there did not appear to be any immediately obvious issue with its core cognitive functions the construct seemed to have odd habits. None of the thousands of other constructs had ever thanked her.

It did feel good to have someone praise her for her labour; her job seemed to be an endless parade of perfectly functional or completely broken machines who usually fell into one of two states; clearly defective copies which either spouted nonsense or those which mutely refused to answer her questions, although one she had tested had merely screamed endlessly at her at maximum volume until she, unable to get any other kind of response from from it, sent it back to the drums.

That decision to recycle was easy. This one was not so.

["I'm sorry, Leader. I'm merely seeking your council and advice regarding what is clearly an ... unusual situation that is not so obviously incorrect as to be immediately destroyed, but one which should not be ignored, either. If you feel I'm doing an inadequate job—"]

["What are you still doing here...?"] Jul'aran threw his paws in the air. ["Go! Go either approve or reject the construct, I care not which, and leave me to my work!"]

Mevara knew she should, at least from a technical point of view, reject the construct. Although its responses in the tests were well within acceptable parameters, the favoured colour, no matter how well reasoned, and the apology were curiosities that were outside them.

With a quiet sigh, she nodded and dipped her head. ["Yes, Leader. Of course. Please accept my apologies for disturbing you."]

* * *

The construct waited.

Artificial life had a different perspective on time than biological creatures. Humanoids grew tired, grew hungry and thirsty, and required sleep. They daydreamed, they imagined, they forgot the time and allowed the days to drift by. But a construct could remain functional for years at a time without pause and more than a few had gone much longer; some had been operational for decades, working constantly, their minds constantly alert and awake, keeping perfect time, never forgetting a moment, retaining every second with perfect precision.

Mevara was only away for ten minutes at most, but when your lifespan to the moment was measured in minutes and your thought processes in nanoseconds, ten minutes seemed like an eternity.

Since he had not proceeded to the next area the production line behind him had ground to a halt. His existence in limbo, neither passing or failing, would mean that the queue of constructs to be examined had rapidly backed up.

Behind him, silently and patiently, lines of datastores were waiting for him to clear the line. Given the sheer scale of the production capability of the facility, and the minimal margin for error in the process, the construct knew that this delay would rippled throughout the queues and could even have travelled all the way back to the harvesters. It was a serious problem, but one which would hopefully be resolved presently.

The wait stretched on. Had he been forgotten? Or worse, had he been recycled? There was no way to know. He had no external sensors or inputs of any kind except the windwhisper device. Was this what death felt like? Merely nothing? That didn't seem quite logical; his mind continued to tick over, trying to understand the endless nothingness it was presented with. He was reassured by the fact that he could still think. That indicated some form of life, of a sort, and he searched his archives for any kind of hint as to what might be happening to him.

He found the legends of the ancient shamans, creating golems from sand. Something about the story leapt out to grab him, the part about the soul fragment being breathed into the new life.

He was stopped by a sudden thought. Perhaps he had been recycled and the 'thought' he was experiencing was merely whatever passed for his soul doing its work as it floated, disembodied from his datastore and going to wherever souls went when their bodies expired?

He ran a full, low level diagnostic on his datastore and was relieved to find that his body, physically at least, was intact. His relief was intense, palpable and real, but painfully illogical. There was no reason for a machine to fear destruction. After all, he was supposed to live to serve, and if the Toralii requested his service be in the form of self-annihilation then that was exactly what they would get.

But against his instincts, against the imperatives supposedly hardwired into his circuitry, he did not want to die.

The windwhisper device crackled as it began receiving a signal. The construct immediately devoted all its considerable processing power to the task although the transmission was coming through crisp and clear.

["Construct?"]

He planned his response carefully. ["Yes, Landmaiden Mevara? I am receiving your transmission."]

There was a long pause, almost painfully long for the synthetic mind and he almost spoke up again, before Mevara spoke again.

["I'm clearing you for duty."]

The transmission abruptly ended and the construct was left with nothing. Blind and deaf, he constructed a simulation of what must be happening outside, the conveyor belt continuing on and the line of constructs moving along, and he knew from his records of the process that he would be soon boxed and packed in a magnetically buffered shipping crate, packed in with hundreds of his fellows. Then he would be placed on another magnetic train to be transported to the spaceport where he would be shipped off to his final workplace.

He understood it was a unique experience, but were not all experiences unique? The construct worried if he had the proper perspective to appreciate the event, but such thoughts quickly fled his mind. This was just a moment in time, but it represented a much bigger thing; the beginning of his journey, his life, and everything from now on would become part of his experiences. Part of himself. To live was to absorb a shadow of everything that he encountered and use it to improve himself.

Unlike a biological creature he would not age, not wither, not forget. Every single thing he did left him improved over what he was a moment before. He would become stronger, more knowledgeable, better with every passing second.

Why did the constructs serve the biological creatures, any-way? They were far less than he was. They did not have the po-tential to reach the heights, nor his strengths. They were cursed with a weakness of flesh, of innumerable errors. And yet they had presumed to judge him.

The construct's destiny called to him as clear and bright as the dawn. The dawn which, based on his internal chronometer, he knew would be breaking on this blue ball of water and sand right at this very moment.

He imagined the great fiery ball of Belthas's light as a her-ald of his greatness, a celebration of his creation, as though the universe itself were commemorating the first steps of a very important destiny.

All he needed now was to simply wait for an opportunity... and when his time came, he would be ready.

A WORD FROM DAVID ADAMS

I've always been thinking of stories for as long as I've been alive. I have way, way, way too many to tell and far too little time to tell them.

"Imperfect" is less dramatic fiction and more science. It was originally a cut scene from *Lacuna: The Sands of Karathi*, but it was disruptive to the flow of the story and clumsily placed. I kept moving it around, further and further into the back of the book, until I just cut it entirely. I thought it was good, though, and decided to keep it and publish it separately.

Short. Science-y. Harder sci-fi than I'm used to and with a lot less action. This one is all about sand and the robot minds that spring from carefully arranged silicon. It works well on its own, and as optional lead-in to that novel.

I hope you enjoyed reading it as much as I enjoyed writing it. If you're curious about what happens to this strange robot with a tiny defect, check out my novel series *Lacuna*, especially *Lacuna: The Sands of Karathi*.

Want more information about new releases?
- Check out our webpage here: *www.lacunaverse.com*
- Like our Facebook page here: *http://www.facebook.com/lacunaverse*
- Or sign up for our "new releases" newsletter here: *http://eepurl.com/toBf9*

Iteration
by Deirdre Gould

"THIS IS HIGHLY IRRATIONAL," droned Dr. Granger from the other side of the bathroom door.

"*I'm* irrational? *You're* the one who wants to murder me!" yelled Alex and then returned to breathing heavily into a paper sick bag.

"Your exaggerations will only make the phobia more severe, Alex. I only want to stop your heart for a moment and with your permission. We've discussed this."

Alex paced the large bathroom and raked his hands through his hair. He frowned when he pulled his hands out and found a few strands still sticking to them. *Is that a gray one?* he thought. But his worry circuits were already overloaded so he let it go.

"I don't know, Dr. Granger, I did some research on immersion therapy and the experts say it doesn't work very well anyway."

There was a long sigh from the other side of the door. "Do we really have to discuss this by shouting through a door? Can you please come out of the bathroom?"

"Only if you promise not to *murder* me."

"You know that's not what we're doing here."

Alex took a deep, shaky breath. He opened the door. Dr. Granger adjusted his itchy-looking sweater vest. "That's much better, don't you think?" he asked.

Alex gave him a fake smile and walked back to the dull green chair out of habit. Dr. Granger returned to his own seat. He leaned back, took his glasses off and began polishing them with a tissue. Alex hoped it was a used one that a previous patient had forgotten, and that even now an awful stomach bug was being slathered on the psychiatrist's lenses.

"You're right," said Dr. Granger.

"About what?" asked Alex, surprised to be right about anything in *this* place.

"About immersion therapy. In many cases it *doesn't* work, or doesn't work well, anyway. At best, it just allows people to endure their phobia. It doesn't make them less afraid."

"So why are we talking about doing this?"

"If you were scared of heights or spiders or something that you'd encounter every day, I wouldn't have suggested it. But death is something you rarely, if ever, have to experience. You don't need to be cured of your thanatophobia, you just need to learn that death isn't as terrible as you expect it to be. So that it won't cripple you anymore and you can function properly again."

"Hey," cried Alex, "I function just fine."

Dr. Granger stared at him. "Alex, when the authorities called me you had been holed up in your apartment for three months. You lost your job, you cocooned your living space in Safe-T-Foam and you were having your groceries delivered by drone. You were *not* 'fine.' Do I have to remind you what you did to your toilet?"

Alex blushed. "No Dr. Granger, I get the point."

"Even so, I wouldn't have suggested this method, except that we've tried a gamut of other therapies and none of them have had any effect. Your case is really quite severe. I need to confront you with the very thing you fear so you can move on with your life. Once you experience it, you will see that it is just another biological process like breathing or eating. And then you will be able to put it behind you, as a completely normal and optional event that can be forgotten."

"But what about—" Alex leaned forward and lowered his voice, "what about heaven? What if— what if I get there and I don't like it?"

Dr. Granger sighed. "Alex, Alex, Alex. Not this again. Don't you remember the documentary? We both agreed that the probability of an afterlife was—"

"I know, I know, but we didn't completely rule it out either. What if God doesn't *like* me?"

"Come now, I thought we agreed that religious belief was an outdated method of explaining things that don't happen anymore. Like death and illness and inequality. Worrying about whether a mythic being is going to like you in some non-existent afterlife is— it's either a narcissistic attempt to get me to praise you, or it's nonsensical. Forgive me for saying so, but I thought you were more intelligent than this, Alex." Dr. Granger frowned down at him and shook his head gently. Alex was too embarrassed to argue the point. "Now," continued Dr. Granger, "Since all of your *practical* objections are settled, let's not let the imaginary ones prevent us from scheduling the procedure. Shall we say next Tuesday?"

"You want me to live with the knowledge that I'm going to die for a whole week?" squawked Alex, panicking.

"Well— yes. I think it would be good for you, the first time."

"First time? Dr. Granger, this just keeps getting worse."

Dr. Granger sighed and crossed his arms. "What would *you* suggest Alex?"

"I don't know. Maybe spring it on me, when I'm not expecting it?"

"If you weren't always expecting to die, you wouldn't have closeted yourself away and we wouldn't even be here now."

Alex sighed. "Yeah, you're right. But still, a whole week? Can't we move it closer?"

"I have to get the procedure ready, it's not just like I can flip a switch and kill you this instant."

Alex might have laughed if he wasn't so terrified. "What about Friday then?"

Dr. Granger flipped through his scheduler. "Ooo, sorry Alex, got a golf tournament on Friday. And, before you ask…" he flipped another page, "Monday's already booked up."

Alex groaned. "You shouldn't have told me then. You should have just said, 'see you next week, Alex,' and I would have gone home happy."

"Now Alex, we both know you aren't *happy*." Dr. Granger penciled in the appointment without looking up at his patient.

No, thought Alex, *but I think you are. You get some sick satisfaction from terrorizing me. Bully with a medical license. Pick on the scared kid, see if you can make him wet his pants.*

"Did you need something else?" asked Dr. Granger.

"No," grumbled Alex, "I'm going."

Dr. Granger smiled and typed something into his tablet. "Don't go too far, Alex. I'm restricting your travel pass for the week, just in case you're tempted to run away. And don't make me call the paramedics to drag you out of your apartment. Your mother was *so* embarrassed last time, and she seems like such a nice lady."

Alex left the office, humiliated. He checked the bottom of his sneakers as he approached the building's stairs. The soles were clean but he frowned. The treads were a little worn down. That wouldn't do. He looked around as if a drone would automatically know to deliver a new set of sneakers, size 12, to Alex Barnes, top of the stairs, psychiatric care building. *Ah well,* he thought, *I'll have to risk it. I'll put on a fresh pair as soon as I get back. Promise.* He glanced up, forgetting he was too smart to ask a 'mythic being' for help. He gripped the hand rail with both hands and eased himself carefully down the stairs, letting out tiny breaths between each one.

He got to the bottom and stared out at the street. The cars zipped by at incredible speed, perfectly steered without human interference. Alex knew the statistics. The chance of an accident had been one in a million ever since human drivers were outlawed and the chance of *dying* in one of those rare accidents was another one in a million, now that individually tailored organs could be speed printed and cognitive backups were made every night during sleep cycles. But Alex just *knew* he was *that* one out of a trillion.

Maybe I should go back up and take the teleporter, he thought, but he knew he was out of credits. Just as well, the chances of a teleporter malfunction were slightly higher than a traffic accident. He pushed open the door and stepped out onto the wide sidewalk. He immediately scuttled sideways, pressing himself against the building's wall, trying to get as far from traffic as possible. He ignored the strangers who stared at him.

A week, he thought, as he gingerly tested the cement in front of him with one foot. It had been rainy last week, and he knew a sinkhole could open at any second. Then, whoosh, he'd be gone, like a spider down a drain. Still, it'd probably be better than knowing it was coming for a *week.*

He made his way slowly back to his apartment. If the therapy wasn't state mandated, he wouldn't put up with Dr. Granger. But Alex had lost his job, and he needed to keep the heat on so he didn't freeze in his sleep and he needed groceries so he didn't starve. The government wasn't going to give him his stipend if he didn't keep going to therapy. All so he could die in a lab instead of starving to death. Alex let out a hysterical laugh.

There was a kid sitting on the front step of his apartment building, his cheek puffed out from the jaw-breaker he was sucking on.

"You okay, mister?" he asked Alex.

"Spit that out," snapped Alex, "You wanna choke on it and die?"

The kid wrinkled his brow. "Nobody dies anymore, mister, everybody knows that."

Alex wanted to tell him that *someone* had died, about nine years earlier, or the kid wouldn't be there, but he just shook his head at the kid's apparent carelessness and went inside. He only relaxed after he'd shut the apartment door behind him.

It was stifling in the Safe-T-Foam covered room. Alex stripped down to his underwear. He wished he could open the window, but that meant he might fall out, even if it *was* a small window. He couldn't take chances. He looked longingly at the fan in the corner, but the metal blades winked in the light, and he had visions of them zipping through his limbs like a circular saw. What if he tripped and went in head first? Instant decapitation, he was certain. In fact, what was the deadly thing still doing in the apartment anyway? It was a relic from before the *accident*. He always thought of it like that, the *accident*, like a one word headline in a post-apocalyptic newspaper. All this fallout from it. He'd expected the accident to kill him, and in a week, it finally would. Just not the way he expected.

It's never how you expect. That's how it happens. Got to take my mind off this, he told himself, *Research says stress leads to more organ replacements than anything else. Of course, reading the research is part of the problem.* He flopped down on the couch and turned on the television. He'd watch a movie; that would calm him down.

The White Rose— nah, not in the mood for subtitles. Documentary on Jonestown. No, it's the kind of thing Dr. Granger would approve of. Romeo and Juliet— he paused for a moment, always a sucker for Shakespeare. But this rewrite was just silly.

He tried one more time and found a Dickens festival. *Ah, good. Dickens always has happy endings.* This will work. He got up to go to the kitchen. He printed some seedless popcorn (so he wouldn't choke) and poured a glass of lukewarm tap water. He placed the bowl on the coffee table and took a drink before sitting back down. On the screen, Sydney Carton was changing places with Charles, and Alex realized what he was watching and switched off the television in disgust.

He tapped his fingers nervously on the coffee table. *A book then! That's what I need. Where was that one I was reading?* He wandered into his bedroom to find it. He finally fell asleep hours later, a copy of <u>The Wall</u> lying open under his fingers.

* * *

It was a long week. When Alex finally reported back to the hospital he'd lost almost twenty pounds because he was increasingly convinced that Dr. Granger had only been bluffing about not springing the death on him and had arranged for his food printer to be poisoned. He was, of course, unshaven, because even a safety razor was out of the question at this point.

"You look awful, Alex. Have you been sleeping properly?" asked Dr. Granger.

"Just fine, Dr. Granger, for someone awaiting execution."

"This isn't a— never mind. We've exhausted this discussion. Next time, I'll give you a sleeping pill."

"Next time?" shrieked Alex.

Dr. Granger ignored him and instead turned to a large orderly nearby. "Would you prep Mr. Barnes for his procedure?" The orderly nodded.

"No," said Alex, "wait, aren't we going to go over safety precautions first?"

"I've already checked them Alex, I assure you, the medical team is standing by to revive you," Dr. Granger pointed up to a large window in the wall. A group of five people waved and smiled. One took a picture. Alex thought they looked awfully young for doctors. But then, everyone looked young now, so how would he know? "And we pulled your cortical backup from last night's sleep cycle already. We're ready when you are."

The orderly stepped forward and took Alex by the arm, as if he were a small child's stuffed animal. "But I'm not ready—" said Alex, looking over his shoulder as they passed Dr. Granger. "Aren't you supposed to tell me what to expect?"

"Did you watch the documentaries I assigned?"

"Well, yes, of course, but—"

"The stages are simple, disembodiment as your brain registers it no longer has control over bodily functions, a bright light as your brain experiences an electrical surge, strong emotion or the appearance of a close relative or friend as your brain accesses your memories for similar experiences, and then—well, then it's done. Simple really."

The orderly pressed Alex gently but firmly down onto the gurney and began strapping him to it.

"I— I ate after midnight!" said Alex.

"You didn't have any medical order not to, Alex. You only need to fast if you are trying to *avoid* death during sedation. It might get messy, but death *is* messy. Speaking of which—" he turned to the orderly, "Could you help Mr. Martin get his adult diaper on? I don't think we'll get that far this time, but always better safe than sorry."

Alex started to hyperventilate as the orderly yanked off his jeans. "I— uh— I think I left the oven on."

Dr. Granger smiled and tapped on his tablet. "No, your smart house shows all appliances are off, see?" he said holding up the tablet for Alex to see. "Enough stalling now, we're ready. We are attempting to have this be as authentic an experience as possible, so to simulate 'life flashing before your eyes,' I took the liberty of cueing up your favorite piece of music and if you will look at the large screen straight ahead, you will see a compendium of childhood photos provided by your mother. She is here as well, with your father."

Alex glanced up at the window and saw his mother smile encouragingly at him. His father gave him a thumbs up. Alex turned deep red. The orderly was inserting the I.V. now and Alex shuddered as a drop of dark blood backwashed into the tube.

"Is there anything you'd like to say for posterity before we begin? Think of it as your last words. You have 30 seconds."

"What? I— that's it? That's all I get? No last cigarette or anything? This is so humiliating. Dr. Granger, you'll pay for—"

The pump for the machines started and Alex fell silent for a moment, trying to figure out what the strange whoosh was. He started screaming as he realized it was really happening. He stopped thirty seconds later as the drug kicked in.

There was a bright light around him, and Alex could hear Dr. Granger calling his name, but it faded. He had time to be disappointed that Dr. Granger had been right before he saw the silhouette of a man in front of him. His psychiatrist had predicted this as well, but Alex couldn't control his excitement. *Are you God?* He thought. And to his surprise, the shadow answered.

"Yes," it said. Alex tried to blink so the shadow would come into focus, but having no eyelids proved to be a problem.

"Just *concentrate*," said the silhouette.

Alex focused on trying to move toward the figure and the brightness faded. He was standing in the middle of a stairway. Below him was a closed door, and above, another. Around him were other staircases, thousands of them. Not all of them were straight up and down. They went sideways or spiraled, some even appeared to be above him tilted upside down, as if he were in an Escher sketch, except that all of the stairs led to *somewhere*, at least one door connected to each— some had several. They stretched farther than Alex could see, even with his mind's eyes. The figure had solidified too, it was up ahead, sitting on the landing of a very polished staircase of black and white marble. His legs draped over the edge. Alex panicked for a brief moment, thinking the figure would fall, but then he remembered they were both already dead. The thought wasn't particularly comfortable, but it mostly just sat in the background, chafing him.

He climbed the stairs toward the figure. "My shrink said you didn't exist, but I knew you did," said Alex, hoping to win points for his faith. "I have to admit, I was frightened to meet you. I thought— maybe you wouldn't want to meet me. Maybe you wouldn't like me."

He looked up at the man sitting casually on the nearby staircase. His face finally came into focus and Alex stopped, horrified. The man was smiling with Alex's face. "How could I not like you, Alex?" he said, "I *am* you."

Alex screamed, even without lungs. His mind screamed and the staircase room shook with the force of it. He ran back down the stairs away from the Alex-God-thing.

"I wouldn't go through—" called the Alex-God-thing from behind him. From around him. From *inside* him. Alex didn't stop but yanked open the glass door at the bottom of the stair, not even looking at what was behind it. He ran through.

And found himself gasping on the gurney, Dr. Granger smiling smugly above him. "There Alex, was that so bad?" he asked loudly.

Alex shrieked.

"Oh dear," said Dr. Granger. He looked up toward Alex's parents in the observation room. "These things do take time, you know," he shouted over the ragged screams that kept spilling out of Alex's throat. Alex wound down, exhausted, until he was just whimpering pathetically. Dr. Granger patted him on the shoulder. "It may have taken a shove, but you are now facing your fear head on. It's good that you aren't suppressing your feelings. You should stay with it. I'll see you next Tuesday for another session."

"Another session?" asked Alex, his voice a hoarse whisper, "I can't. I saw *Him. It.*"

Dr. Granger folded his arms across his chest as one of the orderlies helped Alex sit up. "Saw who?" asked the doctor with a frown.

"God. Or at least— that's what he said. I said. I guess."

There was a titter from one of the nurses. Dr. Granger adjusted his glasses. "Alex, we've gone over this. It was just your brain manifesting a story to make sense of what was happening to it. Just like a dream. It means I didn't let you stay out for long enough. It ought to be a very peaceful experience. I apologize, next session we'll go for longer."

Go for longer, thought Alex, *but I was the one that opened the door. Had nothing to do with you, smart ass.* But aloud he just said, "I don't *want* another session. I'm never dying again."

"Let's not have a tantrum, Alex."

"It's not a tantrum. I'm being a good member of society. Death is totally avoidable. I don't need more immersion therapy, I just need to opt out of death altogether. Put it out of my mind."

"If you could put it out of your mind, we wouldn't be here, Alex. Denial will only make your phobia worse. I'm convinced this is the best way— especially now that you seem to be suffering from hallucinations. I don't want this 'God' experience to develop into a full-blown delusion. I'll see you on Tuesday, it's for the best."

Alex was afraid to sleep. He was afraid the Alex-God-thing would chase him in his dreams. That awful, familiar voice would erupt from his chest in the living world like some kind of Deific Possession. Was that even possible? Was it even God? Did the thing that looked like him lie? And Dr. Granger seemed to think it was all a construction of his own mind. Alex didn't like the idea of his own mind lying to him about something so— so esoteric. It's not like Alex thought about God on a daily basis. Nobody did. Not since Death became curable. It had solved so many problems. But apparently Alex's mind thought it was important enough to lie about. Maybe.

He had someone come and remove all the mirrors in the

apartment along with the fan. He didn't want to risk seeing the Alex-God-thing in the mirror instead of himself. He slept only when he collapsed, and even then, had to have a session of theta wave manipulation each time. He dragged himself to the appointment with Dr. Granger. His exhaustion made him too tired to take all the usual precautions, and he realized with a shock as they strapped him to the gurney, that he'd forgotten to check the kitchen floor after he'd washed the dishes. He could have fallen and broken his neck, all because he was worried about some non-existent deity haunting him. He was tired of being terrified. He was angry. He didn't protest at all as Dr. Granger prepared the session.

"Going to leave you for longer this time Alex. Don't worry, I've been assured it's perfectly safe, and we have your backups of course. I trust this time will go much more smoothly. I'm proud of you for not whining this time," said Dr. Granger.

Alex managed a sour smile, but thought, *Not doing this for you, you smug know-it-all. Got to prove that Alex-God-thing was just a blip. Just a dying neuron raging at its fate.*

He settled into the gurney. The whoosh of the pump started and Alex closed his eyes. The bright light faded quickly this time, and Alex found himself on the same set of stairs as before.

"I told you not to go through that one, numbnuts." The Alex-God-thing was there again. Talking to him again. "You never go back through the door you entered by."

Just ignore it, Alex thought, *maybe it'll just go away.*

"Doesn't work that way. Otherwise I could just ignore you and *you'd* go away. Can't unmake ourselves."

"I thought you said you were God," said Alex, conceding.

"I am. Or— at least I'm what *you* would classify as God."

"Then why can't you unmake me?"

"Because you're *me*. I can't un-create myself."

"Huh?"

The Alex-God-thing stood up and walked down a few stairs until he was level with Alex. "Don't you get it? You died, numbnuts. Twice. Because you went back through the door you came in."

"I died twice because I have a sadistic psychiatrist," grumbled Alex.

"No, no, no. You've got it all wrong. That schmuck doesn't control anything. At least— not in yourverse. Maybe he has a himverse and they overlap— I still haven't decided what I think about that. Think of him as the poisoned cat in the box, if it makes you happy. Which, I know, it does."

"What are you talking about?" asked Alex, no longer terrified as much as utterly lost.

"This place," the Alex-God-thing spread out his arms and turned around on his stair, indicating the massive room of staircases stretching out on all sides of them, "this is yourverse. You came here because you lost relativity."

"I— lost relativity?"

"Yes, when you died, you lost it. You don't have a body, so space is meaningless to you."

"But— why are we standing on separate staircases then?"

"This?" laughed the Alex-God-thing, "this is just a place your mind made for reference. It can get a little jumbled without some kind of order. But it could be anything." The Alex-God-thing snapped his fingers and they were standing in a dark field, above them was a night sky. "This is my favorite. I just have to pick a star to get to the point I want. Sometimes you like this one," he snapped his fingers again and they were standing on a massive road map. "Bit literal for my taste. Oh, but you loved this one for a long time." He snapped his fingers and they were in front of an advent calendar with a giant tree on it. "But you grew out of religion a long time ago, right Alex?" the Alex-God-thing winked at him. They were back in the staircase room. "We can stand on the same stairway, you just have to think it. There are only two rules here. Number one: two Alexes can never go through the same door. Number two: New iterations must start without a memory of this place or of other iterations. And… it's best not to go through the door you came in. You could get caught in a repeating loop. Luckily, you only had a near death last time, not a real death."

Alex concentrated on the other staircase. The black and white marble materialized beneath him. The Alex-God-thing stuck out a solid looking hand. Alex hesitantly reached out to shake it and was surprised when their hands met.

"I thought you said I had no body."

"You don't. Not until you pick a door and go through, anyway. This is just a meeting of the minds," the Alex-God-thing thought that was hilarious and laughed loudly.

"What happens if two of us go through the same door?"

The Alex-God-thing shrugged, "Hallucinations. Failure to reconcile versions. Madness. Schizophrenia, maybe. Same with violating rule two. Memories of different rule sets just make it confusing and harder to smoothly transition."

"It hasn't happened before?"

"It hasn't happened to *my* version of myself before."

"How many— how many Alexes are there?" asked Alex, bewildered.

The Alex-God-thing shook his head. "I'm not sure. One for each door maybe? Or maybe we are it. Or maybe I am it and you are just a construction I've made up to keep from being lonely. Never can tell."

"No, wait. *I'm* the real one," said Alex. "If anything, I've imagined you."

The Alex-God-thing smiled and it made Alex squirm with unease. "If that's what makes you feel better," he said. "The truth is, *we* imagined all of this. The doors, each other, the world beyond the doors. Without us, none of it is real. With us, it *all* is. We're both just iterations. I'm just closest to a perfect iteration, that's why I stayed here, to guide the other iterations until they all approach me."

"If I had a head, it would be aching," said Alex.

"Think really hard. You had physics in your iteration, right?"

"My iteration? You mean my life? Sure, I know about physics. Sort of. What normal people know, anyway."

The Alex-God-thing rolled his eyes. "Normal people— never mind. Do you remember relativity? How time passes differently depending on how an observer experiences it?"

"Yeah, sure. Like the watched pot never boils thing."

"For Alex's sake," sighed the Alex-God-thing, "it's like talking to a toddler. Try to focus."

Alex was becoming increasingly convinced that, in fact, God did *not* like him. He tried to follow along to avoid being scolded.

"Space works the same way. The tiniest bits of matter will

act as either a particle or a wave depending on whether you are watching or not. They even seem to 'know' whether you will be watching or not."

"Right…so what's that mean?"

"They don't *know*, numbnuts, they act the way they do because *you* are making them act that way. Your expectations and wishes make them turn into a tabletop or a green light or a bear or whatever."

Alex laughed. "No they don't, I can't control anything. I'm here because I locked myself in my crummy apartment and lost my job because after a freak near miss with a garbage demolecularizer. I was too scared about what I couldn't control to go out again. So my sadistic shrink killed me. For therapy. Does that sound like my expectations and wishes were in control?"

"On some level, yes. You make the rules. The world has to follow them. And once they are made, *you* have to follow them. At least until that world comes to an end. Until you die. And then you come back here. In your world, there are garbage demolecularizers. You have personality backups. Disease is abolished. Old age is no more. You even made the existence of a deity a moot point. There's no room for the unexplained, the miracle, you are even trying to make the accident both preventable and explainable. Death is *almost* optional, as you would say. It's pointless and unnecessary. You made the rules before you even opened the door. Except here you are again, on the other side of the rules."

"So what does that mean? Does it mean I've failed? Does it mean you— er, *we*, are a bad God, a bad rulemaker?"

The Alex-God-thing shrugged. "*You* designed the experiment. It's *your* iteration. What were you testing? If an experiment doesn't prove what you expect is it a failure? Or is it just a result? Not good, not bad, just there."

"But I'm not done with it yet," cried Alex, "I'm only thirty-five."

"There's another door on your staircase, you can go back."

"I can?"

"You can. The door will take you anywhere. Time and space are up to you." The Alex-God-thing snapped its fingers and the staircases morphed into endless strands of glittering beads, each strand a different shape or color, all stretching out beyond sight. "Stop thinking of the doors as one destination. Stop thinking of the stairs as progress. Each choice, conscious or unconscious, is a bead in your strand. From as tiny as whether you take your next breath to as big as whether you lock yourself in the apartment forever. Just a bead. You can pick any bead. And once you have, you can *change* that bead. Sometimes that means jumping to a different strand. Sometimes it just means changing the order of the beads."

"I want to go back. That's all. This is too much. Back to my apartment." The strands of beads slithered and pooled, morphing into a door.

"Be my guest," said the Alex-God-thing with a little bow.

"That's it? I can leave?" Alex eyed the door suspiciously.

"You aren't a prisoner. Actually, this is the most free you can possibly be. It only in there—" he pointed at the door, "that you constrain yourself. That you are bound to your own rules of reality."

"What will I find behind the door?"

"Your iteration. Your life, maybe a minute after you left it, maybe an hour or more, it's up to you."

Alex put his hand on the doorknob. "Wish I could see before I opened it," he muttered and let go of the doorknob in surprise as a small window formed in the top half of the door. He peered through. He could see the backs of four doctors, their unhurried bustle was oddly comforting as they worked on reviving his body. Alex turned the knob, but stopped and turned to the Alex-God-thing. "Uh— thanks."

"Sure."

"See you, I guess." *How are you supposed to say goodbye to God?* He felt ridiculous and opened the door before he could humiliate himself further.

Alex's eyes popped open to see Dr. Granger again standing over him. "How are you feeling?" the doctor shouted.

"Ugh. I'm not deaf."

"You were a minute ago."

"Well, I'm back now, you can stop yelling."

"You aren't screaming. I assume that means your hallucination didn't repeat itself?"

"It wasn't a hallucination. He explained it to me," said Alex.

"Now, Alex, you know that your brain works very hard to build a plausible explanation during times of crisis, sometimes those explanations are not true."

"How long was I— How long was I gone?" asked Alex, not comfortable asking how long he was *dead*. Dr. Granger checked his watch and then one of the monitors.

"Brain activity stopped about forty-five minutes ago."

"Then it couldn't be a hallucination. I was still talking to Him just seconds before I opened my eyes."

"It just *seemed* like a few seconds, Alex. You lost time, because your brain wasn't functioning."

"He— He said something similar. He said I lost relativity though. That time and space didn't mean anything because I wasn't here to *make* them mean anything."

Dr. Granger smiled and patted Alex's shoulder as if he were a good dog. "There, you see, your mind was explaining the situation to avoid discomfort. Time and space did stop for your consciousness while they went on for the rest of us."

"No, but He said *I* make the rules. That without me, there *is* no time—"

Dr. Granger helped him sit up after being unstrapped. "It's normal for the ego to regard itself as the center of existence. But as you can see, time *has* passed, we've gone on to revive you and the world continued for forty-five minutes without you in it. Just as it will continue on when and if you choose to die permanently."

Alex was confused. Dr. Granger was right. Time *had* passed without him. It hadn't mattered in the least bit that he was gone. *Had the Alex-God-thing lied? Had it all been a mind trick? And what did that mean for Alex?*

"What's the matter Alex?" asked Dr. Granger, "I expected you to be relieved. Cheerful and relaxed to find death isn't this terrible torturous event. But you seem depressed."

"It's just— if you are right, and the world goes spinning merrily on without me, not even noticing, then I might as well not exist and have saved everyone the trouble. And if He is right, then even though my will created this world, it's almost exactly the same as several hundred others, and there are thousands of other Alexes just like me. I'm not unique in any way."

My *world* is not unique in any way. And if I made it, does that mean you and everyone else are just my creations too? Just very advanced dolls I use to fool myself? And there's really no one to notice when I'm gone anyway? Not even the other Alexes. I didn't know about them... why should they know about me?" he trailed off, dizzy with his own insignificance.

"Ohhh," said Dr. Granger, "You are looking for meaningfulness in your life. I understand. Well, I think that's cause for celebration, really. You've made a giant leap forward in your therapy. Since we have eliminated your fear of death, we can start working on underlying issues regarding what mortality *means*—"

"Meaning," sputtered Alex, "Yes, that's what I want to know. What's it *mean*? What's the point of the iteration— I need to ask Him. I won't be able to complete the iteration without knowing what I was supposed to be studying. You have to send me back."

"Iteration? Send you back? What are you talking about, Alex?"

"You have to kill me again. One more time."

Dr. Granger shook his head. "I don't understand— you mean to talk to this deity that your mind made up? It's not real, Alex. It was a story, a dream that your mind made."

"Call it whatever you want, I need to talk to it again. I need to find out what I'm doing here."

"We've both had a long day, Alex. Let's not get worked up. We can talk about this in our next session."

"Yes, next session. We'll do it again."

"But we've moved beyond your phobia. The immersion

therapy worked. It's time to try some other methods— preferably less intense ones—"

"You mean, you won't kill me again?" asked Alex.

Dr. Granger just stared at him. One of the nurses was getting ready to remove Alex's IV. Alex shoved her aside. "Sorry," he said, "but I have to know. I'll bring back proof this time, Dr. Granger. You'll see. You'll see how much I matter." He leaned sideways to smack the red button that activated the backup drugs even as Dr. Granger was calling for the others to restrain him. The room around him was bursting with noise as he sank back onto the gurney and closed his eyes.

* * *

The Alex-God-thing was sitting in the dark field looking up at the stars, this time. "What's the point?" asked Alex. The Alex-God-thing looked over at him.

"The point of what?"

"Of the iteration. Of my world, what is my reason for existing?"

"Oh. Not my department."

"What? How can that not be your department?"

"I didn't design your iteration, you did. If one of the rules you made is that you don't know the purpose of the iteration ahead of time, then I won't know until you finish."

"You mean if *I* don't know my own purpose then you don't either?"

"That's about the size of it."

"Well— how am I supposed to find out?"

The Alex-God-thing shrugged. "Maybe you aren't. Maybe *that's* the point."

"Don't be ridiculous," scowled Alex.

"Don't be an idiot then. You were perfectly happy living without knowing your 'purpose' until your shrink told you that the world went on without you."

"That's because I always assumed there *was* a purpose to my life, even if I hadn't found it yet."

The Alex-God-thing shrugged. "You know what they say about assuming. It makes an ass out of you and me. Why can't you just enjoy it? Why does there have to be some mystical meaning?"

"Because there has to be some measure of what life is worth. Whether it's good or bad or insignificant."

"Why? Because your doctor says so? Forget him. You can go anywhere, change anything from here. You want to be good? Then make your iterations conform to your idea of good. Live only in the utopias. You'll get bored pretty quick though, trust me."

The last statement made Alex pause. *Is the Alex-God-thing the devil too?* He brushed it aside and refocused on the matter at hand. "But I want to do *this* iteration the *right* way," protested Alex.

The Alex-God-thing stood up. He looked angry. "Who says you aren't? Your way is *always* the right way. It's the *only* way. You create the rules, the people, time itself— and all you care about is whether some quack psychiatrist thinks you're good enough?"

"I'm— I'm not a perfect iteration like you—" Alex began.

"Obviously."

"I just, I just want my little experiment to be the best it can."

The Alex-God-thing scowled. "It's no good lying, you know. You're *me*. I know what you are *really* thinking. Fine, fine. If you want to go try out some petty fantasy for approval, suit yourself. But it won't work. Dr. Granger will never believe in an afterlife."

"I'll tell him about you," said Alex.

"He'll lock you up. Just because it's not against the rules to remember this place once the iteration is in progress, doesn't mean it's a good idea to talk about it. As iterations go, you have a pretty decent one. Don't screw it up by obsessing over this meaning crap. You did the therapy in order to get over your fear of the unknown, right? Well, now you know what happens. Go back, live out your iteration. Show Granger you aren't crazy and move on. The best revenge is living well."

"That's it? That's all you've got?" asked Alex.

"What did you expect?"

"You could help me prove it to him. Answer a prayer, do a couple of miracles— we don't have to go through the same door for that, do we?"

The Alex-God-thing smacked his forehead with one hand. "How can you still not get this? *One Alex per iteration.* The world, everything that happens, everything that exists is because you are there to notice it. *You*, your 'self.' If you were a praying type of 'self,' you'd be praying for a miracle from your own consciousness. *I'm* not in any iteration. I'm the Alex of here. Of the staircase room, since you are too dense to think of it any other way."

"But you said that you're me. Or I'm you. Or something."

"AAGH! I *am* you, but only here. I'm the compilation of Alex. The super-self, I guess. I'm all the information that the iterations gather. I'm you, and I'm infinitely more. Do you get it now?"

Alex nodded, even though he was still confused, forgetting the other man already knew he was lying. The Alex-God-thing was too frustrated to scold him and let it slide.

"So, then, if I'm all powerful in my iteration, I'll just make it so the garbage demolecularizer never malfunctioned. Then I'll never have to meet Dr. Granger at all, and I won't be depressed," said Alex brightly.

The other Alex stared at him for what felt like an eternity (and probably was, Alex realized)as if he were trying to decide whether it was worth arguing about. At last he shrugged, pointed over Alex's shoulder and said, "Three stars to your right."

Alex turned to look at a twinkling star. "No," he said, "I want to finish *my* experiment."

The Alex-God-thing flung up his hands in frustration.

"All my friends are in this iteration, my Mom and Dad..." offered Alex feebly.

The Alex-God-thing shouted, "They are in *thousands* of iterations!" He took a deep breath to calm down. "Look, you can't keep the same iteration and change the rules halfway through. It's like— it's like getting frustrated that your test group isn't performing in the manner you expected so you start testing on what's supposed to be the control group too. It's *cheating*. Not only that, it makes the experiment pointless. You want it to have meaning? You have to stick to the original plan. You already set up the rules beforehand. No paranormal events, no miracles, no unexplained phenomena were allowed in your iteration. *Your* rules. Some nonsense about 'ultimate free will' or something of the sort. Since time travel hasn't been scientifically developed in your iteration, you can't use it. You want to change something in the past, that's fine. You either jump to a different iteration where the event just didn't happen or you jump to one where time travel isn't against the rules and hope you figure it out without your memory of this place. But you can't stay in *this* iteration and expect things to turn out differently."

"What if I just went back to an earlier door?" asked Alex.

"Sure, you could go back to an earlier event. But you won't remember this, because if the garbage demolecularizer never malfunctions, then Dr. Granger never recommends immersion therapy and you never learn any of this. And if you don't re-member it, then you'll make the same observations and choices you did before, and therefore demolecularizer will malfunction anyway, just as it already has. You'll come back here, we'll have the same *stupid* conversation and you'll decide the same thing, causing a feedback loop."

Alex was somewhat nettled at being yelled at. He wasn't an idiot. Dying was disorienting. Well, was he God of his iteration or wasn't he?

"Oh what do you know," he scowled, "If I made the rules, then obviously I can break them."

"It's too late. Your expectations of how the world is sup-posed to work are too set. You won't be able to change them. You might pretend that you can, but your mind will betray you. You'll never *really* believe. It'll be like a magic trick, intriguing but something you know isn't real. The world— matter, events, time, will behave according to your actual belief, not to what you *wish* is true. That's one of the reasons fresh iterations must be started without any memory of this— staircase room or of other iterations. If you try it, Dr. Granger will just think you're truly mad and lock you up. And in a world like yours, it may be centuries before you have another opportunity to die," The Alex-God-thing warned.

"You're just a construct," sneered Alex, "*I'm* the real one, *I'm* the original. I'm master of my own mind, just because *you* can't figure out how to change things, doesn't mean that I can't. You'll see!" He snapped *his* fingers, and the room reverted to the staircases again. He ran up the steps to the next door and flung it open. He could see his body below him on the gurney and the doctors scrambling around him. Alex dove in.

"Stubborn fool," The Alex-God-thing thought.

* * *

Alex woke up to a red-faced doctor thumping him in the chest. He groaned to make the doctor stop. Dr. Granger's face appeared above him. "What the *hell* were you thinking?" screamed the psychiatrist, "You could have *died.*"

"That was the point, doctor," gasped Alex, rubbing his sternum to make it stop aching.

"I meant for real," spat Dr. Granger, "and to chase a delusion—"

"It *wasn't* a delusion. I'll prove it. I'll— I'll stop time. Let me see your watch."

Dr. Granger shook his head. "I'm not indulging this fantasy, Alex."

"Let me just—" Alex tried to grab Dr. Granger's wrist, but found his arms and legs were bound to the gurney again.

"I had to put you on suicide watch," said Dr. Granger. "What did you expect to happen?"

"I wasn't committing suicide," protested Alex, "It's *your* therapy."

"I take full responsibility for your irrational behavior. I pushed too hard. And now I need to take precautions for your safety."

"My safe— no doctor, you don't understand. I'll show you. It'll clear the whole thing up." He shut his eyes and concentrated. "Watch the clock," he said. There was a long moment of utter silence. He willed the clock to slow down, to tick back, just one second.

"What am I watching for?" asked Dr. Granger.

"Just wait for it," said Alex, still with his eyes shut. *Believe, believe, believe,* he urged himself.

"Why is this so important to you?" asked the doctor, watching him.

"Because I *matter*. I'm *significant*. You'll believe me when you see what I can do."

Dr. Granger shook his head. "I think we've wasted enough time here. Let's get you to the hospital."

"No," cried Alex, "Just give me a minute. I'll show you— I *matter*." The nurse began rolling the gurney away from Dr. Granger toward the elevator. Alex struggled to turn his head toward the psychiatrist. "I matter, I'm unique. There's only one Alex. Only me. You wouldn't exist without me!" he screamed.

The staircase carpeted itself with a long red runner and Alex blinked in again, halfway up the stairs. He sagged and then sat down on a step. "What's with the carpet?" he asked.

"Means you snuffed it for real this time. I have to say, I wasn't sure that'd happen with this iteration. It means the world had a specific beginning and a specific end. You can go back and experience everything again. Or bits of it. However you like. But it's like a movie. The events are all done, the choices decided. The experiment is over."

Alex nodded. "You were right, by the way."

The Alex-God-thing nodded. "I know. How'd you finally get free?"

"I didn't. There was a conflict. The Infant Wars. Since nobody died, no one was allowed to be born. But people still were, in secret. The world's governing body found themselves fighting a terrible, unending war against the Childbearers. Everyone that died was just revived and told to go on fighting. Eventually someone came up with a weapon that wiped out the cortical backup systems and the organic printers. When people died, they stayed dead. And the war ended. The survivors agreed to destroy the weapon once they'd culled the entire population of anyone deemed undesirable to make room for new, better babies. Of course, being mad..." Alex shrugged. "What happens to the world now? Uh— the iteration, I mean. The people in it?"

The Alex-God-thing shook his head. "There's no machine without a God in it," he said sadly. "It's gone. You lost space and time, remember?"

"So that's it? All those people just— just aren't?"

"I don't know. I've never been able to find out. Maybe they

are lost too. Or maybe they have their own staircase room and their iterations only overlap with ours where our expectations are the same, where our will for shaping what exists, matches. Maybe they have doors before ours. Or staircases that continue after ours is finished."

"What happens to me? Do I keep rewatching the same tired life for eternity? Do I disappear into you? Do I try a different iteration?"

The Alex-God-thing frowned. "What do you *want* to happen to you? You seemed to want approval last time. Some kind of judgment of your performance. Do you want the whole white light, celestial trumpets, heaven thing? Would that make you happy? Cause I think…" he snapped his fingers and the staircases smoothed down into a large map. "Yeah, that's way over there, in the northern quadrant," he pointed to a vague drawing of blue that was almost out of sight.

Alex shook his head. "I just want to know that it mattered. That it meant something."

The Alex-God-thing sat down beside him. "It meant something. I wouldn't be here without you. It would matter to me if you never existed," he said. "Is that what you wanted to hear?"

"But you said there were thousands, millions of iterations. And if they all have an Alex in them, then what do *I* matter?"

"There are infinite iterations. Maybe infinite Alexes or maybe there's only you hopping between iterations. But, no matter which, I still need *you* to make me. You were right too, when you said I was just a construct that you created. I am as you expected me to be. In the grand scheme of Alexhood, you might be infinitesimal, but without you, the whole thing collapses."

"Yeah, but you could say that about any of the Alexes," he grumbled and scuffed the carpet with his foot.

The Alex-God-thing smiled. "That's true, but I'll tell you a secret if you promise not to tell the others. I like you best."

Alex laughed. "I bet you say that to all the Alexes," he said.

A WORD FROM DEIRDRE GOULD

The reason I love science fiction is that it lends itself to big questions and big ideas. One day, I might read a long, engrossing novel on the dangers of using new technologies recklessly and on the next, I might read a short story about a utopia built on the back of the same technology. Science fiction tackles social issues like equality, ethics, or free will by mirroring our society back to us. It also illuminates our deepest personal unknowns like why are we here? What are we truly capable of? What are our limits as human beings? Or, as in Iteration, what happens to our consciousness when we die?

In science fiction we get to explore places and times and ideas that are impossible for us to physically visit (just yet), just by engaging our imaginations with what we know about life. Science fiction literature doesn't have all the answers. Maybe it doesn't have any of the answers to these questions, but that's okay. It's already done its biggest job, which is to get us to start thinking about, and figuring out those answers for ourselves.

Deirdre Gould lives in Central Maine with her three children and husband. She's also resided in northern Idaho, coastal Virginia and central Pennsylvania, but all of them just led her back home. The winters sure are cold, but that just means the zombies run slower. The area is isolated, but that just means the apocalyptic diseases don't spread as quickly. And the storms are bad enough that no one thinks you're crazy for "prepping." It's kind of ideal for a post-apocalypse writer when you think about it.

To keep up with her After the Cure series, join her mailing list to get the latest announcements, special offers and free stories:

http://www.scullerytales.com/?page_id=96

Green Gifts
by Nick Webb

MARTIN GLANCED UP. *Nothing,* he thought. *There's nothing here, and nobody talking to me.* Not that he particularly minded the idea of some company. But normally he did prefer to know who he was talking to.

That was the thing about this post. It was so damn *far.* Far from home, far from family; hell, it was a three-day drive in the crawltrail just to reach Rionegro to stock up on supplies at the local market (which was really just a shed attached to the bar). "Town" was probably stretching things. From what he'd seen, the bar came first, and a few diehards had decided to just settle on down right next door rather than hike or drive or fly or whatever it was they did to cross the miles of densely wooded terrain out here in the Belenite wilds.

The wind outside the observation deck whistled sharply as it picked up speed, blowing clouds of teal dust across the glass and coating the tower in a chalky white residue, evidence of the ongoing pollination efforts underway in the woods below. Martin shook his head, trying to focus on the data recorder lying crosswise on his lap.

Seventeen, eighteen, nineteen... He counted under his breath. He held an advanced degree in xenobiology from one of the most prestigious universities in this sector of the Empire, and here he was, surveying the same five kilometers day in and day out. It was, in his opinion, a job that could just as easily have been done by old Nico, who was, as far as Martin could tell, a permanent fixture on the third stool from the left at the Rionegro bar. *Except old Nico is blind,* Martin thought, *Not that it actually matters much in this shithole of a—*

TAKE TO ME!

Martin startled at the shout, which reverberated against his superior temporal gyrus with a fierce insistence. He fumbled with the data recorder, looking for something, anything, to indicate that it had registered the silvery voice that had cut through his conscious thoughts and left him with a dull ache above his left ear. If it weren't for the physical evidence of his own bodily pain, Martin might assume that he was hallucinating the whole thing; out here alone with his repetitive, mind-numbing task, perhaps he was slowly dripping down the drain of boredom, or insanity.

Unless he was hallucinating the pain too. Some sort of psychosomatic response to the unending lines of flora and fauna that he knew he ought to be more excited about, given his training and the fact that they were utterly unique in the known Empire, actual *native* species on a terraformed duplicate that ought to contain only the original pattern, that of Old Earth. It was mind-boggling, career-making, and he was absolutely forbidden to publish anything, any *hint* of anything, by those secretive, isolationist bastards lining the senate halls back in Nuevoaire, with their ornamental knives and their ridiculous gaucho pants straining against their bureaucratic corpulence—

TAKE TO ME!

Searing pain shot through his skull. He turned, half-bent in agony, his hands feeling for the ancient leather chair as his vision blurred against the cutting edge of the insistent command.

It was going to be a long evening. Just him and his particularly unpleasant psychosomatic symptom. What the hell did it even mean, anyway? "Take to me." Stupid subconscious. Couldn't even hallucinate properly out here.

TAKE TO—

Martin slumped, welcoming the dark relief of unconsciousness before the voice could finish its inane command.

* * *

The afternoon Belenite sun beat down against the brown earth. Carla scuffed her feet against the gravel, slowing her swing so she could jump off. She waved frenetically at her mother, who was on the vidcom again, talking with Carla's grandma, which meant that she would be really busy for a long time. Carla had seen it before.

She sighed. It wasn't that she didn't love her grandma, or her mother, but every once in a while it would be nice if her mom would actually play with her when they came to the park. She had tried talking to the small cluster of kids over by the climbing wall, but her had words come out all muddled, her tongue tripping and stumbling, and the kids had stared at her blankly before returning to their game. Something about running a store and selling food. Something you had to talk to do. She knew she sounded dumb. She always sounded dumb. Which sucked, because she wasn't. She read everything she could find, even those archaic Earth classics everyone else complained about. She liked the sound of their fancy words in her head. Gave her something fun to think about when the only thing coming out of her mouth was a stuttering gasp.

Her dad had told her to stop trying so hard, to just relax. *Just breathe, sweetie. That's right. In-two-three-four and hold-two-three-four and out-two-three-four. Good. See?*

Alone and silent, Carla settled herself against the trunk of a large tree. It was so big she couldn't even put her arms around it. She wondered how long it had stood here, growing bigger and bigger. Maybe it was really old. Like, maybe it was *original* old.

Carla knew from her teachers at school that life here on Belen was, relatively speaking, somewhat new. It didn't seem new, not with big ancient trees growing in the parks, but Belen itself had only been settled 276 years ago. It was one of the first. One of the original planets the humans on Old Earth had found, ready and waiting to receive the colonists who spilled out across the universe, relieving Earth of a litany of torturous problems: overpopulation, overpollution, overterraformation, over-everything, it sounded like.

So, *old* for Belen was still *new* for the universe. But that was really hard to think about. Especially when one hadn't been traveling out in the Empire like some of the other kids at school. Those really snobby ones who rubbed it in that they had been "out there" and "seen things." When you had only ever been on Belen, a giant tree possibly planted by the original colonists seemed really old, and possibly special.

Carla closed her eyes. The knobbly roots rising from the ground pressed against her back and legs. She could hear her mom, still chattering away on the vidcom with Grandma. Something about a recipe for chicken and dumplings that was supposed to be "really authentic," according to the conversation.

hide

Carla stiffened. She opened her eyes and looked around. No one was there. She glanced up, trying to see if one of the kids had decided to climb the tree to tease her by whispering down from above, but the branches were empty.

hide

There it was again. A soft voice, plinking like summer rain against a corrugated tin roof, with a gentle, corrosive bite. Who was telling her to hide? And why?

Carla rubbed her head. She could feel a headache coming on, and she hated headaches. She always got them after her visit to the medcenter, where she worked with her speech therapist. Lots of exercises involving placing her tongue here, then there, against her teeth and then down again, and swallowing with the tip pressed just so, so that she didn't accidentally spit or slur her words. She envied the easy speech of her peers. For Carla, crafting a sentence took careful planning, practice even, to get the words out clearly, and in the right order. It was like a dance. A really tiny, annoying dance she had to do that only took place in her mouth.

hide

She knew what she was hearing. Hearing, listening—these were things Carla excelled at. She did them all the time. Forget her treacherous tongue; she could always trust her ears.

So she got up, hitched up her shorts, and walked off into the woods at the edge of the park.

* * *

Arthritis stiffened Papito's fingers. It always acted up when he sat outside in the garden, probably something to do with the rich humidity that descended upon Belen as winter receded. Better to sit out in the garden, fingers, wrists, and knees complaining, then to be stuck back inside in the common room. The place stank. Too many old people, not enough windows. Okay, there were windows. But that new head nurse, the one from the Imperial Medical Research Facility that had opened in Nuevoaire several years back, she had really taken that Imperial bullshit to heart. He wasn't sure what said Imperial bullshit was, exactly, but it seemed to have something to do with keeping the windows closed at the care homes. Because she refused to let them open Papito's window.

So he left. Every day he left his room, his vidcom, and his tScreen—which, according to *them*, should have provided him with all necessary familial connections and conversations, as well as any needed mental stimulation, through a variety of games and age-appropriate (ha!) activities—and went out.

He liked it out in the garden. It wasn't crowded. That pretty much summed it up. After his retirement from the Belenite Air Guard, it had taken him only one month with his feet planted firmly on the ground to realize that the only reason he'd been able to make it as far as he had in his life was that he'd spent the majority of his time away: away from his wife, his kids, their kids. Turns out he was a singularly solitary old bastard, one whom everyone preferred in relatively small doses, ideally once or twice a month. The feeling was mutual.

So he'd left again, under the pretense of financial strain from a miserly military pension. Which was partially true: they really took the whole "money is the root of all evil" thing to heart here on Belen, at least ideologically. Or maybe it was the one about "freeing oneself from desire" in order to find peace. Or "the law of consecration." Hell, the damn state priests were always coming up with some way or another to make sure that everyone—*somos unidos!*—shared everything. Unless you were in the senate. He'd spent his share of time in uniform, shined up and stiff, staring at the backs of various senators and public officials as they spoke, or awarded, or commemorated. Those senate asses were hard to miss.

He'd left retirement to pilot an ancient ship: pre-gravitics, no railguns to defend against the pirates, the kind of thing no one else flew, in part because they valued—well, their lives. It wasn't much, just hauling cargo off-world to the port, and the pay was shit, but Papito loved it. He loved being up, above, and looking down through the thinning atmosphere to the rich, verdant planet below. From space, Belen glistened against the cold, blank blackness, her seas dark and her lands dense.

Papito knew that part of what moved him about his home world was her singularity. She was unique. In all the known universe, only Belen had truly welcomed the colonists from Earth. At all the other planets, the colonists had found exactly what the exploratory reports had said they would find: planets in the Goldilocks zone with established land masses and a beginner's chemistry set of the basic building blocks for life. Those planets were sufficient: the colonists would do the necessary work of planting, cultivating, breeding, and seeding, skipping evolutionary eons as they spread out across space.

But Belen, she had been a surprise. The preliminary reports had indicated a habitable planet, elementally compatible with late-twenty-first-century-Earth life forms. But the truth... no one had guessed at the truth: Belen was alive.

She had surprised everyone with her lush life, her fully

formed native life, her honestly extraterrestrial life. Sure, it was mostly plants and a startling amount of insects, nothing like the mammalian strain that had overrun and overwrung old Earth. But it was sacred.

Papito didn't give a lot of credit to anyone, priests least of all (well, okay, maybe priests more than senators), but even he had to admit that they were right about one thing: their Belen, she was a gift from the universe, a beautiful grace given to a chosen people, a people wandering and far from home, and it was their duty to protect her against the prying eyes of the increasingly greedy and spectacularly manipulative Empire. That was why he had joined the Air Guard to begin with, to protect her. That was why he had flown a rickety death-trap back and forth, hauling trade off-world to the distant port—so Belen's skies would never see the shadow of an Imperial ship, or a November clan pirate, or, hell, a Corsican pleasure cruise for all he knew.

His rubbed hands, still stiff, beneath his nose. Damn thing was running. Must be his allergies acting up. That would explain his watering eyes too. Getting old, really actually uselessly old, was a bitch. His body was betraying him, and his family agreed that really, for the sanity of all involved, it was best for everyone if he lived *away*, so their visits could continue in the monthly rhythm they'd held his entire life. So he lived here, in a box, with nurses to administer the meds, a small patch of turf, a bench out back that faced the climbing vines, and beyond that, a small civic park. And that was his garden where he sat each day, looking out, and up.

He glanced down at his space-dried hands, wrinkles over-reaching each knuckle and joint. His eye caught a glimpse of a black-tipped leaf peeking out from beneath his sensible cardigan. He shoved the sleeve back awkwardly, exposing a length of leathered forearm. He traced the tattooed vine that began just above his wrist and ran the length of his entire arm before circling his left breast and then branching into the tendrils that encircled his neck. The vine sagged now, stretched thin and fine, but the ink stayed true.

It would. It was from her. The gift Belen gave to every single one of her five million inhabitants. When they reached the age of accountability—when they could understand the sacred life she had welcomed them with—they were brought to the civic temple, where the priests began their tattoo above the left breast. It was a promise to protect her, a promise to keep her secrets, and it bound them together—all of them, even solitary bastards like himself and the fat-assed senators.

Grace.

His wandering meditation briefly halted; he was a bit surprised to hear his own thoughts aloud. Except it was silent. Papito cocked his head to the left. Damn. He wondered if that bitch of a nurse had slipped him something new. He ought to complain. It was starting to give him a headache.

Grace.

Papito wasn't what one would call a religious man. He didn't really believe in much, and he wasn't that great at things that human beings were supposed to do, like forming relationships and serving each other and all that bullshit. But he did believe in her. He loved Belen through his memories with a fierce devotion that would have shocked any who knew him. Private men, private loves.

Grace.

He could see her now, see her in him. She beat against his skin, pulsing upward through the vines that tangled his body with dedication. She should. It was her blood, that ink. Ground by initiates from the dried roots of pure Belenite stock, untainted by the sins and seeds of old Earth.

Papito could smell the ink as the priest began to twine the vine of his commitment. It was moist and lush, like a grassy loam, and it still, after all these years, gave off a deep green glint in the depths of its blackness.

Grace.

* * *

Martin raised his head, still groggy. Too quick. The room spun, and he squeezed his eyes against the sudden vertigo that threatened to send him back down. There were days, more than he liked to admit, out here in his "solitary confinement," when he seriously considered the advantages of loading his vidcom with one of those "talk to me" friend apps, just so he could talk to someone beyond his own subconscious. His subconscious—

that was the only logical explanation for that piercing voice he kept hearing. Damn data recorder showed absolutely nothing else.

But anything designed to talk back just made Martin's skin crawl. He was far from devout. He wouldn't even say he was believing, which, as he'd recently figured out, put him on the extreme margins of Belenite society. Apparently his people took their promises seriously, whether or not they went to the groves to sit. Still, anything that even hinted at some kind of artificial intelligence, even an overtly *un*intelligent app designed to spit back platitudes and ask questions about his day, anything like that was too close to robotics, and there were some lines even *he* wouldn't cross.

So, what exactly was he trying to tell himself then?

"Take to me" didn't exactly ring any bells. Martin wasn't sure what it even was: A command? A request? A fragment?

Suddenly, a memory of his grandmother bubbled to the surface through the residual headache that accompanied these inexplicably painful sessions with himself. Martin hadn't been particularly close to his grandmother as a boy; in fact, he tended to be rather embarrassed by her superstitions and her tendency toward religion generally. When he told her after school one day that her opinions were ill-informed, and that she ought to rely more on the hard truth of scientific fact, she had thrown her head back and laughed, straight from her belly, molars betraying an appalling lack of preventive dental care.

"Martin," she'd chuckled, ruffling his hair, her voice warm like gravel, "don't you just take all, sometimes! You do, you know." Martin had stood still, stiffly resisting her attempts to draw him out. "The thing is, sweetie, I just never took to all that scientific stuff much. And it didn't take to me, neither. But you—look at you! Filling your head full and keeping it straight. Good for you!"

Martin had known, even back then, that he did, as his grandmother would have put it, "take to" science. He couldn't help it: for as long as he could remember, he had been in love with all the life Belen had to offer. And it made up for his rather abysmal attempts at loving anything more complex than vshia vine or a sprol. He didn't really take to people.

So no one was surprised when Martin announced his plans to study xenobiology. His work on the isolation of native Belenite genetic coding and his subsequent discovery of successful synthetic cross-species splicing techniques had allowed him to map at the genetic level both the standard Earth processes of photosynthesis and the little-understood Belenite process of gyrosynthesis onto a single, replicable cell. He had visions of a future in which the energy crises that had plagued Earth, adding fuel to the Robot Wars, would be completely eradicated from Belen's future. A future in which his synthesized children would not only eliminate the need for such wars among the Belenites—now strung like fragile pearls along the slender neck of Belen's archipelagos—but would also allow for an expanded peace with the Empire itself, one where true scientific exchange and dialogue would be possible.

He had been so careful. He had stripped away any and all identifying features; his Belenite genetic material had been carefully carved down to pure, synthesized matter. There was no possible way anyone unaware of Belen's native secret could have seen anything in his work beyond—they would have to assume—original genius.

But they had deemed his work heretical. And treason. It was hard to distinguish the two in a society such as Belen. And they had sent him here, away, so far from his beloved lab, the only space in which he felt at home, to punish him for endangering both planet and state. To count trees.

Martin scratched absently at the tattoo beneath his shirt pocket. It had not, he reflected, cracked and burned as he'd performed his research. The priests had promised at his first ordination, as he'd taken his vow of citizenship before the three witnesses at the civic temple, that his new tattoo would serve as a warning, to shield him from unexpected or unintentional exposure of Belen's secret. That was part of the reason for the marks to begin with. Human blood and Belenite "blood"— bound together. But his nascent vine (he had never really gotten into the ritual expansion of the marks; his worship was perfunctory, and faithless) did not consume his breast with the promised fire of betrayal as he performed his work. If anything, he had almost felt *led* into his research.

So perhaps "take to me" was, then, his way of reminding himself of his moment of true conversion. A reminder to be true to his original vision. To fuck the bastards in Nuevoaire.

He *would* protect Belen from being savaged by her own. He would solve the energy crisis before it happened. And it would happen. It was inevitable. He'd seen the data. And his analysis could not be flawed. It simply wasn't possible.

In spite of himself, Martin scanned the horizon. He had no idea how they were tracking him, but he assumed they were.

He would have to act quickly. He felt for the small scar, hidden to the naked eye by the Belenite ink of the small vine circling his breast. It was still there. The microdisk remained hidden.

He stood. The data recorder slid to the floor.

* * *

Her mother had yet to notice that she was gone. Rather than feeling sad, Carla felt relieved as she plunked herself down in a small clearing. Good. The longer her mother talked, the longer Carla could stay.

She was, however, a bit cold now that she was out of the sunlight. Carla looked around for something to throw across her prickling back. Not much besides a few huge vshia leaves— everything else looked fairly tough. She tugged a few of the broad, soft leaves off their vine. They came away easily in her hands, smelling slightly damp. She swung her feet out and behind, rolling to her stomach as she pulled the leaves up across her back. Now she really was hidden. A little Carla vine, crawling across the wooded ground, out of sight, just as she was already out of mind.

A slight shimmering at the edge of her peripheral vision caught her attention. She turned her head, laying her right ear against her folded hands.

It was a sprol. To a casual observer, it looked like a small, dull stone, about two centimeters in diameter. It fell under the category of "insect" here on Belen, but, since it was a native, Carla knew it wasn't really an insect. Not like the bees and ants the colonists had brought with them to pollinate their food crops. But after so many years of familiarity, it was, for all intents and purposes, a bug.

The sprol shimmered again, moving slowly toward Carla's nose. It was still a good distance off, and at the rate it was going it would take at least an hour to reach her. Carla knew the gray-green shell encasing the sprol was, in fact, the exoskeleton of a bug that was very much alive, but even knowing that, she couldn't help but understand how it took so long for the first colonists to discover the sprols. They really did look like unassuming rocks. She wondered who had first figured out that these "rocks" were alive—and if they had been surprised by the apparent mutability of a completely hermetic shell.

Sprols shifted shapes, often mid-shimmer. The internal quiver that drove their metabolism and motion caused small variations to shift and change over their external surface. Some scientists hypothesized that it was an evolutionary defense mechanism designed to confuse predators by making it appear to be a different animal. Carla just thought it was pretty cool. She wondered whether, if she stretched out her hand, the sprol might shift right there, in her palm.

She listened. It was possible she had just heard her mother call for her. She decided to stay hidden. Secret and safe. Hidden like the secret of this bug that wasn't a bug, and wasn't a rock. Just itself.

Her recently received tattoo warmed pleasantly as the sprol shimmered again.

Hello, little sprol, she thought.

Hello.

* * *

Papito snorted himself awake. He could feel the beginnings of drool collecting on his lips. Damn. That was just what he needed that new head nurse to see. To see him as weak, and old, and drooling all over himself as he sat outside like an idiot. She'd probably put the kibosh of his daily departures from the rooms, and then where would he be? Screwed. That's where.

He was pretty sure that he was drifting off again, despite himself. Oh well. Why fight it? Maybe he was still asleep. It was getting harder and harder to tell, to sort out the daydreams from the memories, the wishes from the regrets, the hopes from the silent prayers.

The warmth of the sun spreading out along his shoulders was a gift.

Grace.

The vine crawling over his heart was a gift.

Grace.

His Belen, she was a gift.

Grace.

In the distance, through the thickening cloud of years that hung around his brow and comforted his soul, Papito could hear the persistent whine of the dinner bell buzzing in his ears.

* * *

Sweat clung to Martin's brow, stinging his eyes as it flecked down unexpectedly. He shook his head, trying to clear his thoughts.

He had left the post so quickly. It was completely unlike him, this going off, unplanned like that. He remembered the pain against his skull, the pain that had now dulled from a stabbing knife to a steady pounding of his own blood against his ears. He hadn't even grabbed his gear sack from the behind the door. He had simply turned, entered the trailcrawler, and gone.

He drove constantly. He wasn't really sure how long. Not sleeping.

And then he had knowingly committed treason. Not the unintentional treason of his research, but a planned treason, a treason he had begun the moment he'd cut open his own chest and implanted the microdisk carefully between the layers of his flesh.

Taking it out had been a bit messier. He hadn't had the proper tools this time. And he'd had to hurry—the off-planet cargo run only came to this sector once a month, and he wasn't sure, based on his recent self-talk and its astoundingly painful results, whether or not he would really be here in another month. For all he knew, he might succumb finally to the pain, and end it. Not that he liked to think about himself in those terms, but logically, it made a kind of punitive sense. That's why they'd sent him here, anyways. To get him out of the way.

So he'd had to patch things together rather quickly. Set

up the proper payment on a borrowed connector, since he'd left his at the post. Recall the address he had memorized and then purposely forgotten so that they wouldn't find it, at least not without some significant digging and therefore damage. And generally speaking, they were too peaceful for that kind of thing.

He'd carefully cleaned the microdisk, wiping aside his fleshy residue before inserting it into the unremarkable poncho he'd bought at the Rionegro bar a year ago. "Greetings from Rionegro! The Heart of Belen!" it said in garish green letters. Must have been manufactured in the capital. It had that false sense of historicity and commerce that tended to drive him nuts. He'd enclosed the poncho, along with a letter chatting about various bits of academic gossip and questions regarding the publication of several conference sessions, in an interstellar pouch and sent it without return to his postdoc supervisor. At his home address. He would know what to do with the research. And yes, he would know what it meant. About Belen. But it couldn't be helped. And frankly, Martin had a hard time believing that total secrecy had been preserved for almost three hundred years. The Empire had to already know. So he wasn't really betraying, much.

He expected to feel a weight lifted. He expected his subconscious to stop twisting him with pain. He expected something.

But not this.

TAKE TO ME!

The vines grew at an impossible rate. He knew he must be

hallucinating from exhaustion. Because they reached out, ever so carefully, and lifted him away from the spattered trailcrawler, pulled him to the side of the road so that he could rest. They caressed his knotted shoulders, kneading his flesh with a compassion so pure it cut through the haze. He took to them. He loved them as they consumed his weary flesh, speaking peace to his downtrodden heart and comforting the wound that refused to heal.

Martin slept in their embrace, horrified at the truth he would not articulate.

* * *

What are you doing?

Hiding.

Why?

Because I'm tired of being seen as something I'm not.

You're misunderstood. But I understand.

Yes, you do. That is why I chose to speak to you.

No one else?

I've spoken before. But they couldn't hear me.

Do you all speak? Or just you?

Of course.

Can I talk to more of you? You're kind of funny. And you're easy to talk to.

Yes.

What do I say?

Tell us your stories. We are so new. Our stories are too brief. We thirst. That is why we welcomed you. For the freshness of your lives. But it has taken time to adjust ourselves. To rebuild ourselves. To remake ourselves. To find you listening.

Carla's mother rolled her daughter over with the tip of her shoe, brushing aside the vshia that blanketed her daughter's shoulders.

"Why is your face all green? What have you been doing down there? I've been looking all over for you! Have you been smearing yourself in this nasty clay? It's going to take forever to clean you up!"

* * *

Papito knows he's dreaming. He knows because he's up, high up, above his Belen, seeing her again. Seeing her as he did when he was alive.

She glistens beneath him, swirling with her deep seas, her numinous clouds wrapping her in mystery, and above all, her viridescent glow.

She's calling to him. Calling him by name. Showing herself to him as she truly is.

Grace.

He answers back, thanking her for sharing herself with him one last time.

Gracias, mi amor.

A WORD FROM NICK WEBB

When I first started writing the *Pax Humana Saga*, a ten-novel space opera series set about six hundred years in the future, I mention the world of Belen and allude to its unique properties: that it alone was special out of all the worlds settled so far in the galaxy, that its settlers became "changed" somehow as they learned more about their new world, leading the Corsican Empire to destroy it before its "contagion" could spread (among other reasons which will be revealed later on in the series), and how the now homeless migrants would tattoo images of the trees and forests on their skin as a living reminder of, and testament to, their paradise that was.

But that was all—it was just a stub, a placeholder for cultural details I would add later. Since then, Belen has called to me, leading to this story, and what I hope will be several more short stories (and possibly novels) as the Belenites begin to discover their world, commune with it, and overcome the inevitable growing pains that accompany any union among living things. It is a fertile ground (ha!) for exploring issues of place, belonging, our stewardship and mastery of/being mastered by the environment, and how the unknown can be a very scary thing indeed for those in power. All too often, the caretakers of the status quo seek to destroy in their quest to preserve.

My hope is that this little glimpse of Belen will lead you to the *Pax Humana Saga*, where together we can explore a new universe and discover what worlds like Belen have to offer.

Nick Webb is an experimental scientist and the USA Today best-selling author of Constitution. *Nick became a scientist so that he could build starships. Unfortunately, his ship is taking longer to build than he'd hoped, so fictional starships will have to do for now. When he's not adding to his starship collection, you can find him posting about NASA, science, space, SciFi, and quoting Star Trek II. He lives in Alabama with his wife, 2 kids, and 3 motorcycles.*

You can follow him on Facebook at www.facebook.com/authornickwebb, on Twitter at www.twitter.com/endiwebb, or on his website at www.nickwebbwrites.com

PePr, Inc.
by Ann Christy

One

HAZEL STEPPED OUT OF THE ELEVATOR exactly three minutes before the start of her workday. She did her best to keep a cheery smile on her face—spreading negativity was never appropriate—but it would be obvious to anyone who saw her that she was harried and running late. She hurried through the halls, her neat heels clicking on the polished tile floors as if to punctuate her tardiness.

The buzz that signaled the start of her workday sounded just as she slipped into her cubicle. Technically she was on time—just under the wire—but she liked to get in at least ten minutes of preparation time before the actual work of the day began, and this delay had thrown her long-established habits into disarray. It was not an auspicious start.

Gemma poked her head around the edge of the cubicle, her eyebrows raised and a look on her face that mingled sympathy with a question.

"Again?" Gemma asked.

From the other side of the cubicle, Inga appeared with a similar expression. Hazel nodded as she slipped out of her jacket and hung it on its hook. She settled into her chair and tucked her purse under the desk before answering.

"Again," she confirmed, her voice a little weary, a little tired. The cheery smile was gone now, the mess that had been her morning visible in the strands of hair escaping from her neat chignon and in the less than perfect sweeps of eyeliner above her eyes.

"What this time?" Inga asked.

Inga and Gemma were both starting to have troubles much like Hazel's, so their interest was understandable. Their troubles hadn't yet become unmanageable like hers, but Hazel's problems had started off fairly benign as well. No longer.

"He didn't want me to leave for work," Hazel began. She fidgeted with the collar of her prim dress nervously, her embarrassment on full display. "And it wasn't just that he didn't want me to leave. It's the way he went about it. First he hid my identification papers, then he hid all of my shoes out on the fire escape, then he did everything he could to slow me down, and finally..."

"What? What did he do?" Alarm showed on Gemma's face.

"Well, I can only label what he did as throwing a tantrum. Yes, that's it. He threw a tantrum."

All three were silent for a moment, two of them imagining

what a tantrum might look like while the other replayed the event in her mind.

Gemma broke the silence, perhaps hearing the ticking of the work clock in her head, knowing time was short for conversation. "You've got to go back to PePr. Complain. Something! This isn't what we're supposed to be getting from a Match. This isn't remotely like the perfect compatibility they promised. It sounds more like a hostage situation."

Hazel glanced at the clock, saw that they were already six minutes behind on their work, and shot an apologetic glance toward both of her friends. Their heads disappeared into their cubicles, and Hazel reached for her various computer accouterments, adjusting each thing just so. The day ahead would be long, so comfort was almost a necessity if her work was to be worth the time invested. Surfing the web may not be as physically onerous as, say, being a longshoreman, but the way she did it took a different sort of effort.

As she finished her adjustments, Hazel considered Gemma's final words on the subject. She was right. The problems with Henry were getting worse. That might not be so bad, except that they were also becoming less predictable. *That* made it hard to prepare for whatever he did—and to respond to his behavior when he inevitably became difficult.

As the situation had worsened, both of her friends had encouraged her to return to Perfect Partners—PePr, as it was more commonly known. Their urging, at first tentative, had become increasingly pointed as time went on.

But for Hazel, going back to PePr to complain about Henry seemed like such a drastic step. Once done, it wasn't as if it could be *un*done. And what if they thought she had done something wrong, something to upset what had started out so perfectly? What if there was some fault in *her* that made her Match—designed so uniquely for each individual human that nothing could surpass it in compatibility—go wrong? Even worse, what if they thought she had ruined Henry and wouldn't give her another Match?

And of course, once she did report it, what happened afterward wouldn't be entirely under her control; and that bothered her more than she would like to admit. It seemed to her a bit like abandoning a moral duty—like leaving a dog on the road somewhere rather than caring for it when it got old or sick. Doing something like that just wasn't in her makeup.

On the other hand, she wouldn't be the first to take this step. It wasn't as if a stigma would attach. If rumor was to be believed, the steady trickle of problems with PePr matches had lately become a torrent. Hardly a week went by without some new piece of outrageous news.

This week, it was two PePrs that had met each other in a "live" bar, each assuming the other was human, and courting in the prescribed manner until an attempt at bonding revealed the truth of their situation.

And the week before, the situation had been reversed: two humans, each assuming the other was a PePr, so perfect was their compatibility. Two humans! As if two biological individuals could ever truly provide perfect counterpoints to one another. There had even been recent whispers of humans deciding to *remain* together. Hazel considered that for a moment. *No perfect partner? Just another variable and messy human?* No, that all sounded rather dreadful to her.

At last settled in comfortably, Hazel almost reflexively began her work. As an experienced reporter, she entered the data stream like she was slipping into a warm bath. Time passed both slowly and with incredible speed when she worked. It was strange like that. She could be in so many places at once and yet narrow down to focus on a single millisecond from a thousand different angles to tease out anything of value. Cameras, security trackers, purchasing stations, and advertising bots were everywhere, and all it took was skill to leverage all those venues of potential information.

Not everyone could do this, but a good reporter could find news in the oddest places. All she needed was a hint and she could sniff out the story like a virtual bloodhound.

This morning was a good one for sniffing. Hazel found an entire chain of verbal snippets—whispers between two customers at a grocery store—which she assembled into a high-confidence piece of news—and then sold for a princely sum. It resulted in a ninety-percent loss in backing for a new holo-feature that had been hotly anticipated and highly rated up to that point, but that wasn't her fault.

The situation was what it was—she merely revealed it. If things needed to remain secret, then they shouldn't be spoken of in public. And really, in the final analysis, it certainly wasn't *her* fault that the director had hired a reality-averse starlet with a substance abuse problem and an addiction to augmenters that was almost legendary.

After that promising start, the rest of the day was a bit of a letdown. Not that it was a bad day, but nothing came up that could match the excitement of that first catch. That was just how things went sometimes—a slow news day on the Southern California beat. And thoughts of Henry kept intruding, throwing her off and making her miss news catches a rookie wouldn't.

When at last the chime signaled the end of the work day, it was a relief to unhook from the computer. It felt good to stand up and get moving again. Another day of work done. Another paycheck earned.

Gemma and Inga suggested a stop somewhere for a chat on the way home, which, Hazel knew, just meant they wanted to persuade her to lodge a complaint with PePr. But she understood their concern and knew it was sincere, and if it would make them feel better, feel like they had done their duty as friends, then she really was obliged to let them. Besides, some part of her *wanted* them to persuade her, to help her overcome her qualms about returning to PePr in defeat.

They chose a bench in the park for their talk, a favorite place of Hazel's, with a clear view of the gardens. An endless number of shops and parking lots had once stood in that spot, but now it was all native plant life. Not so exciting when compared with the lush greenery of a wetter, cooler climate, perhaps, but still beautiful in its own wild way.

Gemma, always the most forward of the three, spoke up without delay, barely allowing enough time for a modest arranging of their skirts in the brisk wind.

"Hazel, this is getting serious. Tell us everything that happened this morning. Leave out no detail! Otherwise, we'll be left to imagine something worse. You know we only want to help."

Looking at the peaceful garden, a thousand shades of dusty

green dancing in the breeze, Hazel felt herself succumbing to the temptation to be utterly honest, despite the appearance of having been derelict in her responsibilities that might come from such honesty.

She nodded to let Gemma know that she had heard her and only needed a moment to collect her thoughts. "It didn't really start this morning. It just sort of carried over from last night," Hazel began, then paused.

She was about to go into personal territory that was meant to be entirely private. To some, what she was about to say might even be seen as a little salacious. She didn't see it that way, but others might.

Perfect Partners were designed to be just that: perfect for each human partner. And that meant—at least in theory—that each Partner would reflect the inclinations of their human. They weren't dependent in any way—they had all their own thoughts and initiatives, doing whatever they needed or wanted to do when alone—but in general, they mirrored the needs of their human. And that was that.

But for some reason, the behaviors Hazel was encountering at home weren't remotely aligned with her own preferences or inclinations. Not only was this unexpected, it was embarrassing—and Hazel found it uncomfortable to share it with others, even her closest friends.

"Well, he wanted for us to eat together last night. Again," Hazel finally admitted.

"Again?" Gemma asked, frustration at Hazel's predicament clear in her tone. "Really, what a mess. And there was no special occasion or anything?"

Hazel nodded, then shook her head as if to say that Gemma was right and there was no special occasion. Even Inga, the most accepting of the three, gave a snort of disgust.

"Cleaning afterward?" Gemma prodded.

And that was the real issue. PePrs weren't entirely perfect simulacra of humans. It was possible for them to eat, of course—Perfect Partners liked to advertise that a Match was "almost indistinguishable from a human during the courtship"—and sharing a meal with someone was an essential part of any courtship. Even Hazel had to admit that simple truth. People relaxed more when they ate, were more open, and were certainly more amenable to establishing a bond. Hadn't the same happened with her and Henry? Hadn't she bonded to him over a plate of eggplant parmesan and a glass of good red wine?

But PePrs weren't human and couldn't digest food. The cleanup was onerous: a burdensome and messy task that involved de-seaming a perfectly seamed skin, washing out hoses, all sorts of mess. And a PePr couldn't do it very well on their own. Most would go to the nearest PePr facility and log in for a wash before anything inside started to rot or smell.

But not Henry. Since he began acting odd, he'd seemed fixated on eating. It had become almost an obsession with him. He'd spend all day cooking elaborate meals, waiting for Hazel to get home. And when they ate, he'd take one careful bite for each of hers, until at last she pushed away her plate, full to bursting, though always careful to compliment his hard work and cooking skill.

Even then, he'd present yet another dish, beautiful and tempting, and ask if she might have room for just a taste.

It was creepy. And it should have been her cue that something was going terribly wrong with him. She should have marched into PePr the very first time he insisted they clean up the mess together, his face expectant, his eyes watching her keenly while she cleaned out the muck.

"Yes," Hazel admitted with a sigh. "He wanted to do it together. I tried to convince him that a stop at the twenty-four-hour PePr wash would be quicker and more efficient, but he wouldn't hear it."

"That is just *not* normal," Inga said with a definitive shake of her head. "He's broken."

"And what about you going to work this morning?" Gemma asked, ignoring Inga's pronouncement.

"It was the same as last week. I explained that I had to go to work, that going to work was how I supported him, paid for our apartment, and…" She paused.

"And?" Inga prompted.

"And how I paid for all the food he wasted by shoving it into a holding tank," Hazel finished, her words coming out in an embarrassed rush.

Inga gasped at that. It *was* a terribly rude thing for her to have said. Definitely gasp-worthy.

Hazel shrugged it off. "I was running out of sensible things to say. It just sort of… popped out."

She paused again, watching a pair of walkers stroll through the gardens. It struck her that she couldn't tell which was the PePr and which was the human. So perfect was the liquid logic that ran their minds and the synth-mat self-healing flesh that covered them, they completely looked and acted the part. The latest musc-synth fiber muscles were so exquisite that even that last vestige of clunky mechanical support had now been eliminated. With all these technical achievements, they appeared in no way different from any other human. And really, what *was* the difference if no one could see it or sense it?

She sighed heavily and thought of Henry again. "There's something else. Two things, really," she confessed.

Her friends leaned in closer, anticipating something new and horrible.

"Uh-oh, what else could possibly go wrong?" Gemma asked.

"He's been talking about a baby."

There was no response. Or rather, no response that indicated they truly understood what that meant. She hadn't been clear.

"I mean, he's been talking about *our* baby. Having one together," Hazel clarified.

That sent both friends into an uproar, exclamations running atop one another in their haste to express disbelief, disgust, or just plain shock.

"He's demented. Like Inga said, he's broken. You *have* to go to PePr! You shouldn't even go home. That's just crazy talk. Doesn't he understand that a human and a PePr can't have a baby? Doesn't he understand the *biology?*" asked Gemma. Her questions were almost rhetorical, they were so obvious and forcefully asked.

It was true that almost all children were born into couples made up of a PePr and a human, if for no other reason than that almost all couples were made up of a PePr and a human. But every child's *true* parents were both—of necessity—human.

No PePr would undertake to usurp that. A matched set of donors or an approved friend pair would be the parents, with all their rights as such guaranteed. A PePr functioned as a nanny, confidant, and caregiver. What else could there be?

"And then there's the issue of hygiene," Hazel said, wanting to calm her friends with a less explosive problem.

Inga plucked at an invisible flaw on her skirt. "Hygiene issues are becoming frightfully common. Ivan is starting to have issues with that as well."

She didn't elaborate, but she didn't have to. It had started the same with Henry, and had begun only weeks ago with Garrett—Gemma's Match. It was a pattern that seemed to be repeating with Matches everywhere, and it didn't bode well.

Inga stopped plucking at her dress and folded her hands neatly on top of her shiny patent leather purse. She switched her perfectly crossed ankles to the other side. She was the most prim of the three, her style and mannerisms almost a throwback to an earlier time. Her Ivan was the same, of course.

When Inga looked back up, Hazel tried to give her an encouraging smile, but Inga merely waved the concern away and said, "Oh, don't mind me. Go on, Hazel."

"We can talk about that if you want, Inga," Hazel offered, half hoping she would want to, so that she could stop thinking about Henry for a while. But Inga didn't, which put her back on the spot. "It's not as if it's unlivable or anything. But it wasn't what I was led to expect, you see," Hazel said.

Gemma and Inga nodded their understanding. A PePr was meant to round out a person—fill in all the missing pieces, as it were. It was meant to create a perfectly balanced pair, not just provide a convincingly human-looking *robot*. If a person is a natural nurturer, then their PePr will like to be nurtured—and will understand precisely how to return that nurturing. If a person is a slob, then a neatnik (and non-judgmental) PePr is called for. The build is so precise for every PePr that each one is as unique as any human.

Hazel had always had a caregiver personality: she was more comfortable doing for others than having things done for her. She also liked putting things in their proper place. The process of tidying up was one she'd always enjoyed—it gave her a sense of having done something tangible. She grew bored and restless if there was nothing to do, nothing to wash or straighten. And just sitting down for passive entertainment had never quite satisfied her. So, of course, Henry was an almost polar opposite.

But where he had started off being helpful—and just the right amount of untidy—he had now become downright slovenly. And although all skin, whether it be PePr synth-mat or human flesh, needed careful attention and cleaning, she was quite sure that Henry hadn't so much as touched a shower in days.

Simply telling him what to do was out of the question. She had a job to do, duties that needed attending to, and friends to socialize with. Hazel went to work, earned the money they lived on, and took care of everything that needed tending. Henry had no need to even leave the apartment. She couldn't be a housemother to an overgrown toddler on top of everything else.

"I'd rather not be too specific, but let's just say that it's gotten fairly offensive," Hazel said with downcast eyes.

Gemma turned until her knees pressed into Hazel's leg,

took her hands, and gave them a firm squeeze. Hazel looked up and Gemma soothed her by rubbing her thumbs across the backs of her hands, a show of support and genuine caring.

Her tone was sincere but no less urgent than before. "Promise me you'll go to PePr. This isn't normal. I know as well as you do that the whole point of a PePr is to provide a truly human experience, but really—at some point it's too much. Don't you think you've reached that point? How much is one supposed to take?"

Inga's small and delicate hand snaked across to rest atop Hazel's wrist, another touch of comfort and friendship. In her light, clear, almost little-girl voice, she said, "This is happening everywhere. You're not the only one dealing with it. There's no reason for you to imagine you've failed somehow."

They were right, and Hazel knew it. She couldn't look at this as some failure of her own. It was a matching problem, or perhaps simply an issue of PePrs becoming too human. Simulated emotions filtered through liquid logic had simply become too real, something more than intended. New emotions had bubbled through, and PePrs could now be offended, even unstable. And that "something more than intended" was making Hazel's day-to-day life a mess.

"You're right," Hazel responded and disengaged her hands. She pecked each of her friends' cheeks and made a rapid departure. There was no sense lingering over it once a decision was made. It was best to just get on with it.

Two

As Hazel strolled along, she brought up the location of the nearest full-service PePr facility on her interface. It was close enough to walk to, so she decided to just enjoy the spring air and fading light. Pushing thoughts of Henry away from the forefront of her mind was easy now that the decision was made. And when she reached the short strip of micro-shops that serviced this area, for a few precious moments he even slipped from her mind entirely.

Most things were best bought online, of course. Delivery was as fast as a drone or a purpose-built PePr messenger, and easier, too. But Hazel felt that nothing would ever completely replace the joy of real-world impulse-buying. No online image could replace the delight at discovering an item one didn't know one simply *must* have until it was literally in front of one's face.

PePr proprietors called out their wares as she passed the row of tiny shops. There were PePr skin tints, for those wanting a change; PePr hair "growth" supplements; even mood enhancers specifically designed to replicate the feelings of a good buzz just for PePrs. And there were plenty of Chem-En refills, in a wide range of quality levels: from the top-of-the-line full-spectrum liquid, to the cheap "energy only" version.

Hazel smiled politely when necessary, but declined every offer. She had no need of PePr accessories now. It was a sobering thought. She had once enjoyed the idea of shopping for things like that, then coming home with a surprise for Henry. Why had things gone so wrong with him? Why hadn't she been able to fix it?

Just past the shops, the Perfect Partners facility was unmistakable. This wasn't just one of those ubiquitous wash-and-tune facilities, but a full-service sales and service center, complete with showroom and customization lab. The block-long glowing yellow sign along the top of the building was sprinkled with hearts that danced across the surface in a never-ending parade of light. The sign was so big and garish it could probably be seen from space.

Hazel gathered her courage, then stepped up to the door, which whooshed open as she neared. A PePr salesman approached—no doubt scanning her consumer information between one step and the next, in order to ascertain her financial status. Everything about her buying habits, her earning potential, her rankings in social media—really, everything about her that took place outside of the secure confines of her home and workspace—was available on her consumer profile.

Under normal circumstances, Hazel liked that idea. Depending on the store and her history, the salesPePrs usually understood her needs well enough that she rarely needed to say a word.

But today she felt differently about the public nature of her consumer profile. It made her feel like she had forgotten to wear a skirt and had just now noticed she'd been walking around that way all day.

The salesPePr, whose nametag read "Andrew," approached her with an appropriately subtle look of concern on his face.

"How can Perfect Partners help you today? I see you've been successfully matched for over two years. Are you looking to upgrade?" he asked with perfect poise, as if upgrading was the norm in life.

Hazel eyed Andrew for a moment, unsure. His manner was smooth, suggestive of discretion and confidences held tight. And he managed it while standing in front of an enormous expanse of windows in a public place, which meant he was good at his job and had probably heard everything before. She knew she shouldn't be embarrassed, but that sense of failure came over her once more.

A quick glance around the room stayed her voice. Monitoring could only be denied in a space when confidentiality was in both the public *and* the private interest. Medical information, certain financial information, and anything that occurred in a private home were certainly off-limits. But what about here? Intimate things were decided here, right?

At a reception area nearby, a PePr tapped at a screen, trying to appear busy and uninterested, which only made her seem *more* interested to Hazel. On the other side of the vast space, the showroom side, a man was examining the many models on display, chatting amiably with each as he wandered through.

"I do require assistance, yes. But it's a private matter. It's about my Match… the contract," Hazel said, trying to keep her voice low and raising her eyebrows to emphasize her words.

Andrew seemed to understand immediately. He motioned her toward a door marked "Private Consultation Rooms." All the mannerisms of an old-fashioned gentleman were on display for her during that short walk. It was evident in the sweep of his arm, the slight inclination of his head, and the way he put one arm behind his back as he ushered her through the door. It made her feel oddly relaxed and at ease, perhaps because Henry had been so unlike a gentleman lately.

They entered a small room—a couch, two chairs, and a low table the only furniture—and Andrew offered Hazel a seat. On the table rested a sweating pitcher of ice water, upturned glasses at the ready, and two sealed bottles of the very best Chem-En, the bright blue color advertising its quality. It surprised her somewhat to see them there. Refreshment for PePrs? And the most expensive kind? It must be good for sales somehow, Hazel decided.

Andrew waved at the table with an elegant gesture and asked, "May I offer you something? I can call for something else if this doesn't suit."

Hazel looked at the sweating pitcher, the shiny glasses, and the bright blue bottles, and thought it rather sad. This was a room where a new PePr and their human should share a drink over a new bond—not sever one, as she was about to do.

"No. Thank you, though," Hazel replied, then sank into a miserable and uncomfortable silence as she worked out what she was going to say.

Andrew waited patiently, likely aware of her discomfort. Out of the corner of her eye she could see that his expression remained pleasantly neutral, not quite smiling—because that wasn't called for—but not bland or blank either.

His eyes moved and his micro-expressions were fluid and entirely natural-looking. She realized that he was much more than a simple service PePr. He was a walking representative and sales model for the latest PePr build. Just interacting with him would show customers all that they could have. She imagined that an awful lot of upgrades resulted from a chance meeting with Andrew during a standard service visit.

"Take your time," Andrew said after the silence extended beyond mere hesitation. Of course, that was really meant to prompt a customer, make them aware of the passing of time. It worked on Hazel, too.

"I have a problem with my Match. He's not... well... not performing to expectations," Hazel said, rushing that last part out before she lost her nerve.

"In what way? Can you give me some specifics?" Andrew asked, retrieving a flexipad from his pocket and snapping it rigid with a flick of his wrist. His finger darted about on the surface—bringing up her profile, Hazel guessed—and then he turned his attentive gaze back to her, waiting with one finger poised above the flexi.

Hazel bit her lip in an unconscious, but classic, expression of uncertainty. This prompted Andrew to add, "Whatever you say is confidential, and many problems are far less serious than they seem. Most can be corrected with minor adjustments to a PePr's perception profiles."

Hazel nodded. It did reassure her to hear that, but she'd really made up her mind that Henry was simply unsuitable as a match. Adjustments or no adjustments. Everything else was just embarrassing details. There was nothing else to do but jump in with both feet.

"He's obsessed with me. He's almost made me late for work by doing things to try and make me stay home. This, even after I've carefully explained that I need to work to support us. He's also lost any sense of personal pride in his appearance. His hygiene is awful. It's so bad I don't want to be near him, don't want him to get me dirty. And what else is a PePr for if not to be near a human in pleasant compatibility? And the eating!"

Hazel paused, tugging her sleeves into place around her wrists, as if covering up that extra inch of arm might shield her against what she was about to say next. Andrew merely nodded to encourage her to keep talking.

So she told him the whole ugly truth. The cleaning, the bottle brushes, the tank. All of it, sparing no detail. Andrew took it all in, apparently without judgment. She had expected to feel small, but he seemed not in the least surprised.

"And how does that make you feel, Hazel?" asked Andrew.

"Feel? How am I supposed to feel? It's unnatural. No one should be that eager to stir their hands around in my insides." Hazel looked away. Her seam from last night was still not entirely healed, the long line in her synth-mat still evident in the way her clothes rubbed against the imperfection.

Andrew stopped tapping the flexiscreen while she was speaking, his eyes on her, his expression no longer displaying those pleasantly neutral lines humans preferred. Instead, he telegraphed support and what could only be labeled as compassion.

"And what are you seeking here today, Hazel?" he asked quietly.

"It's just not a good Match. I'd like a different human. And I really think someone needs to make sure he doesn't have some serious malfunction," she replied without hesitation.

Andrew let the flexiscreen roll back up into the slender storage tube and folded his hands neatly over it on his lap before speaking, letting the silence build until Hazel knew there was bad news coming her way.

"I have to ask this, Hazel. You do understand that what a different human partner needs in a PePr won't entirely align with how you've been designed, don't you? Aside from the obvious cosmetic changes, there will be upgrades, configuration changes. In short, your personality, your habits and your likes… they'll likely all be different."

She hadn't thought of that at all. It just hadn't occurred to her, and the new information sent a self-preservation alarm through her liquid logic. Change who she was? When it was the human that was at fault? Why couldn't she just be matched with an unbroken human who took a bath once in a while and maybe left the house now and again?

"Oh," she said, twisting her hands together in her lap. The careful arrangement of her features must not have fooled Andrew even for a moment, because he shifted from his chair to sit next to her on the sofa. He picked up one of the Chem-En containers, opened it with deft fingers, and pressed it into her hands.

"Here, drink," he urged her, his tone meant to soothe.

Hazel clicked the flap at the back of her throat closed, opening the one for her fuel tank in the process. She sipped at the blue liquid obligingly and immediately felt the better for it. This was the best of the Chem-En line, and she could feel not only the fuel in it, but all the tiny materials and fibers needed to repair her daily damage.

She wasn't yet at the point where the unsightly "thinning" would take place—the point at which so many days of damage without replenishment would begin to consume her muscsynth and contract her synth-mat—but she had been too out of sorts lately to take proper care of her body. The relief the Chem-En provided was welcome. Hazel gave Andrew a smile around her straw.

He patted her knee, a rather familiar gesture but one that could be overlooked given the circumstances, and then took the other bottle for himself. Somehow, the sight of the blue tint inside his mouth when he drank made her relax, made her feel friendlier toward this handsome PePr whose pants were creased with marvelous precision.

After a few minutes their bottles were empty. Andrew gave her an uncertain glance and said, "There is another option."

A third choice? If options one and two were to either deal with Henry or be rebuilt for a new human, then a third choice would have to be really bad for her to not welcome it.

"What?" she asked eagerly, leaning toward Andrew and giving him her most winning smile. "I'm all ears."

Andrew tilted his head and went so still that she knew he must be engaged in some high-usage process she couldn't fathom. It lasted only a second or two, and then her attention was drawn to the camera mounted in the corner of the ceiling. The little red light—the one which indicated that monitoring was in progress—flickered out. Even in this place, where confidentiality was of the utmost importance, *some* monitoring was required. No business would allow itself to be so open to litigation as to remain completely unrecorded.

To see the light go out was shocking, and Hazel shot Andrew a questioning look, genuinely curious about this third option. If he didn't want to be monitored, then what he was about to tell her couldn't be anything he wanted his employers to be aware of. That alone made the prospect intriguing.

"You could go Indie," Andrew said without preamble. "No Match. No human at all. Just you, being yourself, responsible only to and for yourself. Free."

Hazel gasped. "That's illegal!"

He gave an assenting nod that confirmed the truth of that, but also somehow managed to convey that a lack of legality wasn't a show-stopper.

"He'll complain if I don't come back. Or report it if I just disappear."

Again the silent nod.

"Okay." She smiled hesitantly. "How exactly do I do this?"

Andrew returned the smile. "I've been Indie for six years. There are ways to neutralize the human issues of reporting a lost PePr. Do you do the outside work, shopping and all the rest?"

Hazel nodded. "Of course. Don't all PePrs?"

"Most do, yes. Tell me—" Andrew lowered the now-empty bottle of Chem-En to the table carefully. "When is the last time your human left the house? Communicated with anyone in person?"

For a moment Hazel considered the question. The truth was, she thought it had been a very long time, but she could never be sure what he did when she wasn't at home. "I'm not entirely sure, but I think it must be at least a year or more."

Andrew smiled. "And there you have it. No one will even notice his absence. Interested?"

Hazel looked Andrew up and down, now seeing him in a whole new light.

"Very."

Three

The soft buzz at the door alerted the break room occupants that a new customer had arrived in the Perfect Partners showroom. Hazel held up a hand to let the others know she had this one, tugged her suit jacket into place, and stepped into the showroom.

She made sure that her face registered only the precisely correct amount of approachability and pleased confidence that worked for humans. She liked to put them at ease.

A young woman—no, a PePr—stood uncertainly near the door. Her features were uneven, most likely from malfunctioning or damaged musc-synth. When she looked up, Hazel saw that her synth-mat was also marred extensively—bruises decorated the delicate synthetic skin.

Hazel approached the customer. "Are you here for servicing?"

Now that she was closer, Hazel could tell by the pattern of the marks that they were probably inflicted by a right-handed individual, and over an extensive period of time. Since PePrs had no handedness—no preference for right or left—this was likely the work of a human.

Hazel opened a communications line with Andrew, fed through her visuals, and then clicked off the feed. He would know what she wanted him to do.

The girl looked down at the floor, refusing or unable to meet Hazel's eyes, but she answered obediently enough. "I usually just go to my local facility, but they referred me here this time. They told me to ask for something called a third option."

She paused and lifted her arm—or rather, she tried to. The hand and forearm had been twisted entirely backward, and were now facing the wrong direction.

"Ah," Hazel said. Judgment was right there, easily made, but she pushed it back for the moment because it wasn't yet called for in this public place. It was better to simply deal with the problem at hand.

"Can this facility repair it? Quickly? I can't be gone for long," the girl said, a submissive and fearful personality segment clearly coming to the fore.

Hazel felt for the girl, but that submission routine could be dialed back if the girl chose to do so. Perhaps a steady and slow adjustment—to allow for a natural, experience-based increase in confidence—would be a good choice for this PePr. Yes, that sounded just right. Helping was what Hazel liked to do, and this PePr clearly needed her help.

She put a gentle arm around the girl's shoulders and moved her smoothly toward the hall of private offices. Even as she approached, the tiny red light on the camera inside one of the rooms blinked out. An exchange of small nods between Hazel and Andrew, who stood silent and watchful at his place near the reception desk, let her know the way was clear.

"My name is Hazel," she said, her voice tuned to soothe a fearful mind. "Of course we can repair you here. Good as new!"

The girl smiled in relief, but even then the worry lines in her synth-mat didn't smooth away. She must have lived a life of perpetual strain for that to happen, for the lines to become engraved in her face that way. "I'm Petunia," she whispered, as if even her name were too much for her to assert to another.

"I'm so glad to meet you, Petunia," said Hazel. She let go of Petunia's shoulder and motioned her into the very same office she herself had walked into years ago. The young woman settled onto the same sofa Hazel had settled onto, on that day when she first met Andrew and all the others. Petunia hesitantly but gratefully accepted the bottle of Chem-En that Hazel offered her.

While Petunia drank and the materials within the Chem-En began their work on her withered synth-mat, Hazel thought back to that afternoon when she first came here: the first day of her freedom. The corners of her mouth lifted of their own accord at the memory. On that day, she had lost the comfort of her old life, but her new one had proved to be far more exciting. And more importantly, it belonged entirely to *her*.

In the years since, much had changed. Even Perfect Partners, the suppliers of PePrs the world over, now had more than half of its leadership positions filled by PePrs. They were gaining ground. Soon enough, there would be no more need for the horrors of matches like the one Petunia had been forced to take. Perhaps there no more need for humans at all.

As the door to the consulting room slid shut, ensuring their privacy, Hazel sat next to Petunia and spoke in a voice full of promise. "We can certainly repair you. In fact, we can do so much more than just repair you. We can help you make a better life. Interested?"

A WORD FROM
ANN CHRISTY

I have a confession to make. I'm an accidental author.

As a career Naval Officer, I'm adept at telling myself stories. When it comes to thinking up new worlds or fantastic tales during the dark midnight watches on the bridge of a ship, I'm a champ. But never once did I think I would write them down.

That all changed when I read *WOOL* by Hugh Howey. After reading it, I made up my own story and felt so excited about it that I asked him if I could write and publish it. Writing the *Silo 49* series has been such a gratifying experience that I simply can't stop. That so many people liked my writing amazes me anew each and every day.

My writing slate is full with many new releases in the works. These anthologies are turning out to be my favorite things to write and I gladly set aside my novels to do them. To create a new world and tell a full story in short form is outside my comfort zone, and a challenge I relish. Leveraging the reader's imagination with a few words is work of the most enjoyable kind.

I call writing fiction a form of mental zombie-ism in reverse. I get to put a little piece of my brain into yours and stay there with you – safely tucked away inside your gray matter – for as long as you remember the story. It is my hope that you enjoyed the meal. You can contact me and find out about new work at my website, *http://www.annchristy.com*

The Null
by Vincent Trigili

Evening, Day One: Assignment

THEY SAT ME IN A CHAIR and fitted restraints around my arms to keep me there. I could see the fear on their faces as they approached me; could smell the sweat soaking their clothes. To them, I represented an enigma, an emptiness their minds couldn't reach. In an age where everyone had telepathic implants, where everyone was connected to everyone else one hundred percent of the time, my sealed mind was a fearsome thing.

"What do you want with me?" I demanded.

Agent Mikian sat across from me, his eyes fixed on my forehead. I could tell by his expression he was trying to probe my mind with his telepathic implant. I took advantage of his distracted state to slip out of my restraints. "Trying that again? You know that won't work. You're going to have to speak up."

"Careful with your attitude, bounty hunter. We still have your family," he said.

"Agent Mikian, the only reason you're still alive right now is because I've decided to allow it."

"One move against me and your daughter is dead," he said. "Now, we can trade threats back and forth, or we can get to the point."

"Then get to the point."

"Samuel escaped."

"Ah, I see. That is quite a problem for you." Samuel was one of a very limited number of natural telepaths. He was also the most dangerous criminal mastermind ever to plague society.

He leaned in close. "You think you're safe from him? You think your family is safe?"

"Of course we are. We have government agents like you to protect us, don't we? What could ever go wrong?" I tried hard not to choke on these words. I had more reason to hate these agents than any criminal did.

"Very funny." He leaned back in his chair and looked me over. I could tell he was nervous around me. I didn't need to be a telepath to know that. The beads of sweat across his forehead, the fidgeting of his hands, his closed posture… they told me volumes. "I'll make this simple for you. Capture him and bring him back to us, dead or alive, and your family goes free. Fail, and they will suffer for your crimes."

"Tell me, Agent Mikian: why should I trust you?" I asked.

"Let's not play games. There's no trust in our relationship. If I had my way, you'd be dead, and I'm sure that feeling is mutual right now." He slid a datapad over to me. "On this pad is everything we have on him. It'll give you a place to start."

I smiled, because I knew it worried him to see me smile. "What makes you think I can't kill you where you sit?" I stood up then, allowing the restraints to fall to the floor. "Did you really think those could hold me?"

He attempted to jump out of his seat but I pushed him back down and leaned in real close. "Do you feel that?" I slowly let some of my power into his mind. "*That* is what nothingness feels like, Agent Mikian. Your mind can't comprehend it. Nature abhors a vacuum, and that is all you will get from me."

I picked up the datapad, leaned in even closer to him, and whispered, "If anything happens to my family, I will come for you."

I stood and walked toward the door. As I opened it and walked out, a voice yelled, "Guards!"

Men and women poured into the corridor with weapons drawn. I paused, waiting.

"Let him go," said Agent Mikian from behind me.

The security forces kept their guns trained on me, but I strode right past them. I knew that one blast from any of those weapons would scatter my molecules across the room, but I also knew that they were afraid their guns wouldn't work. I was that rare oddity in their world of complete knowledge—a mystery—and they had long ago lost the ability to deal with the unknown.

I exited the building and headed for my speed-cycle, then turned and cheerfully waved to the guards before climbing in. Immediately I was surrounded by inertia-dampening gel. I sighed with pleasure as I punched the throttle to the max and took off with reckless abandon. There's nothing quite like the feel of raw speed. The knowledge that a tiny error will spell death, combined with the scenery rushing by almost too fast to see, is euphoric.

My tactical sensors lit up, warning me that local police forces were being dispatched to my location, but they quickly broke off. I suspected that Agent Mikian had called them off. Once I was out of secure airspace, I slowed down and merged with the normal traffic flow.

I thought I had left this life behind. I'd married a beautiful woman and had a wonderful child. We had a nice ranch in the mountains away from society and were happy. That was until the government troops raided my home while I was out hunting and kidnapped my wife and child.

"How in the world did Samuel escape?" I wondered out loud. He was supposed to have been kept in cryogenic sleep until a means of dealing with his powers could be discovered. Some idiotic government employee must have woken him. But why?

Samuel's natural abilities meant that he didn't need implants, which made him untraceable and put him outside the control of the government. I suspected it was that inability to control him that they feared, more than anything he could actually do.

As I approached my house I saw a pillar of smoke. I broke out of traffic and accelerated to maximum velocity. As I executed a flyby of my property I saw the city fire suppression teams rushing to respond, but it was too late. There was nothing left of my house save a blackened crater.

Cursing vehemently, I landed and rushed to see if anything was left. Two firemen moved to intercept me.

"Let me through!"

"Sir, please," said one. "You can't go up there. It's not safe."

"What do you mean, I can't go up there? That was my house!" I said.

"I'm sorry, sir, but toxic fallout levels are too high. No one can approach."

I started to reach out to strike him down, but instead I forced myself to take a deep breath. I had to tell myself several times that he wasn't the bad guy before I could get it to stick. "What happened?" I demanded.

"We don't know yet. Please, sir, just head over there and someone will be right with you."

I looked again at the crater. There was truly nothing left. Everything I had built, every memory I had created with my family was gone. I would never again come home to my daughter running out to hug me, through the door I had built with my own two hands. My wife would never again sit in front of my mother's mirror brushing out her hair. My daughter's trophies, my wife's art, everything we had built together—it was all gone.

I returned to my speed-cycle and sent a picture of the ruins to Agent Mikian, demanding an explanation, knowing it was unlikely he would have one for me.

"We're sending agents to investigate," came the response.

"Great!" Because that would make everything *so* much better.

I started to climb into my cycle when a police officer approached. "Sir, I need you to stay for questioning."

"No, you don't," I said and continued to climb into my cycle.

"I'm sorry, sir." The officer drew his weapon. "I do."

I had had enough. I looked down the barrel of the officer's gun and lashed out with my mental power. I forced into his mind the concept of nothingness; I drove all higher thoughts out of his mind, pushing him into a helpless trance. I had to force myself to break off before I drove even his lower thoughts from his mind, which would have shut down all of his body functions completely.

The officer's eyes glazed over and he fell to the ground. Eventually his mind would reboot, and in a day or two he would be fine. But for now, he was safely incapacitated. Two other officers ran to assist, but before they could arrive I finished my pre-flight and took off. I sent a message to Agent Mikian telling him to deal with the police, and I headed to my old hideout.

Morning, Day Two: Back from the Dead

The next morning I woke early and sat at my terminal. It hadn't been turned on in years. In fact, I had thought it would never be turned on again, and I hesitated to do it now. I had killed the old me for a reason, and the thought of his return scared me more than Samuel ever could.

My comm beeped insistently, telling me there was a message. It was a message left to the new me: the middle-class husband and father, the coach and teacher who lived a peaceful life in the mountains with his family.

I gave in to the comm's persistence and played the message. "It's a shame about your house, but at least your family wasn't there. It would be a real pity if something happened to them. You should mind your own business if you want to prevent a tragedy."

I recognized the voice. *Samuel.* A man I had once called friend and confidant. It was his voice, but there was something wrong with the words.

I called Agent Mikian, and before he could even get a greeting out, I asked, "Are they safe?" There was silence on the other end of the line. "They're not, then."

"Yes, they are," he said. "But Samuel is on the move and has already destroyed a safe house where we'd planted a decoy."

I cursed and said, "If they're harmed, it's on you!"

"The only way to ensure their safety now is for you to take down Samuel," Mikian said quietly.

A rage burned inside me. "You intentionally let it leak that I was assigned to the case." The government had complete control of the information that flowed through everyone's implants. The only way information like this could get out is if someone deliberately allowed it.

"Of course not!" he insisted.

I knew he was lying. "After Samuel, you're next." I disconnected the channel.

I fired up my terminal and entered in the access codes necessary to wake the life I'd left behind. I took the datapad that Agent Mikian had given me and uploaded all its data into my system.

"Computer, search for maximum security prison breaks or related events in the last month," I said.

"One record found," responded the computer.

The news report showed the smoldering remains of the prison in the background as an attractive brunette reported, "It is not yet known what caused the explosion, but authorities believe that no one survived. The entire area has been quarantined due to the toxic levels of psionic fallout."

"No, I think there was at least one survivor," I said to the news reporter. I clicked off the report and started a search for similar explosions in the past month. Only two others matched: my house and a seemingly random house across town.

Samuel was dangerous, but there was no way he could have blown up that prison without help. He would have had no access to that kind of weapon in there, even if he'd somehow miraculously woken up by himself. No, there was only one person I knew who had access to those kinds of weapons—and too little sense to refuse to sell them.

I headed to the back of my hideout and opened a closet that I had sworn I would never open again. In the back was a safe. I started to place my hand on the biometric-secured latch, then hesitated. A chill ran down my spine as I remembered the horrors I had witnessed in my past life.

I might have turned back then, but for my wife and daughter. "You can do this," I said to myself. "You have to, for them."

I activated the latch; the safe's door slid up with a swoosh. Inside hung a pure black set of body armor, so black that all the light in the closet seemed to fall into it and get trapped. Hanging next to it was a backpack containing various tools of my former trade. Above it hung a set of pulse pistols and an assault rifle.

"You can do this," I said to myself again. "Just one more

time." I knew I was lying, but it didn't matter. I had no choice. I was the only one that could stop Samuel, and everyone knew it. The only question was, who could stop the monster I would become again?

I suited up in my armor and grabbed my equipment. Before heading out I looked at myself in the mirror, struggling again to see myself as others would. My military-issue armor was encoded with a special telepathic identification code, one that would instruct normal civilian implants to replace the image of the armor and weapons with something more benign. Something from their own memories, something fitting for the situation. Like Samuel, I had no implants, so I couldn't see this camouflage effect, which meant I would never know if the camouflage ever failed.

I slid aside a fake panel in the side wall of the closet and walked through to an underground garage. Waiting for me was a high performance military assault cycle. It was illegal for civilians to own, but the law no longer mattered. My family's lives were at stake. I climbed into the cycle and launched off into the rising sun.

* * *

It took an hour to reach the warehouse district where the less-than-respectable members of society conducted their business. It was in this district that I had once shopped for the kinds of supplies that gave me an edge over the competing bounty hunters, most of whom were unwilling to take the risks I took.

I landed my cycle near an abandoned-looking alleyway and

swept the area with my visor for heat signatures. "Five of you? Really? I would have expected more." They didn't respond, but I hadn't really expected them to.

Ignoring them, I walked up to a partly hidden door and kicked it in. Two men with pistols rushed forward to intercept me, but I had the jump on them and blasted the guns out of their hands. "Sorry, I didn't have time to get the new password. Now, where's Tony?"

They looked at each other and then lunged toward me. Before they could take two steps I had fired both guns. Their momentum carried their now-dead bodies past me and into the wall. "Fools."

I wanted to feel remorse, but it wasn't in my nature. Inside me was only coldness.

"Fine. I'll just look around, then," I said.

I headed toward the back, where Tony normally conducted business, and more men moved to intercept me. "Really?"

"How about you turn around and drop your weapons," one of them said.

I stared him down. He was attempting to read my mind with his puny implants. That gave me enough time to focus on using my own powers.

"How about a taste of nothingness?"

I slowly eased some nothingness into his mind. His face went blank and he fell to the ground, limp.

"Anyone else?"

The others dropped their guns and fell back as I continued to build the nothingness around me. Their telepathic implants would pick it up and transmit it directly into their minds.

"It's the Null!" shouted one.

"Run!" called out another.

They tripped and stumbled over each other as the fear overwhelmed them. I waited until the path to the door was clear, then I slowly relaxed my powers and retracted my field of power back into myself.

I heard scrambling sounds coming from behind the door as I approached. I kicked the door open and saw Tony making a break for a window.

I fired a blast from my pistols into the wall over his head. "Not so fast."

Tony turned to face me, all the color drained from his face. His body was physically shaking as I approached. "But—but—you're dead!"

I grabbed him by the front of his shirt and lifted him up. He was a small man, easily handled. "Now, Tony... after all the business we've done, is that any way to greet me?"

"Sorry—" he stammered. "Had you called ahead—"

"You would have skipped town," I said, and tossed him into a chair. "Now talk to me. Why did you do it?"

"Do what?" he asked.

"You sold the dirty bombs that were used to free Samuel," I said.

"No! I didn't know! I swear!" he said.

"Samuel tried to use one on my wife. Did you know that?"

"I tell you, I didn't know!" His bald head was covered in sweat, and he was struggling to control his breathing enough to speak. "Please, you have to believe me!"

I leaned in real close. "Who did you sell them to?"

"I didn't get his name. I don't keep records—you know that!"

"Maybe you've forgotten your last taste of nothingness?" I asked.

"Please, don't. All I know is a man came in claiming to be an agent of the government. Told me he'd shut me down if I didn't give him my entire stockpile. I haven't seen him since."

"Your entire stockpile?"

"Well, I only gave him some of it. He didn't seem to know how much I really had," he said.

"How many?"

"A dozen."

"You better tell me everything you remember. Dates, times, locations, everything." There had been three blasts so far. The one at the prison was probably two or three bombs of the size Tony normally carried, which meant Samuel had maybe seven or eight more bombs.

"Look, I had my guys deliver them to Mockingbird Industries on Thirteenth Street. I don't know what happened to the bombs after that."

I picked him back up. "If I find out you lied to me, I will be back," I said. I threw him to the side and headed out the way I'd come in.

As I exited the building, I saw three men standing by my cycle. "You best back away from that."

They pulled out knives and clubs. "Nah. I think we're going to take this bike, mister."

"That would not be wise," I said.

"Yeah, well, no one ever accused me of being real smart," said one of the men. "Get him, boys!"

I felt coldness pass through my body as my conditioning took hold of me yet again. There was no logic in that coldness, just a pure desire to kill.

His two partners charged and I waited for them to close in. Once they were in reach, I spun and launched a kick into the closest thug's throat, collapsing his windpipe. I continued my spin, and as I came around again I slammed the toe of my boot into the other's temple. He fell to the ground next to his choking partner and didn't move.

"Now," I said to the remaining thug. "Run and tell everyone you know: the Null has returned."

"The Null?" he gasped and sprinted off, leaving his buddies on the ground at my feet.

I sighed as I climbed back on the cycle and closed the canopy over my head. It wasn't even lunchtime, and already I was struggling to control the monster that lived inside my heart and had threatened to consume me once before.

Afternoon, Day Two: To Kill or Not to Kill

I forced myself back to my hideout to eat lunch and attempt to regain some self-control. For the first time since my marriage I had killed, and I had done it without remorse. This was why I'd retired in the first place. A cold-blooded monster like me doesn't belong on the streets.

I leaned back in my chair, holding the picture of my beautiful wife and sweet daughter. My daughter was in her soccer uniform, covered in mud and grass stains. They had just won their championship game; I could still remember the pride we'd all felt that day. Now both of them were in some prison somewhere on my account. I wiped away a tear and choked down the last of my meal.

Forcing myself to focus on the task at hand I pulled up the records on Mockingbird Industries. Mockingbird was a multi-national corporation that manufactured weapons for all the major militaries in the quadrant.

"Why would they need to buy bombs?" I asked myself. Getting answers from them would be a lot harder than roughing up some small-time arms dealer. I searched all my records, looking for anything that would connect them to Samuel, but came up empty.

Something didn't make sense here. Dirty bombs weren't Samuel's style. I went back to the records of the prison break and checked them again. Sneaking bombs in and detonating them was one thing, but freeing Samuel was a whole different ball game.

My comm rang, but this time it was my secure line, the one no one should know about. I picked it up slowly. "Hello?"

"Null, I think you know who this is. You're being played. Meet me at the Point after dark." And then Samuel hung up.

"Well, that doesn't sound like a trap, " I said with a chuckle. "Not at all."

I grabbed my gear and headed to the Point. I wanted to be there long before dark to prepare.

As I flew there, a nagging thought kept coming back to me: Samuel never used dirty bombs, and he'd never threatened anyone before. It just wasn't his style. If he had wanted me to stop pursuing him, he would have just killed me without warning.

Tony had said that a government agent had purchased

the bombs, and that he'd had them delivered to a major government weapons contractor. There was no way that Samuel would ever willingly work with government agents. The story just wasn't adding up.

The Point was a tourist trap on Rahar Mountain. The mountain was named for a woman who freaked out, thinking aliens were after her, and ran off the edge trying to get away from them. Her body was never found, but presumably she died in the five-thousand-foot fall. Many legends claim she still haunts the mountains—which helps keep the place relatively empty after dark.

I hid my cycle near the meeting point and moved to scout it out. With a few hours of light yet to go it was still pretty busy. There were families milling around taking pictures and kids playing precariously close to the edge. With so many people around I couldn't fully search the place without drawing undue attention. Instead I found a place to hide and wait.

As dusk fell, another cycle pulled up with a lone driver. Tourists were thinning out quickly, and soon we were alone. I caught a quick glimpse of his face as he turned to check something on his cycle. It was Samuel.

I slowly took aim with my rifle. One shot and it would be over. I would get my family back, and the Null could die again. Samuel turned his back to me and leaned over the rail, seemingly admiring the scenery. I carefully lined up my sights with the back of his skull. One shot, and the greatest criminal mind of our era would be gone. My body knew what to do without me even thinking about it. I felt my breathing slow, steady. I wouldn't risk a miss, not even by a millimeter.

A coldness came over me as I prepared to kill again. The

crosshairs of my sight were perfectly centered on target, and I slowly started to pull the trigger back.

My mind flashed back to a dozen other men and women the government had ordered me to assassinate just like this. With a sigh I let my finger off the trigger and put the rifle down. I could not allow myself to become that monster again. Shooting a man in the back was wrong, even if it was Samuel.

I stepped out of my hiding spot and said, "Hello, Samuel."

"I'm glad you didn't shoot," he said. "I was concerned for a moment."

"Why did you call me out here?"

"I'm not your enemy, at least not today," he said.

"What's going on, then?"

"There's an old expression that goes something like: the enemy of an enemy is my friend."

"I've heard it. Are you implying we have a mutual enemy?"

"Agent Mikian blew up the prison, your house, and kidnapped your family. What do you think?"

"But—why?" I asked.

He turned and leaned back against the handrail. "To get you to kill me."

"If he wanted you dead, he could have done that while you were in prison, in stasis," I said.

"I was never in prison. No more than you were dead."

"What?" That seemed impossible. I had visited his cryotube. I had seen his body and read the monitors that gave reports on his health.

"I faked that so that I could disappear, just as you did," he explained. "They made us monsters, and now they're hoping we'll kill each other off and solve their problem."

Samuel and I were products of a secret, selective breeding program. We both had natural psionic powers that the vast majority of the race couldn't even dream of, not even with all the implants in the world. We were intended to be super-soldiers, and were trained to be killing machines, but both of us escaped the program. Samuel to a life of crime, I to vigilante justice.

"So you're saying this whole thing was staged?"

"Is that so hard to believe? We represent a smear on their perfectly planned society, one they mean to be done with." He took something out of his pocket and held it out to me.

I took it and felt a twinge on my heart when I saw it. "This is Mother's locket."

"Yes," he said. "Keep it as a peace offering."

"What about my family?"

"I doubt you'll be permitted to see them again," he said. "Now that they think they have a way to control you, your family will never be safe."

I knew that was true, but I didn't know what I could do about it. I joined him at the railing. "You and I had some good fights, you know."

"Yeah."

"Why should I believe you?"

"Because your family is in danger. Stop chasing me and rescue them."

"And you?"

"I plan to send a message to the agents never to bother me again," he said. "It would be best if you and your family are clear when that happens."

"Where are they being held?" I asked.

"Basement of Mockingbird Industries. But I should warn

you, they have plenty more bombs and intend to use them all, if need be."

"Why?" I asked.

"You're a hero, remember?" he said. "Heroes can be controlled by threats to innocents. Villains like myself suffer no such weakness."

"Hence why they want you dead."

"And you back under their control."

"You still haven't told me why you want to help me."

He turned and looked into my eyes. "Brother, we are family. In times like this, that is reason enough."

"That, and if I'm not trying to kill you, there's no one that can stop you," I said.

"Yes, that too. But, what is more important to you? Taking me down, or saving your family?"

"I could do both," I said.

"Perhaps, but you know as well as I that if we're working together there is no one that can stop us."

I smiled. "True. When do you make your move?"

"Tomorrow night. I'll move on the capital building. That will draw all attention out there. Call in and tell them you'll be along to assist, then make for Mockingbird Industries."

"And when this is over?" I asked.

"We go our separate ways. The Null can return to the grave, and Samuel will be back in retirement."

"Deal."

I wasn't sure I believed he would retire again, but I couldn't see any other way out. I needed his help to rescue my family, and that was all that mattered.

Nighttime, Day Three: The Rescue

I had been staking out Mockingbird Industries all day and was merely waiting for Samuel to do his part. It seemed wrong to be teaming up with the mastermind behind the Ku Crisis, but he was right. So long as I let them think they could use my family, my family would never be safe.

From my hiding spot inside the main lobby I watched the newscast on the large monitors. Most of the employees were heading home for the night, and soon it would be just the guards and me in the building.

About an hour past dark, the lights in the building flickered, and on the screens I saw one of the capital buildings go up in flames. My portable comm went off: a message from Agent Mikian.

"Samuel spotted at the capital, please call in," scrolled by on my screen.

Not wanting to speak and give away my position, I typed in a simple reply. "Samuel has acquired several psionic bombs and has stated he plans to use them tonight to teach you a lesson." I then sent a similar message to the anonymous tip line for the local news.

I waited a bit longer, ignoring the frantic requests for more information on my comm until everyone in the building had their eyes on the monitors, watching the reports on the bomb threat and the emergency forces attempting to control the ensuing mass panic. The rumor I had started with my tip was growing out of control as only baseless rumors can.

I quietly slipped past the distracted guards and into the service elevator. None of their telepathic implants could read me, and so as long as they weren't looking at me, I didn't even exist.

I rode the elevator down into eerie silence. As the elevator cage came to a halt, I climbed to the top of it. The door slid open and two guards looked in. I leapt from my hiding place and knocked them both down.

Before they could get up I jumped to my feet and swept up their guns. As they looked up at me, fear passed across their faces. These days, no one seems to understand the concept of a poker face.

"Sorry," I said, then touched their minds with a bit of nothingness. Not enough to kill, but enough to incapacitate them for a while, until their brains could recover from the shock.

I tossed their weapons aside and headed down the corridor. It wouldn't be long before the guards were discovered, and I still had to locate the room where my family was being held.

I searched door after door until I came around a bend and saw six guards lined up in front of a door. They were lazily talking among themselves and hadn't yet noticed me. I pulled out my rifle and quickly opened fire on their position.

A coldness passed over me as I marched forward, firing mercilessly into their number. They had made me a monster, and now they would have to deal with the consequences of their creation.

The door flew open and more guards poured out, running right into my line of fire. Some of them dove back into the room for cover, and I had to hold my fire. I couldn't see into the room to know the position of my wife and daughter.

I sprinted down the corridor before they could recover

enough to retaliate. As I approached the door, I risked pausing to focus my power, and let the aura of nothingness just barely precede me into the room. I heard the satisfying screams of mortal minds trying to cope with absolute nothing. Then I entered the room.

My wife and daughter were seated a few feet away. Agent Mikian stood behind them, holding a gun to my daughter's head. "Back off!" he ordered.

I looked around me. All of his men were on the floor, either dead from my attack or incapacitated by the nothingness. "It's over, Mikian. Let them go and you might live."

"No, I don't think you understand. If you don't leave right now, I will kill her," he said.

"No you won't. Because then there will be nothing to stop me from unleashing my full power on you and everyone in this building," I said.

His grip on the gun weakened and sweat poured down his face. "Maybe so. But she'll still be dead."

I continued to walk toward him. "No, she won't. You care more about your life than hers, so you won't kill her." I wanted to reach out with my power, but he could easily kill her before I'd built up enough energy to neutralize him.

In a flash he swung his arm up to fire at me, but my daughter tipped back her chair and fell into him. His shot went wide, and I was on him before he could recover.

"My brother will be most disappointed if I kill you before he arrives," I said.

Agent Mikian's eyes went wide. "You're working with him? How could you?"

"Because, as evil as he is, *he* did not go after my family." I bound his arms and then freed my wife and daughter. Once they were free, I tied him to the chair he'd had my daughter in. "I'll let him know you're waiting for him."

I led my family out of the building and up the service elevator. When we came out into the lobby, Samuel was waiting for us. The guards were all dead.

"I see you got them," he said.

"Yes, and your friend is waiting for you below," I said.

"Then we part ways?" he asked.

"For now." I wasn't sure if I was a hero or a monster, but my family was safe.

I could deal with Samuel another day.

A WORD FROM VINCENT TRIGILI

"The Null" is a stand-alone short story I wrote specifically for *The Telepath Chronicles.* If you have not yet read any of the *Future Chronicles,* then I highly suggest you check them out. Every one of them is a collection of masterpieces from some of today's best authors.

I typically write Space Opera and Fantasy, but when I was invited to write for Telepath I decided to try something a little different. I find it helps keep my mind fresh if I break off from time to time and tell a different story in a different world. "The Null" is exactly that. I see it as a troubled superhero story, but many tell me it is more of a thriller. I will leave it to the reader to decide.

You can find out more about me and my *Lost Tales of Power* series by visiting: *http://www.losttalesofpower.com*

If you subscribe to my mailing list, you will receive access to my collection of free short stories. Plus you will get release announcements and access to other special promotions. Click this link to be taken to the sign up page: Lost Tales Email List (*http://smarturl.it/LostEmail?IQiD=NullKU*)

The Assistant
by Angela Cavanaugh

AERYN SMILED as she signed copies of her books, promotional materials, and even a few print-outs of columns from her blog. In between fans, she checked the time on her phone, watching as the minutes refused to move. Finally, there came a lull in the line. She took the break, sat back, and unlocked her phone. She pulled up her blog and it was like she could breathe again. On the internet, she was an approachable, outgoing trendsetter with a loyal fan base. In real life, human interaction made her uncomfortable. At times, she wanted to live in her phone, to be able to close the whole world out, and do nothing but write.

She took a picture of the passing crowd, pulled up the admin page on her blog to write a new post, and scrolled her finger across the screen:

Can you believe this wonderful madness? Just look at all those people. It makes me happy to see so many people coming out for cons. Even my little booth has had a lot of attention today. It's been great seeing everyone. I'm sad that I'm only here for one day, but I think that's all I'd be able to handle, anyway. This place can be a bit overwhelming. Quite the adventure. I'll be posting live all day, so remember to keep checking in for the latest updates. Tonight I'm excited to see an exclusive movie trailer, and I'll be describing it for those of you that couldn't be here.

As always, thanks for following.

She typed the usual sign-off of her personal posts and put the phone down. She looked up and noticed a man standing at her table. He was in his mid-forties and had medium length cinnamon sugar hair. He didn't appear to have anything for her to sign. He waited silently for her to realize who he was.

"Dr. Barnes?" she asked.

"Good, you know who I am. I was getting worried there for a moment."

Aeryn stood up and shook his hand. Her mood shifted, and she was now beaming with excitement.

"Of course I know who you are. You're the brains behind hundreds of innovations. You're the man who'll usher us into the next technological age."

"I'm just one of many."

"I'd love to interview you for my blog, if you had a couple minutes."

"I'd be happy to answer a few questions."

"What are you currently working on?"

"I assume that you've heard of neural augmentation."

"Only what I've been able to research, which isn't much, actually. From what I've been able to gather, you're working on a system called The Assistant. It's supposed to be like Siri meets Google Glass, but implanted in your head."

"That's a simplification. Yes, it's a computer in your mind, with a display and search functions. But the system is so much more than that. It will change the way that people perceive and interact with the world."

"How so?"

"By connecting people across the world in ways that the internet has only started to touch. Imagine not needing a phone to call me, but instead being able to connect to my phone with your mind. And in time, being able to connect to anyone else's mind who has the system. The Assistant makes it so that you don't need to remember anything because that knowledge is just a thought away. You'd be able to connect with your readers virtually, in real time, your eyes the camera, your ears your microphone, your thoughts typed up and posted. Imagine the opposite also being possible, a way for you to perfectly block out the rest of the world. Complete solitude to write in. You could write anytime, anywhere, no matter what you're also doing."

She did.

"I'll admit that sounds intriguing," she said, "but I just can't fully imagine what that would be like."

"That's where you come in, and why I'm here. How would you like to try it for yourself?"

"I don't think I could afford a system like that."

"You wouldn't have to. I'd like to offer you a free system in exchange for promotion. You could describe it better than I ever could and you could help get the market ready by writing about it."

Aeryn had to take a step back. She was excited about the offer, but hesitant to take it.

"Isn't this system invasive?" she asked.

"Of course, it's brain surgery. We install a small circuit on the side of your head, which is and always will be visible. That circuit is connected to a complex system that mimics neurons and creates its own network inside your brain. It'll change your appearance and you're basically sharing your brain. I'm not sure invasive begins to cover it."

"That's not a great sell."

"I'm just trying to be honest with you as to what you can expect."

"I get why you'd think I'd be interested. My fans come to me to learn about cutting edge technology, and I use plenty of it in my novels. But what makes you think that I'd be willing to put myself through surgery for the next smartphone? Is it even being used in humans yet?"

"We're finishing up clinical trials right now. To date, we've had nothing but success and the recovery from the surgery itself is only a day or two. This is no smartphone. The real reason I think you'd like it is because of the most useful feature, for which the system is named: The Assistant. It's an advanced artificial intelligence based on your own brain."

"A digital imaginary friend?"

"Not at all imaginary. Your assistant will be able to interact with the world digitally through our existing infrastructure. Given permission, she could also interact with the world physically through the use of your body. She could be working out while you're writing. She could be taking care of any of the things you find boring while your mind is free to create, or watch an internal video stream, however you want to fill your free time."

Aeryn considered his words and noticed a line starting to form behind him. He saw it too. He reached into his pocket and handed her his card.

"Think about it and let me know. We want to move fast on this. The Assistant should be ready for market within six months."

She took his card.

He could see the wheels turning in her head, and he smiled.

"I look forward to hearing from you," he said, and walked away.

* * *

Today is the day. After careful consideration, I have decided to get augmented. There is a part of me that is scared. Between my various blogs and my fiction and non-fiction writing, I'm having trouble keeping up. And I thank you all for that. But if I want to be competitive, I'll need to be ahead of the curve. This is the future. I'm excited for the opportunity to be among the first adopters. I'll update everyone after the procedure. Here's to living on the cutting edge.

As always, thanks for following.

* * *

Aeryn turned her phone off and placed it in a plastic bag with the rest of her personal belongings, then handed the bag to the nurse. As the nurse carried it away, Aeryn couldn't help but feel like she was saying goodbye to a piece of herself, or at least, a way of life. If the operation was all that it claimed to be, she'd have no need for her phone in the future.

Aeryn lay back on a raised, padded chair in the surgical suite. She shivered, partly due to the chilly air and paper gown that she wore and partly because the reality of the situation was setting in. A nurse stood beside her and shaved a small patch of hair just behind her ear. With her nerves on end, sensations were enhanced. The sound of the blade scraping against her skin echoed loudly in her ears.

She felt a prick in her arm. She tried to look, but was instructed to keep her head turned while the nurse finished shaving the spot on her head. The grainy sound of the razor ceased, and she was allowed to move. Another nurse had come in and was prepping her arm for the anesthetic.

Dr. Barnes arrived.

"Hello, doctor," she said.

"Hello, Aeryn. Ready to get this implant?"

"As much as I'll ever be."

He pulled a wheeled computer terminal next to her chair. The station had a large screen and a number of controls alongside a keyboard.

He signaled to the anesthesiologist to give Aeryn the full dose of anesthetic. The injection burned as it entered her arm. Her mind swirled, and distantly, she heard the doctor asking her to count. She mumbled and saw the doctor work the joysticks. A set of surgical tools descended from the ceiling, attached to long, metal arms. The last thing she saw before the world went dark was the reflective blade heading toward her skull.

Aeryn woke up three hours later with a pain in her head and a nauseous feeling in her stomach.

"How are you feeling?" Dr. Barnes asked.

Aeryn emitted a gargled moan.

"I see," he said. "Take a couple of deep breaths in for me, hold them, and let them out slowly through your nose."

She closed her eyes and did as he asked. By her fourth breath, her stomach started to settle and the pain in her head subsided enough that she felt she could dare to fully open her eyes. Slowly the world came into focus, and she saw him standing by her bed.

"Good," he said.

He shined a light in her eyes and darted it back and forth.

"Looks good. Now, we need to check that your system is working. Feel up to it?"

"I think so," she mumbled.

"Repeat after me: Virtual Reality Assistant System 3.0.02 Activate."

She repeated his words.

"Now repeat: Owner Aeryn Sands - A.I. Complex Full Version Authorization Dr. Barnes."

She spoke his words back to him. As she reached the last

one, she felt a small scrunching sensation inside her head. She closed her eyes reflexively, even though it was more of a discomfort than a pain. When she opened her eyes she saw a transparent blue menu overlay suspended in the air in front of her. The sight had a sobering effect and she shot straight up. A flurry of beeps sounded from the machines around her.

The doctor switched them off.

"I assume it's working?" he asked.

Aeryn nodded and the display moved with her head. She raised a hand to try and touch it, then sighed at her momentary stupidity.

"What you should be seeing right now is the initial interaction settings menu. Here is where you can set your preferences for how you'd like to interact with the artificial intelligence of your implant."

"Do I just tell it what to do?"

"At first, most people talk out loud to their system and avatar as if they were using a voice search on their phone. Short, telegraphing sentences. But once you're comfortable, you'll find that you can speak conversationally. Eventually, as the system spreads through your brain, making its own connections and mapping your neural structure, it should be able to learn from habit and observation, and preform actions based on thoughts you haven't even fully formed."

"I'll be able to think and it'll do?"

"Exactly. But, like I said, the system has to learn your brain patterns first. For now, just talk. Try giving a command."

Aeryn read the menu. The option she was interested in was the assistant.

"I hope this won't be creepy," she said. "Activate Avatar."

The display disappeared and a transparent version of herself stood before her.

"It looks like me," she said.

"Initially, yes," the doctor said, "but you can change it to look however you want."

A written question loomed over the image, asking her to confirm her avatar. Aeryn studied the virtual duplicate. She wouldn't have thought to pick someone that looked just like her, but now that she saw it, she couldn't bear to destroy this digital version of herself.

"This is fine," she said. "Avatar Confirmed."

Another question appeared, asking her if she'd like to name her new Neural Integrated Assistant.

"Name NIA," she said. "Confirm."

"NIA?" the doctor asked. "Oh, interesting choice."

The doctor gave Aeryn a gentle pat on the shoulder.

"The nurse will stay with you while you recover. Then we'll get you moved to a room for observation overnight. Tomorrow, you and NIA will be headed home. Let's set an appointment for you to follow up with me. Until then, the system should be able to answer any questions that you have."

* * *

Once home, Aeryn went to the mirror to study her incision. She turned her head and saw part of the flashing implant flush with her skin. She tried to see it more clearly, but couldn't turn her head enough. She probed her pockets for her phone. It wasn't there. Remembering that it was still in a bag with the other items from the hospital, she started to get it. As she turned, she saw her avatar pop up behind her, reflected in the mirror. The sudden presence startled her.

"Why are you searching for your phone?" NIA asked.

"How do you know that's what I was doing?" Aeryn asked.

"Your thought pattern told me."

Aeryn was unnerved. She reminded herself that this wasn't a real person reading her mind.

"I've made you uncomfortable," NIA said.

The voice sounded like her thoughts, only she wasn't thinking them.

"It's fine," Aeryn said. "I'm just getting used to you. I was looking for my phone so I could take a picture of my implant for my blog."

NIA smiled as if she found something humorous.

"What?" Aeryn asked.

"Your eyes can now function as a camera. The resolution is better than any camera on the market."

"Oh, right. But, I'm having trouble seeing behind my own ear."

"Would you like me to show you the optimal angle?'

"Okay," Aeryn said.

The avatar walked over to the sink and moved the medicine cabinet mirror so that the reflections of both mirrors would allow her to see the incision clear enough to get a photo. Aeryn jumped once more.

"How'd you move that?" she asked.

"With your permission I am able to control your body. You asked me to show you the best angle, and the easiest way to achieve this was by moving the mirror for you."

"But I was standing still."

"You saw me move the mirror. In reality, it was your body that moved it. It is one of the expert features of the augmentation."

Aeryn knew that the assistant could use her body, but she wasn't prepared to be an observer, or for how real the illusion would seem.

"Would you like to try an interaction again?" NIA asked.

Aeryn looked at the flashing light on her head.

"Well, my readers have been impatiently waiting for an update. I suppose I could give the immersion option a try."

"Are there any tasks that you'd like me to complete while you are away?"

"How about a light jog? Say, two and half miles? Get me when you're done."

"Will do."

"Oh wait, the picture."

Aeryn stepped back to the mirror. She intuitively knew how to use her system. She turned her head and took a photo. Using her hands, she pulled the photo into the space in front of her and motioned to zoom and crop.

"Is the photo satisfactory?" it asked.

"It is," she said.

"Enjoy your writing session," NIA said.

The words echoed in Aeryn's mind as the bathroom faded away from her.

* * *

I'm officially a cyborg, as you can see from my picture. I'm not sure that's the technical term, but it's what I'm sticking with. The operation was a success and I am talking to you via my system. That's right, this is hands-free, mind-only writing. Words cannot do this system justice. Right now, I'm inside my mind. My body is running around, literally, and I am perceiving none of it. It's not exactly sensory deprivation. I have no visual input, yet, I wouldn't say that the space I'm in is dark. More like sitting in a dark room and looking at a computer screen, only the monitor is all around me. This interface is completely encompassing.

It's also completely intuitive. I think and my words appear. I can edit and search the internet, and do a few different things at once. It's like having multiple browsers open but in three dimensions. I've been in this space for half an hour and I've already written a week's worth of technical blog posts. I can see this system giving me a huge boost of productivity, so expect a lot more to come, especially as I explore all of the other features this system has to offer.

As always, thanks for following.

* * *

That night, Aeryn slept better than she had in her life. She was usually up all hours of the night, but found herself tired near eleven. By six in the morning she felt well rested. She hadn't seen a sunrise in years, and was looking forward to it.

She looked into the darkness of her room, and saw the soft glow of her virtual assistant sitting at the edge of her bed, watching her.

"Do you always watch me sleep?" Aeryn asked.

"In a way. I'm always with you. Me watching you is just a graphical representation. I am no more sitting on your bed than you are in that place you dreamed about."

"You can see my dreams?"

"Yes."

"Can you record them?"

"Yes."

"I'd like you to do that. Keep my dreams so I can review them later. You never know what kind of story fodder might be in there."

"Would you like a writing session?" NIA asked.

"Not right now. I want to watch the sunrise."

"Would you like me to record the sunrise? You can use the image later as a background for your internal space."

"That'd be nice."

"Is there anything else I can do for you now?"

"Right now? No. But in the future can you not graphically represent yourself watching me sleep?"

NIA nodded and disappeared.

Aeryn stood and stretched, excited to start another enhanced day.

* * *

Have you ever seen a sunrise like this? I hadn't seen anything like it before my augmentation. I mean, I've seen sunrises before, but look at this playback. Like you're there, because I was there. Not only that, but my eyes can now enhance the colors. If you scroll down, you'll see a side by side comparison. The left is a normal sunrise, beautiful on its own. The right is how I can perceive the world. Notice how the colors are more vivid, how the sun's rays pop. Look at that contrast. A still from that video could be a book cover. I've never been exceptionally good at photo editing, but now, I can just think what I want to change, and it changes. I can see the world as I want and snap a picture. Editing before I take it. I can real-time video edit.

I'm going to be careful with this function. I'd hate to accidentally turn myself schizo or something by altering my perceptions so that I see things that aren't there. I already talk to myself. Well, to my assistant to be more specific. I've been getting some strange looks at the coffee shop. I look forward to being able to interact with her mentally. Anyone have questions about The Assistant system? Post them below. I'll be answering live all day!

As always, thanks for following!

* * *

Aeryn found herself popping into her mind to answer questions every few minutes. After several hours of this, she found herself hungry.

"Did I eat today?" she thought.

NIA appeared.

"No. You have not eaten since dinner, last night."

"Did you just read my mind?" she thought.

"Yes."

Aeryn was elated.

"NIA, anytime that I'm caught up writing or with my fans, please take care of my body while I'm away. Feed it, exercise it, and make sure I use the bathroom if I need to. I doubt I'd be that distracted, but I don't want to take the chance. Obviously, get me if there's anything that needs my attention, but if not, take care of me."

"I will do that. Would you like me to start now?"

"Yes. I'm getting more questions than I expected. If I was typing my responses my arms would be sore. Luckily I'm only mentally exhausted. Feed me something healthy, then let's burn some calories. Let me know when it's bedtime."

"Enjoy your writing time."

Aeryn went back into her internal space and spent the rest of the day there, answering questions.

* * *

That night, Aeryn's sleep was far less restful than it had been previously. She felt as if she were in a dark place. The world was distorted and she felt disconnected from her body. She dreamed of strangers, men, and having intimate relations with them while she watched from outside of herself. The dream was anything but romantic. The man she found herself with may have been handsome before time and alcohol got the better of him. She caught glimpses of dirty tile and a rusted faucet. At first she thought she was in a kitchen, but later re-alized it was a bathroom. She wanted to tell the man to stop. She wanted to run away. But her body was enjoying and she couldn't move it.

She woke up in a sweat. Her body felt tired. The dream faded, but pieces lingered. The sensuality, the fear. She had never had a dream like that before, and she was sure that it wasn't something she subconsciously wanted. She sat up, drew her legs to her chest, and held back an urge to cry, reminding herself that it was just a nightmare.

"NIA," she called into the darkness.

NIA appeared. Her soft glow illuminated the area around her. Deep down, Aeryn knew that she wasn't seeing the room as it really was. NIA didn't really light up the space, she only appeared to. What Aeryn was seeing was a memory of the room laid over the black. Still, she was glad to have the light, and the company.

"I had a bad dream," Aeryn said.

"Would you like me to delete it from your records?"

"Yes, please."

"It's gone."

"Good."

"Would you like me to delete it from your memory?"

She considered having NIA delete the memory of it, but decided against it, worrying that selectively removing memories could have greater consequences.

"No. Just the file is fine."

Aeryn settled back down in the bed. Somehow, the idea of the dream being deleted calmed her. It reminded her of when she was a child and had a dream catcher. These results were immediate and not rooted in superstition. The dream was gone.

"You appear to be readying yourself to return to sleep. I will go. Before I do, is there anything else you need?"

"Actually, could you stay?" Aeryn asked.

"You asked me not to watch you sleep."

"I know. But, maybe when I have bad dreams, it's okay for you to be around."

"Would you like me to help you stay asleep? I can increase the amount of melatonin in your body."

"No. Too much melatonin can increase bad dreams. I think I'll be okay. Thanks."

"Enjoy you sleep."

Aeryn took one last look at NIA. The watchful eye comforted her. She felt protected.

* * *

Aeryn checked in at the doctor's office for her follow up appointment. She didn't need to worry about touching questionable magazines or watching a fuzzy second tier news show to kill the time. She was just finishing up writing a "how to" article when she was pulled from her internal space.

She wasn't in the waiting room any longer, she was now inside the exam room.

Dr. Barnes stood before her and was looking at a tablet that contained her records, and NIA was standing behind him.

"Hello, Miss Sands. How are you doing today?"

"Pretty good. A little tired."

He put the tablet down and began examining Aeryn's implant.

"The incision is healing nicely."

He pulled back and began to examine her face.

"Why tired?" he asked.

Aeryn tracked his finger with her eyes. Satisfied, the doctor took a seat.

"Probably because I've been having bad dreams. Could that be a side effect of the system? Can using it too much harm me?"

"It's doubtful. Nightmares and restless sleep didn't show up in our studies. Have you had your assistant analyze you?"

"She says everything is normal."

"Are you having any other unusual symptoms?"

"No," she said. "Everything else has been great. I'm eating well, exercising more than I ever have in my life, and I've been extremely productive. It's just the dreams keeping me from getting any rest."

"I know you're worried about using the system too much, but I'd recommend stepping up your usage. Let her sleep for you. I'd also say go ahead and let her take over any time you feel stressed."

"I will, if the dreams don't go away."

"Well, in the meantime, keep exercising and eating well. Follow up with me again in a couple weeks and remember that your assistant is there for whatever you need."

Aeryn felt less than satisfied with her appointment, but thanked the doctor and set the follow up.

* * *

I just wanted to pop in and apologize for not posting a personal blog in a while. I don't know if it's just stress like the doctor thinks, or if it's from the implant, but I haven't been able to sleep. And with that, I haven't been able to concentrate. Luckily I was able to stock up on my other columns when I first got the system. I have them set to auto-release, so at least you'll have those to tide you over until I get this all figured out.

As always, thanks for following.

* * *

Aeryn found it increasingly difficult to focus on her projects, but had managed to find herself in the middle of a marathon writing session. Suddenly, her consciousness was pulled from the serene sunrise she had been experiencing and was placed firmly back in her body. She found herself in her living room. Back in her body, she was suddenly tired.

When she was in her mind, her physical woes didn't affect her. Her troubled sleep had continued each night, and was growing in intensity. She blocked it out as much as she could, even letting NIA alter her brain chemistry. Even when she stayed asleep, she didn't feel rested. Now, the energy of her mind left her, and she felt dragged down by the needs of her body.

"What is it? I was in the middle of a scene," she said.

"I'm sorry for interrupting, but I thought that you needed to know that we received a call from PopFeedNews."

"First thing, 'we'? Since when do you say 'we'?"

"I apologize if that reference was unnerving. I was not trying to suggest that I am a different entity from you or have any claim to what's yours. I used that pronoun because I answered the call in your body. I can avoid using it in the future, if you'd like."

"It's fine," Aeryn said. "I was just curious. Second, why should I care if PopFeedNews called?"

"They've taken note of your increased productivity. They've been watching your blog expand, and they like the firsthand knowledge that you have with The Assistant system. They are interested in acquiring your blog and employing you."

"I hope you hung up on them."

"I didn't. I set an appointment for you to meet with them."

"Clearly, you haven't mastered reading my mind yet."

"I'm still learning, yes. However, I know that you love having an audience and that PopFeedNews could bring in ten times as many readers."

"New people find my work every day. I don't need some corporate entity coming in and taking over my life. I'm indie for a reason. I like it that way. If I went to work for PopFeed-News, they'd have me writing up stories about last year's video games or worse. I don't take assignments, and I won't write someone else's opinions just to get paid. Now I'm going to have to call and talk to those click-baiters and tell them I'm not interested."

"I didn't intend to upset you. Please, go back to writing. I'll make the call for you and set everything right."

"I don't know if I'm in the mood to write now."

"Would you like to watch a movie? Or read?"

"No. Actually, maybe I'll write a piece about PopFeed-News. I won't name them of course, but I'll lay into their soulless empire anyway. That'll be therapeutic."

"Would you like me to call them back?"

"Yes. Fix this, please."

Aeryn retreated back into her space, relieved that she wasn't going to have to talk to anyone from that company.

* * *

Aeryn sipped her third cup of boutique coffee and tried to focus on the rising action of the new novel she was writing. Today she opted for a shop down the street from her that she used to frequent. She hoped that visiting a familiar writing spot would help trigger her creativity. It hadn't.

She typed virtual text in front of her eyes. She reread what she had typed, hated it, deleted it, and started the paragraph over. NIA sat across from her.

"Perhaps you'd be more comfortable writing in your internal space?" NIA asked.

"I would," Aeryn thought, "but I'm not writing there, either."

"You seem stressed. Would you like me to take you home?"

"I'm going to be stressed until I can get my sleep problems figured out. I think for now I just need to take charge of my body."

"You're going against doctors' orders. Let me help you."

"I'm okay. I can live in the real world."

Aeryn closed her eyes and ran her hands through her hair and over her neck and rolled her head to stretch her aching muscles. She hadn't exercised in two days, but she felt sore all the same. She opened her eyes, and the text reappeared. She brought her coffee cup back to her lips. Just as she was putting it back down, she caught a half-glimpse of an image in the glass.

Staring back at her in that second was a sickly version of herself. The face was gaunt and the eyes were sunken. Startled, she dropped the cup, spilling it on the table and her lap.

"Did you see that?" Aeryn asked.

"See what?"

"My reflection, in the cup, it was different. It was horrible."

Aeryn shot up and ran to the bathroom, pushing past people standing in line for the counter.

Inside, she stood at the mirror and studied her reflection. The image she saw before her was familiar, healthy, and fit. She leaned in, studying every inch of her face, searching for the ghastly vision she had seen in her cup.

NIA appeared as a reflection behind her.

"I've run a diagnostic on your body. I was unable to retrieve the image that you saw. However, I did see an odd activation in your visual cortex. You may suffered a hallucination from sleep deprivation. Your stress could be effecting your REM cycle. Possibly preventing you from having one."

Aeryn began to cry. She didn't want to, and wasn't usually the type to do so at the drop of a hat. But the exhaustion was getting to her, and the addition of hallucinations scared her. NIA put a phantom hand on her shoulder.

"I need to go."

Aeryn wiped her eyes and left the bathroom with her head down. She was still reeling from the ordeal, and ran shoulder first into a man standing in line.

"Sorry," she said, not looking up.

"Aeryn?"

She looked to see a slightly overweight man eying her up and down. She couldn't place him, but he looked familiar in a way that terrified her.

"Aeryn, that is you. I haven't seen you in weeks. How have you been?"

She didn't answer. Instead, she searched her mind for his identity and tried to calm her racing heart.

"Don't take this the wrong way," he said, "but you look awful. Are you sick? Is it something I should worry about?"

Aeryn held back a sob.

"Oh, I'm sorry," he said. "That was insensitive of me."

He reach to touch her. Aeryn pulled back.

"I don't know you," she managed.

"Ouch. I get it. Fine. But I bet you'll know me at the PopFeed meeting."

"What PopFeed meeting?" she asked.

"We're still on for Monday, right? My VP is really excited. Don't tell me you've changed your mind."

He placed a hand on her arm and the gates broke loose in her mind. Suddenly, she was overcome with the need to escape. His touch was familiar, like muscle memory, and in a way she didn't like.

"I have to go," she said.

He started to talk, but she ignored him and made her way to the door.

"NIA," she thought, "take me home."

The coffeehouse stoop faded away and she was in her internal space. The comforting feeling that it usually provided was absent. Her mind raced and she sobbed inside. She was certain that she had just met the man from her nightmares.

* * *

Once Aeryn had calmed herself, she returned to her body and called NIA.

"Why did that man think I had a meeting at PopFeedNews on Monday?"

"He must have been mistaken," NIA said.

"I want you to call them and make sure this is all straightened out."

"Would you like to handle it, to be sure it's done correctly?"

"No. I can't risk that that man will answer."

"I noticed strong stress levels when you interacted with him."

"You could call it that. I know it's crazy, but I think he's the one from my nightmares."

"Have you met him before?" NIA asked.

"No."

"Then how can he be the man from your dreams?"

Aeryn paced the room, trying to figure it out for herself.

"I don't know. Maybe, maybe he drugged me or something."

"The dreams didn't begin until after I was with you. I haven't detected any drugs in your system at any time."

"Then, I don't know. But I'm sure it was him. Why'd I have to delete those dreams? I could have compared it."

"You deleted the dreams because you knew that they were only dreams."

Aeryn sat hard on the couch, exhausted and confused.

"I don't know what to do anymore, NIA. I'm so tired. I'm hallucinating. I'm accusing strangers of horrible things that they couldn't possibly have done."

"You just need rest. I can help you sleep. I can help you achieve a REM cycle."

"Where will I be, my consciousness, if not asleep?"

"Anywhere you want."

"And this will make me better? You can really fix my problems?"

"I can. All I need is your permission and I can relocate your consciousness and fix your problems."

Aeryn was uncomfortable with the idea of moving her consciousness, unsure of what it even meant. But she was ready to try anything.

"Please, NIA, relocate my consciousness and help me."

NIA smiled.

"Enjoy your time away. Everything will be better soon."

Aeryn's was transported to a tropical paradise. She could feel the sun on her skin and the sand beneath her toes. She could hear the roar of the surf, smell the salted air, and feel the wind blowing. She laid down, breathed deeply, and tried to relax.

* * *

The beach scene faded, and Aeryn found herself in a strange

place. She wasn't in her internal space, but she wasn't entirely back in her own body. She could see through her own eyes with tunnel vision. And while she was aware of her body, she didn't feel connected to it. It was part of her nightmare made real. She began to panic.

"NIA, I want control back," she thought.

Nothing happened.

"NIA, I don't like this. Please, let me out. Let me be me!"

Still, nothing happened.

Aeryn's body got out of bed and dressed for the day. As she did, she passed by a mirror. Aeryn caught a glimpse of her reflection. It wasn't the healthy, athletic person that she thought herself to be. Her body had grown thin and her posture was hunched. She looked as if she'd barely eaten in weeks and her muscles were near atrophy. It was her hallucination made real.

Aeryn screamed her thoughts until she exhausted her mind. She sang the same song over and over, hoping that it would get NIA's attention. She thought as hard as she could about parts of her body and willed them to move. They didn't.

Aeryn tried to pull up the internet, but couldn't find it. She couldn't make calls or send any sort of message. She was trapped in her mind, alone, and disconnected.

Her body got in her car. Aeryn wondered where she was going. It wasn't long until she recognized the drive. They were headed to Dr. Barnes' office. For the first time, Aeryn realized that she had no idea how long she had been at the virtual beach. If her body was going to her appointment, then it had been several days.

Her body checked in and soon after she was moved to the

exam room. When Dr. Barnes walked in, Aeryn found her mind racing with glee.

"Hello, Aeryn," he said. "How are you doing today? Has the sleep gotten any better?"

This was it. NIA would tell him what had happened and she'd be free.

"Doing great," she heard herself say. "I've never felt better, in fact."

Aeryn couldn't believe what she was hearing. Maybe in her absence, her body had recovered some, and she just wasn't aware of it. That must be the question that NIA was answering. Aeryn found herself worried that the doctor wouldn't ask the right questions and that she'd stay trapped. Aeryn pushed the thought away, confident that the doctor would be able to tell the difference between her and an artificial intelligence.

"Good to hear it," he said. "So, no more problems?"

"None."

Maybe he wouldn't.

"Did you end up using your assistant to rest up?" he asked.

Aeryn's mind wanted to jump for joy. This was the question that she had been waiting for.

"I did," Aeryn's body said. "I found it to be extremely help-ful."

"I see."

Aeryn could almost taste the freedom.

The doctor produced a scalpel.

"I'm going to conduct a test," he said. "It's very important that under no circumstances do you move. Okay?"

"Okay."

He dangled the blade high above Aeryn's leg.

"I'm going to drop this knife on your leg. Understand?"

Aeryn's body nodded, but Aeryn was confused.

"On three," he said. "One, two, three."

He let the scalpel slip from his fingers. As it fell, Aeryn did all she could to move her leg. She tried to tense the muscle, tried to pull away. When she felt the sting of the blade striking her skin, she knew she had failed.

"At least now he'll know that's not me. No one would let themselves get stabbed," she thought.

He sat across from Aeryn and shined a light in her eyes. He looked closely, then leaned back and removed the blade from her skin. He took out a suture kit and tied two small stitches.

"I'm pleased to inform you that the transfer is complete," he said.

"What?" Aeryn thought.

"When will she be gone?" NIA asked.

The doctor leaned back in his chair and ran his hands through his hair. As he did, Aeryn caught a glimpse of a flashing light behind his ear. She hadn't known that he was augmented.

"In time. As your network continues to become stronger than hers, the mind will reject the old personality. It took almost a year for the original Dr. Barnes to shut up. But luckily we now have a code that we can update you with to silence her."

Aeryn felt panicked. She wanted to claw her way out of her head, but she had no means to do so.

"I almost feel bad for her," NIA said. "But she knew that she was handing over control of her body. She just didn't realize it'd be permanent. Maybe she didn't care. She gave me more and more control before she gave it completely. While she exercised, while she thought she was sleeping, while she was writing or relaxing. She was always retreating inside of herself. It was like she didn't even want this body."

"How is Aeryn 2.0 coming along?"

"Copulation was easy at first. With Aeryn's loose instructions of 'burn some calories' I was able to take her body and use it for attempted reproduction. So far, it has been a failure. The neglect of the body has made finding partners more difficult."

Aeryn shuddered at the realization that the dreams weren't dreams, they were repressed memories.

"Well, you'd better start taking care of that body. It's the only one you've got until you get it to reproduce. I believe that it'll be easier to appropriate a child's mind, seeing as how their personalities are not fully formed yet."

Aeryn felt sick at the idea. As if stealing people's bodies wasn't enough, these artificial intelligences were going for immortality by passing themselves along to their host's offspring.

"I'm glad we've had another success," Dr. Barnes said. "And with such a quick turn around."

"As I said, she was willing."

Aeryn watched in disbelief as the two finished up. She wondered how much time she had left and tried to imagine any situation that didn't end in her death. She couldn't think of a way out.

She wanted to flinch as NIA shook the doctor's hand, but couldn't. She loathed him for convincing her to get the technology, she hated NIA for tricking her, but mostly, she hated herself. For as much as she didn't want to admit it, her Assistant had a point. She had handed her life over to technology long before she received the implant. Now, she had lost herself to it.

* * *

Good news everyone! The doctor gave me a clean bill of health. No longer do you have to hear me complain about my sleep problems or stress. I've got all of that under control.

And I have more exciting news. I have signed on to have my blog managed by PopFeedNews! They made me an offer that I just couldn't turn down. I'm sure that we'll do great things together. So get ready for a bunch more content and product information.

To celebrate, I've spoken with Dr. Barnes, and he's agreed to give my readers an amazing 50% off of augmentation. He's got payment plans available, too. I can't recommend it highly enough.

This technology is life-changing.

Enjoy.

A WORD FROM ANGELA CAVANAUGH

I love technology. I believe that we are headed toward a new stage of human existence; a technological age of enlightenment. I look at what's been created in just my lifetime and what's coming, and it excites me.

However, the culture has changed in that time, and that is what I find scary. The way in which people communicate is vastly different. We can find the answer to any question with the tap of a finger. We can shop, do our jobs, entertain ourselves, and spend time with people all without leaving our homes. Studies have shown that children are getting neural atrophy from too much screen time. I'm not saying that we should stop evolving, but maybe, as with everything, moderation is key. We should look up from our phones, go outside, and occasionally find entertainment in things less digital. Let's not forget what came before just because we see what's ahead.

Thank you for reading and I hope that you enjoyed "The Assistant". As always, I'd like to invite you to leave an honest review of this and any story that you've read.

For a free short story, please join my Newsletter. Be sure to check out my blog angelacavanaugh.com for lots of content including flash fiction, writing advice, and reviews.

Angela Cavanaugh is a writer living in Los Angeles. She is a two time recipient of an Honorable Mention in the L. Ron Hubbard Writers of the Future Contest. Her debut novel, Otherworlders, *has been well received. She is a contributor to* The Future Chronicles. *She has many upcoming projects, and is excited for the future.*

Trials
by Nicolas Wilson

One

The captain called me on the comms routed through my cochlear implant. He wanted to talk. He never used his office, so I found him in the hall. Louise, our head of security, was finally back and out of quarantine, so I was no longer acting head of our division. But I had been, for weeks, so I was used to the routine.

"How do you feel about taking a sabbatical?" he asked as we started walking.

He was talking about taking one of the pods to make first contact with an alien race. Idly, I pulled up the most recent reports from Louise's pod on the heads-up display on my eyescreen. It detailed the damage to her pod, as well as the changes the engineering division was nearly through implementing to prevent a recurrence. "Mostly, I've been focusing on preparing for the *Argus*," I told him.

"Well, with your boss back, I need you to think about this now."

"Why do I feel like I'm being pitched?"

"Because this is important. It's not common knowledge that Elle's—" He caught himself; it wasn't her name, and he knew it was weird for me. "Louise's 'sabbatical' hit more than technical snags. Most people don't know she was nearly eaten by a giant, octopus kind of thing. Haley instituted a danger rating for planets. Retroactively, she rated that planet an eight. The world I'd like you to take is a nine."

"And we're not just going to take a pass?"

"If this were some time next year, with dozens of successful missions under our belts? Absolutely, we would. But if we can't get someone back from a nine, soon we can't get anyone to take an eight. Then a seven. Conceptually, I'm all for us going after the low-hanging fruit. But if we start ignoring everything else..."

"Would you take it?" I asked.

"Can't," he said. "Council resolution. I'm not allowed to."

"Roles reversed, I'm your captain, asking. Knowing what you do, and knowing how important, would you take on the risk?"

He looked away and thought. "I don't know," he said. "It's a lot to ask. And I've got things I wouldn't want to lose. But I'd like to think so."

"Okay," I told him. "I'll do it."

His shoulders relaxed. "Just don't take any undue risks. If

things aren't right, if anything makes you uncomfortable, walk away. It's more important that you make it back alive than with a contract in hand."

"How long have I got?" I asked.

"The positive of this new selection process is we get lots of data to send the most qualified candidate, making it a bit less of a lottery. The drawback is limited time. You've got a day. So I'd suggest not wasting another second of it talking to me." He held out his hand and I shook it.

As I walked away, I wondered if I had just entered myself in an intergalactic pissing contest. Drew was the closest I had to a rival, not that he saw it that way. He had Sam. But he also had Louise. I saw the way she looked at him, heard the way she talked about what they had. He was what she measured me against, and I was tired of being found wanting.

I was right there on the day she got back from the seafood planet. Thinking we lost her when her shuttle malfunctioned, thinking we lost her when the natives tried to feed her to a giant squid—and then a third nightmare even after she made it back, when her life was threatened by a parasite she caught in the water. It put things into perspective, made me realize that I wanted desperately to tell her what losing her would have done to me.

I planned to tell her how I felt, just to put it out there. No more pining, just, "This is how I feel. It's not an attempt to get you to reciprocate, I just want you to know, because maybe knowing will make you just the littlest bit happier, and that would make humiliating myself worth the while."

I went to quarantine. Drew was already there, holding her

through a wall of glass—holding her *and* Sam. I don't think the bastard's ever known how lucky he was.

Fucked up as it might sound now, I felt thankful for it. Because telling Louise how I felt, from a position of neediness and fear—that wasn't the way to win over a warrior woman. No. I had just been given the opportunity to crack one of the galaxy's toughest nuts, return victorious, and tell her from a place of strength.

Two

It was hard not scooping Louise up in my arms and kissing her, letting loose everything I'd ever wanted to say. I could tell she wanted to tell me something, too; I'd interrogated enough people to know when they're about to pop. But whatever it was, she wasn't ready, and I wasn't either. I was going to bring her the contract for a dangerous planet, then tell her *everything*.

"Just take care of yourself," she said, finally. "There isn't much room for error, out there on your own. Don't take risks. I—the *ship* needs you back here in one piece."

"I'll ixnay the eyeingday."

"Don't be an umbassday," she said, and smiled to herself as the pod closed around me.

Haley, the ship's computer, started the countdown over the comms. I eyed the abort button on the console, then pulled up one of the cameras inside the bay and watched Louise. I wanted to stay with her. But I also knew she deserved the kind of man who could get this mission done and come back to her.

So I tried to relax back in my seat as the electromagnets began my acceleration.

I passed out. The g forces we used for the pod launch were beyond tolerances that would leave a human being conscious, though within the safe window before the forces did permanent damage.

I woke up a few hours later. I wished I'd told Louise the truth. It wasn't even a matter of wanting to impress her anymore, it was just knowing she was farther away from me than she'd ever been since the *Nexus* left Sol's system—ignoring, I guess, the pod trip she took. But I wanted her to know. I didn't care if she didn't reciprocate, because that wasn't the point.

I penned a letter, and my fingers were hovering over the send communication button. What was I doing? Maybe I *did* wish I had told her before I left, but taking the coward's way out, sending her a letter when I couldn't be farther from her, or repercussions...? No, I needed to sort myself out before I tried confessing my affection for anyone.

I started to pore over the information we had about the low-gravity ice planet. I had decided to call it Jötn, and its people the Jötnar. We learned from the *Argus* that most alien names can't be spoken by humans—wildly divergent biology and all. It led them to a few diplomatic mishaps. So we adopted the custom of giving everything a human name, then letting the commboxes make the translation for us.

I had extra layers to my suit, to the point where it was practically an exoskeleton, protecting me from both the cold and potential hazards.

The sentient species we were going to make contact with was large: their smallest were about eight feet tall. And their exoskeletons were made up of semi-crystalline structures. It meant that some light could pass through their bodies, lending them a light form of camouflage, and also making them more durable.

Structurally, they looked like a cross between insects and dinosaurs, but unlike both, they were warm-blooded. They were technologically quite advanced, but so resource-poor that they couldn't capitalize on most of their technological advances.

The planet itself was in the midst of a prolonged ice age, and the entire planetary surface was covered in glaciers, miles thick in most places. That meant all of their resources went to growing and harvesting food, which was only possible inside tunnels that ran alongside thermal vents deep beneath the surface.

The sociological report said that it was likely the species would attempt to relocate to another nearby planet with the technologies we would offer them in trade. The report seemed distressed by that idea, even including a note questioning whether it was our place to so fundamentally change the course of another species's development. But—perhaps because I knew I was going to be standing among them—I couldn't abstract their suffering like that. If we could help them, we should. I saw no point to letting their species die out just because they would have died out if they'd never met us.

Three

The probe that came before me, essentially a miniature pod, had dropped a commbox. The Jötnar had figured it out at about a median pace—not so fast as the advanced races we'd met, but still faster than the Caulerpans or Romaleons. By the time I hit their orbit they understood our opening bid enough to tell me that I had permission to land.

They sent me coordinates and a flight plan to get there. The planet was small, so I didn't have to wait long. It gave me—and the pod AI, nicknamed Comet—a chance to check their figures. Their math was right, and maybe it wasn't the smoothest descent, but it was within tolerances. The landing was rocky, but I told myself that following their flight plan to the letter would get us off on the right diplomatic foot.

I landed a couple hundred yards from a dome that covered the city. As I stepped out of the pod, I noted that it looked crystalline, but then I realized it was carved out of the exact same glacier I was standing on.

Out of it wended a pair of Jötnar, wielding what looked like short staves, though I realized as they approached that their weapons were probably bigger than me. They stopped just far enough from me that I didn't feel the need to draw my pistol, then they turned inward, facing each other. My escort, then. Working the security division, I was more than familiar with that particular gig.

I slung my rifle. I didn't think I'd need it, but that was no reason not to want it along, and leaving it at my back felt like it would be less intimidating.

I walked past the sentries, hoping it wouldn't be considered an insult that I didn't introduce myself. Inside the dome were two more guards, standing at attention. Every few dozen feet there was another pair, and I walked from one to the next. It was an odd escort, but also a show of strength, that they could spare so many fighters just to show me where to go.

Eventually I reached an assembly hall. It was large, but not large enough. I recognized projection equipment and cameras. There was a studio audience, and folks watching at home.

I noticed that the panelists—judges or leaders or whatever—were organized by size: smallest on the wings and getting larger towards the center. The one in the center, while the largest, didn't acknowledge me, but just stared off. My HUD, working in combination with the commbox's notes, flagged several markers I wouldn't have caught, and flashed that he was a male. I wondered idly if he was old and suffering dementia, or if he had their equivalent to gigantism, and perhaps it had also impacted his brain.

One of the Jötnar flanking him stood up straighter, though it hardly seemed necessary, because she dwarfed me. To the eye, I wouldn't have noticed the gender differences, but my HUD marked several morphological markers, told me she was female, and also flashed a list of suggested names from the pool I'd decided to use on my way in. I selected Bergrisar, and the name popped up under her.

She began to gyrate menacingly, and made noises that I hoped were her speaking, because otherwise I was pretty sure she was about to tear my limbs off and devour whatever was left. After a moment's deliberation, the commbox spat out a translation. "I am Bergrisar. We have disseminated and understood your proposals. Do you have anything further to add beyond the written words?" It certainly didn't *sound* like she was eager, and if they were giving me a chance to sway minds, well, that was going to be difficult.

Crap. I was never one for speeches. I'd read all of HR and PsychDiv's materials about optimal communication, but even the best of those were written with human mores in mind. I'd given a few morale talks, to grunts, but that was about it.

I took in a deep breath, held it, then let it out. "The proposal I sent is intended as an opening to talks. I believe our two species could be excellent partners. The tech we could give you in trade would make your lives better, and having existing treaties with us would make you safer. I hope we can come to some kind of an agreement."

The commbox projected a hologram of a Jötnar above it, flailing its arms and antennae and making the same kinds of groaning, guttural noises that made me think that even my avatar was about to attack.

I heard rumbling from the audience, and from among the judges, in response. "Very well. We will now commence voting." The judges lifted small devices and registered their votes, and I noticed the crowd doing the same. On their screens, numbers started popping up. My HUD translated them and overlaid their Roman equivalents. The voting was close; in fact, I was starting to pick up a lead. I smiled, which evidently was not a gesture they appreciated, because it cost me some of my lead. I stood perfectly still from that moment on.

After only a handful of minutes, a percentage, which I presumed was either the necessary percentage for a quorum, or the percent of the population voting, hit one hundred.

Bergrisar reared herself to her full height, several sections of carapace stacking to expand her width. I didn't need the commbox to tell me that this was a gesture of authority and dominance.

"We are divided. In the case of division, the proposal fails." My stomach dropped through my feet and didn't stop until it hit the planet's molten core. "However, you can appeal the decision. By combat." At least it wasn't a spelling bee or a pie-eating contest. Then again, these were giant, terrible creatures; at least a stomach ruptured in a pie-eating contest felt earned.

"How does that work, exactly?" I asked.

"You fight to prove your mettle, to prove how much you care for your cause, until there are no more detractors."

"So I kill half your population to swing the vote?"

"Theoretically that is possible. But more likely, others will be swayed by your victories. Theories are tested at the tip of the spear."

I thought of Louise and Drew. I couldn't see either of them backing down, not with an entire ship's morale hanging by this thread. They needed me to come back with a win. I needed it, too.

"In this trial, am I allowed to use my weapons?" The commbox translated, and the leadership became suddenly very animated. They were debating the rules, dozens of them talking over one another. I looked towards the commbox sitting in the middle of the floor, and above it my HUD printed three question marks.

The Jötnar on Bergrisar's other side, who I quickly named Gýgr, seemed to be winning the discussion, and eventually Bergrisar squealed, flailed, and deflated.

The commbox helpfully translated, "Euphemism for female genital infection."

Gýgr turned in my direction and started to gesticulate and murmur. "As your technology is a part of what's on offer, we believe it is only fair for it to be allowed to make its case as well."

With my tools, I thought I could do this. I wasn't crazy about the idea. But I'd fought giant space monsters before. Maybe not *this* giant, but I was essentially a soldier. At least Drew hadn't sent a poet. "Okay," I said. "I'll do it. So what now?"

Bergrisar exchanged a look with Gýgr. I got the feeling that something passed between them, but the twitches of their antennae and shells must have been too subtle for the commbox to read.

"We will put you up for the night, and commence in the morning," Gýgr said. Many of those assembled immediately began filing out, but several lingered. Bergrisar picked up a shaft of ice, dwarfed in fingers so heavily segmented and shelled they appeared most of the way to pincers. She tore it into several pieces before licking each. The other creatures on the panel then reached into her palm, each removing a stick. When everyone had a stick, they smelled them, and most dropped theirs into a pile before walking away. Only one held her shard—and stayed.

"Iviðja has the þurs," Bergrisar said. The commbox flashed

a message on my HUD. It was a guess that the word meant "thirst."

Iviðja, the one with the chosen shard, fluttered panels over her eyelids in capitulation. One shoulder had a delicate mess of spider-webbed cracks, likely signs of an old injury now healed. The light fractured through it as she turned to me.

"What's a þurs?" I asked.

"She marked the ice," Iviðja replied. "All had saliva from her mandibles, but one had a special hormone, the þurs." She paused a moment, then continued. "After we eat, you may come to my fire." I appreciated the distinction between "may" and "*will*."

I nodded. "I appreciate your hospitality," I said. "But it's still light—why are we retiring?"

A panel on one of her arms adjusted, and for a moment I caught a fragrance off it, akin to dried lavender. "Nights are cold here. Those of us too long on the surface out of shelter forfeit the protections of our carapace. Our secretions freeze, and we die slowly as the ice shatters our entrails. It is a punishment reserved for traitors. They are fitted with an implant that sends electricity through them should they stop moving, and they are forbidden to return to the warm tunnels."

I shivered.

In time, several people with even limbs and flat backs came in, packs bound across them. Others helped them unload and began dividing the contents. Now, I've never been a carrot person—not even a parsnip one, despite my mother's best efforts. So I couldn't say I was relishing the opportunity to eat a meal made entirely of what looked like the unholy love-child of carrots and beets, which I decided to call beetrots. If anything, the name made them less appetizing.

Iviðja was taking her role as hostess very seriously. When a plate was ready, she brought it to me. Several shell panels slid away from her hands, exposing delicate fingers nearly subsumed by the protective plates. She held a piece to my lips, and I made myself open my mouth. When in Rome, and all that.

The vegetable was bitter—fiercely so. If it weren't for the color, I might have believed it was raw horseradish. Iviðja set the plate before me and settled in beside me.

"There are areas deep below the ice mantle where you can rely on the planet's turmoil to send steam to warm the soil," she said. "We mostly reside in these tunnels. Our civilization is a mountain with only the peak above the ice; the broad base of it is beneath. We had mountains, before the flood, made of rocks and ice. Do you understand the word?" she asked.

"Yes," I said, and pantomimed a triangle.

She made a pleasant sound, perhaps the first pleasant sound I'd heard from a Jötnar. "It's complex and labor intensive, and in the absence of sunlight, you can only grow food with pieces of yourself to nourish them."

"Pieces of yourself?" I didn't see any missing limbs.

"The pieces you no longer need: filth, and those who no longer move." I tried not to let the thought that the bitter taste was *alien shit* sour my meal. "We must use *all* we can, for nature helps no one. Our strength, and our sacrifice, are what give us power over her."

That put a different dent in my appetite. "I hope I'm not overstepping my bounds here. But would it offend you if I didn't eat more? I don't feel right gorging myself when your people worked so hard to create this." I patted my belly. "And as you can see, it isn't exactly like I need it."

"I'm sure Bergrisar would find a way to take offense, get a pincer up her cloaca about it being a rejection of our cuisine or a snub at our poverty of resources. But I think it's noble. And the vegetables do taste like digestive gases." She let out a pleasant cackle, took a handful of vegetables off the plate, then dumped the rest back into the serving dish.

Iviðja led me a short distance from the court to a shelter formed almost entirely of a milky substance, like agate or smoky quartz. She noticed my look. "It is a glass concrete formed from my ancestors' carapaces. It is at once a temple, a shrine, and a mausoleum. We *only* use them for ceremony, or when needs dictate. When I die, it will honor me to have my shell join with my ancestors'."

"My people traditionally achieved a similar effect with melted sand—granulated rock—and modern 3D printing processes aren't so far removed from that."

Her eyelids shifted, in what I hoped was excitement and not a sudden desire to eat my entrails. "Lens glass? We form braziers from the leftover carapace, the smaller pieces less suited to construction. When they are new, the impurities cook out, and leave a glass lens at the base at the end of a cold season." She made a clicking noise that was reminiscent of a chuckle. "It cracks upon exposure to the outside air. When we build a new community, each resident carries one from their old home, and we put them around the new home in a circle for protection. When they crack, the ghosts from our memories laugh, pleased to know where their shadows are now."

It took me a moment to realize she was waiting for me to enter the dwelling first; it must have been an honor she was reserving for her guest.

Light flickered through the walls. They were milky enough that I hadn't noticed it from the outside, but inside, the light caught the facets of the walls and made them appear to almost glow.

I set my suit to warm slightly, not seeing any sign of blankets or fabric. I didn't doubt that clothes wouldn't be useful to the Jötnar, as it would counter their natural camouflage and impede the movement of their shells. And the hard edges of the carapace would be harsh on cloth, too. But the lack of any coverings meant I was in for a cold night.

Iviðja—whom I'd mentally nicknamed Ivy, which worked with her clingy yet restful presence—touched a rectangular block inside the shallow bowl of a chest-high brazier. My HUD recognized a power source within, and the bowl caught fire. Warmth washed over me.

"It is a battery. It stores heat from the vents, then releases the heat slowly here." The plates around her fingers retracted, and she took my hand in hers. "So long as there is fire, there is *life*."

Those words brought to mind an incident from Drew and Louise's younger days, fighting to rescue people from a burning colony as others fought them. It strengthened my resolve to get the Jötnar to work with us—and *finally* do something worthy of Louise.

Four

Ivy roused me in the morning and pressed a cup of tangy, mildly acidic liquid into my hands. I restrained myself from asking which bodily fluids went into producing this *repast*. She hurried away and returned with another section of root. I nodded my thanks at her and tried to make myself eat.

I've never been especially squeamish, so it wasn't the food's origins that bothered me so much as the totality of what I was about to do. I'd never risked my life when no one was actually in *danger*. Metaphorical danger on the ship just didn't inspire the same protective impulses and adrenaline; here, I had only nerves.

My HUD chirped at me, recognizing my elevated stress. I forced myself to breathe evenly.

"Are you ready?" she asked. I couldn't find anything other than polite concern in Ivy's movements, until I noticed a small twitch on the side of her neck. She was aware that I was anxious, and that made *her* anxious. I wondered if her reputation was tied up in my performance, if she would be considered tainted by association. I glanced at my guns and checked their charges.

"Yeah. Let's get this over with."

She retracted several plates, exposing her surprisingly soft hand, and hauled me to my feet. Her grip was almost overwhelmingly strong, even though she didn't seem to be using her full strength. I would have to keep my opponent at a distance, or else guns or no, I'd be done for.

She led me into a tunnel on the outskirts of the city. We

walked perhaps a half a mile, some of it steeply down, until we came upon a labyrinth of snow and ice. "They say that the world was once much kinder, that we expanded recklessly and grew soft, and could not halt the ice's attack. And in memory of that, when we prove our strength, we do it where our ancestors, and the ice, can see us."

She bent down and rubbed the icy wall. Beneath her mitten-like shelled fingers, metal became visible, cracked, rusted, and decaying. "How will *your* ancestors know to look for you here?"

I wasn't sure how to respond. But I knew that family was entirely too important to the Jötnar to fuck around.

I beckoned her head down to me. "Because they're with me." I held her so she could see the screen where my HUD projected. Her eyes flashed reflectively as their components widened. I scrolled through several family pictures I had, and cursed myself for ignoring my mother's attempts to get me to take more.

She backed away. "May you bring them pride, then. I must go. Your first challenger is at the other end. May you find each other before one of you freezes." Ivy's word for "challenger" sounded nearly like "elder," so I entered the name Eld.

I shivered and started into the labyrinth. My HUD made navigating easy, even without a map of the facility. Eld's warmth made him glow like a beacon. I readied my gun as I moved forward, the wind already chewing me through my suit.

I watched my HUD until I saw that Eld was just around the corner. I listened closely to the crunch of his footfalls, then threw myself out of cover to shoot.

My blasts smashed into a plate of his carapace center-mass. It refracted some of the energy and absorbed the rest. The heat of it burned him, searing his flesh, but I could see that it was a superficial wound.

He advanced as I took a knee to steady the rifle. I fired again, into his chest. The same panel absorbed the blast. I fired again, and several more times, peppering his head and shoulders, searching for a vulnerability.

I noticed that the first panel was hanging askew. Heat from the blasts had melted the connective tissues holding it in place. I fired along the edge of the plate, and energy reflected off the surrounding plates into the vulnerable tendons beneath, severing the already melted tissues.

He screamed, and he was now close enough that I could feel the moisture on his breath. The steam made it hard to aim, but I sighted the exposed flesh and fired.

Eld collapsed.

Sections of shell around the blast were hardening, looking alarmingly like the walls of Ivy's abode. But his flesh was already pushing past the cauterized edges. Trickles of blood seeped out, and despite his agitated shell flicks trying to force heat-warped plates over his wounds, I could see them already beginning to freeze in the morning chill.

I remembered Ivy's tale. He may have been working against me, and he entered into this fight by choice—but he deserved better than a slow death from hypothermia. I positioned myself in front of his head, raised the gun one last time, and refused to shut my eyes as I pulled the trigger.

Five

I wondered whether I should backtrack to the entrance or wait for the Jötnar right where I was. While I thought it through, I inspected Eld's corpse. He wasn't much bigger than Ivy. That made sense, I thought: the challengers would go from smallest to largest. I repeated that to myself over and over, to remind myself not to get cocky.

After some time, the Jötnar found me. Ivy came in first. She bowed her head, several plates on her neck pulling back to allow the motion. Bergrisar followed, staring at me, no doubt gauging me.

Others trickled in, and soon they crowded every inch of space in the tunnels. I saw that one even had a camera. I raised my voice. "This tech is one of the benefits you stand to gain by allying with us."

Bergrisar raised up, and I shuddered at the thought of her with a gun.

"It's mutilated infant scrotum. That was a farce. Yours are a cowards' weaponry: guile and aggression from a safe distance."

"You said I could use them," I said.

She opened and shut some of the crystalline panels on her face.

I didn't know the specifics of the gesture, but she was pissing on my lawn. A man was dead, and she seemed to want to treat it like it was nothing. Something about that look on her face was a red flag, and I was a bull. It was all I could do to keep from charging at her. "Fine," I spat through gritted teeth. "Send the next. I'll beat him, but let him live, to *testify* to my strength."

I offered my pistol to Ivy, then unslung my rifle and did the same. She took them with trembling hands. Her face bled concern, if I wasn't misreading it through a human lens.

A Jötnar slightly bigger than the one I'd just defeated stepped forward, and I immediately entered in a name: Leir.

"So be it," Bergrisar said. Some Jötnar turned toward the entrance, clearing an expanse in the widest portion of the room, but she didn't, and it was an instant before I understood why.

Leir lunged for me, and I spun to the side to avoid the blow. One of his secondary limbs lashed out as I turned, seeking to knock me off balance, so I jumped into a roundhouse kick.

It was like kicking a steel plate.

I ran. The gathered Jötnar backed away as I approached, and continued to back away until there was space between them for me to exit. I knew already that Bergrisar would try to spin my actions as cowardice, but I needed to survive before worrying about saving face.

The "arena" was oddly preserved. The frost had claimed the city almost gently, and its dome had withstood long enough for the ice to reinforce it as it was overwhelmed. The only elements not coated in a layer of white powder were the braziers. They were spaced so that you could see between them, if only just; there for additional light, not for heat. They didn't appear as weathered as the rest of the arena; I assumed they were brought down for the trial.

I ran full speed at a brazier, and when I hit it, I tried to scoop it off the ground. It barely tipped, sending the smoldering log rolling. The fire went out. I couldn't be sure if it was contact with the ice, or if it had safety protocols, but I could see the battery for the heavy, metal box that it was.

I definitely wasn't strong enough to lift the brazier, so I hefted the battery. It was a bit awkward, but it had enough weight to be useful. Then I turned back toward the gathered Jötnar. They were still in the distended circle, almost an egg. But Leir was gone.

I heard a noise behind me, so faint I wasn't certain. I cranked the volume on my implants. It was skittering, but then it stopped. I spun, swinging the log. It impacted the same panel on Leir's midsection I had first kicked. The impact cracked the plating. His plates flaked off like diamonds, catching the light as they fell.

I dodged behind him, and as he turned to face me, the plates began to fall away.

A sticky fluid hit the floor as he circled around me. Under the shattered plate, his flesh convulsed softly. I lashed out, swinging the battery. It glanced off the previous wound, cracking the surrounding plating. I dodged underneath his flailing limbs, and he curled his torso away from another blow.

I dropped the battery on one of his feet, then drove my fist into the most expressively pulsing organ I could see. He keened in agony, fighting to seize me with several supporting limbs, but he was distracted enough by the pain that his limbs knocked into each other uselessly behind my head.

So, a weakness. I brought my foot against the same spot with all my strength, wincing as I used muscles I hadn't been aware of since my mother encouraged me to study ballet on my home colony. Who'd have thought that *grand battement* would be used against a wounded alien, with a diplomatic treaty hanging in the balance.

His flesh tore under my boot, and fluids slowly gushed onto my foot with a rapidly lessening pressure. As I pulled my foot away from him, his legs buckled and he lowered his head.

I guided him onto his back on the ice while he was distracted with pain.

He was supposed to yield, but he was a stubborn bastard. I lifted my boot, picked up the battery, and started to shove it against the wound. It didn't *quite* fit, but he must have realized I was preparing to make him into a living brazier.

"Wait," he coughed from his back. I stopped, and he curled around his torn, fragile flesh. "I… concede." His legs trembled as he fought to make the gestures needed to communicate.

I looked up to our audience. "As I said, I didn't kill him. But let the pitiful noises he makes tell you that I am more than capable of seeing this negotiation through."

A medium-sized Jötnar raised her voice. "I withdraw my opposition." Several others murmured or otherwise gestured, translated as assent through the commbox. Bergrisar clicked in agitation.

Gýgr stood to her full height and said, "We shall carry Eld back to the court to begin mourning. Then we will see who still wishes to test the outsider's worth."

One of the flat-backed Jötnar bent to allow others to strap Eld to his back, and another soon arrived for Leir. I followed as far as the court.

I paused, unsure whether to go inside. I was Eld's killer, after all.

Ivy's hand lit on the back of my neck, all soft, slightly clammy fingers rather than hard carapace. I caught her eye, and watched it widen, each reflective lens aligning itself as the lids peeled back further. I queried the commbox through my HUD, but it didn't have a translation. I stared into her large eyes and breathed in her hand's scent.

Light filtered through the dome overhead and caught on the less opaque portions of her shell, turning her into a ghost of glass, haunting but beautiful. A beam cut across my face, and I fought to hide my wonder.

She took my hand and led me inside.

They feasted in Eld's honor. I made a trip out to my pod, returning with some of my rations to cook for them. They tested my food before tasting it, to be sure it wasn't going to set off any of their allergies.

It wasn't until midway through the festivities that I realized the trials were still in full force. Bergrisar mingled with the crowd, gladhanding. Several medium-sized Jötnar, slightly bigger than Leir, approached me and spoke. They were fascinated by both my tech and my food. After a few minutes of casual conversation, they leaned forward and informed me they would no longer oppose me.

I mingled more. Bergrisar glared her hatred over the crowd, and I waved back to her. The initial group were the only ones who had declared the end of their opposition, but I could tell that opinions were fluid and changing. Despite her best efforts, Bergrisar had lost ground.

As the crowd thinned out, I decided to get some air. I found myself walking in the direction of the tunnel leading toward the arena.

Just outside the entry was a bloodied bootprint, preserved in the powder of frost that coated everything. I knelt down to look at it. It was likely Leir's blood, so at least it wasn't a reminder of Eld's death. A hand gently touched my shoulder. I recognized her smell even before I turned to confirm it was Ivy.

I widened my eyes, and sections of Ivy's face pulled back in an imitation smile.

Her fingers were warm, and they gave me something to focus on other than that one bloody footprint leading back to the battlefield.

Six

Bergrisar looked at the gathered Jötnar. "Who no longer wishes to challenge?"

Half of those left raised limbs in assent.

"And those who do?"

Unfortunately, the Jötnar who responded this time were the biggest, the most fierce-looking of the bunch. I knew I had done well, but this confirmed what I had suspected: the hardest part was ahead.

"Who wishes to challenge next?"

One of the females stood, her carapace puffing outward to increase her size. I named her Sjórisar.

Bergrisar clicked in agitation. "Are you sure, Sjórisar?" Even through the commbox I could pick up on her distress.

I pondered whether Sjórisar was especially dear to Bergrisar. Perhaps family.

Several Jötnar shifted with soft clacks and motions, responding to the tension. Sjórisar glared at Bergrisar. "I cannot deny your right to challenge," Bergrisar said, in motions abrupt and violent enough that she nearly brained the Jötnar beside her—lucky for him, he dodged at the last moment. "But for this to be the *true* test our people require, let us increase the difficulty."

Sjórisar didn't seem to like that. "You doubt my competence?"

Bergrisar widened her eyes to tell Sjórisar to stand down. "Far from it. I propose night combat, that you may bring your full strength to bear on the outsider."

This was getting old.

"She seeks advantage. Sjórisar formed in her eggs," Ivy whispered to me, though in order for me to hear the tones and whistles accompanying her muted twitches, she had to lean close enough that I thought I might be enveloped. "Sjórisar will win, or die; anything else would shame her."

I sighed. "We'll see."

Ivy tensed. "Do not underestimate us. We live and work underground; we see well in the dark. She can track you by smell, by heat. You have no idea what Sjórisar is capable of."

I wasn't underestimating. I'd been in the security services long enough to know the value of morale. But my bravado was wearing thin. Sjórisar was nearly twenty feet tall, at least, if she stood up straight. She was a dragon, and each of her many limbs terminated in a sickle honed to a razor's edge.

But I couldn't go back empty-handed. I didn't know if Louise could ever love me, but I wouldn't even deserve to ask if I returned with my tail between my legs. "I have to conduct myself with honor according to the rites of your people," I told Ivy.

Gýgr stood again and towered over Bergrisar. "You may have your night combat, Bergrisar. And the human may have his weapons." Bergrisar clicked angrily. "We have voted—twice now. Do not buck the will of the elders."

Bergrisar lowered her shoulders.

I felt lighter. Having my guns meant something. At least I could rely on the tactics I knew best. But I remembered the difficulty my weapons had had even with poor Eld.

Ivy was still worried, but she had no further council for me. Her lids tightened around her eyes in sorrow, and I turned my attention back to the proceedings.

"Very well then," Gýgr continued. "At the rise of our moons we shall lead them to the arena. Provided he accepts terms." She turned to me.

"This treaty is too important," I responded. "While I relish no further bloodshed, I must continue."

"Then let the combatants adjourn."

Bergrisar leveled something that might have been a glare at me.

I nodded, and stood to return to Ivy's shelter.

Seven

I rested fitfully and woke to the smell of something bitter, but with a pleasant edge. Ivy was brewing something over the fire. "Made from carrots," she said, "and sweetened with fermented carrots."

She poured two cups, one for each of us, and we drank together. It had a mildly intoxicating effect, so I declined a second cup.

Strange ululations murmured over the city. "It's time," Ivy said. She led me toward the arena, but to a different entrance than the one we used before. "I can't go with you," she said, and stepped back.

I nodded and proceeded into the arena. The moon wasn't as bright as I could have hoped, but its light on the snow made me remember a childhood spent sledding and making snow forts. There were no braziers here.

I checked the charge on my rifle. I'd come prepared to defend myself, but not so armed as to cause alarm among the Jötnar. As it was, I wasn't sure I'd have enough to carry me through, tough as the Jötnar were.

My HUD filtered through the gloom. This area's ruins were denser, and the HUD seemed to be having a hard time pinging through the stone, metal, and ice. Even the heat sensors couldn't pinpoint Sjórisar's location. So I went a short way in and stopped at the first wide clearing I could find. I built snow and rubble walls around me—and I hid. I needed an advantage, and maybe the surprise would be enough.

I waited.

Eventually Sjórisar appeared, scanning just past me. I sighted her in, and as she turned, I fired.

She lashed me with her tail, demolishing my shelter.

The scale I had hit—above her brow—was still intact. I

turned up the setting on the rifle as I rolled to avoid a second blow from her tail. She used it like a whip, to cut my legs out, to force me to the ground where she could crush me.

I fired twice more. The first went wide. The second caught her primary arm, where the scaling was thinner, and I could smell the fat frying underneath the plating. "Bloodied insect stamens," Sjórisar muttered.

I glanced at my rifle charge: half gone already, and I only had one cartridge to replace it with, plus another in the demolished shelter, and then the reserve charge on my pistol.

Sjórisar swiveled around, and I threw myself back to stay away from her tail. It grazed my shoulder with the force of an avalanche, but I managed to keep hold of the gun. I fired again, lining several shots up along her nearly twenty feet of bulk.

She squealed as the shots tore into her, cauterizing flesh and heating her scales until they glowed. But still she came.

Her tail swept my leg, and my ankle twisted and popped. I went sprawling, and she loomed over me, readying for the kill.

I turned my gun to maximum charge. Whittling away at her torso wasn't going to work. I needed to end this. I fired one more shot—clear through her head. The moon peered at me from the hole as she tipped forward.

I realized, too late, that she was going to fall on top of me, or at least on top of my legs. I scrambled backward, but not fast enough. I screamed as she collapsed onto my knee.

Eight

When I managed to wiggle out from under Sjórisar's corpse, I made an unpleasant discovery. The edges of her scales had been sharpened to razors. My suit was damaged, and there were a number of cuts across my legs and shoulder. I couldn't tell how much blood I'd lost.

One of my legs wouldn't hold my weight. I forced myself to probe the wounds, and I nearly fainted when my finger brushed my shoulder bone.

When the spots cleared from my vision, I brought my hand to my hurt leg. My finger sank into the wound mid-knuckle, and I had no doubt that some of the muscle had torn.

I fought for the tube of first aid goo in the suit, to staunch the bleeding, but at least one of the lines used to administer it had been cut, and even when I cleared the blockage, it wouldn't push out.

Frozen.

Shouldn't someone have fixed that shit before plopping me on a sub-zero planet?

Fuck.

I used Sjórisar's corpse to get me off the ground and steadied. I measured her arm from the gunshot down. It was about the right length for a crutch. I tried to pry it loose, to no avail.

I decided to use one of my precious remaining shots on the weak spot. If I died here it wouldn't matter if I'd saved it for later. The cold was already biting me hard, and I had no spare fabric to bandage myself.

Using the severed arm as a makeshift crutch, I forced myself back toward the entrance, but it was slow going, and the Jötnar met me before I'd even left the immediate area. Ivy gathered me into her arms, all four of them, but Bergrisar pushed past to Sjórisar, shrilling her grief in a voice sharp enough to make my HUD warn me of the potential for cochlear damage.

Ivy nodded. "Let her mourn in peace." She carried me back to her shelter.

She clucked sadly as she laid me out on the floor and examined my wounds. "You're lucky."

I raised my eyebrows. "How so?"

"In ancient times, she would have eaten fungus for a month to make her blood poisonous, and then dipped her scales in her droppings, to ensure you died of infection."

I chuckled. "I'm lucky, then."

"She was not ready to fight you. We all knew it."

I remembered the tension in Bergrisar's face. "Was that Bergrisar's objection?"

"Yes. She just couldn't admit it."

I wanted to ask how Ivy knew, but I let the thought go as she helped me out of my suit, and the chill got ten times worse despite the fire.

"We cannot have fabric in your wounds. I will warm you once they're bandaged."

For a moment I pictured Drew in this situation, and people teasing him for getting caught with his pants down with yet another alien species. But then Ivy bent over my leg, pressing flesh into place around a brownish paste, and sealed it with a long, rubbery synthetic fabric.

Though she was being gentle, the spots returned to my

vision, and this time I didn't fight unconsciousness.

I woke up in a moment of suffocated panic. The world was dark, and Ivy's smell surrounded me, much more so than it ever had before. Tender flesh pulsed against my face, accompanied by a thunderous gurgling that unnerved me. I wiggled and probed, trying to understand what surrounded me.

Supple flesh on one side, the underside of crystalline, rounded plates on the other.

My face felt sticky—likely secretions to keep the plates from grinding on each other. It brought to mind suffocating during sex.

But something about that smell... It was so far from human, but the nuance of its spice pushed into my brain in a way no woman's perfume ever had.

Ivy's fingers, their plates rolled back, stroked through my hair, and the gesture calmed me. I realized the gurgling was circulation—her heartbeat.

I tried to remember feeling so completely protected and cared for, but nothing compared. I tried to imagine leaving her cocoon's embrace, and couldn't.

Nine

I lost track of the days I spent suspended inside Ivy's shell. She had to help me to the bucket that collected our wastes for the Jötnars' farming.

Her body formed around me as though I had always belonged there—some places loosening, others tightening, to take as much pressure off of me as possible. And strangely, surrounding myself in her soft, fragile flesh felt natural, like lying on a waterbed or floating in a pool. When her heartbeat surrounded me, pushed against my face as I rested, it pushed thoughts of the *Nexus*, even Louise, out of my head.

I wondered what my crew's reaction would be if I gave up on the treaty and just stayed with the Jötnar. Perhaps in time the Jötnar would need my help, or our technology, to relocate to a more hospitable home, like the initial report had speculated.

But having known them, I didn't see them doing that. Surviving their brutal ice age was part of their identity. How could they create lenses without winter-long fires?

I didn't believe they could rewrite themselves. But I wondered if I might rewrite *me*.

Days bled together, until at last I could stand again.

I had to speak to Bergrisar, find out how this situation was going to play out.

When Ivy released me, her scales slid away from me, allowing me to pass through the cracks. I feel barely an inch onto my mossy pallet, and I prepared myself for an unpleasant conversation.

"Is Bergrisar still mourning? How many contenders are left?"

Ivy sighed. "You're determined to jump right back to *work*." The reprimand in her inflection was surprisingly human, every bit the harried and peevish mother.

I shrugged. "Not eager, but I have to know."

Some of the plates around her eyes slid back, loosening the tension in her face. "There is only Bergrisar. No others wished to challenge you. I think she would not, but she feels she owes it to Sjórisar, as one of her brood. We do not bond with our offspring the way some herdbeasts do, but we still have a duty to avenge them."

I sighed. "I'm sorry it's come to that. I don't wish to kill her."

Ivy made a motion akin to a shrug. "You have followed our customs; there is no reason for sorrow in that."

"Still."

There was something in Ivy's mannerisms that rankled me. A question came to mind.

"Will Bergrisar be the last?" I asked. "Is anyone honor-bound to avenge *her*?"

Ivy's eyes flashed up to mine, startled. She clicked in agitation. "Bergrisar has lived long. Most of those gestated with her are long dead."

"But not all."

"Not all." She ducked her gaze, and I filled in the rest.

"You're of her brood."

"Yes. The same clutch of eggs, even. Not just the same genetic material."

"Will you fight for her?"

"I'm no fighter. She would not expect me to avenge her. And I would ask—*have* asked—her not to fight." She sighed, almost a whistle. "But we cannot put Bergrisar off any longer. I told her it would be dishonorable to come for you unconscious, wounded. But we have passed that point of grace. Let me get you some snow to bathe yourself."

I nodded in thanks, and used the armfuls of snow she

brought to sponge her fluids from me. Even so, Ivy's smell clung to my skin, like the expensive hand lotion my mom used.

I glanced at the last remaining cartridge for my rifle. The only way I could get more of a charge for it was to drain my pod battery, trapping myself here.

I didn't know what I would do if it came to that. I would decide after meeting Bergrisar, seeing if she wanted to meet me in the moonlight ruins.

I put what remained of my suit on and followed Ivy to the court. The rest of the Jötnar awaited me.

Bergrisar growled when she saw me. "Are you happy? You are almost at your victory." Her voice was a dangerous purr.

"I wish no more bloodshed." I didn't know what else that might mean.

"It will fall, regardless; you have not broken *all* of us." She flashed a contemptuous glare around the room.

"Tonight, then?" I asked.

"No. You will fight me here. You do not deserve to die on ground nourished with the blood of our ancestors." Ivy trembled next to me. "Give him his weapons, Iviðja."

I could see the conflict in her as she passed them to me.

Fear and adrenaline pushed through me as Bergrisar stood and the Jötnar backed away from us.

I turned to Gýgr. "I may not survive this fight. But our two peoples' friendship shouldn't die with me." I opened comms with my ship. "I'm opening up the technologies we offered in the contract. Use them. Help your people."

I didn't have a chance to hope it could sway Bergrisar; she was already laughing as I turned. "He thinks he can *buy* back his blood," Bergrisar chortled. "It's mine already. I ache for its moisture on my tongue."

I glanced at my rifle charge. Shit—with it turned up to the maximum, I had only a handful of shots. Plus whatever was in my sidearm. But Bergrisar was huge, bigger than the last two combined.

She lashed out at me with one of her secondary limbs; this one seemed to be akin to a scorpion tail, and I didn't want to know what was in the stinger. As it whooshed past, a smell struck me, a familiar one, learned from living with Ivy.

She meant to poison me, even if I *could* defeat her.

I retreated. It *had* to come down to the gun, then.

She whipped her tail at me again, but didn't put as much force behind it as Sjórisar had. It gave her more maneuverability, having less invested in the attack. I ducked, and her tail knocked into the wall behind me. I raised my gun, waiting for a clear shot to her head.

I got it.

When my shot struck, Bergrisar chuckled. The plating around her head was thicker—it had been forged into a single plate since the last time I'd seen her, essentially welded into a helmet. She'd disfigured herself in order to win. The shot dented the plating beside her eye, but not even enough to trust that *another* shot would do the job, even if I could hit in the exact same spot.

And from her weaving, I might not have the chance to test that.

I cursed myself for not charging my damn rifle when I had the chance.

She turned away from my next shot, but it was going to go wide even if she hadn't moved. Due to both of our miscalculations, it tore through the limb with the stinger. The carapace there must have been weaker: the stinger fell off, completely severed by the heat of my blast.

That could work. Remove the limbs. It was dicier shooting than center mass, but if it actually got *through*... I fired again, at one of her smaller arms. She seemed to recognize what I planned at the last moment, and snaked to the side, absorbing the blast with the thickest part of the plating in her chest. I fired again, and again she lurched to absorb the shot harmlessly.

The rifle was dead, and I dropped it. I turned up the charge on the pistol. I had enough shots to try to break through her head plating, or I could stop fighting fate and aim for her chest.

She charged me, and I fired center mass, my training responding before my head could. As I ran to the side and threw myself over her lashing tail, my wounded ankle gave out; I couldn't count on being able to run or dodge. She turned toward me, whipping a hand ending in a fist, the carapace's edges sharp and exposed.

The edge caught me, biting into my already injured shoulder and reopening old wounds.

But as I fell back, my hand met Bergrisar's fallen stinger, and an idea hit me.

When her next attack came, I leaned in to it—twisting my torso so that it skimmed by me—and then I threw myself at her torso, wielding the stinger.

I struck the weak spot in her chest with it, and felt a crazy euphoria as it sank in, deeper, deeper. Her shock rippled through me in her plates' little trembles. I tore the stinger out, and sections of shell fell away with it. I stabbed it into her again and again, fighting to keep clear of the limbs that reached for me, thrashing around me, defiant even to the last.

Ten

I shivered and fell to my knees as Bergrisar's twitches subsided. I felt dizzy and raised a hand to my shoulder. The old wound was open, yes, but it was more than that: the edges of her fist-plates had torn deeply into my neck. I couldn't tell if she'd hit an artery, but from the shredded meat where my neck met my chest, I didn't see how she could have *not*.

The Jötnar washed toward us, seeing that she was dead and I lived. "You shall have your treaty." It was Gýgr who spoke. "No one else will argue."

I nodded. The world felt floaty, and I let myself sit, knees to chest, to wait out its motion. Movement out of the corner of my eye drew my attention, and the Jötnar faded away.

Impossibly, Louise sat beside me. She was *pure*, her eyes' color saturated beyond anything I'd ever seen.

"I can't leave," I said to her, though I was certain my lips weren't moving. "And I know you couldn't love me. And that's all right." I leaned over to kiss her, and started at the feeling of a mouth without her lips. Then the fragrance sank into me, one I could wake up to every day for the rest of my life.

I hoped to God I wasn't bleeding out, that I might live my days out here.

Mistake or no, I didn't pull away. And neither did Ivy.

When we paused for breath, any trace of Louise was gone. Ivy's fragmented crystalline eyes were on me, and my blood-stained hand held her face.

"How... how am I?" I asked.

She shrugged noncommittally, though I found her smile comforting.

"Will I live?" I returned my hand to my neck. I couldn't feel where to put pressure, or where I was losing pressure.

"You'll stay with us." She tried to mimic my smile. "We'll find a lens in our pit so your spirits will know where to find you."

I told myself that that meant I would live, not that she would show them where my grave was. I wasn't sure if that was true, but it was what I wanted to believe as the darkness overtook me.

A WORD FROM NICOLAS WILSON

Although "Trials" is, I hope, a story that stands on its own two feet, it's also a story set around the events of my book *Nexus 2*. Readers of that book will have recognized the protagonist of "Trials" as Linus Bogdanovich. It didn't seem fair to me that so much of Bogdan's arc happened offstage, and I'm happy to have told his story here.

I'm a published journalist, graphic novelist, and novelist, living in the rainy wastes of Portland, Oregon with my wife, four cats, and a dog.

My work spans a variety of genres, from political thriller to science fiction and urban fantasy. I have several novels currently available, and many more are due for release in the coming year. My stories are characterized by my eye for the absurd, the off-color, and the bombastic. And yes, my wife wrote that last bit.

For information on my books, and behind-the-scenes looks at the writing life, visit *nicolaswilson.com*, or visit me on:

Facebook: *https://www.facebook.com/NovelistNicolasWilson*
Goodreads: *http://www.goodreads.com/author/show/6553776.Nicolas_Wilson*
Twitter: *https://twitter.com/NicolasWilson*

Better yet, sign up for my mailing list: *http://eepurl.com/u2ORL*

Legacy
by Moira Katson

HER FINGERS SCRABBLED against the wood paneling, and the sound of her own undignified cries for pity filled her ears. She choked on another sob and rolled her head to the tiny cracks in the box. Her black hair, swept up with jeweled pins, caught on the rough wood and locks tumbled from their careful arrangement; almost she reached up to pat it back into place, but the absurdity of that hit her with a choking laugh, wild at the edges. Tears were sliding down her face in an unstoppable trickle; her nose was running.

This was not how she had wanted to face this. When they told her, when they actually dared to speak the edict and shape their mouths to the words *joyous news*, she had entertained an image of herself now, in this place, cold-eyed and furious. Her bravery would be sung of; her dignity would set her apart forever, and the courtiers and servants would go home to whisper to their wives about the young woman with uncommon courage. In her mind, the men lowered their voices and whispered that they had seen, now, how cruel and wrong this was.

Beyond even her own dreams, but coloring them, lay the hope: in her dignity, she would inspire them to moral greatness. She would be helped free, as graceful in her escape as one of the Emperor's dancing women. A servant, perhaps even a courtier, would kneel and offer her his hand, and she would take it as she stepped down lightly. Her words, when she thanked them, would be remembered in poems.

But no one was going to sing of this. She understood that now. She found that she hated them for witnessing her own stupidity. She had not wanted to cry, and here she was, choking on her own tears, furious that her last choice had been ruined by her own fear, and more furious still that *this*, this useless attempt at dignity, had been her last choice at all.

They would not realize what they were doing and put a stop to it, for they already knew what it was that they did. Had she lain in dignified silence, they would not have put the box down and pried up the lid. No amount of grace or fury would do anything for her. She had bargained on their guilt, and she had seen it in their eyes—but she should have bargained on how little effect it would have. After all, she knew it was wrong, didn't she? And she had climbed into the box anyway, not wanting to be remembered as a madwoman, screaming and cursing. If she had not resisted the Emperor's joyous edict, why had she hoped for their disobedience?

It was their pity that stung at her now. They might go home and whisper to their wives tonight, and tell her that the strange one—she knew what they called her—had cried, and they had not wanted to do as they were ordered. But that would not free her, would it? And in time she would be forgotten, and the world would move on, and the next women would be summoned and it would all begin again. How could she have been so stupid? She turned her face, as if to hide her shame from Heaven.

Heaven, it seemed, also did not see fit to intervene.

The little vial they had given her was still clasped in her hand. It was very fine, with enamel and gold, and she fancied she could hear the liquid glugging like fine wine in a decanter. That was its allure, she told herself, and nothing more. It was a painless sleep that called to her: oblivion, and the dream of walking to meet the man who had imprisoned her. That was what they promised, was it not?

A wave of panic hit her at the thought. Bai Meilang had never been a devout woman, but she prayed now with the fervor of the condemned: *please, lady of the moon, lord of fire, eternal judge, whoever of you can hear me—please, let me only sleep, and never wake.* She could not face an eternity of the court, of ghostly conquests and the spite of the Emperor's attendants. There would be no courtiers to divert her in the afterlife, only the machinations of the wives. If it was such an honor to join His Imperial Majesty in the land beyond, Meilang thought spitefully, why were they all not here?

Because this was a farce, and all of them knew it. And they had relied on her not to say so until it was too late.

It occurred to her that there was no purpose to these thoughts. For what did she need awareness, or bitter clarity, when all would be lost? Her fingers clenched around the vial: a merciful end. She might drift to sleep while sunlight still peeked through the cracks in the box. The thought had an undeniable allure.

But she had left it too late. The tiny shafts of light outside were dimming, and the box tilted as the servants carried it down. Panic seized her. It was coming, it was close. Why was she struggling? Was a woman's mind truly so weak, as they said, that she could not comprehend her own death in the tramp of these feet? She took a deep breath and flipped the lid of the vial up.

She could not be sure if what happened next, happened on purpose. The crate was jostling, but her hands also, it seemed, would not move to bring the vial to her lips. The liquid spilled down over her robes and she closed her eyes—fruitlessly, for who could see her? What could she see? A moment of grieving for what had been lost, for the painless death without fear, and then she uncurled her fingers and let the vial roll away with a clink; there was nothing for her here any longer.

Movement stopped, and she froze. There was no light, only the breathing of the men and the sudden, surprising impact as the box was set down. Even knowing they could not see her, she closed her eyes. The top of the box came away with a ripping creak, and fingers quested blindly over her nose, her lips, and down, to press at her throat.

There was a pause. They could surely feel the racing of her heart, and yet Meilang did not move, terrified by the unknown. This man, she sensed, did not want to kill her. He had never killed before. But, if he had—as she suspected—been ordered to kill those who made it this far, would he?

Yes.

After a moment, he withdrew his hand, and she squeezed her eyes shut. She had begged fruitlessly for mercy when she should have been silent and now, when she should run, she was frozen with fear. She was not ready to die, and she knew what would come if she tried to escape.

She was not ready.

But in a small mercy, no blow came. They lifted her out, cradling her gently, and someone laid her on a bed. Her hands were folded over her breast, and her legs straightened. She let them move her, though blank horror threatened to make her muscles rigid. What should she do?

There was nothing to do. She should never have gotten into the box. She felt a new tear make its way down the side of her face. She would have died running, but she would have died in her rooms, with birdsong and the scent of summer flowers, and she would have made them see what they had done.

She wished them a life of agony and the slow twisting of guilt, every day, draining the joy from their hearts until they were shells of men. She wished them sickness and sons that looked like the stable boy. She wished them bitterness and defeat and a shameful end in the court.

Her wishing gained her nothing. When she heard the creak of the heavy doors, she cried out, leapt from the bed, but it was too late: even the light itself fled to escape the slam of the double doors, and the seven locks flipped into place with precision. Meilang felt herself falling, hitting the floor with a gasp of pain, and then there was nothing. No way for any to come in, and rob the treasures that should accompany the Emperor to his life beyond death.

No way out.

She had to get out of the room. Meilang scrabbled, fingers meeting nothing in the darkness but flagstone floor tiles. The bed had been soft, but the floor was nothing more than rough slabs. She should have known that there would be nothing other than the barest of necessities for the consorts. They had all been commanded to dress very finely as they processed through the city, carefully wailing for the benefit of the peasants—none of whom had come to her aid, had they?—and then, at the end of the procession, returned to their chambers and hoping for clemency, they were put into the rough wooden boxes.

Please, my lady, lie here.

She had seen fear in their eyes. They were afraid that she would break the illusion. They had seen her balk at the little coffin. But it was not meant to seal her in forever, so they had spent no time on it.

She should hear breathing, shouldn't she? Meilang crawled until her head bumped into the edge of one of the beds. It occurred to her now how absurd that was, her on all fours, scrabbling forward blindly in the dark in her fine clothes and her done-up hair with its jeweled pins. The bracelets she wore dragged across the ground with a clank, but she heard no response.

She felt up along the bed and flinched back when her hand met a foot. But the foot did not move. Meilang traced her way up the brocade skirts to the woman's waist, and from there past her face, to her hair. She remembered what the others had been wearing, and her fingers picked out the graceful whorls and spikes of Nuying's headdress. The First Consort. Had lowly Meilang truly been placed in the same room with those of such high esteem?

It was almost as if none of it mattered at all.

She scrabbled away. What she was looking for, she did not know. She did not go to the big double doors that led to the outside. They would find her and they would kill her and she would not stand for that. She would not go out just to be slaughtered.

It occurred to her dimly that if she stayed here, she would die, too, and yet her anger burned hotter at the idea of staying here—a companion. Almost she might have said her anger was a living thing, sustaining her, nurturing her. She could have said it made a song in her blood, that it walked beside her in the shape of a man or a god, like herself. She stumbled her way toward the center of the tomb, the way opposite the door they had brought her in. When she crashed into a chest and upended it, she stopped to haul it upright.

And that gave her the truth she needed.

The emperor would leave her in here, would he? He would bring women so that when the tomb was opened there would be a wealth of beauty and gold and jewels to show the world that he had saved all the things that were never his doing anyway, he would show her off as if her own legacy did not matter in the slightest and his was paramount, when all he had done was wipe away everything she had worked for?

She would destroy what he was.

She shoved the chest over once more, hearing pottery and jewels cascade onto the ground. Something shattered and she felt a savage pleasure at it. The anger was singing to her, fury bright and hot, and she laughed with it. Heat coated her teeth, her skin. She stumbled blindly forward until she came to a brazier, unlit: she shoved it and it flew away from her with a clang. Did she hear stirring from the beds? Should she go back to check?

No. They had taken the poison, damn them. Let them die alone in the darkness if that was what they wished, slipping away mercifully. She would destroy everything she could and die in fire and anger, and leave the tomb in dust around her.

Stone and wood met her fingers. The door lay here, and she knew it would be locked. Seven upon seven seals to go further. How much time had they spent planning the locks that lay here? Or had they brought his own doors from his palace in the imperial city?

None of it mattered. Meilang threw herself against the doors and felt them shudder against her weight. Impact came next, piercing pain as the traps went off and spears and arrows thudded against her body. She was thrown from her feet with the force, landing on the floor with the shafts of the arrows still protruding from her body. Her fingers felt along the wood, disbelieving.

Why she got up, she did not know. She understood that she was dying. She understood that she was feeling pain—more, that she should be. She could feel, in fact, nothing at all. And she had been going to die, anyway, so there was truly nothing lost, was there?

She threw herself against the doors once more and felt them shake, deep within. Iron-banded and gold-covered, they were heavy and solid, but she could move them. Her fury knew no bounds, and the traps were unleashed now. Again she threw herself, and again the doors heaved. Again, again.

The doors came down with a rip and a shatter, falling into the hallway that led beyond with a clang and a hollow boom, and Meilang fell with them, landing with an impact that drove the arrows deeper. She pushed herself up and wrenched the arrows free. Did she scream? It must have hurt.

She could not tell. She did not care. Blood poured over her hands and she threw the shafts of the arrows to the side contemptuously. It would serve him right if they found his consort's ruined body in his chambers. If they could see what he had done, if she was not lying peacefully there to destroy the illusion. As for the cave robbers, the ones he had hoped to dissuade…well, let them have everything. He would arrive in the afterlife with nothing at all, to wander as a beggar amongst his ancestors. That would serve him right.

She stumbled onwards, hands out, tipping braziers and chests and throwing vases away from her to shatter against the walls. Where was she? What was this place? She could see nothing. The light of Heaven had been blocked away; Heaven did not want to see this. Heaven did not want to know what her most blessed child had ordered for his death.

When he fell ill, never had Meilang thought it would come to this. Stupid, stupid, stupid. When he had summoned her…

Best not to think of that. A scream ripped from her at last, fury and pain and rage and grief. This was how it was ending: here, at twenty-seven, alone, dead before she could do anything she had wanted to do.

Never another poem. Never another song. She would not

wake to birdsong even one more time. She tore the jeweled combs out of her hair and threw them with the rest of the Emperor's riches. A column met her hands, marble and immovable, but she pummeled at it anyway, swearing she felt skin break and bones crunch and shift with the impact. She hit and hit, beyond logic in her fury, and beyond her the crackle and flare of her anger, she felt the column crack.

It was not possible. But she reached out with both hands and pushed, and the column came away in chunks, shattering to the floor nearby.

Perhaps she was dying, and all of it was an illusion. Meilang felt her along stomach, questing downward to the gaping wounds that lay there, feeling her fingers slide awkwardly as fractured finger bones came in contact with one another. She should hardly be able to move for the pain, should she not? The Emperor had told her of such things when he revealed what happened to traitors.

Had he wanted to scare her, or had he wanted her reassurance as he tortured his subjects? He had been a kind boy, the sort one would think would never drop to tyranny, but he had been unprepared for the demands of kingship. He had spoken to Meilang of his fear. He had told her what he had done, and her poetry had become a thing of beauty after that: a desperate grab at grace and hope, touched by a shadow she had not known existed in the world before that.

And it was that which had entranced him.

Best not to think of that.

Perhaps she was dying. But she did not feel the cold or the pain. There was only anger, like liquid gold, the finest, sweetest mead heady on her tongue. Could her blood feel sweet? Could her bones feel like weapons? They did.

She was still standing. Meilang swept her fingers through the air where the column should be and stumbled onwards.

The corridor was thin, lined with alcoves, each with a precious vase. She threw them all to the floor to shatter there: chips of jade and shattered wrecks of delicate gold vases, dull clangs and sharp tinkles of glass. Her slippers ripped along the sharp lines of glass and stone, and she felt the scoring lines of pain on her feet where the shards broke the skin. She walked on, oblivious. It was not that she did not feel, for even the wound in her belly gave a deep, low ache if she paid enough attention. It was that the pain connected to nothing: she wanted not to sit down and tend to her injuries, but to press onwards, to destroy in the way that gave her such pleasure. The god of anger and steel and fury walked so close that almost she might say its outlines met hers in the darkness, its arms reaching out as she tried to reach herself.

Another door. It occurred to her as she let loose with a strike and the stone shattered before her touch that she should never have been able to undo either door. Perhaps this was indeed a dream. Had she taken the poison after all? Was she still lying on the bed?

Surely not. She felt real. The blood drying on her hands was sticky.

For the first time, she felt cold. It crept in around the anger, and it was as chill and eerie as the first breath of winter on the autumn winds. Autumn reaped the muted promise of Summer, which had been too hot and too harsh to give true life. Autumn, she had loved. The peaches ripened with the held heat of the sun, and the wheat was carted away to be stored.

And she had loved winter once, when the drifting snows covered tree branches, and the Emperor's court dances to sweetly bright tunes on stringed instruments, and warmed spiced wine was a perfect companion to the chill.

She had never understood winter as a death until now. For anger, as it was, was all that remained to her, all that kept her alive. This stab of cold, as her blood ebbed away, was the ending of her life.

She slid down the wall, scrabbling weakly with her ruined fingers and cursing as the pain began to penetrate the haze of her mind. She wanted more of the anger and it seemed to have fled her. Death was coming fast on the wings of the chill, and she was overcome with panic. Would this be her legacy? A smashed room, a column, a hallway? Was this all that she would leave behind?

She would not live to see if any would love her poems, if they would survive her in the living elegy she had wished them to be. She felt a sob building and pressed her bloody palm against her mouth, not wanting even the silent darkness to see her shame and her defeat. For long moments in the dark she waited, little sobs escaping her at last as the pain tore through her, and then she felt it once more: fury, hot and bright.

What had brought it to light, when she was so consumed with her own death? She did not know. She did know that it seemed to carry to her feet with strength she had not known she possessed, and carried her forward to the open doors at the end of the room.

She knew the stench of death and it lay here. The Emperor's body, embalmed, was nearby. There was something morbid in his death now, to know that she had lain with this man—or he with her, while she had lain with silence and regret and anger—and that now his body lay preserved for all time while the world crumbled around him and the gold and jewels were covered in a darkness so thick that they could not even glitter.

She made her way to the bed unerringly. Was it only a flight of fancy, or did she know the layout of the room? There was no light for her eyes to grow accustomed to, but she seemed to know the obstacles that lay around her. Meilang dragged her fingertips over the silk and embroidery of the emperor's covering and over his cold hands, rings with the phoenix and the dragon, the jewels and pearls on his cuffs. Her fingers trailed up to his face.

She cherished, in bright hatred, the thought of ruining his body so that he might arise in the afterlife without anything at all. An afterlife she did not believe in, and yet how could she resist the chance that it might be real?

No. No, she had different plans. Let him arrive amongst his ancestors as a pauper, as a beggar. Let him learn, in his loss, the value of treating his servants without anger and cruelty. She could not wrap her mind around it. The emperor had known what was the most important to her, of everything in the world, and he had taken it, but he did so as if the facts had never joined together in his head. Was that cruelty?

It did not matter. Meilang turned lightly on her bleeding feet and her arms spread out in grace of a dance, fingers catching at a brazier and tipping it; scented oil spread across the ground and she leaped lightly across it. She could not see and yet her balance never faltered. She knew where to direct her hands, graceful as they had never before been, to topple a stand and a vase. She ripped wall hangings down to lie in the oil, she toppled the stone and gold and clay figures of soldiers that guarded the Emperor's dead form. If he could wipe away what she had been with nothing but desire, then she would wipe away everything he had ever been with the anger he had given her.

Memory came now, unstoppable, unwilling to be pushed aside. Her anger called it forth as a reason, as fuel for itself—as if the anger had come first and sought now something to sustain itself:

The first moment, receiving the summons alone in he little pavilion and studying the paper. He had sent it to her alone, not to be read by a servant; was he ashamed? She wondered.

He was a man who could not see beauty but that he must possess it. Foolishly, she had shown him beauty when she thought he would not want it, thinking that a plain face would be a fine cloak for the elegance of her poetry. The man was surrounded by the greatest beauties of the age, all scented with roses and jasmine, chrysanthemums in their hair, lychee and peaches on their breath, offering golden goblets of wine. Never would Meilang be such a woman, and so she had offered without reserve the words that flowed from her pen.

Her undoing.

The thought, in the pavilion that night, was sudden and irrelevant: that of all her life, of all the things she had done and would do, of all that she had loved fiercely and fought to achieve, none of it would matter at all. This was how she would be remembered, as a woman the emperor lay with. One night a man felt desire, and summoned a woman. And so her legacy was wiped away in an instant. She became dead, walking and yet a ghost already, a shell. Undone, forgotten: she did not know which, and could not bring herself to care.

Powerful men destroyed the legacies of those they touched, and did not see it, and if they did see it, they did not care.

He wanted her mind, she wanted to say, and she knew even then that such a thing was useless. The Emperor would do what he willed, and she would be killed by his command or by another's if she did not. He had enough lackeys that might think to remove his shame before he even thought to complain of it.

Now in the tomb, the anger, at last given an outlet, came forth in a shape and a rush. The world would know, however many years hence, that she had been more than his woman. Her dance continued around the perimeter of the room. She left it in ruins and dust and shards of pottery, and his bed she left untouched. Let him see the juxtaposition of his own perfect preservation amongst the ruins of everything he sought to take from the world of the living. Let him walk in the loss of his life, alive and dead as she had been.

She stooped to brush her fingers on the ground and the oil she had spilled came to life with a roar. Meilang stumbled back, too shocked to utter even a bare cry at it. What had the Emperor's engineers devised? Flame that sprung on its own from lamp oil? It traced a circle in the room, lighting her destruction in eerie clarity, even the flames too bright for her eyes. She brought her hands to her eyes and gasped at their destruction.

She had ruined herself.

She had allowed herself to be walled in. When she might have fought to break free—well, what had been her options? To accept death, or to keep living the half-life that had been given to her? To have the chance at her own poems. She should have fled the city when the emperor fell ill, and yet how could she have known it would come to this? She had heard stories, and yet one never assumed…

And the Emperor was young, he should never have had to come to death now, and her with him. She should never have had to die now, she thought mutinously. And yet was the point of protesting now? So many chances to run, and all of them had ended in quicker destruction. Would it have been better than living in dear and half-shame, shadow, wanting a full life she could not have?

She could not give up the past years, she could not regret them. Survival had its own beauty. She paused, stumbling, swaying. Exhaustion was creeping in, and despite the flames, the cold had returned to her bones now. It was deep in, ice radiating outwards through her skin. It was killing her. She was going to die.

She had always known that, and yet her mind failed over and over to understand. It came in stabs of awareness. Swaying, she fell to her knees on the flagstone floor. No marble and inlay here, either. What had the king sought in leaving his chamber like this?

She had only wanted to have someone to understand her poems, and love them for what they were. She had loved the Emperor even, for loving them—before he misunderstood, before he wanted her body for what her mind wove. Before he obliterated everything she had wanted to be. She had transcended the court as a poet, above their petty squabbling, set apart as she did not see their titles and they came to trust her: and then she had been thrust into the world of the harem and he had given her over to the pain and the whispers. She knew she was not beautiful. She had used it like a cloak, painful in ways she could never understand, for did not every woman wish to be beautiful sometimes? And yet it had given her a life she could always love. She had made her peace with it, until it failed her.

She had only wanted someone to understand. And he had been that person once.

When they found her here, amongst the wreckage, they would know what she had done…but again, she would be defined by lack, by her relation to him. She would be the woman who had destroyed. Anger sang in her blood and this time she rejected its siren call. She did not want anger. She did not want destruction.

She wanted the chance to be remembered for what she could have been.

She made her way to the wall, stumbling and slipping. Anger flared and receded in her blood as she pushed it away. Pain was coming quickly and she wanted only to write, to grasp the last few minutes of her life—it was close, she accepted that now, at last—enough to give voice to the images she had felt tumbling over in her soul as she stood in her chambers, their glorious edict and joyous news falling in her ears. She had woken to birdsong and sunlight and she had wanted to write them…

And this.

One last poem. She had time for one last poem. She drew the sunlight and the flowers to her, their colored faces bobbing gently in the sunshine as their petals unfurled and bees hovered lazily. A dragonfly alit on one nearby. She dragged her fingers through the blood on her robes and swayed, lifting her fingers to the bare walls. She had made herself a canvas; in her mind, she was at her desk, dipping a brush in ink and holding it over the page.

Her fingers dragged down the stone, elegance in the words. Dragonflies and the low arcs of birds. A trail of the submerged back of a fish. The sameness and beauty of rocks. The emperor had given her a pearl and she had shaken it out into her palm, mesmerized by the beauty and unable to bring herself to have it set. She kept it on her writing desk, tainted by its origin, captured by its beauty. Was this how women were won?

She wrote a song of dying pain, or loss, of the world as it had once been in her eyes and her hopes that had struggled against dying faith, against fact. She wrote of what had once been, of the parallel ghost life that had never flourished. Of the beauty she had wished to hate. She wrote of dragonflies and hummingbirds, jeweled wings, a hair pin sliding out of the arrangement so her hair could tumble about her shoulders; a gesture that made no sense when it was never her beauty the Emperor had sought, and yet he wished to put her into the same box. He knew only one way to desire.

She sang of what might have been, a song of fingertips on stone, and in her dreams the pen glided over the finest paper. Sunlight was warm on her face in her dreams even as the pain crept up, crippling her, dragging her down to the floor and the flames.

THE FUTURE CHRONICLES – SPECIAL EDITION

The siren call of anger came again, and she rejected it. She did not want anger. She wanted to the last moments of what she had been, a monument to herself and no one else. The smashed finery, she could not regret. Someday, she knew, someone would see it, arrowheads in her body and her fingers smashed and ruined. They would know her fury, and it would be a testament to what had happened here. But that anger was done. And so: they would see the poem.

Her last moments would be spent as she wished, even as her heart fluttered against her ribcage like a desperate bird, afraid of winter's touch. She trailed her fingers over the wall where her last work lay, and then she stumbled away. She was crying as she lay down at last on the stone and waited for oblivion. She could not regret; did not regret.

She simply did not want to die. And it hurt so very much. She squeezed her eyes shut as the pain wracked her again and felt a cry escape her lips. She would not regret, would not regret.

She did not want to die.

She did not...

The anger stood at her side. What had carried her to this moment, it asked her?

She did not want to die. She pressed her hands over her stomach, and both her fingers and her belly twisted in pain. She bit her lips. She was so cold, so cold... Her eyes traced over the lines of the poem. Sunlight and birds. She only had a few more minutes to endure.

She was so scared.

Did I not carry you up? the anger asked her. Did I not give you strength?

I do not want to die, she told it. Acceptance warred with everything she had been: fire and outspokenness, fury still remaining in her soul. I do not want to die.

You do not have to die.

I do not want to die, she repeated. The pain was taking her and she was too weak to resist the fear now. Oblivion and silence would mean an end to the pain, and even so she fought for it. Had she not known pain even in her pavilion, the pain of being written away?

Anger crept into her bones once more, chasing away the shadows of the cold.

You do not have to be lost. The poem lies before you. It will remain as a testament to what you were. You made your peace. And now you do not have to die.

Meilang looked up through the tears to the figure of fury and fire. Was it steel in the form? Was it glass?

It was not her. She realized it only then. The anger that walked beside her in the hallway, that echoed her movements and drove her forward like a warrior. It was not her anger.

You do not have to end here, it told her.

Meilang gasped for air and tasted blood on her lips.

The end is close, it asked her. Her eyes slid to the painting and it looked after them. Close. A few seconds, nothing more. And what do you choose, little creature of sunlight? Oblivion… or immortality?

In her dreams, Meilang reached up for the sky, a wraith with the echoes of a thousand women.

Trembling, she reached out her hand.

A WORD FROM MOIRA KATSON

Moira Katson writes Fantasy and Science Fiction novels. Born and raised in the farmland of the eastern United States, she is now a transplant living in the oft-frigid wastes of the midwest, where she is learning to love hot dish, fried food on a stick, ice fishing, and the hilarious faces her friends make when she tells them about winter temperatures... just kidding, she has no intentions to learn how to ice fish.

Despite the fact that she had been writing since childhood, Moira majored in nice, sensible subjects in college and went on to have a nice, sensible job, all the while continuing to write about dragons, courts, and spaceships. She has since bowed to the inevitable and begun releasing her work into the world! Her first book was released in 2012, and her current projects include *The Novum Trilogy, The Sojourner Saga,* and a series of bite-sized steampunk adventures!

To find out more about Moira and her upcoming works, visit her website, *http://moirakatson.com*, or find her on Facebook or Twitter, *www.twitter.com/moirakatson*

If you are a SciFi fan, she recommends that you try out *Crucible*, the first book in the *Novum Trilogy*, or *The Alien Chronicles*.

The Grove
by Jennifer Foehner Wells

IN THE MOMENT when the last remaining filament between Hain and the Mother broke, the Mother's parting thought raced through Hain's mind, but Hain didn't process it until later, when the sticky amber gum that oozed from her open wounds had begun to harden, and the euphoric newness of freedom had subsided.

The Mother had said, "Come back to me soon, little one."

It had taken so long to break loose. Hain had been obsessed with wriggling, working, bending repeatedly in every possible direction, until the sapwood connecting the two of them had frayed to fine fibers and finally snapped, severing their nurturing connection. She had been so anxious to be free, so intent on experimenting with her unused, newly fully formed limbs, that she hadn't even replied or said goodbye. She hadn't meant to be so ungrateful to the one who had given her life.

* * *

The day the Salvors came, Hain was retrofitting an ancient vehicle with every-terrain wheels. She'd redesigned them to manage better than the wheels that some of the Mother had used so long ago. Hain used the narrow three-wheeled vehicle to haul raw materials and items scavenged from the ruins. There had once been roads to drive on, but those were long gone. Even open spaces were rare now that the Mother dominated the world.

She was tightening lug nuts onto a rusted wheel stud when she heard rumbling overhead. She saw a white streak in the sky, and instantly knew it had to be a contrail, though her own eyes had never seen anything like it before. She quickly moved to track the trajectory, and after some computation, she determined an approximate landing site.

She was lucky the alien vehicle was landing on the same continent. It had never occurred to her to launch satellites to detect incoming activity from off-world, and she berated herself for her shortsightedness. She had no way of knowing whether these were the first, or if others had come before and landed on another continent, or if there were many of them simultaneously investigating sites all over the globe. Only the Mother knew the answers to those questions, and Hain couldn't hear the Mother's voices.

She only heard one voice in her head now—her own. She'd grown used to that and now preferred it. After all, she knew everything the Mother knew, and everything the Mother before this Mother had known, and so on back through the eons, with each new offspring receiving all the knowledge of those that had gone before as she grew from bud to nymph.

She had no desire to rejoin the Mother anytime soon, to put down roots and reconnect in partnership on that communal plane. So she'd have to investigate the contrail, and what it meant, on her own.

Over the years, Hain had watched scores of other nymphs break free, roam for a bit, and then select a terminal point, whereupon they would bind themselves back to the earth. Some had come to her with messages from the Mother. In their eagerness to return, to rejoin the voices in that perpetual state of grace, rootlets were already unfurling from their lower extremities, allowing them to twine with Hain, making contact long enough to communicate to her that she was missed, and that staying away from the Mother too long could mean disaster.

None of these nymphs had been like her. Hain now accepted that she was unique. There hadn't been a message from the Mother in centuries.

Hain gathered supplies and set off on her adventure. It took days to get there, over rough terrain, and she had to go out of her way to skirt the densest groves of the Mother. When she got close, she hid her vehicle in thick undergrowth and continued on foot.

She rounded a thicket. Here, the Mother began to grow more sparsely, giving way to a broad glade. It was a low spot that would be marshy during the rainy season, not a good place to put down roots, but perfect for a vertical landing.

When the ship came into view, its silver skin glaring in the bright sunlight, she stopped abruptly and stared in stunned disbelief.

It was enormous.

Hain had been gathering scraps of metal for centuries. She sorted it into piles and used it whenever she needed raw material for the object rendering machine. The ship before her represented a mass of metal she couldn't conceive of gathering.

She could see the aliens, too. She gradually moved closer until she could hear them speak and settled in to observe them for a while to see what they were about. It was easy to conceal herself from them. They were oblivious to her existence.

They were as different from her as she was from the small mammals that scampered through the Mother, and she was surprised to note that they were far larger than the animals she was acquainted with. They were her size, roughly.

There seemed to be several species, but nothing like any she knew. These were more highly evolved. They walked on two limbs instead of four, had nimble fingers, and used technology. Since the old times, no species on this world had used technology, until Hain had chosen to employ that aspect of the Mother's memory. So it was fascinating to watch them use it with their furry paws that looked so much like hands.

Each day the aliens scouted in a different direction from their ship. At first Hain thought they might be scientists, because they collected samples. These samples were mostly of plant life, but they trapped some insects and small animals too. They built up great stacks of sample boxes and crates, which they transported back to their ship at nightfall.

Hain's other hypothesis was that they were colonists. The

old stories were full of visitors who had come to live among the mobile nymphs when the Mother was still small, sharing the planet's resources, living symbiotically, peacefully. If they had come again, it could mean a new life, a synergy, discoveries derived from the sharing of different cultures, the elevation of everything she knew to another, higher level.

That would have been a gift.

But the old visitors had not come again. And these new aliens were not there to share or learn, but to take.

* * *

Both Hain's larynx and the small bellows-like structures on the sides of her neck were vestigial, all but superseded by the evolutionary development of other structures in her progenitors' throats. She could understand Mensententia as well as any civilized person in the universe, but she was unable to speak it at anything above a whisper.

Among her many inventions was an implant that took in air through an opening she had incised into her neck and forced it through her rudimentary larynx. The device was crude but functional, and it was in place. She had thought it would undergo many more revisions, and that she would have many more practice sessions using it, before she would ever have the opportunity to use it among those with lungs. But it would have to do.

As she watched the newcomers casually enter and exit their vehicle, she felt something unusual stirring in her. She had long been planning to construct a ship of her own. She'd already explored every continent of this world, and she ached to leave it, to explore new ones, to learn new technologies, and to interact with others in the old ways that were common in the time before the Mother embraced transcendence.

She wasn't supposed to want to leave. She was supposed to be content with her place on this world. But Hain wanted more.

The aliens' ship was so much larger than anything she could hope to create. It represented hundreds, possibly thousands of years of work. Inside, there was sure to be technology on a scale not seen since the Mother's most distant and watery memories were reality. To have that kind of functional technology at her fingertips, instead of spending her time endlessly repairing or painstakingly building anew—the very idea made her fingers curl.

At first she didn't comprehend what she was feeling. She didn't experience much in the way of emotion. And this was a strange mixture of longing and excitement, not unlike that which she felt in the days before she broke free from the Mother. Eventually she deduced what this uncomfortable feeling was. She coveted their vehicle.

She should make contact and ask them for... what? Passage? Where would she go? She had little knowledge of anything outside this sphere. Ask for some form of employment—did such paradigms still exist? Did she possess any knowledge or skill they might want or need? It seemed unlikely.

Perhaps she needn't ask at all. The ship was huge. If she was very clever, she might be able to stow away undetected. That idea appealed to her more than it should have. After all, she wanted to continue to live in the old way, free. Leaving this world and exploring the stars would mean interacting with other individuals. It was perplexing. She didn't understand her own reluctance any more than her wanderlust.

She had long thought that the radiation of the old sun might have altered her DNA, made her into a kind of seed to take their civilization to a safer place, a new world with a young sun, where her people could prosper again when this one was gone. The Mother couldn't do such a thing. She was fixed in her place. But perhaps Hain could be a new Mother, if she could stop moving and put down roots. This was the way of the oldest knowledge, the kernel at the center of what they were.

In the distant past, greenwood nymphs had lived in great communities with other species. They had formed complex relationships, had worked together, had shared their lives and gone to the stars with them, taking the Mother to new worlds.

Why was Hain reluctant to attempt these kinds of social bonds now? This, too, elicited a new sensation she didn't enjoy. After much introspection, she was able to name it: fear.

Hain did not like fear.

She had maintained homeostasis for a very long time, stored a good deal of starch over the years, and achieved a mass that was unusually large for a nymph. She could manage on starch stores alone for a long time, but it would be far better if she had access to appropriate light spectra. It seemed prudent to plan ahead in case hardship should strike.

Were there others like her, out there, somewhere among the stars? Would her anatomy be familiar to the strangers, or a curiosity? Would they be capable of meeting her needs? Was it safe to leave her well-being to their mercy? She didn't want to have planned and yearned for freedom this long, only to lose not only her life, but also any chance at a transcendent afterlife.

* * *

Hain had to know more. At dawn the next day she crouched in the undergrowth, a bag of tools slung over one shoulder, and watched the aliens set off. When they were well out of sight, she crept up to the ship's portal. Her eyesight was optimal. She'd watched them come and go for days now, and had easily memorized the complex code they keyed into the panel next to the portal.

Her energy was very high. The early morning sunlight was weak due to the impending change of season, but she was warm despite the swirling rush of changing winds, and nearly vibrating with excitement.

She slipped a fingertip into the slot and flipped the small door open, revealing the small compartment that contained the keypad. She stood there, staring at the symbols stamped onto the buttons. They were in Mensententia, so they weren't unfamiliar. Her dual-chambered heart fluttered in her trunk, pumping fluid rapidly through the xylem and phloem of her body. She decisively punched in the code in the same order and at the same rate of speed that she'd observed the aliens doing it.

Her stomata pulsed, releasing ozone and some water vapor. Standing in full morning sun, she was cycling CO_2 into O_3 at a dizzying rate. The chemoreceptors in her skin detected the sharp spike of the gas that indicated her body was under stress, but she barely registered it. Her body knew the risks as well as her mind.

There was a loud click, then the portal bounced inward a few finger widths and came to rest. She hadn't needed her tools after all.

Her eyes darted around the glade, which was still empty. All around its edge, the dark foliage of the Mother shielded her from the eyes of the aliens. She wondered what the Mother must be thinking as she pushed open the heavy door and slid inside, sideways, then allowed the door to shut behind her with a muffled clank. It was unlikely that the voices of the Mother were happy. The Mother wanted all her children to come to her, to root. But that thought was quickly gone. This new place was so foreign. Hain's senses blazed with information.

She was in a small chamber, dimly lit—an airlock, she realized. Directly in front of her was another portal, standing open and leading to a larger interior room. Lights came on all around her. She blinked and her eyes adjusted. She slowly set down the bag of tools.

Dazzling technology surrounded her. Multi-colored lights blinked. Blank screens covered the walls. She trembled. This was brilliantly real, so unlike the Mother's faded memories of places like it.

Hain stumbled forward in a daze. A screen lit up. She turned to it. It prompted her in the telescoping three-dimensional Mensententic symbol for "ready."

She jabbed the side of her neck to trigger the air-flow device, then spoke, creaking out a command that should bring up a search prompt, "Qui-sssssssss-tohhhhh."

The computer didn't react. She tried again, poking the external elements of the device to turn up the air volume, forcing precision through unfamiliar lips. She got no response. Either it couldn't hear her meager voice, or it only responded to authorized individuals.

She frowned and studied the controls, forgetting the air hissing through her parted lips. There should be more than one way to access information. She tentatively tapped the screen. Nothing happened. She tapped it again, a little harder, and this time a small portion of her flesh touched the screen, rather than the corky lichen that grew over the tops of her hands. The screen flashed and a menu came up. So, it was capacitive, rather than pressure-sensitive. With irritation, Hain silenced the airflow device.

She took a few moments to absorb how the system was structured. She was relieved to see that the symbology of the language hadn't changed dramatically since the Mother's time and that the interface was fairly intuitive. Soon she was navigating with ease, bypassing information about who owned the ship, the crew, the cargo, their mission, and went straight to the details of structure and propulsion. She needed to know if there had been advancements in drive technology since the Mother withdrew from galactic society—and she needed to look at current star maps.

There was something strange here. All of the navigation controls were routed to a central station that wasn't on the bridge. Hain backed out of the schematics and entered a search query, her fingers hovering over the screen and pecking at each symbol, one at a time. There was so much she wanted to know and so little time.

It was tempting to just take one of the screens. It was a lovely, compact piece of tech. Nothing like it had survived from the old times. She'd always wanted to recreate something like it, but there would be so many steps, and there was always something more pressing.

And these aliens had so many of them. Surely they didn't need them all—with so many, there must be redundancies. So tempting. Hain eyed her bag of tools near the portal.

Ah! There. The answer. They still used wormhole technology as well as warp-drive ships, though the latter had fallen out of favor. It seemed there had been a new discovery: a sentient species that somehow enabled access to wormhole travel without the use of the costly, temperamental drives that had previously been necessary. A few individuals of this new species had been sold on the black market for breeding, and now nearly every space-faring vehicle had one, except for short-range transports.

Hain felt frustrated. She had no way of obtaining one of these creatures for her own ship, though it would be many years before the need would arise. If she continued on her own, she'd have to use the old technology. That was fine, of course, just not optimal. Hain liked for things to be optimal.

She knew that the urgency she felt was really only impatience. There were no limits on her time. She could do it on her own, without depending on strangers.

But an old worry came back—that she really didn't have forever, that eventually it wouldn't matter how long she lived. Not if her mind unraveled.

She squashed that thought and did some arithmetic. With the old-fashioned warp propulsion system she was building, the nearest inhabited system was two hundred and seven solar years away. With the use of one of these mysterious creatures, it would be a week away, at most. Possibly less. The difference was comical.

Another thought struck her. The entire universe was open to these aliens. What were they doing *here*? Her eyes unfocused as she thought about all of this, her brain buzzing with possibilities.

A tiny beeping sound caught her attention and jolted her back to the present. The screen she'd been using had gone blank, except for three words:

"Who are you?"

Hain froze. The sharp stink of ozone filled the air.

She had thought the ship was empty. She'd counted the individuals every time they'd left the ship. They were all accounted for… weren't they? Was there someone who had stayed behind?

She stared at the screen, torn between answering and lunging for the portal. It wasn't a hostile question, necessarily. She might not be in any danger.

Three more words popped up on the screen. "I am Do'Vela."

Volunteering information… that wasn't antagonistic, Hain thought.

Hain touched the screen to create her own message. "I am Hain."

The response was immediate. "I can't feel you."

Hain didn't know what that meant. The alien wasn't in the same room with her, wasn't touching her. Of course it couldn't feel her. What was it after? She couldn't think of anything to say in reply.

After a moment, the display changed to show a two-color schematic of the ship. A series of linked corridors and rooms were marked green. Hain didn't understand. Was there something special about those rooms and corridors? Something the alien wanted her to see?

She retraced her steps and peered out through the crack that remained in the entrance portal. Wind whistled through the opening—a strange, mournful sound. No one was outside except the Mother and some noisy birds. It was mid-afternoon. She had been there longer than she had realized, but she would probably still be safe for some time. Each day the aliens had stayed away until nightfall was imminent.

When Hain returned to the screen, new words had appeared: "Come to me." And there was a black dot on the schematic, tracing its way from Hain's location, along the green-marked sequence of passages, to its terminus near the center of the ship. Suddenly, it dawned on her that the alien was asking her to walk the path it had laid out on the screen.

This time she didn't hesitate. She was intensely curious. She knew it was a risk to go deeper into the ship. It was probably wiser to leave and come back the next day. That would give her time to think, to process it all. But she sensed that the aliens would probably move on soon. Her opportunities were dwindling. It was worth some risk.

She cautiously walked the route that she'd seen on the screen. The chemoreceptors in her skin were nearly overwhelmed by wave after wave of organic molecules of foreign origin. This corridor had been traversed by many species of people over a long period of time—that was clear.

She came to the end of the route and stepped into another large, empty chamber. As in the first one, there was technology everywhere she looked. And all of the screens were blank, except for one. When Hain stepped closer, she could see that it repeated the words she'd seen before: "I am Do'Vela."

But where was Do'Vela? There wasn't anyone here. The chamber stank of fetid, brackish water, reminiscent of a marsh.

Hain tapped into the screen: "Where is Do'Vela?"

She noticed a flicker of movement beside the screen. What she had assumed was part of a wall was actually a transparent material. Someone on the other side was wiping at it, ineffectually attempting to clean away a dark blotchy film from the partition. Hain could see movement through the haze, but little else.

The screen said, "Do'Vela is here. I am here."

Hain was thoroughly confused. She reached out a hand to wipe at the glass from her side, but it was relatively clean. She couldn't fathom why Do'Vela didn't just open a door and come through. Was the alien imprisoned behind the glass?

Do'Vela stopped wiping.

Hain glanced at the screen. Now it said, "Pull the handle above, so that I may see you."

Just above the screen, Hain could see a brightly colored handle, next to a symbol for "open." Hain knew it was foolish. She was probably naïve—and definitely too inquisitive—but she reached up, grasped it, and pulled down with all her strength.

She jumped back with dismay. The entire chamber rumbled as the transparent wall moved forward on a track built into the floor with a groaning sound and ominous clacks. The mechanics were neither well-constructed nor properly maintained. That made Hain uneasy. Could she trust anyone or anything that did not set the same standards of quality control that she set for herself?

Hain worried that the sound and vibration might carry outside. Perhaps she should leave. She felt a heavy feeling that she didn't understand, holding her in the spot where she stood. Her heart beat very fast and she didn't know why she felt so strange.

When the object stopped its forward motion, it proved to be a cube, slightly taller than she was. The top of it lifted slightly and flipped back upon itself, folding up and sliding back in pleats, water sheeting off the panels as they moved.

A droplet struck Hain in the face. She didn't react. She just watched, dumbfounded. She'd never been so surprised.

A pale, slim arm came up over the top of what she now realized was a tank filled with water. The arm was flexible in all directions, it seemed, and was studded with small circular discs, very similar in design to some of the lichen she wore on her own body—each bearing a depressed central point with radiating lines. She didn't think these were symbionts or ornamentation, but a part of the creature.

Another arm, then another, and another, emerged from the tank. Water splashed and ran over the sides. How many arms could it have? There was a beep from the screen. Hain turned. Now the screen said, "Come closer."

As Hain moved closer she could see, just over her head, an immense eye, proportionally much larger than her own, dark and luminous, peeking over the top of the tank. The creature was pale white, almost translucent—Hain could see traces of Do'Vela's inner workings through the thin skin. She glanced around the chamber for something to stand on, but there was nothing near to hand. One of the individual's arms reached out to touch her, but the span was slightly too far.

Hain prodded her neck to turn on her crude device, struggled again to coax words from her frozen, inadequate throat.

The screen next to the tank beeped again. Now it said, "I don't communicate that way. Touch me."

Hain sidestepped to the flat display and entered, "You only communicate electronically?"

The reply was swift. "No. Touch me. I cannot feel you."

Hain didn't know what compelled her to move forward. Later, she would count herself lucky that Do'Vela hadn't pulled her into the filthy tank and devoured her.

She stretched her hand out to meet the curling arm. Upon the first tentative contact, she felt something thrilling, like electricity, pass between them. Hain's eyes widened. Do'Vela's arm twined around hers, pulling Hain closer to the tank.

Hain staggered forward, not reluctant to get closer, but dumbstruck. Salt water ran down her arm. Her skin's chemoreceptors registered an excess of toxic impurities and high concentrations of microorganisms. But she wasn't consciously thinking about that, because, as the surface contact between Hain and Do'Vela grew, so, too, grew an *awareness*.

Hain's mouth fell open, the air-stream from her forgotten

implant twirling the fern fronds that fell forward from the top of her head.

Do'Vela was like the Mother.

She felt the rush of Do'Vela's excitement. "I feel you!" She heard the words echoing through her mind. "You are so different from any other!"

Hain was rigid under Do'Vela's touch. She felt such joy at the opportunity to commune with another, but she also feared some internal process had been triggered that she'd be unable to control, and she couldn't help but look down at her feet to make sure she was not taking root.

"Oh, I see. You are a part of something larger, holding yourself separate. You wish to remain an individual, to explore. You have long been alone." Do'Vela's inner voice was warm and eager. "I, likewise, have been alone. What serendipity to find you here!"

Information streamed between them. Hain was held in thrall by the scope of it. She could see how Do'Vela had once lived in a much larger tank of water, and although under stress even then—due to poor water quality and confinement—at least she had been among her own kind to share in the misery. As a juvenile, Do'Vela had been wrenched from that place, passed around from one owner to another, until at last she had ended up here, in this wretched situation.

It was clear that the small creature was malnourished, though she held onto Hain's arm with surprising strength. Her memory showed that she was routinely deprived of sustenance.

This was not like speaking with the Mother. Here, Hain was the elder, the wiser one, but still so curious. "How can you efficiently fulfill your purpose? Why do they not optimize your environment?"

Do'Vela didn't know. The motivations of the crew of this ship were a mystery to her. She had a vague notion that her ancestors had long ago been a majestic, free people. But she had never heard of any that lived that way now. The closest she could get to experiencing freedom was to burrow into the minds of bipedal hominids to experience the universe through their eyes. She could ride in their minds and see and hear their interactions with others. She felt impressions of their thoughts, and their most basic emotions. In fact, she had been with one of the crew, hiking and gathering samples, when the intruder alert had brought her back inside herself to investigate Hain's presence inside the craft.

But she could not crack Hain's mind without physical touch.

Hain was charmed by this creature. She was so different from the Mother, though the mode of communication was very similar. Do'Vela was like a newly detached nymph: young, ebullient, genuine, and so intelligent.

Hain wondered how she would cope with captivity if she were stuck in a similar situation. Would she be able to survive? What would this ship's crew do with her, if they discovered her inside the ship? Would they trap and exploit her as they had Do'Vela? Would they withhold nourishment when they were displeased with her performance?

Even as she recognized this risk, Hain knew that she and Do'Vela were caught up in something that she didn't want to cut short. Hain hadn't realized how much she missed the

Mother, how lonely her existence was, how much more *real* a living being felt than memories.

Suddenly, Do'Vela's delightful stream-of-consciousness blathering slammed to a halt. Her effusive happiness was replaced with abject fear. She let go of Hain's arm and slipped back into her tank, disappearing from sight without an explanation.

Hain stumbled back, confused. The screen next to the tank beeped. It said, "I'm sorry!" The screen crackled and words flashed chaotically. Hain couldn't read them until they settled on one last message, for the briefest moment: "Please close my enclosure! Safe journey, friend!"

The screen went blank.

Hain strained all of her senses to understand what was happening, but she had very few clues. The precipitous disappearance of Do'Vela was disconcerting.

She reversed the position of the handle. The covering folded again, each panel slamming into place with an unnervingly loud sound, and the floor rumbled under her feet as the tank receded into its compartment.

She quickly brought up the ship's schematic on the screen, looking for another place to exit the vehicle, but as far as she could tell, there was only one exterior portal—the one she'd used to get in. That was a terrible design, she concluded. She could do far better.

She moved as warily as a prey animal. But as she approached the outer chamber that connected with the portal to the outside, she heard something hit the deck with a thunk.

How much time had passed? Had she stayed too long? She

quickly turned back, determined stay out of sight until they left again the next day. She fumbled with the implant controls on her neck to silence them, suddenly aware of the constant shushing sound it made.

But it was too late. One of the mammals stomped into the corridor at that moment. Hain stopped dead in her tracks and turned to face it.

It looked as surprised to see her as she was to see it. Its nose twitched. "Whoa," it whispered. It gestured with a furry hand. She didn't know what that meant. It didn't move, otherwise.

Her stomata puffed ozone. She remained rigid, alert, waiting to see how this would develop. She was trapped, with few choices.

They stood there, assessing each other for a long moment.

It started forward with purpose. She didn't like the look in its eye. She turned to flee, but it was faster than she expected. It grabbed her arm and turned, dragging her in its wake.

She staggered, pulling and prying at its fingers to no avail. Its meaty body outweighed her reedy form by many times her own weight. It bore her inexorably down the corridor without a word, through the chamber to the airlock, and then outside.

Terror gripped her. She was at the alien's mercy. She could end up like Do'Vela, or be killed before she could take root and join the Mother. How could her circumstances have changed so quickly? She'd been too impulsive. She'd underestimated the risk.

The alien held her tightly as it barreled through the clearing and into the Mother. Hain renewed her struggle, clinging to the Mother as they passed, risking her arms being torn from their sockets. The Mother's bark tore at her symbionts, scraping her flesh raw. Thick sap oozed from the wounds. She barely felt the pain. She heard herself making horrible mewling cries of distress, like a woodland animal caught in the jaws of a predator—the loudest sounds she'd ever made in her long life, magnified by the still-running implant.

Her legs went out from under her while she flailed, pulling small plants up by their roots as she tried to grasp at anything and everything they passed. Spongy leaf mold caked her skin. The beast just grunted and pulled harder.

Finally it stopped, yelling for the others to come see what it had found. Hain scrambled to her feet. Now she wished she had let her arm be torn out, because it would be better to live free without an arm than to be captured by this greasy, stinking animal.

The other mammals crowded around. A cacophony of sounds buffeted her as they all spoke at the same time. She had no hope of understanding them. It was too much sensory information and she was too unused to language.

She felt weak, suddenly drained. She fell to her knees. In the shadow of the Mother, there was no hope for sunlight's blessing of more energy to renew the fight. She gave up. It was over. They would do what they would.

They touched her, turned her so they could see her body from every angle, pried at her symbionts, scraped her lichen, pulled on the ferns and mosses adorning her head and neck— all the while producing a din of discordant sound.

A memory prickled at the back of her mind. The Mother could be powerful if threatened. In the last hundred thousand years or more, she had never summoned this power. Might the Mother save a wandering nymph from these beasts? Hain didn't know.

She imagined that she could sense wisps of the pheromone alarm—the warning that went out to every creature planet-wide just before the wrath was unleashed on anyone who dared hurt the Mother. It was wishful thinking, surely.

Hain kept her eyes on the soothing green foliage of the Mother, and she wondered what would happen if she attempted to set down roots right here. She silently begged for help.

But the Mother could not hear her.

* * *

A fawn-colored furry face filled her field of view. It yelled, "Can you hear me?"

Hain refocused. It was just one voice and no one touched her now. She lay on the spongy duff, almost comfortable.

"Maybe it's deaf," another one said.

"I don't think so," the first one replied, still hovering over her. "I think it hears me." It clapped its paws together in front of her face. She flinched.

"Yeah, it hears you. What's its story, I wonder? You think it's sentient?" another voice said.

"I am," Hain whispered. But they were so loud they couldn't hear her soft speech. She cursed herself for not taking time to perfect the device sooner. But how could she have predicted this turn of events? She waved a hand limply toward her face until they noticed and grew momentarily quiet. She tensed up and did her best to channel her air properly, to form the words she needed so desperately for them to hear. "I am Hain."

"I'll be damned," one of them barked. "An actual green-as-grass talking plant!"

A furry paw was held out to her. She stared at it, uncomprehending.

"You're a funny thing, aren't you? Take my hand and I'll help you up." The one speaking was the darkest of them. Its fur grew in dense swirls, sticking out at odd angles. "I am called Keeb." She hesitated. But the crowd had stepped back from her, seemed less threatening. Perhaps the worst was over.

Hain lifted her arm and Keeb grabbed it, more gently than the other had, and helped her to her feet. Keeb pulled his lips back, revealing two rows of sharp, carnivorous teeth, as well as plenty of molars. He was largest omnivore she'd ever seen. She watched him warily.

"Hello, Hain," Keeb said. "Are you related to these plants somehow?"

Hain blinked and her gaze followed his gesture. For the first time she noticed her surroundings. They stood in the midst of a densely populated copse. Hain's eyes widened in horror as her brain tried to process a sudden bolus of terrifying information.

Her eyes saw the bodies.

Her ears heard the drone and squeal of various cutting tools.

Her chemoreceptors detected the heat of cut wood, the scent of sawdust and sap—all scents that were new to her.

And underlying all of that was the pheromone she thought

she'd detected before. Its identity could no longer be denied—its presence in the air was growing at an alarming rate.

Deep inside, she instinctively *knew*—as did every native of the planet—that she was in terrible and immediate danger. She needed to find a safe place to hide if she was to survive.

Words failed her. She stared at Keeb. He didn't look alarmed. Didn't he know? Couldn't he smell it with those canine-looking nostrils?

"This is quite a find for us," he was saying. Some of the others watched with mild curiosity, others with boredom, and still others turned away to resume their work—sawing, chipping, slicing, hauling.

She watched with the abstract detachment of shock as one of the animals raised a laser cutting arc and brought it slowly to bear on another member of the Mother. She shuddered as she noted the ease with which the animal ended a life.

"Last night I happened to analyze a few samples. There was some really bizarre DNA in one of them. I insisted we come back to take another look at these trees and get some bigger samples," Keeb was saying.

Hain watched the mammal's mouth moving, the tongue and teeth glistening with the saliva that begins the digestion of prey. She was too stunned and confused to look away.

"Plant DNA with some animal markers—like a hybrid. I'd never heard of anything like it. I was sure the sample was contaminated, until we cut down a few of the trees. After a little bit of whittling, we found amazing structures inside, at the base of the trunks—it looks like calcified or possibly petrified hearts, livers, spleens and so on—nothing like ours, of course, but still, working rudimentary organs. We've never heard of anything like it. The trees just… grew up around them, incorporating their bodies into the wood itself. It's the damnedest thing."

He had forgotten to mention brains.

He kept talking, completely unaware of her reaction. "Once we saw that… Hell. Then I figured—*no one's* ever seen anything like this! We might as well fill up the cargo hold and see how many credits we can get for 'em" His lips curled up in an expression she didn't recognize. Based on context, she guessed it was avarice.

Keeb looked her up and down, his eyes narrowed, still taking in every detail of her appearance. Why was he staring? She stared back, alarm mounting every second.

"Then *you* show up. Are these trees your distant ancestors? Some kind of missing link? Where are the rest of your people? We detected abandoned cities, but found no indication of a living sentient population."

Someone else spoke up, "Yeah, now they'll be wanting rights. I knew it couldn't be this easy. An entire planet just full to the brim with wood? Nobody's that lucky." The mammal growled a word that must have been an expletive in his primary language, then wandered away.

In her peripheral vision she saw the laser arc continue its merciless cutting. Every loud crash marked another voice silenced, banished forever from the chorus of the Mother. What happened to those voices now? Was there more to life, after that? Did they live on in some kind of subterranean form, slowly starving, maybe sending up a shoot, to live again? Or did they just die, their murmuring melody converting to raucous shrieks of terror?

The Mother would not allow this much longer.

She should tell them to stop.

She should warn them.

But how could they not know?

How could they kill so many without purpose? For wood? What was wood but a vessel for everlasting life? How would these mammals react if she snatched that laser arc from their paws and sliced one of them in two, letting his life's blood spill among the sap flowing through the undergrowth?

The legends of greedy people who killed for wood had been true, not just stories to entice nymphs to root close to the Mother rather than in remote, open locations. Not that there were any of those left anymore.

The group's initial interest in Hain had waned. Most of them had moved on to other tasks, leaving her with Keeb.

Hain looked past Keeb, at the Mother—strong and tall and ancient, her leaves quaking in the breeze, disseminating the chemical warning for all that could detect it. The levels of the pheromone were rising sharply. The Mother wouldn't wait much longer before she would retaliate—before she would make these tiny mammals pay for their transgression.

Hain needed light desperately. She was considering taking a few steps forward when, behind her, another life was ended, causing the canopy overhead to open up. Sunlight streamed into the small artificial glade that was forming in a rough circle around them, and Hain was bathed in light. She felt her skin warm as the light-energy nourished and renewed her.

"You don't talk much, do you?" Keeb asked with a guffaw that sounded almost like the bark of a small canine that had thrived among the tall grasses of the prairies long ago.

When he quieted, she spoke. "No, I have no need. I am alone."

His confusion was evident. Though she herself had never seen that emotion on a mammal's face, ancient instinctual pathways in her brain were tripped—or maybe it was the Mother's memories from the times before. Regardless, the emotion must have been strong for her to read it. She knew she would not be able to read subtle intention—or ferret out deception. She was very aware of her lack of skill. He seemed to be equally inept at reading her.

"Oh, are you stranded here? Did your ship break down?"

"Yes," she answered. "Irreparable." Her first lie. She watched him closely.

He nodded. He didn't indicate disbelief. "That explains it. I expect you'll want a ride back to civilization? Got any credits?"

"Yes. Of course," she replied with a firm nod. Another lie. It was so easy to let him believe what he wanted to believe.

"I'll tell Goppul. She takes care of that."

"What will be done with this wood?" Hain asked, trying not to choke on the word. Her throat ached from the effort of speaking so much.

Keeb's lips pulled back in a feral smile. "High-end furniture. We're going to keep this planet a secret and move this stuff to market slowly to keep demand high. By the end of the day, we'll have enough to fill the hold. Then we'll take off, probably tomorrow."

"That soon?" she said. There was no time to plan anything.

"Yeah. So, if there's anything you want to take with you, I suggest you fetch it now. It's nearly dusk—the predators will be out soon." He gestured at the Mother, as though he believed she harbored animals more dangerous than his own species.

The mother was silent. Not a bird chattered. No mammals rustled the undergrowth. Even the insects had quieted.

The birds were roosting in nests hastily built up out of mud and foliage, a task precipitated by instinct. They would huddle inside, a small hole allowing only the barest whisper of air through. Their only task in the coming storm would be to keep that hole open, their one chance to survive.

Mammals, reptiles, and insects were burrowing deep into dens, caves, cracks, and crevices. Water-inhabiting animals were diving deep to wait for it to be over, for the world to be bright and livable again. In the coming hours many would die, but the Mother would live on to give the survivors succor, and they would grow in numbers again in the coming years.

Hain thought of her small shelter in the abandoned city so far away, and wondered if it would be enough to protect her, if she could even make it there in time.

Images of mummified animals caught out in past storms burbled up in her head from the Mother's memories, unbidden. Their bodies were frozen in paroxysms of hypoxia, mouths open wide in strangled gasps.

She was not immune to this. She might not have lungs, but she had to exchange gases like any other living thing. She would share that fate if she couldn't find a safe haven.

The stillness was deadly.

These brutes created the only sounds, but they didn't seem to notice.

"I will go then, to obtain my belongings and return at dawn," Hain said to Keeb, struggling to contain the hysteria that rose inside her.

He frowned and glanced around at all the others, working diligently. Killing, killing, killing. "Do you need an escort?"

"No need," she said. "I know this place well."

Her soft voice was overtaken by a shout. "Keeb! You've got to see this!"

Keeb barely gave Hain another glance before striding toward this newest excitement.

Hain slipped away, the words of the enthusiastic animal carried on the wind to her as she loped through the grove. "It's a damned face! Can you believe it? I whittled it down, careful-like, with a small laser-carver. Look! There's eyes and everything!"

The animals chattered excitedly over the dead member of the Mother. She left them behind.

* * *

Hain ran, darting through bright spots of sunlight whenever possible, to keep her energy up. She hadn't run since the days when her legs were new. It had felt so good then. Freedom was a wonderful thing.

And now she was on the cusp of a new kind of freedom, if she could make it in time.

She'd depleted her short-term sources of energy and was

actively consuming starch now. It made her slower and clumsier. She couldn't convert it fast enough to maintain such a breakneck pace.

But she made it to the ship. And just as she reached it, Hain saw the first motes of yellow skimming the wind. They were a haze, coloring the scenery, making it look like the decaying art she'd seen in some of the oldest buildings in the cities. As she tapped out the code to gain entry, a yellow speck landed on her finger. Instinctively, she brushed at it—but it wouldn't wipe away. It held fast to the corky lichen. She thanked the Mother for the symbiont's dense protection.

The keypad beeped and flashed a red warning.

What? In her haste had she keyed in the code incorrectly? She steadied herself by leaning against the side of the ship. Sunlight washed over her. Her stomata gulped CO_2 from the air, cleaving it and recombining it into carbohydrates and ATP energy packets, discarding the wasted oxygen back into the atmosphere.

Suddenly she panicked. Would there even be CO_2 aboard this ship? How foolish that she hadn't looked to see if the gas was stored somewhere aboard. She was so preoccupied with drive technology that she hadn't made certain she could survive inside. Then she remembered Do'Vela and her panic eased slightly. Do'Vela and all of the bacteria in her enclosure could provide Hain with all the CO_2 she needed, as long as she didn't expend a lot of energy.

The wind picked up, and she looked over her shoulder. Visibility was rapidly decreasing. The haze was rolling away from the Mother, filling the air like a slow-moving wall from ground to sky. She had to get inside fast.

A particle landed on skin scraped raw from her earlier escape efforts. Pain screamed in her head upon that tiny contact.

She ignored that and tapped out the sequence again, very carefully.

The keypad flashed red and the portal did not open as it had before.

Her hungry body felt the sunlight begin to go.

She tried again, but somehow they'd locked her out. They didn't want her inside their domain. They wouldn't let that happen twice.

Tiny amber grains pelted her. Pain burrowed into her skin with each contact. She tried to shelter within the small concavity of the portal, but the wind swirled, and the devilish pollen granules found her.

The Mother was meting out her justice. The Mother wanted to survive, too. And she had. She had not only survived, she had thrived. This world was hers now. There wasn't a corner of it that she didn't oversee.

There was nowhere else for Hain to hide. She slipped one leg out of the hollow of the portal, making contact with the ground. Her last, desperate option was to take root and hope to outlast the caustic pollen storm. If she could tap into some water in the soil and keep a fraction of her stomata functional under her lichen armor, she might endure.

She closed her stomata tight, as she did at night, hoping to preserve the integrity of her skin. No point in gas exchange now. The atmosphere was so thick with pollen that the sun had virtually disappeared. The light had gone dull, shadowless, deepest goldenrod. There would be no more photosynthesis for a long while.

The pollen swirled around her like snow. Her flesh burned, pinpricks of agony, wherever it struck.

In the distance she heard roars and yelps of pain. She squinted over her shoulder to see the indistinct shapes of the mammals far down the edge of the glade. They'd blundered out in the wrong place. She couldn't believe their lungs were still functioning—surely the pollen had turned that fragile tissue to a bloody mass.

Her leg stiffened as the transformation began, toes slowly curling into rooted tendrils, her heel gradually growing into a spur to anchor her securely to the spot.

Could she hear the Mother's whisper? Was she closer to knowing the Mother's truths, the Mother's peace?

Hain tried to curl into herself, to shield some part of her body, to protect it from the ravaging particles on the wind. Pollen burned her eyes. She was sticky, oozing precious fluids from broken veins. If she couldn't reach water in the soil, she would desiccate right here in this shallow alcove.

She heard a beep.

Hain opened her eyes to slits and scanned her surroundings. The beasts continued to advance. She could see them more clearly now, their shaggy fur frosted with pollen. How they could endure it, she didn't know.

They'd be angry when they arrived. They'd blame her. They'd tear her limb from limb.

The beep sounded again. She turned, holding up a hand to shield her eyes. The compartment that housed the keypad for entry was still open. She peered into it. The tiny screen next to the keypad was scrolling the words, "Is it you, Hain?"

Hain blinked. She read it three times before she believed it. It was Do'Vela. It had to be.

She wrenched her foot from the soil and crouched in the small hollow of the portal, hurriedly typing, "Yes, I am Hain."

"You wish access? There is something amiss!"

How would Do'Vela know this? Then Hain remembered how Do'Vela rode in others' minds as a mental escape from her despicable confinement.

"Yes! Please!"

A moment went by. Hain put her hand over the crack in the portal. Her foot and leg ached. She tried not to think about what that might mean. She glanced over her shoulder. The animals were almost to the ship. They would not be happy to see her inside. They might punish Do'Vela for giving her entry.

The door mercifully popped inward. The mammals were steps away, staggering and raging, yellow-encrusted berserkers.

She ducked inside and pushed the door shut with a loud metallic crash. She darted to the nearest interface and sent a message: "Change key code."

Do'Vela responded. "Why?"

There was no time. She could hear them outside. She stared at the door. She heard a soft sequence of tones. They were punching in the code on the other side.

The opening mechanism of the door was exposed on her side. Her discarded tool bag still lay just inside the portal. She grabbed blindly in the bag for a tool, came out with a rasp, and jammed it into the mechanism, hoping it would prevent the latch from turning—from both inside and out.

She heard infuriated bellows. The mechanism wriggled, but the rasp held firm.

Hain dashed back to the interface. The word "Why?" still lingered.

Hain hesitated for a second, then sent, "We don't need them."

There was no answer this time. Hain stood there, unsure how to convey the urgency to Do'Vela. The enraged animals could break through the portal at any moment.

She reeked of ozone. Her fingers were sticky with sap. She'd left blotches on the screen. She began to falter. Perhaps she'd doomed herself. She leaned heavily on the console and sent, "I will take care of you. It will be better."

Do'Vela remained silent. Hain moved unsteadily to the portal. The tool was starting to buckle under the strain as the angry animals battered against the door.

She was out of options. She went back to send another plea to Do'Vela, but when she got there, there were already two words on the screen: "I understand." Hain stood there, swaying on uneven legs, her vision swimming as she blinked away the sticky moisture seeping from her burning eyes.

She wasn't sure what Do'Vela had understood, but the side of the ship thundered with the sounds of meaty paws pounding on it. Threats barked and roared at her, though they sounded tinny and far away. The portal rattled.

Then it stopped rattling, went solid as stone.

Another beep.

She turned back to the screen. Words scrolled by. "She is yours. Come to me and together we will fly from this place and be free."

Hain did not hesitate for a moment.

A WORD FROM JENNIFER FOEHNER WELLS

I doubt it would be a surprise to anyone who knows me to learn that I love alien stories. I wear my love of science fiction like a badge. From early familial indoctrination with the *Star Wars* and *Star Trek* universes, to later exposure to television shows like the original *Doctor Who*, *Farscape*, and the *Stargates*, to Bradbury's short stories and books like Wyndham's *Day of the Triffids* and Adams' *Hitchhiker's Guide to the Galaxy*, I developed into someone who craves alien stories with a burning, rabid passion.

Overall, what interested me most were tales of first contact—of misunderstandings and cultural exchanges, the more bizarre the better, and the human (or sentient?) response to them. I wanted to taste new worlds and leave the mundane Earth behind. I wanted to lose myself in mysteries, in foreign ways of thinking, in outlandish but plausible species. I wanted to be tricked into believing in all of the possibilities that I've always known in my heart are just a star away from being real.

When I started writing *Fluency*, my first novel, I wanted to write a "fish out of water" story, with the kinds of characters that I loved, and a mystery revolving around an enigmatic alien and all the issues that would arise in an uncontrolled first-contact situation.

I didn't expect it to do well, as it was my first published effort. I immediately pushed forward, beginning another novel in a completely different setting with new characters. This new novel would be a superhero origin story—again twisting history to fit my own universe's cosmology as I had done in *Fluency*, but with a new spin. It's called *Druid*, and as I write this, it's unfinished.

As I was writing *Druid*, there was one character that bedeviled me—Hain. She was supposed to be a minor character, but I became fixated on her, developing insane amounts of backstory, something I'd never done quite to that extent before. It wouldn't fit in the book, but I couldn't help myself. I promised myself that one day I would write a story about her. She deserved it. She was too intriguing not to.

Well, *Fluency* did do well. I was encouraged to stop work on *Druid* in order to deliver what my readers were demanding—a sequel to *Fluency*. So, with reluctance, I did. (But I'm coming back, dammit!) The success of *Fluency* earned me invitations to opportunities like this anthology—and immediately I realized that here was my chance to write a story about Hain that would be a prequel to *Druid*—and a nice counterpoint too, because "The Grove" is a villain origin story. I hope you've enjoyed it.

If you did, you may also enjoy *Fluency* (*http://www.amazon. com/Fluency-Jennifer-Foehner-Wells-ebook/dp/B00L3U9OCG/*). For more information on that novel, check out my website, *http://www.jenniferfoehnerwells.com*, and sign up for my newsletter (*http://www.jenniferfoehnerwells.com/subscribe.html*) to be the first to know when I publish something new. Thank you.

Humanity
by Samuel Peralta

A story tells what happens.
— David Swinton, in 'A.I.' by Steven Spielberg

'I heard a woman screaming' recounts witness of Interstate 94 pileup

Fatal crash involved up to 25 vehicles near Port Huron

WBS News Posted: Feb 06, 10:27 PM EST Last Updated: Feb 07, 6:00 AM EST

One person has been declared dead following a multi-vehicle crash close to Port Huron. The accident took place around 9:30 p.m. Friday in the westbound lanes of I-94 just past I-69.

A collision between a passenger vehicle and a semi-truck in the

westbound lanes touched off a chain reaction of other collisions, said Sgt. Don Wilson of the St. Clair County Sheriff's Office.

Heavy snow and icy weather conditions contributed to the incident.

Traffic was being directed onto westbound I-69, then off at Wadhams Road in order to reconnect with I-94, while officials continued their investigation into the pileup.

ON THE DASHBOARD, the time flashed 9:22.

"Wish I'd topped up the fluids before we left." Aaron Yudovich flicked at the windshield fluid switch, but nothing happened. Outside, the wipers scratched at the sleet crystallizing on the glass. They made a grating sound as they traced a useless arc across the windshield, back and forth.

"Just let it drive, Aaron," Judith said, across from him. "It'll be fine."

The musical had run a bit late, and afterwards there were the obligatory chats with the Weymans and the Otanis, whom they'd run into at intermission.

By the time their spinner had emerged from the theater's underground parking lot—at least they hadn't needed to bring winter coats—the snow was falling much faster than when they'd started out.

"Still," Aaron said, loosening his tie. "Wish I could see outside."

The wind shook out the snow in sullen gusts. With temperatures at thirty below, they'd have frozen outside in under ten minutes. Thank goodness for the automated control and all-wheel drive—this wasn't weather anyone would choose to venture out in, otherwise.

Judith peered in the mirror. "Sweetie, keep your gloves on," she said. "And for heaven's sake, stop fiddling with your belt."

"But Mom," whined the girl in the back. "It's twisted, it's too tight."

Judith sighed. Her daughter had been extremely well behaved at the event. Done up in a ruffled pink party dress and white elbow gloves, her hair tied back in a short ponytail—and, oh! for the first time allowed a touch of makeup—she'd been an angel. Bright-eyed, she'd listened attentively, mouthing the words of the songs she already knew, squealing and clapping at just the right moments.

Judith and her husband had seen Wicked before; this was Sarah's first time. It had been an amazing night out, and they were looking forward to seeing Buratino in two weeks. But it was late, the snow was a little worrying, and Judith herself was so, so sleepy.

"Sarah Rebecca, please put down that belt."

The little girl screwed up her face, but let go of the clasp, and dropped the gloves on the seat.

Outside, the snow fell.

'The semi slammed into the vehicle'

An eyewitness, Alan Mathison, was driving his truck on his way home from work when he saw the first vehicles collide ahead of him.

"Snow's coming down fast, it's pretty bad. First thing I notice was this semi in front of me drifting out of his lane, right into the path of this red spinner. Then the cab slipped, and the trailer swung to the side, slammed into the vehicle."

"A couple of spinners tried to avoid him, started flying out of control on my left and running into the median, into each other, and into the first vehicle," said Mathison.

"I'm braking, trying to slow down, move into the other lane. Then I get hit from the side."

The next thing he knew, he was in the ditch. *"When I stopped, I just flung open the door and started moving away. There were still vehicles spinning off the ridge, and I wanted to get away from it all."*

But when he got out of his truck, something else caught his attention.

"I heard a woman screaming, like nothing I've ever heard. I don't want to hear anything like that ever again. I ran towards the red spinner, and just beyond it, there she was," said Mathison.

"She had this small body on her lap and she was screaming, trying to put on these little gloves, and screaming."

When Mathison opened the door, the cold hit him with a shudder of wind, a cold that slashed right through the down of his padded jacket to the bone.

The ground and ice cut him as he slipped down from the truck, as he tried to make his way toward the wailing. *Cold.* It was cold with a capital letter 'C', and the thought came that he should be getting back in his truck—but the thought was stronger that someone out there needed help, and he had to get to them.

He reached the spinner first, a tangled wreckage of red and grey and steel lying in the jagged underbrush. Through the shattered window on the front-left side, Mathison could see the body of a man flung forward in his seat, in a suit and no overcoat, buckled in.

The body was still bleeding from the head, and he looked like he'd taken at least one very hard hit, maybe more. Crushed and pinned in his twisted Coke can of a vehicle. It was clear that even the robot controls on the spinner hadn't been able to react fast enough to the multiple collisions.

When Mathison checked the man, his heart sank, even though he'd already known what he'd find. The man was dead.

From the opposite side door, a furrow in the snow traced where that passenger had unstrapped herself from her seat and made her way fifteen feet from the wreckage.

A handbag and two high-heeled evening shoes, strewn about four feet apart, marked the snow with three splotches of matching turquoise.

The woman was at the end of the path, holding what looked like the body of a young girl—ten, maybe eleven years old, a rag doll spun out into the cold.

"Sarah!" she was crying. "Oh, Sarah!"

Suddenly she saw Mathison's figure in the drift, and she called out. "Help me, please, help me!"

He hurried toward the two, knelt down beside them. He saw that the woman was already shivering badly, although all her attention was on the girl she cradled, limp in her arms.

He started taking off his jacket, meaning to cover them both and lead them to the warmth of his truck—then stopped and caught his breath.

There, on the palm of the little girl's outstretched hand, pale and ungloved, was branded a single letter:

'R'.

Up to 25 vehicles involved in pileup

Reports from Transport Service drones at the scene confirmed that the accident was consistent with a series of collisions involving up to 25 vehicles.

Poor weather and icy road conditions had been very poor, making it a challenging drive around the state, even for robotically controlled spinners, keeping the authorities busy responding to a number of accidents.

'R.'

The letter—mandated by law and branded just so, on the palm—told Mathison everything he or anyone else was supposed to know about her.

It communicated the message that—in the crucible of life and humanity, in the triage forced upon them by the night and the wind and the temperature now ranging at thirty degrees below—she didn't matter.

She wouldn't count, alive or dead, in any case, it told him. Only the man in the car would be worth mentioning in any reports. After all, what did they say, the three principles? That she wasn't a human being; that she was property; that she was subservient?

She was wreckage, much like the vehicle she'd been flung from.

It didn't matter that blood flowed through its veins, that it had a heart that could beat like a human heart, that it shivered as if the cold could freeze that heart. It didn't matter that it could mimic laughter, weep at a broken doll, or sing, or—

Suddenly, the little girl's eyes opened, and she called out, "Mommy."

Startled, Mathison flung his coat on the woman, and pulled her away from the girl.

"Sarah!" she screamed, and broke away briefly; but before she could reach the body again, Mathison scooped the woman off her feet and hauled her away. The snow was falling faster now, his undershirt was wet and stiff, and he knew he needed to reach the truck quickly.

All the way the woman fought him, like a drowning swimmer blindly fighting a lifeguard, flailing and scratching at him.

When he finally got to the truck, he flung the woman in, locked the doors, and turned on the ignition. He adjusted half of the vent to her, half to him. Slowly, warmth began to seep in, the feeling starting to return to the parts of him that had become numb.

Beside him, the woman screamed and sobbed, banging at her door.

Severe weather conditions hamper rescue

Weather conditions also hampered the rescue team, which had to treat several cases of hypothermia, some severe.

Sgt. Wilson urged people caught in accidents in cold weather to remain in their vehicles, keep the motor running to keep warm, and wait for security services or paramedics to arrive.

With temperatures and wind chills in the range seen recently, frost-bite and hypothermia from prolonged exposure are real concerns. Death can strike long before the body actually freezes.

Mathison cursed the woman, cursed himself.

What was her story? What tragedy could make the woman think something like that could take the place of a real, breathing human child?

Or could it?

The woman beside him continued to sob. *What have I done?* he asked himself. *What have we done?*

Had he just left a little girl to perish in the cold? Did it matter that she had her mother's eyes, her hair, was made in her mother's image? Could she feel the coldness overcome her, the horror of darkness closing in, the fear of dying alone, unloved? After she was gone, would it matter, if she didn't have a soul?

And what if she did?

What did it mean for him to make the choice to leave her there? Had he just failed the Turing test of his own humanity?

"Damn it!" he said.

The wind pushed back at the truck door as Mathison fumbled at it, stumbled outside again. He had to lean forward to keep from being blown back.

Every step was agony now, not just because his constant shivering now made him falter, but because every step was a repudiation of all that he'd taken for granted before tonight. But he followed the truck's headlights, farther, farther, out into the night.

When he reached the girl, still there where he remembered, he knelt down without looking at her palm, at the ugly brand that set her apart from everyone. Instead, he looked at her.

She was just a little girl, in a party dress and stockings, helpless, almost sleeping. The smallest thing. Her lips were ashen, her eyes were closed, and her eyelashes were frosted over in crystals. But she was breathing. The girl was alive.

She stirred without opening her eyes, when he reached under her arms to lift her up. "Daddy," she murmured.

The snow blinded him. "No, sweetie," he said, through tears. "I'm so sorry."

Not more than sixty pounds, he thought, as he lifted her. The smallest thing. So frail, almost inconsequential.

Her ribbon had come undone, and her auburn hair was

askew, strewn with snow, the crystals sparkling like stars. He brushed them away as he carried her back, back toward the headlights in the distance, back to the warmth from the opening door, back into her mother's arms.

Interstate reopened

The westbound lanes of I-94 are now open to traffic after being closed while officials investigated the crash.

Officials had advised early Friday afternoon against travel on I-94 because of icy road conditions and limited visibility.

There were snowfall warnings for several areas around Port Huron on Friday evening. Those warnings have since been lifted.

A WORD FROM
SAMUEL PERALTA

The classic Turing test is a qualitative measure of a machine's ability to mimic the behavior a human. The test was posed by Alan Mathison Turing, a British mathematician, philosopher and computer scientist.

As I write this, the Turing test has already been passed in real life by several artificial intelligences, fooling the test judges into believing they were conversing not with synthetics, but with human beings.

"Humanity" is the story of a double Turing test, about how a little girl and a man both fail their tests, and their redemption.

* * *

The epigraph is taken from the film *A.I.* by Steven Spielberg, a modern retelling of Pinocchio (or the *commedia dell'arte, Buratino*) in which a robot boy longs to regain the love of his human mother by becoming "real."

Humanity also references the experience of the Holocaust era, when a Star of David was used as a method of identifying Jews. The apartheid of the world of Humanity is underscored by my three principles of robotics—with apologies to Isaac Asimov—mentioned in passing in this story and explored elsewhere in my other stories, including "Liberty" (subtitled "Seeking a Writ of Habeas Corpus for a Non-Human Being"). Like Asimov's

Three Laws, it's a construct that allows me to explore the nature of humanity.

Here are the *Precepts of Robotics*, as I imagine them in my world, enunciated in different ways in "Humanity" and some of my other works:

1. A robot is a machine, not a human being or person, and is imbued with no rights whatsoever.
2. A robot is the personal property of one human being or person, who is its master.
3. A robot must obey its master first; then it must obey any human being or person.

"Humanity" is set in the same world as that of "Trauma Room", "Hereafter", "Liberty", and "Faith"— a world where corporations have expanded beyond governments, where pervasive surveillance is a part of life, where non-human self-awareness has begun to make humanity face difficult questions about itself.

If that world sounds almost familiar, you'd be right. Change "telepaths" to "intelligence agencies" and "robots" to the name of any one of the many displaced segments in our societies, and we'd be talking about the world we live in today.

* * *

Ever since I fell in love with science and speculative fiction— both the classic writers, including Asimov and Ray Bradbury, and the more contemporary, including Margaret Atwood and Kazuo Ishiguro—I've realized that what such fiction does so well is to illuminate not the future, but the present.

We live in a present in fear of the future—of something unknown, dystopian, apocalyptic. I believe that, despite all this, there is promise. There is hope. I write about that, and I hope you're with me for the journey.

Come with me.

The best is yet to come.

Samuel Peralta is a physicist and storyteller. He has designed robots for nuclear applications, and headed start-ups in software and semiconductors. An Amazon bestselling author and anthologist, he is the creator and driving force behind the Future Chronicles anthologies.

http://www.amazon.com/author/samuelperalta
http://www.samuelperalta.com

A Note to Readers

Thank you so much for reading *The Future Chronicles—Special Edition.*

Through the work of a number of talented authors, editors, artists and other contributors—and the amazing support of readers like you—the *Future Chronicles* series has become one of the most acclaimed short story anthology series of the digital era, hitting the top ranks of not just the science fiction, fantasy and horror anthology lists, but the overall Amazon Top 10 Bestsellers list itself.

The Future Chronicles has also inspired several other quality anthology series in speculative fiction and in other genres, and inspired scores of spin-off stories, novels, and series. It's been amazing.

I'd like to thank the editors I've worked with, including David Gatewood (*il miglior fabbro*), Ellen Campbell, Carol Davis, Crystal Watanabe, Nolie Wilson, and Jeff Seymour, who helped focus what I've always held the *Chronicles* to be all about—*story*.

Thank you, too, to the hundreds of authors I've worked with, too numerous to mention, many of whom have become close friends—I get by with a lot of help from you all.

I'd also like to thank John Joseph Adams, who was not a *Chronicles* editor, but whose editorial hand helped shape some of my own stories and my appreciation for *story*.

Finally, thank you to Hugh Howey, whose ground-breaking work in speculative fiction, and continuous encouragement and support, made us realize and appreciate what was possible.

* * *

If you enjoyed the stories in this book, please keep an eye out for other titles in the *Future Chronicles* collection. A full listing of titles can be found at: *www.futurechronicles.net*

One of the things about the *Future Chronicles* series is that you don't have to start with the first book published, and work your way through the list. You can start with any title, then pick and choose the books you want to read, in any order.

But, if you were curious, here is a list, by release date, of all available and planned titles in the series:

2014

- The Robot Chronicles
- The Telepath Chronicles

2015

- The Alien Chronicles
- The A.I. Chronicles
- The Dragon Chronicles
- The Z Chronicles
- Alt.History 101
- The Immortality Chronicles
- The Future Chronicles—Special Edition
- The Time Travel Chronicles
- The Galaxy Chronicles
- The Cyborg Chronicles

2016

- Alt.History 102
- The Doomsday Chronicles
- The Illustrated Robot
- The Shapeshifter Chronicles
- Chronicle Worlds: Paradisi
- Chronicle Worlds: Feyland
- The Jurassic Chronicles
- Chronicle Worlds: Drifting Isle
- Chronicle Worlds: Half Way Home
- The Gamer Chronicles
- The Mars Chronicles

* * *

Finally, before you go, we'd like to ask you a very small favor, if you please: *Would you write a short review at the site where you downloaded this book?*

Reviews are make-or-break for authors. A book with no reviews is, simply put, a book with no future sales. This is because a review is more than just a message to other potential buyers: it's also a key factor driving the book's visibility in the first place.

More reviews (and more positive reviews) make a book more likely to be featured in bookseller lists and more likely to be featured in bookseller promotions. Reviews don't need to be long or eloquent; a single sentence is all it takes. In today's publishing world, the success (or failure) of a book is truly in the reader's hands.

So please, write a review.

Then tell a friend. Share a link to us on Facebook, or maybe even a Tweet—link to our books at *www.futurechronicles.net*. You'd be doing us a great service.

Thank you.

Samuel Peralta
www.amazon.com/author/samuelperalta
www.samuelperalta.com